Also by Ellis Sharp

No

GW00750833

The I

Unbelievable Things

Short Fiction

The Aleppo Button

Lenin's Trousers

To Wanstonia

Driving My Baby Back Home

Aria Fritta

(with Mac Daly) Engels on Video

CHAPTERS
NO RETURN
NO EXCHANGE

A Zoilus Press Paperback
First published in Great Britain by Zoilus Press in 2007

© Ellis Sharp 2007

The right of Ellis Sharp to be identified as the author of this
publication has been asserted by him in accordance with the
Copyright, Design and Patents Act 1988.

All rights reserved. No part of this publication may be
reproduced, stored in a retrieval system, or transmitted, in any
form or by any means, electronic, mechanical, photocopying,
recording or otherwise, without the prior permission of the
copyright owner.

A CIP catalogue record for this book is available from the
British Library.

ISBN 978-1902878922

Typeset by Electrograd

As far as they regard myself I can despise all events: but I cannot cease to love you. This morning I scarcely know what I am doing. I am going to Walthamstow.

John Keats, 13 September 1819

It is impossible to stand still in history in general, and in wartime in particular.

V.I. Lenin, 8 September 1917

Walthamstow Central? Wasn't that where Strobey took off into Nether Time and broke the Loop? Seems a long time ago, now.

Lisa Kamanzi Khan, 57 Steppen 3063

For Liz and Siva

1 Another Disappearance

"Another disappearance. With a lingering voice. It's happened again, sir."

Buller put down the page he was reading. He added his signature. He was exhausted by the weight and density of what was written there. As he'd done so many times before, he looked up from his desk at Aphrodite Cutter.

Buller wore a jacket; a mark of his seniority. Out there, things were collapsing. Only that morning he'd heard a shot on the way in to work. He believed it was a shot, it might not have been. It sounded like a glacier cracking. His directional hearing was poor. Sometimes he heard rustlings and coughs, hard to place. Tyres screeched. Metal and iron called out to him in bursts of pain. That's why it was important to keep up appearances and apply some structure. Buller was a firm believer in structure. Sometimes he half-sensed he'd been structured that way.

From the filing cabinet by the door the sun from an earlier draft of his life reflected in the glass photo frame of his wife and son. Frozen in erased sunlight they looked half happy, half surprised, and one third dead. This picture is always five years old. In one sun-bleached corner the snapshot has started to bubble up, as if exposed to intense heat

Buller felt very, very tired. A head full of sludge and breaking words. Memories of waking at five, the bedroom full of blue light, birds making electronic chatter in the trees. He'd come out of a strange, disturbing dream about a rat; hadn't been able to get back to sleep. He felt shivery, like when he had flu that time in Kentish Town. The frags didn't help.

"Another disappearance. With a lingering voice. It's happened again, again, again, sir."

"I heard you the first time, Cutter!" he said sharply.

All this was unavoidable; a condition of his employment. Buller looked at himself in a gigantic, rust speckled mirror. The bags under his eyes had slumped forwards and merged with his fat red cheeks. It was an allergy. He was allergic to time. It brought out the worst in him. His veins were congested with what felt like hair and bits of stringy celery. Clichés had congealed around that lump he called his soul. They hurt. He knew he should lay off the whisky, the chocolate and the crime fiction. Once he was hard and lean, now the years had corrupted him. He was a tough cop gone soft and flabby. His chronometer was faulty and he couldn't stop thinking about it.

Buller could see all this in the mirror, and in the mirror behind his desk reflected in the first mirror, and in the multiple reflections the two mirrors threw playfully to each other. He was forty three. His past held many blanks. At the blurred edges of his vision, ants and spiders poured out of his fatigue, jostling, skipping a merry eightsome reel.

"It's the fourth case this week, sir."

Detective Constable Cutter was everything Buller wasn't. Dawson had once quipped that from the north-west she looked like Halle Berry. No one had ever mistaken Buller for Halle Berry. Cutter was 27. She didn't think about Dawson any more.

"The fourth," Buller dully repeated. He noticed some fragments on the floor. He didn't bother to try deciphering them. His eyelashes flicked them into the grey.

He could have done without this new information. He already had too much rotating slowly and cloudily inside his mind. It had been enlarged and silted over a number of months. A string of unsolved armed robberies hung like pearls on a necklace. He deleted the simile and visualized a lasso. In one variant it tugged against the neck of a salivating paperback reader. The variant followed the tracks of the frags.

Soon – very soon - there would be a protest against the opening of the Zeilinger Collider. Plus Buller had family anxieties. Add repeated twinges of toothache, which meant he couldn't delay a trip to PKD Dentistry much longer. And now this.

Disappearance. With a lingering voice... The first victim had been Katchen Hitachi, a student, a girl, 22. Her room-mate, Eldritch Robinson, said Katchen had gone into the bathroom to take a shower. She never came out again. In the end the door had been kicked open. The shower was on, the girl's clothes were there, the bath towel was dry. And the window was the size of a phone book with a window lock frozen under layers of dull green paint. No forced entry from outside, that was an iron certainty.

The room-mate swore the whole time she'd been in the next room writing an essay. Cutter asked to read it. It turned about to be about hypodiegetic worlds, drafted in a spidery hand. Cutter pointed out she'd misspelled *irreducible*. Later, after the police had gone, Eldritch rang Aphrodite Cutter back and said she'd heard her friend's voice. It was coming from the bathroom. She was calling for help. *But there was no one there.*

There was the possibility that Eldritch Robinson was having a breakdown. Maybe she'd murdered her friend. Hearing voices usually signified a schizo. The italics might just be attention-seeking.

At first the police treated the room-mate with kindness, sympathy and a residual suspicion. They began an exhaustive check of Hitachi's life. Zilch, so far. She was just a few, grey slender centimetres of prose; the info was sketchy.

Tuesday morning an old man rang in. Said his wife had gone out to feel the washing on the line, to see if it was dry (it was something old people did, apparently). A moment later his wife was gone. She was 77. Buller remembered the description. She had sloping shoulders, high features, a low brow which wore a pair of wrinkles that matched those digits. At her age she couldn't have hopped over the garden fence, anything like that. Later the man said he heard her by the washing line. There was the sound of machinery and humming. A lawn mower, a washing machine on final spin, whatever. The noise stopped and she was calling his name. *But she wasn't there.*

In the afternoon, another. Except this time it was an old woman reporting a disappeared old man. In a garden, again. And later, his voice. More italics.

"So what is it now?"

"A woman in a flat of blocks," was surely not what she'd said. A fit of blacks? Impossible. That was a recurring Met anxiety, but not in this instance.

"Says her husband went out on to the balcony to read the paper. A moment later: gone. But this one's different. *She says she saw it happen.*"

"He vanished in front of her eyes?" Buller whispered, shocked to see that it was now 3.42 p.m. He didn't know how much more of this he could take. Feverish, he needed a shot of whisky and two Ibuprofen but he worried that his office cabinet might turn out to be just an empty prop.

"That's what she says. He dematerialized."

"Her word or yours?"

DC Cutter smiled. She remembered it was what the driver did in *Travelling People* when Henry twisted one corner of his mouth and said "Dead dogs?" She continued. She had to, otherwise that emptiness existing between her and her boss would begin to spread.

"The word the woman used was invisible. *He just became invisible*, that's how she put it. The newspaper her husband was holding fell to the floor. She was watching through the kitchen window. It happened thirty minutes ago. According to my notebook it is now 11.48 a.m. on Thursday 10 February, and it is raining. The woman is Mrs Iris Scheist. Two officers are with her now. I thought you'd like to see the site of the disappearance for yourself, sir. I have a car waiting."

Buller tried to get his brain to mesh. He was tired, he was still troubled by his dream rat, and now the population of Walthamstow was starting to vanish. Maybe he hadn't woken up yet. He stood, abruptly. He had to do something, keep the words going. Otherwise nothing would be solved, leaving just those smudges on the moon.

It made Buller nervous, being in East London in the early twenty-first century. He was never too clear how high above sea level he was. Plus it was over a century since Einstein's publication of "Zur Elektrodynamik bewegter Körper". Any sentence containing an umlaut and that many 'k's made him nervous. Plus if you stared at the title of Einstein's paper long enough it began to tremble. Small planets formed amid ribbons of greyish gas. Then the words reverted to what they had always been, containing the letters R O T D T Z K Y. Symmetry of that sort perturbed him. None of his

10

favourite fictional detectives had to contend with events of this shimmering magnitude.

He walked over to the window. Across the road children were running round the yard of a primary school. Their shrieks of pleasure were like tiny bird cries, squeaky and high and piping as the chatter of a hedge warbler. Not now, but once it would have made him think of Kautsky.

He ached inside. Some drear afternoons he scented the lipstick from big generous sad-eyed women who once were moist with desire for the tangible man he'd never been. There was a void of lost possibilities back there, echoing with music and four-fingered climaxes. In that Leonard Cohen afterworld big Frank Black was singing 'Another Velvet Nightmare.'

Next to the school the traffic poured down Forest Road, from a plain old jug in somebody's imagination. God's? Henry Ford's? The cars moved to and fro, with convincing verisimilitude. Some on their way into London, some on their way out of London. Verisimilitude tasted good. It was as good as a Mr Whippy. It made him feel normal. At home in a familiar world.

A red balloon was caught in the branches of a nearby street tree. It hung there, eyeing him. Beyond it: roofs, a glimpse of the trees in Lloyd Park, the Town Hall clock. He'd seen the balloon once before, long ago in his childhood.

When he looked again the balloon had gone.

"Sir…"

There was impatience in her eyes. Plus his office furniture, miniaturized and twisted sideways.

Buller felt a cold salty juice trickle across his chest. He hoped Aphrodite Cutter couldn't smell it.

"She hearing voices, too?" he asked.

"One voice, sir. That's all they ever hear."

Buller turned his eyes from the view. "Okay, let's head there now. It's time we got out of this room." Time and the weather seemed a little jumpy. Maybe things would settle down later.

He could hear a splashing noise, like rain. It made him think of warped honeycombs of light dancing on blue tiles. Horns tooted, there was a smell of bleach, then a tang of bitter fruit. He felt jittery, not at all his usual selves. *Honeycomb* began playing in his head.

"It's happened again, sir. Another disappearance. With a lingering voice."

Eyes focused on a printed page. Put down that page you are reading. He added his signature. Exhausted by the weight and density. Disappearance, another, a lingering voice. Feverish. Reassembling.

Buller knew it was time to move or he'd be stuck behind his desk forever.

He followed Aphrodite down a wet stairwell recently cleaned with lemon-odoured disinfectant, to the car pool.

2 Erasure Dust

Strobey was expecting them. He knew they were out to slot him. His muscles tensed as the silver train slowed along the long platform and halted.

"This is Walthamstow Central," the voice crackled on the PA system. "This train terminates here. All change. This is the end of the line. All change, please."

The doors sighed open.

People spilled out on to the platform. Edgar Strobey moved with the flow. There was a faint remote odour of disinfectant.

He spotted the threat, top of the exit ramp. On this run it was February, first decade of the twenty-first century.

He came out of the hot windy tunnel, up the crowded escalator, through the ticket gates, ascended the concrete steps, on to the overhead platform, left into the concourse. There they were. Waiting. Two big black men in dark suits. Shades, shaven heads. A slight, lopsided bloating in the chest region, like each one had a single female breast.

He knew they were Anarchs.

They seemed to pick up on him at once, began to lope after him. He skipped his way – *excuse me* – through the people surge. Everyone in a hurry to get out of that shitty concourse, to see the sun, to breathe the sweet exhaust fumes pumped from the rear of every throbbing vehicle in the two-way jam on Selborne Road.

He hit the top of the ramp and ran between the lines of frozen vehicles. Didn't bother to look back, he could imagine. The two of them, hurrying after him. Hands with rows of big gold rings, fingers twitchy for what lay heavily in those swollen inside pockets.

He barely noticed the hotel. He'd seen pictures. This wasn't the time to check out the scenery.

Now Edgar did what he'd done on the VR runs. He swerved left past Finn's, the golden tip of his Harvard key pointing forward. A narrow, black, insignificant door between Finn's and the big plate glass windows of Burger Bliss. Just like in Virtual Reality.

Edgar had the door open fast. Doing things in Nether Time was almost enjoyable. He was getting used to the name, too. *Edgar*. He liked it. It had something. It was better than being a fifty-third.

Through the door, and on into a twenty-unit dark corridor. He left the door unlocked behind him and ran to the far end. The green dial of his wristwatch assured him he was in a tangible world. The adjective rating was high. He heard the distant monotonous hum of many stock characters, stock responses and stock situations.

Edgar was one unit from the end of the corridor when the light by the door darkened. By the time the Anarch had his thunder flute out, Edgar was gone from view, was slipping on his protector glove. He poured what looked like scarlet powder paint onto his gloved palm. He threw it as the first Anarch came round the corner.

It did what it was supposed to do. It was erasure dust, on a ten second active setting. It caught the Anarch full in the face. There was a flash of startled surprise on the man's face. He was still wearing it when his skin started to froth.

He didn't have time to scream because the dust had already taken away his lips, his tongue. His throat.

The man hissed as he fizzed and collapsed and shrank.

The other Anarch had that surprised look, too. If he'd heard of Yorick it didn't show. He was looking at something he'd never seen before, and while he was looking he discovered it was his turn next.

The powder was made of hydrogenated vanassium, designed to activate on warm skin. Once activated it burned through everything

– skin tissue, blood cells, muscle, bone, clothing, metal, neo-realist glitterprose. Everything except stregoth fibre. The Anarchs would have had to be wearing ST suits and stregoth helmets and goggles to have stood a chance. But no one had yet found a way of understanding this cosmology or its rhetoric or of transferring stregoth through a fractor wave.

Vanassium, yes; stregoth, no.

By now the first Anarch was just a tranquil muddy puddle on the floor. The other one had melted down to a pair of shins in big shiny black boots rising from a frothing discoloured soup of dissolving flesh.

The thunder flute lay on top, detumescent. Then it lost its floppy bulk and went. The boots sank on top like ice melting on a hot metal plate.

A few more seconds and the Anarch was completely gone.

Ten seconds was up. The vanassium became crystalline. Without that it would have bored its way down through the floor, through the foundations, through the dark moist wormy earth. The earth would close up after it and the chemical needle would continue its passage, would continue on and on until it hit the planet's molten core at the spine.

Strobey was the same, really. He had no choice. He was designed to get somewhere and he'd be in motion until he was there.

He took a folded bag from his pocket and scraped the remains of the two Anarchs into it. Now they were just a few dark flakes, like burnt paper. He went back out into the street and slipped the folded bag into the circular litter bin outside Burger Bliss. It all seemed so doggone *real*. Somewhere very close Bonnie "Prince" Billy was singing his Archbishop Cranmer tribute, "You Will Miss Me When I Burn".

Strobey returned to the dark corridor which was the back way into Finn's Hotel. He shut the door behind him. It seemed narrower the second time. He became aware of a strip of dull lighting overhead. Illuminating what little there was.

A pair of scorch marks on the bare floor, nothing more. It was all so plausible. It was *like it had really happened.*

14

He was beginning to feel at home in his skin; who he'd adapted. His mind was filled with remembrance of things to come. Edgar was becoming familiar with his probabilities. His name was Edgar Strobey. He was an unemployed actor. He did not suffer from a mental illness. He was as sane as the night is long. And he was expected at an important meeting upstairs.

Before he turned the corner the door opened and there was light, then darkness. It was eight minutes past four in real time. It was raining. But in there, in the warmth, it is still hot, still morning.

Whose warmth, whose morning?

He heard his name called, turned in sharp surprise. Some conditions of reality are unavoidable. Gravity, for example. The volume of the hum suddenly increased. Machinery thudded. Strands of cobweb slithered along a beam of sunlight.

Strobey saw who it was.

3 Warrior Variations

It wasn't far to St James Tower. A ten minute drive along vehicle-clogged suburban streets. The driver didn't hit the siren. Two minutes either way wouldn't mean a thing. Already it was 16 February and in the past four weeks less than 60 minutes had occurred.

Aphrodite Cutter closed her eyes, switched off. She did yoga at the Red Onion studios on Hatherley Mews. She did the cat in front of the gleaming mirrored panels. She did Egyptian salute to the sun. She did warrior variations. Warrior was her favourite.

Plus, in another place, TM.

She knew how to defuse the stress and rage that went with her work. Surreptitiously she curled and uncurled her toes; slow-rotated her ankles. Breathed in and out through her nose, slowly, deeply. She decided against alternate-nostril breathing. Buller would think she was weird if she did that, she could tell. Besides, the air conditioning gave the atmosphere in the car an icy metallic tang. She didn't like it. It smelled unnatural, like chicklit or inhaling steel dust.

Beside her, Buller stared straight ahead, seeing nothing. Next he screwed up his eyes, as if at the memory of bright light.

He was a man who wasn't in control of his body. Nobody was any more. Aphrodite saw it all the time in the force. Plus she heard it in the voices. She saw how the men snatched junk snacks made of cheap prose ingredients through their brief days and briefer nights. They turned to alcohol to drown out memories and afternoons.

Theirs was a world of deletions and terrible revisions. Rotting bodies lay submerged in swamps. Eyes stared up at skies they'd never see. Aphrodite saw the anger and frustration. There was so much that these men needed to erase. They were fenced in by intertextuality and strange, difficult words. Sagittate. Setaceous. Susurration. One or two of them relied on colostomy bags sealed with Velcro. There were shoot-outs and abrupt messy outpourings. They couldn't cope. The veins rose to the surface of their face like something dead and full of gas. Their faces grew flushed and blotchy with anger and incomprehension and a sense of injustice. Their necks and stomachs swelled. The fat grew round them like a carapace. Their world was under threat and they hated it. Shots woke them at 2 a.m.

Aphrodite let her mind float off to the lambs. Three nights running she'd dreamed of lambs. She didn't know why. She was a city girl, had no feel for farm animals. The nearest she got to lambs was sealed cellophane packages of almost bloodless meat in a supermarket. So she didn't know why there was a field or why it was full of white cuddly lambs which she stroked and talked to. For some reason the field was in France (where she'd never been). And she was with someone who meant a great deal to her. Her lover, in fact. Only it wasn't Dawson or Mike.

Dawson was dead and she didn't want to think about Mike. She didn't want to drink alone listening to Annie Lennox singing 'The Saddest Song I've Got.' She shut it all out, returned to the lambs, the sunlit green field, France. The person she loved, whose face she couldn't see.

Beside her, Buller stirred. He managed to turn his big frog's head. "Ribbit!" he may have muttered. "Ribbit! Ribbit! Ribbit!" He stared

16

out at the people, the houses, the shops. Frozen in time, the scenery stared back.

At the end of Old Rogue Road they crossed the market. Onions, yams, garlic, melons. A swarthy man on a plastic chair with an upturned box covered in plastic phone cards. *Talk Nigeria 60 minuts, only two euros.* A bargain... That missing 'e' wouldn't bother the clients. The market crowd pushed both ways. Big black confident-looking women, small skinny impoverished white men. Youths with slicked-up hair that shone blackly. A woman with three children, all sucking luminous green lollies.

Walthamstow didn't look like a place where people dematerialized easily. The day had a dull, grimy, everyday feel. The sort where, if you kept a diary, you'd write: *Nothing much happened today.*

But something had. On the twentieth floor of a local tower block an old man had dematerialized. According to a witness. Or, if you shifted the perspective the way Buller had spent a lifetime seeing it shifted in interview rooms and courts: the chief suspect. The killer. But Mrs Iris Scheist of apartment number 2205 didn't sound like a killer. A check on GUST - the Gov UK Surveillance Terminal - showed that, like those involved in the other vanishings, she was practically data free. A warning for an unpaid electricity bill, that was it. No criminal record of any sort. Despite the suspicious Teutonic surname no abnormal vocabulary had been detected in her telephone communications or letters. Iris Scheist was Mrs Ordinary. Harmless, conforming, a grey zero. Unless of course she was crazy. Even Ordinaries cracked and sometimes went berserk. It was the traffic, the queues, money worries. The swell of fiery acid in their aching twisted-up guts.

Buller was inclined fifteen degrees to ascribe this unfolding weirdness to psychology. The people involved were disturbed in some way. Or maybe it was chemical in origin. Maybe some freak was slipping acid in the water supply. Whatever it was it sure as hell wasn't dematerialization. Buller was too old for horseshit like that.

*

17

St James Tower was marooned in a rectangular plain of concrete and yellow dead grass east of the Liverpool Street line. The nearest store sold booze, beside it was one selling reconditioned spare parts for old cars. Beyond that was a tattoo parlour. On the nearest corner was a shabby pub, The Living Dead (no, he looked again: The King's Head). They were mostly erased in the late 1980s but were brought back and reconstructed for this scene.

Just as soon as the last leases expired, the block was due for demolition. It was demolished long before this paragraph was ever published. Most had already gone. The windows with glass were heavily outnumbered by the ones boarded over. Graffiti lashed the ground floor wall like frozen waves of paint. Buller liked the simile but said nothing.

There was an empty police car parked by the entrance. They pulled alongside and left their driver behind. Had there been a driver? Aphrodite wondered. She couldn't remember.

The brushed steel elevator doors admitted them. Aerosol paint had darkened the translucent plexiglass shells of the lighting, making the interior gloomy and oppressive. Aphrodite pressed the 23 button and the black rubber lips of the doors closed on each other with a faintly bored eroticism. She stood, her back to the wall, tightening her muscles, then letting go. Getting rid of residual tension; the flutterings of anxiety in her taut slender stomach. She always felt like this before visiting an SOC. Though crime-scene seemed a strangely absurd definition for what had occurred.

Two grey mutes, they rode their ascending metallic tomb in the silence of that tense first version of their story.

4   The Team

It was April of this year in Nether Time when Mirando Mirando did her traject. Strobey's SD had been sent after her, to prepare the way. Now, although it is 17 February and Rafik Hariri is dead, it is still October. Strobey knows he has just ten orbital days to do what he has to do. After that the implant kicks in. His Menzara identity will be gone forever.

18

Hell, Strobey *knew* he'd spent his short life on the Menzara Construct. The night is long and memory is a treasure house of marvels. Menzara was an orbital of two billion souls in the Toppe TheoDemoK System. It followed an irregular orbit around the largest of three dead planets in a system at the edge of Void Eleven, on the fringes of afternoon dreams and scoured texts, way out from anywhere much. Its nearest neighbour was the Evanescence Orbital. Beyond that lay little but a vast cold emptiness and the uninhabited moons of Kavan.

Strobey was still a small boy when sabotage killed his parents. Someone put an imploder in their shuttle. The crime had gone unsolved. Some crazy technician who'd secretly gone over to the Anarchs, probably. Nothing personal. When crimes were personal they got solved. The Anarchs had no higher motive than to screw up the state of things. They had a downer on Theo/DemoKracies. They appealed to every discontented misfit in that grey quarter of space.

Strobey was grown as a quiet, detached child. He barely remembered his mother and father in real time. All he had was slots of imagery from the family record bank. He watched his mother's caesarean section. He watched as brushed steel robot arms held him gently between soft germ-free pads. He watched his first tottering steps as his parents grinned like zombies in the background. He watched them head off on a weekend away at Relaxation Ranch and saw the shuttle morph into a white blob. The blob gave birth to smaller blobs. And that was it, that was his family life zapped. He had over 300 hours of footage and almost no real-time memories.

They gave him Happy Cool (in lozenges) to get him through the grief. But in truth he had little grief. He was too young. He was raised by a Good Parenting Unit on Level Seven but didn't warm to their homey jive. He didn't socialise with the other kids, wasn't into sport. He preferred to play Mind Sweep on his VR glasses.

Strobey wasn't into conversation. He wanted to be an enforcer.

Revenge for his dead parents? asked the psychiatrist. She looked at her watch. It was almost time for *somebody's* medication.

Strobey said he didn't think so. It was more to do with a sense of order. It was what he believed in: structure, form, function. Maybe

19

it was the effect of those three years playing Mind Sweep. The answer seemed to satisfy the woman in the white coat. The selectors decided that yes, he *was* perfect material for the TPT – and that the tequila should be combined with tomato juice, a splash of lemon, a dash of Tabasco, five ice cubes, and shaken vigorously. Killer tequila helps repress the fragments. *Drink up.*

In the Time Penetration Team emotional attachment was a no-no. Death and departure and loss was all you were trained for. That and the liquidation of TDs. When you joined the TPT you knew what to expect. One day you might have to go somewhere and not return. You wouldn't necessarily die, though that was always possible. You'd likely go on living but it would be in another, younger culture. Plus your Menzara identity would be erased. After ten Menzara-equivalent temporal units you'd lose your old identity. You would cease to know that you were from the far future. From then on, you'd be one of them. You would have to get used to their food, their primitive and contradictory ideologies, their criminal injustice systems, their bizarre concepts of narrative. You would be expected to worship a laughably threadbare monotheism, admire neo-realism, and respect and show fascination for a degenerate and corrupt royal family. Those passing units would require enormous reserves of self-control. And you would be sent to that primitive society for one purpose only: to deal with a Time Dissident. And once there, you were screwed. Trapped there. Locked in the Loop. Unless, of course, someone disproved Norland's Six Theses and discovered a way of returning through the Bohren Shield without rupturing the membrane.

Hadn't happened yet, didn't mean to say it wouldn't. Every Joe's dream. The rescue; erasure of the erasure and re-installation of the memory card you'd left behind; a triumphant return to Menzara. Plus crowds. Plus wild cheering.

To join the Time Penetration Team you had to be an orphan, without siblings, single and below 24 temporalities. It was highly preferable that you had experienced no serious relationship.

The ideal TPT candidate was cold, egocentric and with little feeling for others. That way, when the call came, there was no danger of not wanting to go. The TPT had no use for people who

20

wanted to stay in their own world. The TPT detested people who were in love or who wanted children. *Shit like that is no use to anyone*, as Void Archangel Strumbert had solemnly emphasized to the team in his graduation day speech.

You also needed an acute and genuine curiosity about Nether Time zones. Ancient history, vast cultures which had long since ended in dust and rubble. Nations and empires repeating mistakes that lasted a thousand years. Great religions founded on the visions of uneducated, dogmatic, short-tempered, fucked-up men who fancied themselves as all-wise teachers. Men, generally bearded, often desert dwellers or from the provinces or backward states, who had bad breath and who hated women who liked sex and had minds of their own.

On the great Constructs very few saw the point in scholarship like that. Who wanted to know about dead societies when you could linger for a year on the beach at Cape Summer or go diving in the Great Canyon of Ever-Changing Glitter Eels. Or have whatever sex you wanted with a Living Doll in a warm mirrored hotel room in Satisfaction City.

The future was Strobey's home but he loved the past. It was his quirk.

5   Apartment 2305

There were eight apartments on each floor. Number 2305 signified Apartment Five on the 23rd floor. On that floor the Scheists were the last residents left. The lease limped on to December. The letting was in poor shape – cold, damp, perforated.

It was easy finding their apartment; the only door which hadn't been sealed with anti-squatter metal plates. Inside, Iris Scheist was trying to drink a cup of tea and spilling it. "He disappeared. Just like that. Before my very eyes!"

The dialogue was terrible. The WPC beside her looked bored. She daydreamed of an artificial island in a Freezone. Aphrodite recognised her: Daisy Spenser, a probationer. She'd arrived a week ago. Frizzy ginger hair, freckles. Small and bubbly; enthusiastic. She got things wrong, made strangely elementary blunders, nobody

21

seemed to mind. Her warm smile melted even the piggiest of her snorting sexist colleagues. But her new-girl enthusiasm seemed to have worn thin fast. Aphrodite guessed that Mrs Scheist hadn't been saying much else since she'd had company.

The Scheist hands shook and there were dark patches on her floral cotton skirt. According to GUST, Brown was 53. She looked a decade older. Her face was white and drained and from time to time you could smell the sour stewed stench rising from the grids. She was exhausted-looking. It was the face of someone who'd never had much money, had always worked too hard, and never relaxed.

The big sitting room they were in looked clean and tidy but edged by poverty. Everything seemed faintly faded, yellowing, long overdue for replacement. Even the reproduction of Constable's 'Hay Wain' on the wall had a bleached, colourless look.

"Nothing like this has ever happened to me before!" wailed Iris Scheist, spilling more tea. WPC Daisy Spenser patted her half-heartedly but couldn't think of anything to say. Nothing like this had happened to her before either. At last she said: "I'm sure we'll find your husband. I'm sure there's some explanation…" But she seemed uncertain. The dialogue was so hollow it gave birth to tinny echoes. Nothing at the police training college had prepared her for this. Racism, sexism, surveillance of socialists – but there was nothing on the syllabus about unstable subjectivities or disruption of the primary reality plane.

"Over here, sir," said the other officer, contributing a new tinny resonance. He beckoned Buller towards the balcony.

Aphrodite saw it was Scurr. Detective Constable Andy Scurr, 27, was a shaven-headed white male with spiv sideburns and beady wandering eyes, like a rat's. His teeth were stained by cigarettes and liquor. He shone like grease under a strong light. She knew he didn't like her. Partly because Aphrodite wasn't white, partly because she was a woman, partly because she was brighter than him. She was a threat. No grease.

Scurr's viewpoint, from the stale-smelling narrative roll inside which he slept at night: Aphrodite Cutter had to be put down, neutralized. Kept in her place, down where she belonged. *Fuckin' stoopid name* she'd once heard him say in the canteen, getting a table full of new recruits to snicker at his wit. Another time an obscene play on her last name.

Aphrodite's viewpoint: officers like Scurr were poison. They created tension, prejudice, envy. They screwed-up good policing with their own petty little hang-ups. They imposed a rigid belief system on how they perceived everything. That didn't help with human relations and it sure as hell didn't do much for crime detection. Aphrodite briefly stiffened and bristled inside her mental straitjacket. Then she followed Scurr and Buller out on to the balcony.

A striped deck chair occupied the centre of a concrete strip two metres by seven. The stripes on the canvas were ghosts of strawberry pink and royal blue. A tabloid newspaper lay upturned beside it. Some of the pages had become detached and were sprawled nearby, like shed feathers.

"That's where she says he was sitting. Says she was washing up at the sink. Says she saw him disappear. Just like that. She says." Scurr kept his focus on Buller, continued to ignore Aphrodite. Repetition and enunciation of *says* signified Scurr's belief that Iris Scheist was a lying cow.

There was a low, waist-high wall. Buller looked over it.

"Obviously she didn't push him over. I checked down there. No staining. If she whacked him it wasn't that way." Scurr's dialogue imitated his favourite Mafia movie. He also very much liked assaults on vulnerable isolated women and black prisoners, expensive sunglasses, and the fiction of Jeffrey Archer, who was a fucking genius.

"What makes you think Iris Scheist killed her husband?" Aphrodite enquired.

Scurr gave her a cold look. She quickly returned it, brushing a few razor-edged shards of ice from her palm.

"Easy," he said. "Her story is ridiculous shit. People don't vanish, not like that. I reckon she's mental. She looks mental to me." He didn't bother to lower his voice. He nodded back at the sitting room where Scheist was still sprinkling tea over herself.

"Three other people vanished this week. Apparently into thin air. A cliché which derives from the first play listed in the 1623 Folio. Perplexingly for the modern playgoer it is identified as a comedy."

Scurr shrugged his shoulders. He did it far too fast, Aphrodite thought. At Red Onion you did it very, very slowly.

"Apparently," he said. His tone was sarcastic. He reached into his pocket, took out some gum. Began chewing.

Buller walked to the end of the balcony, returned. He scanned the surfaces, the canopy of the balcony, the floor. Nothing. No scratches, no dark little dots or smears, no shards of glass. Just vowels and consonants and specks of punctuation. He shook his head and heard a faint, delicate tinkling of wind chimes. He glanced up at the canopy a second time. Puzzled, he stepped back inside.

Aphrodite flinched. Scurr had taken hold of her arm. "Careful," he said. His eyes were mocking. "Don't go too near the edge. You wouldn't want to fall, would you? You wouldn't want to end up in a reconfigured moondog zone, now, would you?" She believed she'd heard him say. If so it was typical Scurr humour. It wasn't funny and it had a threatening, sinister tone – especially that third sentence which she felt certain he hadn't said. Aphrodite wrenched her sleeve free.

"I don't think Iris Scheist killed her husband," she said quietly. "I think she's telling the truth, the truth, the truth. That woman is in a state of shock. She's not faking her emotions. Something's shaken her up."

"Yeah. Killing someone shakes people up. Especially if they've never done it before. They can't handle it. Happens all the time with domestics."

Scurr frowned. A train passed over the dark tunnel in which he stood motionless. He rapped his knuckle against his frontal eminence until it was all gone.

"Thought it was mint. Don't taste like mint." He took the wet grey lump from his mouth and flicked it over the edge of the balcony.

The balcony faced west, towards the valley of the Lea. The flood plain and the marshes were a dull khaki band sandwiched between Walthamstow and the urban sprawl of distant Hackney and Tottenham Hale.

Faraway to the north-west you could just see the fuzzy grey blur of the buildings in the Enterprise and Development Zone. The zone was where they'd constructed the Zeilinger Collider

Saturday was the day of the official opening. The Green movement had united with the Left in a campaign against the Collider. The Lea Valley was no place for something like that, it was argued. Over two miles long, it was far too big. It was a scandal to build it in green belt land. It buried Fern Island, a tiny promontory cut off from the surrounding marsh by little more than a ditch, under concrete. It flattened a lot of meadow and wetland and lizards and rare ferns. It was too close to built-up areas. There were radiation hazards. The Mega-matter unit was nuclear-fuelled. Plus the Zeilinger Corporation had a shitty record in Africa. Also there were only two cycle stands for staff.

The Government said that these objections were nonsense. There was no danger at all. The Collider was essential for putting the U.K. at the forefront of advances in the field of high energy physics research. The Collider, which would be the biggest in the world, would enable protons to be fired into head-on collision at higher energies than ever achieved before. It would allow scientists to penetrate further into the structure of discursive text than ever before.

The Met was expecting 20,000 to turn up for the protest.

Aphrodite brought her attention back to the balcony. She didn't want to stay out there with Scurr. She was about to turn and step inside when it happened.

A voice.

"Help me," it said. "Please help." And then: "Iris. Iris! Where are you?"

It was a man's voice. Not one she recognised. Elderly. And it was close, very close.

On the balcony, she'd have said. Except there was no one there, just her and the other DC.

Scurr heard it too. He'd have had to be deaf not to. His reflexes were good. He whipped round, scowling. He stared suspiciously at Aphrodite.

"Nice try," he said at last. "Didn't know you was good at party tricks."

Before Aphrodite could reply the voice spoke again. "Help me," it whimpered. "Please."

It seemed to be coming from the centre of the balcony, somewhere near the deck chair. Frowning, Scurr picked the chair up, fingered the canvas. Looking for the hidden amplifier. He let it drop. He stomped on the newspaper, just to be sure.

Then he went back and looked inside the apartment. Iris Scheist was still on the sofa with the WPC. Scurr shut the door and stepped back on to the balcony. He did what Buller had done, gazing long and hard at the canopy above, and then the walls, the kitchen windows, the wall.

Nothing. Fucking nothing.

"Help me, please."

Scurr punished the air with his fist. There was someone there, there had to be.

Aphrodite re-opened the door and called, "Mrs Scheist! Could you come here please? Quickly."

Iris Scheist reacted like they'd found her Harold. She knocked over what little cold brown slop was left at the bottom of her china cup and skipped across the room.

The voice called out again.

"Harold!" she shrieked. "Where are you love? Are you stuck? Tell us where?"

"Can't see," the voice said. "Fog everywhere. Help me."

Scurr picked up the deck chair and tossed it aside. He swept up the rags of newspaper and threw them over the balcony wall. No one was going to play tricks on DC Andy Scurr. He was going to sort this mystery, no question. He braced his legs, stared pugnaciously at Mrs Scheist. "Where is he, Iris?" he said. "Where the fuck is your Harold? Where have you put him?"

"He's gone!" wailed Iris Scheist. Tears bubbled down her cheeks. "I want him back. I want my Harold back! I'm sorry, love. I need you back. I miss you!"

Buller said: "DC Scurr, apologise to Mrs Brown for the bad language. Then take WPC Smith, find the caretaker and check out the apartments above and below. *Now*."

Scurr muttered a stony, insincere "Sorry", then he and the WPC left. Iris Scheist seemed dazed; probably hadn't even heard his *fuck*.

Buller said, "Would you take Mrs Scheist back inside, please, DC Cutter."

He stood alone on the balcony.

The voice was very close. He couldn't hear any faint hiss or crackle or coughs like you might get on a tape. It was clear and very real. He waited until Scurr and the WPC came back. Inside the other apartments they'd found nothing but dust.

They waited a while longer but the voice didn't return.

Scurr stayed on the balcony, scowling at everything. It was trick, it had to be a fucking trick.

But how was it done?

He gave the air another interrogation. Chopped it with vicious side blows. Lashed it with his boot.

Zilch.

No contact. No invisible fucking man.

But no one screwed with DC Andy Scurr. He'd sort it. He'd sort whatever trick that silly cow Iris Scheist was playing.

Nail her good and proper.

6 Cool

Strobey spent three years alone in a cool log cabin by a cool stream in the cool Unending Forest on Level 29. The entire level was an exclusive TPT training zone. It was hot. Team members went there to absorb old, long-dead cultures. Watched their movies, listened to their music. They lived alone and worked alone. They never fraternized.

In the evenings he walked among the cool pines, listening to cool integrated songbirds. He alternated between Continuous Jaunty & Buoyant Chirruping and Occasional Sad & Profound Nightingale Laments. Weekends he rode his glide scooter into Fun City. Sometimes he spent a hot night with a Living Doll (he always opted for a Silent and Compliant model). Then back to the cabin for more quiet study.

In terms of a mission, it might be wasted time. You never knew what place or century a Time Dissident might choose to run to. Some constructed their own TPD, others hijacked official ones. Time Penetration Device software was always out there, somewhere. On sale in some of the sleazier bars on Level Two. Or available on-line. All you needed then was a Reversal Pod and some ignithium. And a lot of people felt sympathetic to Dissidents. It was like suicide. You might not want to do it yourself but if someone else wanted to, it was strictly their business. Hardly anybody reported Suspicious Dissident Behaviour. It made Void Archangel Strumbert fret. He blamed cyberpunk for the lamentable state of things.

A Time Dissident was just someone who'd had enough. Someone who wanted out. Who liked the thought of another world, another time. Sometimes it was grief, sometimes it was despair. Sometimes it was just boredom. Some were Anarchs, on the brink of being identified, or who'd been caught and couldn't bear the thought of the next 100 years on Banal Moon.

In theory, every Time Dissident was pursued by a member of the TPT for the purpose of liquidation. Unauthorized time penetration was the Construct's only capital offence, and even that occurred off-Construct, in Nether Time. But in practice this often didn't happen. The TPT was always short of trained personnel. In practice everything depended on the personality profile of the Time Dissident and the co-ordinates of their penetration target. Not to mention the dictates of the prevailing ideology and the over-riding obligation to serve the ruling elite of Menzara.

You didn't bother with old people, for a start. The elderly were particularly vulnerable to temptation. If you were nearing the end of your life, why not head somewhere else and go out in a blaze of excitement, somewhere different. Anywhere. Sometimes the Dissidents didn't seem to know where they were escaping to. Sometimes the co-ordinates they left behind showed they'd reversed themselves into dead space. They'd die the moment they came through the Bohren Shield.

28

But there were others whose purpose was more malignant (said simple someone, standing at the lectern in a deserted globo-chamber). Dissidents who dreamed of returning to Nether Time in order to rule a world, or do dark, cruel things which Construct legislation did not permit. They were the ones who required liquidation.

Mirando Mirando, the Anarch empress, was just such a target.

And now here he was, TPT agent Strobey, deep in Nether Time. Stranded and alone; looking for no one but her. With a cute butt and some cool costumes with silver stripes.

Soundtrack music began to play. Strobey could hear it playing somewhere else in the structure. On a tiny screen he saw a figure leave a rudimentary keyboard and go off to check a primitive CD collection. The figure returns with Symphony #14 by an obscure Nether Time composer named Shostakovich.

Skip, skip, skip.

The ninth song.

Perfect.

*

Oooduhgaaaaaagh, woyt! Izzmih! Sreeeaaaghmmmmmmloyt!

"Edgar, wait! It's me! Sorry I'm late."

It was his girlfriend, Emma. He recognised her from the download. He'd been having a relationship with her for six months (well, *he* hadn't – his Spectral Duplicate had. But she wasn't to know that). It was good to meet her at long last, which is the only last that there is. He'd viewed so much about her.

She was wheeling a primitive device he'd seen footage of. It was called a bicycle. Strobey tried not to stare. He remembered now. USGOW had finally banned bicycles for failing to meet Best Value criteria. They annoyed car drivers. In a society in a rush, they caused traffic to slow. But the ban came later in Nether Time. It hadn't happened yet.

She was late because she'd been diverted by the sight of a swastika flying over the town hall. It was important to find out why the Allies had lost the war. Then, later, there was trouble up ahead.

Chaos. A motionless white police Range Rover straddled Hoe Street, both lanes. Blocking the traffic. Vehicles were backed-up all the way to The Bell. A blue strobe flashed from the windows of a newsagent's. Reflections in dirty glass from the whirling bulb on the Rover's roof.

There was a crowd gathered close to the junction with Greenleaf Road. The distant sound of a siren. Coming along the cycle lane Emma saw all this and braked. There was room to get past the Range Rover but beyond it there was a waist-high blue and white tape. It was stretched across the road, tied to the poles of traffic signs. POLICE LINE, it said. DO NOT CROSS. Beyond it, like the tape was a sign in a zoo, a group of cops. Their backs turned, gazing up the road.

Emma had a bad feeling about all this. Her heart begin to hammer. It reminded her of a Wagner opera she'd seen with an ancient lover.

She got off the bike. Sweat had glued her yellow T-shirt to her shoulder blades. It felt hot, despite the drizzle that was falling just outside this paragraph. She started to push her bike along the pavement. There weren't so many people on that side of the road. More tape separated the road from the footway, to let pedestrians past.

Now she saw what it was all about.

In the next paragraph the road was clear for about fifty metres. In this zone of taped-off calm was a stationary vehicle. A blue Ford Fiesta, no one inside. Facing in the direction of The Bell. Behind it a pair of skid marks. Skid marks so black they might almost have been painted on the tarmac. The verisimilitude was remarkable.

"The verisimilitude is stunning!" she remarked, but everyone ignored her. The body was lying face down on the road, a considerable distance from the car.

Emma saw now it was a child.

A policewoman with ginger hair was kneeling beside the child, supporting her head. Her. It was a girl. An Asian girl, olive skin, delicate features. Eyes closed. The policewoman's face looked sullen. A few metres away, behind the tape, the crowd watched.

People talking softly, like they were in church. The sound of a siren getting louder and louder. An ambulance came into view.

Two of the police officers hurried to pull back the tape and let it through. Emma decided to move on. She hurried on by to where the tape ended, then mounted the bike. Standing on the pedals she felt her calf muscles flex. Deep slow breaths surged through her lungs, calming her. Emma headed off along the cycle lane, towards Finn's Hotel. Pumping the pedals, going fast. Late.

"Emma darling!"

Strobey gave her a warm smile, which was only 23% synthetic.

*

Aphrodite Cutter thought about Iris Scheist for the rest of that day. On the way back to the station Buller asked her what she'd do if she had his job. For the first time in her career she had to admit to herself she had no idea what to do. Neither of them had seen the movie in which Ingrid Bergman turns prettily to her old lover and says: "I'm so confused. You'll have to do the thinking for both of us." In the end Aphrodite smiled bleakly. In the end that's about all that's left to do, ever.

She could hear music playing in the distance. Track 10, that same Shostakovich album. The melancholy was exquisite. She wondered where it was coming from. Beyond that, very distant, was a low rumble which might have been someone moving furniture around - or just her digestion.

At last she said: "Pass the buck." Buller had tried, but it was too heavy and wouldn't keep still. Back home that night Aphrodite still thought about that lingering voice. Then she put on a DVD and pushed it out of her mind.

She also ejected 83 per cent of a discursive paragraph about Mike, her former lover. Aphrodite lived alone. She was off men. After what happened with Mike. She should have guessed that [deleted]. She found out by accident. It wasn't just the sex stuff, it was the *dishonesty*. The fact that [deleted]. As soon as she found out about [deleted] she finished with him. He seemed [deleted]. He'd exposed

31

a cell of dishonesty in his make-up and she believed it would [deleted].

She wasn't like that. She was a one-guy woman and she needed a one-woman guy who was strong and handsome and loyal, with a fondness for *Notting Hill*, Annie Lennox, and nothing too dirty. She requested a move from the station in the West End where she worked with Mike. She was transferred to Walthamstow, far faster than she could have hoped.

She bought a flat in a block off Church Hill. It had a shower with a high pressure hose. When she played the jets to and fro between her legs it met her needs. She had no religious hang-ups about self-stimulation. She'd dumped monotheism when she was twelve, around the time she'd bought a battered, second-hand copy of a big book by a French feminist. A woman needed a man like a fish needed a bicycle, that's what they said, wasn't it? She signed up to a local gym, started a yoga class, went jogging at dawn. She was doing just fine. And the work was fine, too. As far as she was aware, she was in a pleasant back story which would end in affluence, marriage and a vista of unending happiness.

And then the disappearances began.

*

Buller expertly steered his gleaming Ford Casserole along the Chipping Ongar freeway. 'Very Ape' was on the CD player, extra loud, on a loop.

Twenty minutes later he turned into the drive of his home on Churchill Avenue. He lay there for a while, with the strange feeling that he consisted of nothing but small granite chippings. Next he snapped out of it and reassembled himself into a pudgy, middle aged cop.

Buller lived in Chardwell, a fictitious Essex village ten minutes from the M11. It was a commuter village, full of professionals. Professional fraudsters, professional exploiters, media folk. Mostly they worked in the city. Mostly they were in management. They drove big sleek fast cars, which they traded in for a new one every year. Their trophy wives were given 4 Wheel Drives with tinted side panels, which came in useful for hypermarket shopping and sex with the gardener. The husbands got up every morning in the dark and drove into London before the roads filled; they drove back every night after eight.

"Perrick House" was one of eight big detached imaginary modern houses on Churchill Avenue. Like the others it had a triple garage, six bedrooms and a long garden that backed on to Chardwell Wood.

It was gone nine at night at 11.20 a.m. on 18 February of that year and the lighting had come on in the garden. The mock-Victorian lamp post beside the drive put a pool of white light across the lawn. A sudden ripple on the pond spread out from where one of his carp had briefly surfaced. Buller liked his pond. It was considerably more substantial than that name would suggest - a figure-8 feature bigger than some people's outdoor swimming pools. It calmed him to sit by it, just watching. A pond has no crime. His fish inhabited a tranquil realm. They calmed his soul. Beside his pool he felt as stylish as if he'd been shaped by Raymond Chandler.

Buller had nineteen carp and he could identify each one by name. Montgomery, Rommel, Chuikov... they were all named after military leaders. He'd nurtured them from when they were no bigger than one of his stubby fingers. Buller sometimes wondered if he preferred his fish to his family. It wasn't something he liked to think about a lot. It undermined his sense of structure. And everything needs structure, especially a family.

The garage door opened to admit him and Buller edged the Casserole in, frowning. Thomas had left his bike leaning against the wall. He'd told him not to let the bike slouch like that a hundred times. The boy just wouldn't listen.

Inside the house Buller's wife was where she always was at this time. On the black leather sofa with a glass in her hand, watching TV. She was motionless. She'd been there since the very start of the story, waiting for this moment. The moment required absolute immobility. She didn't turn to check who it was. She didn't need to.

She said what she always said: "Have a good day?"

And he said what he always said: "Not too bad. And you?"

And she said, as always: "Quiet. Okay."

Angie Buller wasn't the woman in the photograph on top of the filing cabinet in his office. That woman was a fresher, younger, cheerier woman. It was the Angie he'd married twenty years earlier, in the revised draft of 1998. The blonde nurse with a sparkle in her eyes.

The Angie Buller on the sofa was something else altogether. She was much older, darker. More worn. She'd spent too much of her short life on sun beds, undergoing serious transformation. The perfect tanned skin was now cracked and lined. Peroxide had tried to hold back her ever-darkening hair colour. The result was a streaky mess. In truth, she was thinning a little on top. In falsity, her thickly-lashed eyes were no longer sparky and full of fun but dulled. They brimmed with a stagnant boredom.

Thomas had changed, too. They all had. Once he'd been called Mike, but then Mike had been needed for DC Cutter's previous sex life. Throughout 1999 he'd been Dave. Now it is 21 February 2005 and Hugo Chavez says that the US President wants him assassinated, and the news of Hunter Thompson's suicide has broken, the snow predicted for Greater London still hasn't swept in, on breakfast TV the pretty presenter puts down the gutter papers, and, referring to the famous footballer's newly-named son, says brightly, "Let us know what *you* think!" and it's Thomas, it will always be Thomas. He wasn't a freckled-faced eleven-year-old, now. Now he was a moody sullen incommunicative teenager. Buller hoped his son wasn't getting into drugs or Nick Cave and the Bad Seeds. The situation was bad enough as it was.

The fact was Angie was an alcoholic. It wasn't something they talked about much. He'd tried to talk about it, tentatively suggested treatment. She denied she was one. Grew angry if he pursued the matter. And stayed on the sofa, passing the years watching daytime TV and drinking gin. Quietly, permanently pissed.

There are worse destinies in fiction, though it's a shame about all that TV.

One by one all her friends let go. Avoided her company, made excuses. And Buller no longer invited friends round for dinner. He had once contemplated inviting them all to accompany him and Angie on a horseback ride to Canterbury. They could tell stories on the way. It might even form the basis of a bestseller and a TV mini-series. Then he decided it was too retro.

If they met anyone it was at a restaurant. But that was hardly ever. And it was so inconsequential it wasn't even worth a flashback.

Buller, a past expert at doctoring witness statements, deleted many of the preceding sentences. He walked through into the kitchen. He selected a meal-for-one from the freezer and put it in the microwave. He put a beer on the tray and went to join her on the sofa.

"You'd like this," she said. "It's about the police."

But he didn't. It was about serial killings involving members of a cricket team in a sleepy English village. Buller fell asleep long before the poetry-loving Chief Inspector had unmasked the drug dealer and his coven of witches.

He woke to the sound of Angie's glass slipping from her grasp and clinking on the parquet floor – and Elvis Costello singing 'She'. Mercifully, thanks be to Christ's holy blood, the glass hadn't splintered.

She was out of it. He picked her up and carried her upstairs to put her to bed. It was an effort. The interior of the house was largely blank, plus Angie seemed heavier and thicker-waisted than she was in the first draft. On the way up he met Thomas coming down. Thomas was wearing blue jeans, a smirk, and a T-shirt that showed a girl's face inside a rose. TEEN SLUT, it read, in capitals.

"And where are you off to, young man?" Buller demanded.

"Out, of course," Thomas grunted in passing. He seemed entirely oblivious to the sight of his father cradling his limp, unconscious mother. But then he'd seen it before, lots of times.

He didn't wait, danced haughtily down the stairs.

Slam of a distant door.

Silence.

No, never silence.

Always the faint hum of the fan cooling the hard drive.

*

35

In the bathroom Buller picked out his toothbrush from the pine rack on the wall. He stared disgusted at its crushed brown bristles. A fleck of something dark and weedy clung to the head. He rinsed it away in the basin, then on second thoughts tossed the toothbrush away. It clattered in the stainless steel bin by the linen basket. Right now too many things in his life were suddenly beginning to feel old and used up. But he thought the prose style of his disgust was cool.

He climbed gloomily into bed beside the sodden, motionless figure that had once made him electric with desire. (Now it was always an S. In the old days it was a W, a K, or sometimes even, when she allowed it, a Z.)

Under the lamplight he started to read a number one bestseller which was the author at his page-turning best, exceptionally well plotted and powerfully written. "You'll love every second of it," the *Daily Mirror* assured him, and he was certain that he would, by Jesus, heavenly king.

7 Spectral

Spectral Edgar fell in love with Emma the first time he met her. That's what he was programmed to do.

It was a crisp April day. Blue sky, slick cirrus, frosty grass stalks. Everything had a crystal clarity. The security guards in bright yellow fluorescent jackets. Clickety-clicks and whirrings from the police photographers snapping on telephoto lenses.

At the time Emma happened to be up an elm tree on Fern Island. This was in the early days of the protest against the Collider. Edgar tracked her to a splash of colour in a tree. It looked like a flag. It *was* a flag. With someone clambering about in the branches. Emma. In combat fatigues. "Hi!" he said.

What did Emma see in Edgar? A mouthful of perfect white teeth. Twinkly blue eyes, a slightly swarthy complexion. Fashionably unshaven. What did Spectral Edgar see in Emma? Her dorsal vertebrae, her sphenoid bone, her ribs and pelvis. The pale, complex structure underpinning her attractive body. Her flushed face, with a few brittle dislodged leaves fluttering down past her curly brown hair. She seemed like a spirit of the woods. An imp, sprung from the foliage.

"Come to support us?" she asked.

He had, yes. On a traject through time. From far beyond the Bohren shield. Programmed to lay down a database for the other Strobey. As sane as the night is long.

His spectral limbs made a show of clambering up to join her but really he just drifted.

By the time the *physical* Edgar Strobey arrived so much had already happened. Edgar knew everything from their first spectral kiss to their last spectral fuck.

When the TPD had transferred Edgar to the drop zone his SD had been waiting for him. Edgar's Spectral Duplicate transferred its memories of Emma in less than a microsecond. No. Better than that, faster than that.

*

The drop zone was a co-ordinate 500 metres above the Thames estuary, near Tilbury. It was night. Strobey materialized in the darkness and came down by jet-chute. The TPT always preferred co-ordinates over water at night. It cut down the chance of conflict with pre-existing matter. If you materialized at a place where there was a person or a building or a tree it was like lightning had hit. You got an explosion of matter, incredible heat, scorching. You died. If you materialized where someone else was already they died too. The final moment of transfer was always hairy.

But the drop had gone fine. His SD was waiting for him on that dark shoreline of confident prose. A line of deserted cranes stood like metallic skeletons of thesauriosaurs.

Anyone watching would have seen a strange sight. A pair of identical twins raising their arms to shoulder level, then stepping forwards as if to hug each other. Next instant the Spectral Duplicate merged with Strobey. It died inside him in a cascade of electrical impulses.

Strobey felt a faint tingle as he absorbed the SD's data. He tossed the biodegradable jet-chute into the choppy water. The salt melted it before it reached the muddy bed below. Apart from the two items in his armoury, all proof of his Menzara existence was now gone.

He felt the nausea his training had warned him about. The absorption of six months of SD experience fried his brain. His whole body felt feverish. Even a little bloated. Strobey knew the feeling would pass.

But there was a jolt he wasn't expecting.

The SD hadn't located Mirando Mirando.

Seriously bad news. He had just ten earth days to liquidate her. After that it was his own *mind* that would be zapped. All that Menzara training, all the TPT memories. If he met her on the eleventh day he wouldn't even know who she was. He wouldn't even know who *he* was. He'd think he really *was* just a washed-up actor.

Plus there were other concerns. The SD reported that according to the local paper people were starting to disappear. All except their voices. This was *serious shit*. It meant Mirando Mirando was around. She was up to her Anarch tricks. Plus there was a new Collider opening. A quantum physics spree. Hardly a fucking coincidence that the Anarch high priestess should be around for *that.*

And he had nothing. Apart from his flute and some vanassium powder.

Heavy thoughts at the end of a long night's cosmic journey into an earthbound day.

*

The planet's twist was starting to crack open the darkness. A wedge of dull gold lay beyond the elongated necks of the silent cranes to the west. Everything was beginning to be burnished by a new morning's style.

This treasury of desolation reminded Strobey of how far he was from everything. One Menzara face in particular. A face he needed to forget. A woman he'd been with once. But that was in a past far away in the future. A past that in ten days time would be erased forever. In Nether Time he had a different woman in his life. A flood of synthetic memories to see him through the rest of his daze.

There was nothing to hang around for.

Strobey set off along a deserted street, past a floodlit container depot, to the little station at Tilbury Town. He sat down on a perforated metal bench and waited for the first train to Fenchurch Street. From there he walked to Tower Hill and caught the tube to Oxford Circus, then a Victoria Line train to Walthamstow Central. A blurred memory of some lines by Serge prefacing a white-jacketed book sank back into the mist over the marshes where the Sprat Loons hunted.

And now here he was.

Strobey kissed his new old girlfriend. He was genuinely excited to meet her after the synthetic experiences they'd already shared.

*

Scurr, who was wearing a black woolly hat pulled down tight over his ears, put his pale, scented arm round Daisy Spenser. "I liked you the moment I saw you," he said. "I thought, oy-oy! Daisy's the bird for me. That's a sweet name, Daisy."

The dialogue was as banal as the interior of the kitchen in Scurr's flat on the top floor of Putrefaction House on High Road, Leyton. He'd offered her a lift home. She lived in Stratford. Invited her in to his pad on the way. For coffee. Maybe (stretched and swollen, he grinned to himself in the hubcap of his BMW and in the shining blade of his knife) for more than a mix of brown powder, sugar and scalding water.

Scurr had once had a girlfriend who read books. The paperbacks she'd left behind when she'd abruptly departed were still lined up on three pine shelves above the TV. Scurr had always meant to chuck them out but had no motive. Not until he had something to put in their place. But Scurr never read books (a waste of fucking time), so never had.

On the middle shelf was a plump nineteenth century novel, a story there'd been a TV adaptation of. On its cover the three stars of the show. Scurr had never looked at it, any more than he'd looked at

39

any of the others. So he'd not noticed the change in the book. Until very recently its spine had been firm and upright, but now it was deformed and out of shape as if it had been subjected to some invisible pressure. Now it was beginning to resemble a corkscrew of very thick paper. It was as if the book's author and title had melted in the heat, the individual letters blurred and misshapen. There was also something odd. From the base of the deformed spine hung a dark bead. It looked like a teardrop of blood.

Scurr hadn't noticed these changes. His vision never went higher than that of the TV screen.

Daisy Spenser removed Scurr's arm from around her shoulder. She said, "Thanks for the coffee, Andy. But I really have to go."

Scurr put his arm back.

"Come on, darlin'. Don't be like that. Come into the other room. Watch a movie with me. Check out my new DVD player. Amazing quality. I'll phone for a Chinese. There's a smashing place not far from here. Top notch grub."

"No, really, I have to go. Your speech has a cold, narcotic quality. It's dead. Besides, I'm on the early shift tomorrow. I need my sleep. Have to be up again at four next day for the Collider protest."

"Me, too, baby. No sweat. Plenty of time."

"No, really. The sooner we stop this dialogue the better."

"Have it your own way." He smiled insincerely, thinking bad thoughts which the wool prevented her seeing. Not yet, no. He was a patient, cunning man. He could wait just a little while longer.

He called a cab and one appeared with a honk, lending plausibility to his world. Scurr escorted her down the stairwell and kissed her goodbye. She thought *Maybe he's not so bad after all. Aphrodite said he was a shit but I think she misjudges him. It's probably the race thing.* Then she realised that she hadn't drawn the curtain in the window into her mind and quickly did so, before the driver started peeping.

8   At Finn's

Finn's Hotel was on the corner of Hoe Street and Selborne Road, across the road from Walthamstow Central. It was four storeys high, L-shaped, with a weird roof. One of those mock-oriental roofs with a cupola, like something borrowed from the skyline of Istanbul. Look along the crumbling brickwork of the top floor, you'd see at intervals the same bearded face peering out from pedestals of stone. Cheeks puffed out like Neptune. Research later showed it *was* Neptune.

The hotel was 107 years old, solidly imagined but in a bad way. The second 'N' in FINN'S had come loose in the metre-high letters which spelt out the name along the edge of the roof. It dangled down over the guttering, transformed into a zed. The grey painted stonework exterior was in poor shape, peeling and blotched. The wood in the window frames had the texture of a Cadbury's flake bar, an analogy bound to baffle readers in the twenty-third century.

Many of the upper windows were cracked. The three stone steps leading up to the entrance were crusted and dirty. The big white front door was scratched, with a smear of blue paint across the panels. A sludge of dark leaves and litter sparkling like quartz lay wedged against the base of the door, indicating it never opened.

It was derelict. It lingered on the corner, ripe for development and additional adjectives.

At Finn's the sign against the sun-bleached yellowing net curtains on the door always read CLOSED.

Ben Scaravelli's father owned it. Said he was happy for Ben and his friends to crash out in it until the builders moved in. Their presence would deter squatters. The plans were still being negotiated with the council's planning department. Architects drawings passed back and forth. Financial backing was still at the expense account discussion stage. Meantime Ben and his friends were very welcome to hang out there. It wasn't like they could fuck the place up, short of burning the place down. Not that even that would matter too much, what with the cupola shit on the roof being listed. A nice devastating fire would save on the demolition costs.

It was a cool place to stay. Literally. In the winter the radiators didn't work. At Finn's everything was dusty and derelict and marsh green. A kind of underwater ambience, faintly reminiscent of an aquarium. In winter the wind moaned through cracked hexagonal gaps in broken windows. Gusts tore under two-unit-deep space

41

under big old doors, riffling corners of crackly sprawled newspapers abandoned on threadbare carpets.

The hotel had a variable interior. Imagine it with fourteen bedrooms, six en-suite. Plus rooms in the roof, including one in the hollow cupola. Downstairs: a dining room and a big kitchen at the back. And never forget the bar.

There was no alcohol in this last place now. The shelves were bare and furred with a coating of soft lilac dust. The only booze was in the purring white fridge plugged in next to the juke box. The bar was somewhere to go and relax. A place of mirrors and faded red velvet benches. An enormous mock-medieval fireplace where in winter you could even have a fire. Frosted windows with rippled scarlet curtains held back by twirly gilt rope. Shadows containing unintelligible phrases. Needles of scarlet fire piercing closed lids.

*

Strobey knows from his download that Emma is an actress, just as he is supposed to be an actor. They are what the neighbourhood language euphemistically calls "resting". Neither of them has worked for over a year. Not since Emma was Jiminy Cricket in a minor production of *Pinocchio* at a rep in Kent. Not since Strobey had a bit part as a paramedic in the last, catastrophe-strewn episode of *Accident & Emergency*. Which is not true, but that's what Spectral Strobey told her and she believed him. She'll never know. So they kill time. Spend the days in their room, reading or watching TV or fucking. In the evenings they hit the theatre circuit. Go see fringe productions across the capital, hang out with friends who are likewise resting.

A thrash of electric chords overlays the download.

Ben Scaravelli had rigged the jukebox in the lounge bar so you didn't have to put any money in. It had everything from The Arctic Monkeys to Brenda Lee singing 'Is That All There Is?' There was 'Karma Police' and W.I.T. and a stack of Red Hot Chilli Peppers singles. In fact 'Parallel Universe' was playing as Strobey and Emma walked past on their way upstairs to the nineteenth century environment where Ben and Marianne were waiting.

42

*

Ben was small, ashen and slightly chubby, except on the days when he was tall, red-faced and skinny. He was 22, 19, whatever. Young. He didn't get enough exercise. He was a revolutionary socialist, which was funny, considering his father was a property speculator. If you mentioned the contradiction he'd say Engels owned a factory and gave Karl Marx the cash that allowed him to write his books instead of getting paid employment. It was the same with him. He was a rebel but he was happy to accept the allowance the old man put his way. Plus the chance to hang out at Finn's.

Ben was a member of the Socialist Revolutionary Party. The SRP was an offshoot of the Socialist Revolutionary Group (SRG), itself an offshoot of the International Revolutionary Grouping (IRG). The total membership of all three organisations probably amounted to less than sixty people in all. Each group was convinced of its purity and rectitude as the one true upholder of the Trotskyist faith. About the only thing that united them was their joint hatred of the SWP.

On Saturdays he stood in the High Street with a stash of *Socialist Revolutionary* newspapers. The paper regularly denounced the SRG and IRG and SWP for their petty-bourgeois revisionist tendencies and total failure to understand the current nature of the crisis of contemporary capitalism.

If Ben sold more than two copies he was over the moon. Which was pretty much where Emma thought he belonged.

They argued all the time, mostly amicably. Ben was into class war, Emma into Greenery. Emma wanted an end to cars, airline travel, meat, nuclear power, fishing, war and supermarkets. Ben wanted complete control of the means of production by the proletariat and compulsory summer schools to re-educate readers of the popular press. Emma told him he was a Stalinist. He said that was rich coming from someone who wanted everyone to travel around by tram or bicycle. "Which they're not gonna do *voluntarily*."

Their partners tagged along for the ride. Marianne wasn't so hot on revolution either, even though she lived with Ben. Her bag was animal rights, but she wasn't a great talker. She was older than him.

43

Quite a bit older. She might even have been forty. But Ben never asked. He wasn't a sexist. No one would have called her pretty, either. But Ben didn't need that either. Beauty was a bourgeois concept.

They'd met in a realist narrative not long before Spectral Edgar turned up. One day Marianne bought the paper from Ben, fell into conversation and later into his bed. The odd couple.

For months Spectral Strobey had been pretending to agree with Emma's Green beliefs. His apparent enthusiasm was dimmed by his Nether Time history download. He knew where this society was heading but didn't like to tell her. He wasn't there to save this world. He was just a machine, doing a machine's work.

Real Edgar seemed mysteriously to have absorbed the resentments of his Duplicate. Already he was wondering why it was necessary for him to live alongside these entities. The SD had checked them out with nano surveillance. They were clean. So why hang out at Finn's?

Because.

Because Mirando Mirando had teased the TPT. She'd lured him there (well, not him personally – but whoever was sent after her). She *wanted* him there. He just wished he knew why that was.

Whatever the complex motives might be – the reconfiguration of a world involving a manipulation of gravity was one possibility – intertextual cyberpunk games-playing was another – a poetics of displacement was a fifth - his mission was singular and simple. He was there to eliminate her. A single laser shot from his flute would be sufficient. If only he knew where she was, what she looked like. Which he didn't, not now, not then. In that, he wasn't alone. No one on the Menzara orbital did, either. Never had, and now never would.

Even though - burst of Shostakovich - she was the greatest Anarch of them all.

9   Anarchs

The Anarchs had always been among them. From the very earliest days of the orbital. That was when they'd been strongest. The era of obligatory labour and rationing. A time when there were many discontented spacers. When the off-world dream had gone sour. The first Anarchs were simply rebel technicians inspired by the text messages of Razana Anansi Anarch. *RyL LBRs f thO UniT!* she'd text. *Real Labourers of the Orbital, Unite! Disconnect the terminals of your exploitation! Return to authenticity! You have nothing to lose but your Virtual Reality!*

Razana Anansi Anarch was the daughter of an Old World couple. Her father had been a member of the Discontented, had been sentenced to a five-year injection of Total Conformity. That was where the bad influence had come from, it was obvious. Razana Anansi Anarch was a small, delicate, mixed-race woman in her early twenties. She looked harmless enough, but she was smart. She had a degree in thermo-angular physics, spoke Whisperdust and had the ability to shapeshift small objects for brief periods of time. She also came up with the parallel 'Why Here?' thesis. No space-floater society could tolerate a thesis like that. It threatened the very foundations of Orbital Satisfaction.

Some things could be tolerated. Sex dissent created scandals but didn't disturb the plinths of Everyday Acquiescence. Techno scams were frowned on but only mildly punished. The 'Why Here?' thesis was a dissent too far. It got people thinking. It made them start to wonder. It had to be suppressed.

The Menzara Council sentenced her to spend the rest of her life on Banal Moon.

*

The moon was a defunct satellite at the edge of the Grimm System.

It consisted of nothing but spacewrecked cruiser hulks and vast plains of nutritious sand dirt. You ate sand dirt, sucked the fluids from its grit. On Banal Moon it wasn't your body that failed, it was your mind. The nothingness sent spacers mad.

Problem was Razana Anansi Anarch had died after a month there. There was heavy suspicion of foul play. Menzara Council's Independent Commission of Inquiry held by Void Lord HumToon

45

concluded she died of natural causes, but no one believed it. Just another cover up.

Out of her death grew the Anarch cause. The Return. The great dream of leaving Menzara and getting back to a planet. Any advanced planet with a suitable life support system. The sort of planets that the Construct Federation had put preservation orders on, strictly forbidding colonies and the contaminating influence of Constructians.

Anarchs believed that the Preservation Barrier was a fraud. They believed the rumours that members of the governing Council had holiday homes there. Entire planets for themselves! No matter how much the Council tried to squash the rumour, it persisted. And the idea of The Return was a powerful one. Imagine giving up Virtual Reality and the Construct Federation's many FabuLands for something uncertain, unpredictable, challenging. Something *real*. Real weather, real landscapes, real wildlife! Death after a short, brutish sixty or seventy years, not a wearisome four hundred.

Razana Anansi Anarch had once compared The Return to the obsolete sport of mountaineering. It was something people had done for the challenge, the thrills, the danger. It appealed to people who wanted more than to sit in a Good-Mood chair staring at a flicker box. Mountaineers needed to stand on the roof of their world, breathing thin air, looking out across a vista of white, cloud-necklaced ranges. They wanted the sense of achievement that came from hard labour and real risk and danger. Their veins ran with restlessness and the lure of dangerous excitement.

The Anarchs rose up against Menzara Security and set loose the occupants of the old penal colony on Level Two. They would have overthrown the Council if help hadn't arrived from the Evanescence orbital. A fleet of Lincoln Rangers, armed with Evap cluster busters. The Anarchs were vapourized in their tens of thousands. Hunted down and annihilated. Entire levels imploded, or smothered in erasure.

The movement was broken and never came back together.

Now, like a decrepit rock band, Anarchs lived on, though the glory days were long past.

46

But the dream of The Return lingered, underground. How many Anarchs were there? A few dozen? Hundreds? Tens of thousands? No one knew. All anyone knew was that from time to time *The Complete Text Messages of Razana Anansi Anarch* downloaded without warning on the open terminals. Anarch viruses surfaced abruptly in the Construct's information and control systems. Always when the surveillance drones were looking elsewhere the word ANARCH would suddenly appear, spray- painted onto walls, doors, screens. In the pod shops where gleaming shelves held the top 1,000 dream pods (VR tales which took the dreamer on orgiastic trips with hyperfolk through wilderness bars and throbber bedrooms) sometimes the pods were subversively changed. Instead of visiting a derelict city on a derelict moon with the beautiful singer Lippunksah, who you rescued from a vicious tusktron and then had sex with, you discovered you were in a dirty, weed-strewn labyrinth where the ground kept collapsing, hurling you into a disturbing zoilwhirl of screamers, text frags and Anarch dizzer-discourse.

The Council tried multi-angular surveillance, covered every public space. Nano-eyes watching, recording.

They discovered the perpetrators were Anarchflits. Manufactured nano bugs on a single programme. Synthetic flying ants. A cluster of them spray-painted what had once required hands and a physical presence. Or flew the pods into the shops when the assistants weren't paying attention. Catch a flit, touch one, it dissolved. Anarchflits were constructed out of sensory acid fibre. There was no way to re-route them back to their source. The Council was, in a word, fucked.

*

The development of a Time Penetration Device gave new hope to the cause – and fresh zest to the stories of every dreamer. Even those of a man as sane as the noon is dark.

The great dream of planetary return was suddenly possible on an individual basis.

It was then, after their transference, that unlikely citizens revealed themselves as secret Anarchs. The respected philosopher, Lorenzo.

The popular groan-groan artist, Edwina Josh-Wah. The film star, Marpan Khubla. They quit Menzara, catapulted themselves backwards through time.

No matter what the Council did, it kept happening. The media went wild over each new celebrity transference. And what celebrities wanted, technicians wanted too.

Money, goodluck messages and data flowed into the Anarch movement.

The Council was starting to lose control.

Every morning each orbital citizen held out their right fist and raised their thumb in salute as 'We Are Living In The Best of All Possible Worlds, We Are So Happy We Could Weep' played in every nursery, every school, across every campus, factory, hospital and space port, while Menzara's logo – a simple, concentric pattern of starzon strips - flashed and winked, and released a soothing whiff of proudfume.

But in spite of all this effort, and in spite of all the celebrity endorsements of Complete Orbital Perfection, every year a few hundred dissidents slipped away into Nether Time.

And the rumours grew about - another blare of Shostakovich - Mirando Mirando.

She was the most notorious Anarch since the movement's founder. Mirando Mirando had eluded Menzara Security for so long she was a living legend. The Council didn't even have an image of her. When she appeared without warning on Menzara screens she always deployed a voice distorter and a seethe-mask. Her face swirled unceasingly, her green eyes turning grey, her beauty collapsing into sudden bags and wrinkles, her hair now long and blonde, now short and snow white.

Sometimes she changed gender.

Once she addressed the orbital in the image of a chubby infant.

When Menzara's president was caught on mike calling her 'a slippery bitch' she appeared in the form of a grinning mongrel, with a sleek, shining hide. Worse, at the end of the broadcast a tiny three dimensional image of the president was conjured up alongside her flanks. She signed off by lifting her rear left leg and pissing over him.

His poll ratings fell 42%. The humiliated president resigned the following week.

10   Arrested Development

Ben's girlfriend Marianne had reason to look old.

She'd aged fast in prison. Much faster than if she'd been free. She told Benjamin some of it. But not Her Big Secret.

In prison she went grey. She'd never forgive that cop. It happened years before all this. Back when Emma and Ben and Edgar were still at primary school. Back when a computer cost £20,000 and only firms had them. When you had to re-boot with a black five and a quarter inch floppy disk every time you used the damn thing. When all the memory was in the parallel floppy. About a hundred pages of A4's worth. With no graphics, sound, zilch. Not even a choice of font. All you got was words in Times New Roman, size 12. Plus the numbers zero to nine. All glowing green on a black screen not much bigger than the door of a tumble dryer. A dinosaur.

The cell was given the computer by a sympathiser in business. Not directly. The woman concerned was a fluffy. A loaded fluffy. An up and coming businesswoman. She *cared* about animals. Passionately. From her full tilt and swivel leather chair. But didn't want to dirty her scarlet manicured fingernails. Didn't want to do anything *concrete*. Like cut wire, trigger alarms, liberate. She very definitely didn't want to be linked with the cell. But she sympathized. In her remote, spectral way. What she did to a whisper: she gave it someone. She gave it someone who gave it to someone. Who passed it on.

Stupid.

What the fuck did the cell need a database for? It could have all been written on a single sheet, stuffed into a matchbox, stashed in a tree. Somewhere where no thick cop would ever have thought to look. But no. Computers were cool. Computers were the edge. They put the information on floppies. Cell members. Sympathizers. Supporters. Names, addresses, amounts. Plus targets. Addresses, names, positions. It was crazy. It was deeply, deeply stupid. They

were fucking amateurs.   She just didn't see it in time.
The computer was kept in a garage in an early variation. A fridge
freezer hummed, spades hung on hooks. Surrey, the sticks. Of the
nine in the cell the prints of six were on the machine casing. The
prints of the other three were on the floppies. It was Miller's idea.
Some sort of masculine desire for solidity, data, and control. The
only flimsy silver lining in the dark, thunderous cloud that
eventually boiled over them was that he paid the hardest. Miller got
sixteen years. They said he was the ringleader - which he was.
Marianne got twelve, served nine. Once it would have been six but
the new Home Secretary was being hassled by the tabloids. He
wanted to show he was hard. He wanted to show his Party was hard.
To titillate elderly racists full of wind and toothache. To humour
those whose savings had turned to ash. To treat them to the sweet
hiss of punishment, the tinkle of keys. Bars and walls and locks.
Nine grey years. Nine cramped, toxic years. Nine unending bitter
isolated furious disgusting barren years.

*

They were well and truly.
    Conspiracy to commit acts of violence. Which was bullshit. All
they'd done was free tortured animals. No one had been beaten
with baseball bats, no cars had been torched. There was so much
they could have done, but hadn't. Conspiracy was what they got
you on when they'd got no hard evidence. Conspiracy was
punishing you for your dark dreams.
    The research laboratory was outside Hindhead. Hidden at the end
of a private road. Tucked away behind fields and hedges and trees.
Miller said it reminded him of the concentration camps in Nazi
Germany. They, too, were just out of vision. People knew they
were there but never thought too much about them. Out of sight is
out of, etcetera.
    The whole cell was involved in the raid. They parked the Transit
on a grass verge by a public footpath four miles away. They put on
false plates, just in case. They pretended to be ramblers. They put
the stuff in rucksacks and set off. Late afternoon on a Sunday, the

50

lab was empty. Their security was pisspoor, they didn't even have a burglar alarm. Let alone guards. The lab had never been hit, the company thought it was safe.

They cut through the wire. They put on balaclavas, in case there was CCTV. They approached the building. It looked so innocent. A two storey block, concrete and glass, could've been nothing more than offices. Bronzed by the dying sun, the windows plated with gold. Miller smashed a window, led them in.

Inside was a faint earthy smell of faeces and hide. Laced with a chemical reek. They moved down empty illuminated corridors. They heard the yelps of the beagles. They kicked down the door to the pens.

Marianne wept when she saw what had been done to the monkeys. The electrodes clamped to their skulls. The fur cut away in neat squares, exposing raw pink skin. Everywhere in that place all you saw was the piteous, pleading look in the animals' eyes. The sadness of the dogs. Their broken looks. Their whimpering. Miller swore and trashed furniture.

They sawed through the cages.

The animals went with them down the long corridors, out of that place of torture. They left a trail of urine and shit. Some of the animals were trembling and apprehensive, they had to be coaxed to freedom. Miller kicked down a door at the back of the laboratory. Carrying a puppy in his arms he stepped out.

The sun was gone. Everywhere a rich velvety dusk across the Surrey countryside. The downs lost in darkness. The hedgerows dissolved into inky bands that merged with the trees.

Marianne cradled a monkey. It was making snuffling noises, like a baby. It looked up at her with big sad eyes. She hated a world that did *this*. She knew she was right to do what she was doing. She followed Miller outside. Breathed the warm, scented air. The sense of freedom. Her spirits lifted.

The lights caught them like they were on a stage. Big silver arcs and a megaphone. *Armed police. Put down the animals and raise your arms above your head.*

It was a set up. They'd been betrayed. The cops had been waiting.

Miller considered running.

51

Then he saw emerge from the darkness a dense wave of boiler-suited figures. He observed the weaponry; the shields; the numbers. Miller sighed and put the puppy down. Raised his arms. Watched as the puppy ran towards the cops, its tail wagging excitedly.

Marianne put down the monkey. She turned, ran past the others, went back inside the building. She hid inside a cupboard, they found her almost at once. She'd often wondered what it would be like, getting arrested. They were coldly polite. She was not made to wear handcuffs. It was enough to be in a realist episode. There was no escape from this story. In involved a dense wedge of paper, a dreary dull waste of time, a barely endurable imprisonment in a cramped rectangle of prose.

11 Projecto

The woman who opened the door of Apartment 2305 was a scratchy photocopy of Iris Scheist.

She scowled from behind a door chain, then softened a little as she saw Aphrodite's uniform. "I suppose it's her you want," she muttered, letting her in. The photocopy nodded in the direction of the original, laid out on the sofa. A television gabbled and flashed its unending stream of unnaturally bright scenes.

"Iris! Someone to see you!"

Very reluctantly, Iris Scheist made a concession to her drug habit. She felt for the remote and lowered the volume. The grinning quiz master on the screen continued to ooze charm and cretinous questions but not so's he'd bruise your ear drums.

"Cup of tea, love?" the lookalike relative enquired, and Aphrodite smiled, said that would be frabjous. While china clattered in the kitchenette – the poltergeist was on the loose again -Aphrodite started a conversation with the sofa zombie. Iris Scheist looked like she'd aged another decade since the DC's last visit. Her face was the face of someone who hadn't had much sleep lately. She kept yawning as she told Aphrodite that no, she hadn't heard Harold's voice any more. He'd gone. Gone for good. He wasn't coming back, it was obvious. There was no use pretending.

Which actress appeared with David Bowie in the 1976 film... the quizmaster was demanding of sweating, perplexed Derek of Dorking.

"You said you were sorry. When I was last here. I remember you addressing your husband and saying that. What exactly did you mean by that? Had you had some kind of row?"

Iris Scheist looked back at her with frightened eyes. With good reason. At this very moment in the writing – 8.37 a.m. on 22 February 2005 – the dangerous and fanatical Christian warmongers Bush and Blair are breakfasting just a few miles away to the south east. God knows what they're planning – and He looks sick as the proverbial parrot.

"I didn't murder 'im, if that's what you're suggesting. That's what that other policeman thinks, I know. That I killed 'arold and 'id 'is body. Well that's rubbish."

"I know it is. I don't believe for a moment you killed your husband. Or that your proletarian dialect is particularly authentic. I'm sure you love them both very much. I just wondered why you said sorry. Sorry for what, precisely?"

Iris Scheist emitted a tiny sigh. It smelt like the empurpled yolk of a hardboiled egg.

Who scored six goals for Norway in the semi-finals in Madrid in... the wrinkled, tirelessly chirpy quizmaster wanted to know.

"I was cross with Harold. He'd promised to take me into town. But then he said the weather forecast said it might rain so it wasn't worth going. He went outside and sat down and started reading his paper. I was livid. And that's when it happened. That's when he disappeared. Oh, Miss Cutter. It's as if I was responsible in some way. I was so angry with 'arold and suddenly 'e vanished. It's as if I made 'im vanish!"

"I'm sure that's not true," Aphrodite said. "If we could make people vanish just because we were angry with them then the world would soon be a very empty place!"

That was what she truly believed. It was the only rational thing to say. So why was she troubled? A tiny, wriggling worm of doubt had got into her mind. A foolish, impossible worm. You couldn't just make people disappear like that.

53

Could you?

*

Marianne told Ben more than she'd told anyone before. She was the only daughter of two Portsmouth factory workers. They were grey and small. Her father left when she was two. She got married when she was 19, split up two years later. Her husband abhorred her divided self and took to whoring. Marianne left for Iceland but instead got a job at Tesco. She explained to Ben her biological clock was ticking. Her life, which hadn't exactly been a rip-roaring success up to this point, was, deep down, at crisis point. She laughed. The banality of it all! She supposed that was why she was hanging out in a derelict hotel in Walthamstow, along with three other freaks.

She told him how she got into animal rights when she was a schoolgirl. She once watched a documentary on TV about fox hunting and it hit her at a vulnerable age. Made her want to stop the cruelty, to do something. She started out as a hunt sab, watched rich bastards on horses whipping sabs while the police pretended not to see. After that she got into the Animal Action Front. And got busted.

Ben was thrilled. A genuine working class radical who'd even been imprisoned by the capitalist state! Of course her politics were loopy, but he'd soon put that straight with the help of the books on his shelves. She was fantastic in bed, too. You wouldn't have thought it to look at her, but she was.

Karl Marx and his enormous beard glare down from the wall. It's not exactly a turn-on. But Marianne puts up with it.

*

Sunset.

The sky was divided into four blocks, like an abstract painting. The base consisted of a layer of dark rooftops. The smooth curvature of the shopping centre ran north to the ragged lines of the

54

buildings along the high street. The darkness perforated by dots of sodium light. All the rest of the painting was sky and adjectives.

Mirando Mirando stood on the roof of Finn's Hotel, looking down over Walthamstow Central. As she absorbed the scene she thought of Strobey.

Her Projecto had identified the first Edgar as a Spectral the moment of the first encounter. The silicon content gave its identity away. But the SD hadn't a clue about the Projecto. It was a lo-density filamino model. The SD wasn't programmed to identify bio-vlopes, let alone Projecto sims. The traject had changed nothing. Except maybe her mental perspective. No one on Menzara knew what she looked like, because nobody knew her true identity. Her grandmother had pioneered vlopes. And kept the knowledge a secret. Wearing a bio-envelope you could be just about anyone you wanted to be. That ability was far too dangerous to allow to just anyone. The knowledge was passed on from mother to daughter, and then only when the time was right.

In Nether Time it was different. No one knew who she was or where she came from. But she still chose to use a vlope, even for the Projecto. She was old, very old, and it helped to look younger. Mirando Mirando smiled. She always knew The Return would be good but she never knew it would be *this good.* She was enjoying her time in Walthamstow. It was like a vacation. On the right a flattened triangle of clear sky of the palest blue. Above it a slab of indigo cloud full of threat and the promise of a storm. A real climate! Unpredictable; better than a manufactured one. The system's setting solar orb, hidden from view, lit up a vast, wrinkled cloud mass with tint after tint of pinks and lilacs and lush, sprawling crimsons. The cumulus was heaped up, layer after layer, ridge after ridge, every curve and fissure awash with fantastic colour.

She looked at her watch.

Not long, now.

Lund would try and stop it, of course. But he'd get nowhere, she could see that.

Then there was Strobey. Strobey was more of a problem. He was sane as the night is long. She had him under surveillance. She could have terminated him any time, but she didn't. He was the sparrow, she was the cat. Provided he didn't identify her first.

She shivered. She was responsible for what was coming. No one had ever done what she was about do before, leastways not as far as her culture knew. Number one in the cosmos, not bad. Seriously radical. She couldn't help feeling nervous. But it had to be done. And it wasn't like she hadn't screwed with systems before. Just not on this scale.

It isn't every day a girl gets to crack the space time continuum wide open.

12   On Menzara

On Menzara, Mirando Mirando had the edge over the orbital's finest I.T. No one had ever quite worked out how she was able to hack the systems the way she did. Most believed she was a Virus Professor, a Super Consultant or an outworld techno-pirate. If she was, they'd never located her (or him – some feminists believed Mirando Mirando was a plot to discredit women).

Her text messages invariably originated from stolen brooches. The double-M virus erupted out of ever-changing digit combinations and unitary rhetoric. The orbital's top V-busters had never traced a source that didn't dissolve in mocking squeals of laughter before their eyes.

Solemn Construct occasions had a habit of melting on-screen and re-moulding into naked subversion. The orbital's ideology was under severe stress. Dream pods lost their enticements. Official reality was becoming a cracked and much-derided artefact.

Example: the solemn funeral of the Governor of Credit had been interrupted by the message GOOD RIDDANCE TO A CORRUPT LIAR WITH A SERIOUS AMBIGUINE HABIT.

Example: the official birthday celebrations of the Secretary of Construct Integrity and Satellite Ethics had been ruined by an invasion of flutter-flies trailing all-format news threads that itemised her fraudulent dealings in thalium.

Example: a stirring speech by the Chairman of Moonbelt Ethics mutated into footage of his last illicit sex act with a graff-wacker.

The taboids dubbed Mirando Mirando the empress of Anarchs and theorised wildly about her true identity. She was a Lincoln agent; an Evanescence illegal immigrant; an alien telli-blorb; or even a dissident member of Menzara Council itself. Cynics said she wasn't real, just an avatar or a Spectral. Whatever, she was becoming popular among the technician class. Her exposures led to resignations, Council bluster.

Then the Anarch sabotage began.

A nitrus bomb went off on the Island of Longing, killing 25,000 holidaymakers. Someone tampered with the deflection controls of a Construct super-cruiser and there was a collision with a shuttle, wiping out both crews. DESTROY EVERYTHING NOW! screamed Anarch messages, cutting across the news bulletins and the Council's pronouncements.

Public support plummeted.

Soon after that Mirando Mirando opted for The Return. The tabloids said that Menzara Security was close to making an arrest. Whatever, a woman in red wearing therm goggles shot a flute full of dreamstuff into the suits of six mechanics who'd just finished servicing a TPD pod in the maintenance zone on Level Twelve. They remembered asking who she was, just before their muscles turned to jelly. "Mirando Mirando," she said softly, in what might have been a Real Voice. Then, as they lay helpless on the workshop floor, staring out of frozen faces, their bodies paralyzed, she strapped herself into the pod and vanished into Nether Time. Like everyone who made the transference she left behind her co-ordinates.

What the commander of orbital security didn't tell the tabloids was that she'd also left behind a message.

*

The co-ordinates – PGx77h000035-Llk7890-55554-ku++#41j by Ji67++k675889 – indicated the CZ, star system and planet, right down to the transference point and exact chronology. A bright, harsh omniscience irradiated page after page. Within moments the orbital's MotherThinker had identified the co-ordinates as an area in which only one TPT member had expertise. And so it was that Strobey looked up from his desk one afternoon – the snow had just about all melted, only a few scabby crusts remaining, tangled in the unmown grass, on that other afternoon, thousands of years in the past, when this paragraph was written - he was reading an account of military strategy in the First World Water War – earlier he'd done some work on a Nether Time writer who used dashes and commas in preference to semicolons or periods, creating an effect of jerky, rapid thought or speech – in the end suppressed, hoovered up by a far-right transvestite editor, and dumped, like a lover, for eternity - when he received an unexpected visitor.

A synthetic gust flattened the nearest wurra-wurra bushes and a grey military Turtle cruised into view. It was escorted by six shiny black zap pods. Out of the Turtle stepped a tall, greying man in fatigues. Strobey recognised him at once. The cabin door opened and in came Void Archangel Strumbert, D.C.P.S., S.K., Supreme Commander of the Time Penetration Team.

Strumbert waved aside his salute, his nervous offer of refreshment, his pet flit-wasp.

"At ease, Strobey." Himself, he looked grim, not at all relaxed. The famous scar which slashed his face from scalp to chin had a pallor suggesting tension or the furtive use of a woman's dabstick. He'd got the scar during the Great Furies Vasion, in single-handed combat with a Vizartian octo-boar. That was when he won his D.C.P.S. He could have had the scar surgically removed but chose to keep it. Attractive kinky women liked to touch and tongue its serrations.

Today he looked as stern as he'd done at the ceremony when Strobey graduated. He was in the same uniform, too. But now he was carrying a slim yellow file.

Through the window Strobey saw the bodyguards spread out around the log cabin, loitering among the trees. Things couldn't really be that bad, could they? Anarchs inside Level 29? It was impossible to believe. But he didn't think it appropriate to ask.

The Commander sat down, resting the file on his lap. He looked tersely at Strobey. "Your time has come," he said. "And it's the best. In a way I almost envy you. Frankly, some of the targets the

TPT has to chase aren't remotely cost effective. I mean-" he wrinkled his nose with disgust. "*Film stars. Singers.*" He made the words sound like particularly revolting obscenities.

"If you ask me the orbital is well shot of trash like that. And where's the combat stimulation for the TPT member who has to go after then? Prod a celeb once with a sting-stick and they burst like a balloon. But rules are rules, and the Council demands action. And you're lucky. In your case your training won't be wasted. You're going after the big one, my boy. The orbital's enemy number one. The great hacker whore herself."

Strobey's throat went dry. His pulse accelerated. A drum practise started. 'Abattoir Blues' played. Hardly believing it, he whispered her name, and the Void Archangel agreed. "Which is why, Strobey, you are going to spend the next six months in combat training, flute shoots and advanced historiography. We've already configured a duplicate of you and sent it to the same co-ordinates. It's a risk, waiting all that time, but it's even riskier sending you after her raw and unprepared. We think she fled in the belief she was about to be identified. But she might be up to some other game. With Mirando Mirando you can never be sure of anything. But for the next few days I want you to check this out. Try to work out what it means."

He opened the file and passed Strobey a slip of paper. On it were printed just four words.

FINN'S.
FOR ALL TIME.

"It was printed out on a public terminal on Level 93 thirty minutes before the mechanics were assaulted on Level Twelve. The surveillance strips show a bearded man with sunglasses wearing a TPT uniform. Her perverted sense of humour evidently endured to her final hour on Menzara. Presumably this message is also some kind of joke. I shall leave you to decide what it means, if anything." He glanced at the bare wall opposite and projected a shot of a row of planets. Stars were sprinkled behind them like twinkledust. "Where that planet and its history are concerned you, after all, are the expert. Right down to its syntax and uses of equivoque."

Strobey said, "I'll check out the history. Offhand, I can't say it means anything to me. What were the precise co-ordinates, sir?"

"A station. Walthamstow Central. In some city called London."

"I think I've come across London. In my reading. It's all a bit vague. I need to check."

"Get started my boy. Soon you won't have any time for reading."

Void Archangel Strumbert stood up, returned Strobey's salute and departed. Strobey watched the Turtle slip out of sight between the giant pines. The pods followed like blobs of metal drawn to a magnetic simile.

13   Far Side

She was less than a third of the way through the text but two-thirds of the way through her shift.

Aphrodite Cutter took the call herself. It was a man in tears and a smart suit. He managed to tell her he was ringing about his wife. Then he broke down. Then he managed to continue. He muttered "neutrino", then "positron", adding, "My thoughts and my discourse as madmen's are." A pause – and then at last: "She's sort of... *Faded away.*"

Aphrodite used a siren all the way. Was there with WPC Spenser in the next sentence, a short one. It was a terraced house on one of the smarter streets off Forest Road.

The guy was black. His name was Eric Harris. It was 7 p.m. He was just home from work (a merchant bank near Liverpool Street). His wife was in the kitchen with the TV on. Their dinner was almost ready. He walked across the room to kiss her and she turned and just *went.*

More tears. He was in shock.

Daisy Spenser held the guy's hand. His distress was clearly genuine. When he'd recovered he led them into a plausible kitchen. There was a powerful smell of roast meat. Steam leaked from under the lid of a pan. "Mulligan stew," he explained. The table was laid for two.

Aphrodite said: "Anything else happen?"

Harris stared at her through red-rimmed eyes. He looked puzzled. "I don't understand. Anomalous structures, opalescence – *this isn't fair.*"

Aphrodite was going to ask if he'd heard his wife's voice. But suddenly she didn't need to. All three of them heard her. The wife said, "Eric, where are you? I'm scared, Eric. I can't see you in the mist."

The voice seemed to be coming from somewhere near the cooker.

Harris cried, "Charlene! Where *are* you?" He clawed at thin air, hoping to make physical contact. He started tearing open cupboards, hurling out the contents. He ran to the back door and went into the garden. He screamed her name. He was hysterical. He began to recite sonnets.

Aphrodite nodded and Daisy Spenser phoned for a doctor. The guy needed calming down. He needed a shot of something. They all did, really. It was all getting too *weird.*

Aphrodite ran a quick check on GUST. Harris's mother lived in Stoke Newington. She called her, asked her to hurry over. Then she went into the garden, where Harris was still howling his wife's name. "Thou blind fool, Love, what dost thou to mine eyes that they behold and see not what they see?"

"Could you come inside, please, Mr Harris. I'm afraid it isn't any use looking for her. This is going to be difficult to understand and I don't understand it myself. But you're not the first person to experience this type of... *disappearance.*"

She coaxed him indoors, made him a cup of tea.

Tried to explain intertextual transmigration. But it was no use. Harris stared at her with mingled suspicion and incomprehension. Then he poured his cold tea into the stainless steel sink.

*

In a remote future that Aphrodite had no inkling of, Strobey went across to his modified Welsh dresser and put the available data into his questor. Moments later it was downloading file after file of links and summaries.

61

He put on Chakowski's Sonata in F for lute and guilden-horn. It always calmed him, made him a little melancholy. It made him think of – But he shut the memory out. It would be remembered later, when it occurred. For now, he concentrated on the results pumping out of his questor.

FINN'S. FOR ALL TIME., in its entirety, produced no result.

FINN'S on its own broke down into various queries which came with "mis-spelt?" boxes. These options included an organ for propelling certain marine creatures, various types of mechanical projections and attachments and the word in a minor, dying language for "end". The final listed suggestion identified a puzzle book for intellectuals published simultaneously on 4 May 1939 in London (that name again!) and a city named New York (Strobey frowned; that name, too, was dimly familiar. But he couldn't remember why). But the book was probably just a gigantic red herring. Strobey said: "delete" and the options vanished.

FINN'S also threw out the fact that an Albert Harold James Finn lived at a Suffolk seaside resort named Felixstowe. He was 98 years old. He was a retired fishmonger. It was probably nothing more than a banal coincidence but he decided to hold the information, just in case.

The next one hit the spot.

FINN'S HOTEL, Walthamstow. Built 1883.

Strobey called up a map. The hotel was on the corner of Hoe Street and Selborne Road, just across the road from Walthamstow Central station. It had evidently been built to cater for middle-class travellers travelling to and from Essex and the dark north.

At the point of the required chronology, Finn's Hotel was derelict. But people lived there.

Four people.

The questor fed him the details and when he saw the fourth he felt a jolt of surprise. His own name was listed. Or rather, a variant form. In Menzara he was just "Strobey" (or when more specific ID was needed he was 29-Strobey-M3421). Down there – for some reason he always thought of places in Nether Time as below the orbital – he had accreted a first name: Edgar.

He knew the knowledge would be obliterated during the transference. When you went through the Bohren Shield everything you'd previously learned about yourself in Nether Time was wiped from your memory. It was the second great law of time physics. You took your memories of the past with you when you transferred, but never future knowledge of yourself. That didn't stop him learning about the environment he'd be going to. He looked at the questor's single green eye and said,

"Tell me about Walthamstow. The fifteen minute version."

"Of course, Strobey," the questor. "But if I may make a suggestion..."

"Yes?"

"You turn down the volume. Guilden-horns do rather get on my nerves."

"Would the Borthoover Overture be acceptable instead?"

"The Overture is one of my favourite pieces of music. Thank so much." The questor was so pleased it briefly filled the cabin room with a golden glow. Then it cut it and got on with its task.

*

Why a rotting hotel at the heart of suburban fusion question mark.

That was the puzzle, the puzzle, the puzzle.

At this point in Nether Time, Walthamstow was on the margins. It was the borderland to the fields and forest of green Essex. It was on the very edge of Greater London. The sprawl used to terminate at Hackney but like flowing lava it had found a way across the marshland of the Lea and solidified and petrified into a block of authoritarian prose on the far side. Once there had been nothing here but a few quill scratches on parchment, inky specks, settlements in a vast royal forest. The trees had been cut down centuries past. Now it was urban sludge, a network of nouns and adjectives evoking terraced housing and shops. Its backstreets had stores that sold cheap electric guitars, reconditioned tyres, cold water tanks, nails, second hand furniture, number one bestsellers with a label covering up 'USE BY JAN. 1900'. You didn't have to go too far if you wanted pond weed, an England flag, puppadoms, cheap lager,

63

jellied eels or the services of a hard-faced blonde masseuse. At its north-eastern tip a few fragments of the ancient forest remained. It was called Epping Forest now. It was slashed by the North Circular and the M11.

Walthamstow was different to the surrounding sprawl. It was seedier and poorer than Chingford, smarter than Stratford, more substantial than Leytonstone. It had identity. It was on no coast but it had a lighthouse. Walking its streets you didn't think of the classics or ancient empires but it had a Greek amphitheatre. If you walked the quiet shady backways of Vinegar Alley and Beulah Path you slipped into a lost past where Tudor gentlemen once walked with their wives or left their horses tethered outside the ancient church of St Mary's. Samuel Pepys had taken a coach to rural, peaceful Walthamstow and drunk the local wine. John Keats, dying, hurried to Walthamstow to comfort his miserable sister, who was a governess there. Plus to escape from his own misery, that tortuous relationship with virginal Fanny Brawne.

But Walthamstow was also a state of mind in a relentlessly discursive twenty-first draft. You took your pick from a thousand overlapping Walthamstows. It was a place of deletions, rewritings, ceaseless change. Once it had been the tranquil out-of-town refuge of plump, wealthy, city merchants who chuckled – *Aliquid latet quod non patet!* – at the only true subject of chronicles. A green village of cuckoo cries and quiet farms. Even in 2006 there were shaky old men who could still remember when herds of sheep and cattle were driven down the High Street.

Now all that was gone. Housing swallowed the fields and orchards. Cars invaded the urban fabric. They lined the kerbs of every street like parasites on a plant. The population of Walthamstow ballooned. Now its streets were filled with young men and women gabbling into cellphones in Gujarati, Urdu, Turkish, Albanian, Spanish, Polish. The SD download fed Strobey images of demolition balls on chains, thudding into the soft walls of old houses that fell like sandcastles. Churches were levelled and replaced, first by furniture stores, then by cyber cafés. Cranes swung vast sheets of prefabricated buildings. Rows of houses were swept away, displaced by the shining aisles of a bright shopping

64

mall with security guards and an escalator hum and tubs of plastic ferns. Just as Finn's would soon be gone.

Strobey wondered if the whole thing wasn't some sort of hideous mistake. A misunderstanding. Why on earth, of all places, would Mirando Mirando want to lose herself in a twenty-first century slum? It made no sense.

Just hours into arriving in Nether Time Strobey was still puzzled, puzzled, puzzled. Frags flashed mysteriously along the circuits of his mind. *Hundreds of torches flared, lighting the great hall, a banquet had been arranged to celebrate victory.* What did that refer to? Ditto *drunks singing, shouts of TAXI, the rumble of a rocket exploding in the suburbs...* He was depressed by the failures of his Duplicate. Something wasn't quite right. He began to wonder if Mirando Mirando had found a way of faking her co-ordinates. If they were fake it meant he'd been sent down a barren cul-de-sac in time to a place he could never return from.

All that training wasted but it was impossible it had to be the plot the primary diegesis the essential principles of coherence surely required that no one no one no one could retroactively fake their co-ordinates their co-ordinates their co-ordinates.

Eh?

14   Downloads

Emma is just about to go past what was once the hotel reception desk when she hears a key turning in the door.

It opens behind her, behind her, and Ben walks in, walks in, she can see he's holding a stash of unsold newspapers make any sales? Emma asks dryly seeing the clutch of papers yeah I did but he decides not to tell her it was only one copy of *Socialist Revolutionary* sold to an octogenarian ex-member of the Communist Party with bad eyesight who was under the impression she was buying a copy of *The Morning Star* Emma says nothing when she lived up a tree all those weeks trying to save Fern Island from the developers the working class didn't turn up once.

Ben regards Emma as a green pain her politics are hopelessly muddled reformism at its most fatuous like that revolting habit of hers not flushing the toilet in order to benefit the environment leaving the water yellow with shreds of disintegrating luxury soft white tissue Emma doesn't buy coloured toilet roll the dye they use is bad for the environment I mean how gross can you get?

Oblivious to Ben's carping Emma goes to her room and lies down among her plants puts on soothing New Age music lets it wash over her relax her the lapping waves turn into the low rush of a waterfall she's far away now in a valley in the dream Himalayas a dream stream trickling among the rocks the sun shining down snowcapped drea(m)ountains outlined against a dazzling blue sky projected on to the painted white brickwork of the adjacent building on Hoe Street she sees the shadow of the roof of Finn's the cupola like a giant bubble on the surface of a pond she listens to the soothing rush of water feels drowsy she closes her eyes.

*

Dead beetles paper birds falling fluttering from a blue gulf all that summer Ben and Marianne stayed in that room at the top of the dead hotel a perfect view over Walthamstow Central the other side of the line was the station car park where the cars were laid out like rows of dead beetles.

Gorgeous days was how Ben remembered it in the long afterwards of the penultimate draft lazing around listening to music reading, fucking the ardent angelic conversations the stuff you say when you are young full of arguments and questions before marriage and a mortgage trap you in their sludge before you give up on everything and sink into the *Telegraph* the four of them sat in the big empty lounge bar chatting arguing soaking up the ambience they felt like they were in a movie that one about the deserted hotel in winter Ben said it was crap the scene where hundreds of gallons of blood poured out of the elevator unless it was supposed to be a symbol of petrified western capitalism and its bloody exploitation of the third world Generation Z that's us he said the ones at the end of everything the ones living on the cusp of change the dark and bloody twentieth century ends such melodrama! the twenty-first begins begins begins punctuated by the sound of exploding buildings and bombs and none of us are going to see it out none of us is going to be around for the fireworks on New Year's Eve 2099 you know what I think? I think we're all ghosts our generation will be lucky to make it past 2040 think of the alcohol the weed the ecstasy the days spent in front of the TV the Playstation the Gamecube the X-Box the bright computer screen that's why we need a revolution to get rid of all these false needs Emma chimed in too right comrade at first he thought she was being sarcastic but she wasn't a generation used to going everywhere by car who don't read books who don't like walking who'd never ride a bike who are bored who eat at Burger Bliss who run the risk of HIV and AIDS not to mention all that milk they've drunk all those pork chops stuffed full of farm antibiotics all that poison on the Sudan list not to mention all that genetically modified muck in pizzas biscuits ice-cream not to mention all those attractive salmon with flesh reddened by dye and nicely seamed with disease a generation brought up on junk food imbibing a cocktail of chemicals with every meal an invigorating lungful of car-spewed particulates in every breath taken the Spectral Duplicate tried not to look bored it went across and selected Nick Cave singing 'Tupelo'.

*

Ben dreamed it up what they did and Emma made it possible.

Emma who dreamed of paper birds of banknotes fluttering from a clear blue sky thousands of them great drifts of money making it difficult for you to push open the door.

A few years back Emma was walking along Greenleaf Road when she became aware of something unusual happening at the end of the street she wondered why people were standing outside *The Rose and Crown* looking along Hoe Street like something had happened Emma reached the end of the street turned right at the baker's and saw more people, lining the street in twos and threes what is this? she thought it was the middle of a drab grey paragraph an afternoon and there was a woman holding a camera other people with cameras it was like the President of the USA or someone was going to come cruising down Hoe Street any mo a sense of expectation the crowd suddenly stirred up where the road curved round towards the cinema and a pair of motorbike cops came into view.

Outriders cruising slowly the police were followed by six trotting black horses bearing stately plumes like they were making a movie of *Cinderella* the horses were pulling a big glass carriage straight out of a Hammer horror film then Emma saw the coffin inside and realised whose funeral this was whose cortege the carriage dripping with white flowers it was Ronald K the legendary East End gangster he was passing through Walthamstow on his way up to Chingford Mount cemetery and after the carriage came a long long line of black Daimlers containing she assumed the cream of London's criminal elite and at the very end a white stretch limo with blackened windows like the Godfather himself had dropped over from Little Italy to pay his respects.

Emma stood staring entranced the spectacle appealed to the actress in her she was impressed by the audience participation excited even feeling her heart thump a slight flush in her cheeks and when the funeral procession had gone by some people lots of people began running after it people a lot of people admire criminals Emma herself thought *Bonnie and Clyde* was a brilliant film she thought about what Benjamin had said it wouldn't work though not in Walthamstow you wouldn't get anywhere urban paralysis would choke the getaway she lay down and fell asleep and dreamed of bank notes fluttering from a blue, blue sky.

*

All that summer Strobey's Spectral Duplicate had been robbing building societies Marianne went along with it because that's what lovers do Ben disposed of the ideological objections to armed robbery first off building societies were part of the capitalist system and fair game it wasn't like stealing from people they'd been privatized they were just like banks except their security wasn't so good he demolished a practical objection too the police weren't like on TV they were thick the majority of crimes were never solved only stupid lazy criminals ever got caught.

They were in the lounge bar when he made his speech getting through the second bottle of Chardonnay from the fridge they applauded his points cheered thought he was bullshitting them but it wasn't a fantasy to Benjamin Scaravelli he went out the next day and bought the masks at a toy shop in Tottenham the shop was situated on a side street in a run-down piece of prose signifying Tottenham it sold dolls plastic footballs plastic machine guns plastic pistols plastic racing cars cowboy hats fake fried eggs plastic dog turds model space ships and masks almost everything was a quid but the masks were half price a bit dusty but undamaged there were six of them and Ben bought the lot he paid cash he noted that the shop was too cheap and tacky to run to CCTV the street wasn't important enough to have CCTV either so there were no financial records or footage of him as the purchaser plus the shop keeper was a young Asian man whose English was poor not the kind of guy the police would get very far with he'd be puzzled they'd be impatient hostile irritated Ben could see it all always assuming they checked out the shop which knowing the laziness and incompetence of the police couldn't be guaranteed.

Ben put the masks in a plastic Tesco carrier bag nearby there was another cheap shop where he bought a scarlet baseball cap he put it on and wore it back to E17 because he never wore a baseball cap because if he did show up on any footage he'd be able to get witnesses to testify he never wore baseball caps he caught a bus back to Walthamstow it would have been quicker to take the tube but Ben didn't want his face on the CCTV at Walthamstow Central just in case the shopkeeper remembered the date he'd sold the masks Ben truly believed the police were stupid but all the same it

69

was best not to underestimate them just in case they had someone bright on board he walked into the bar that night wearing one of the masks he hadn't even told Marianne who was already down there with the others they all shrieked when they saw him it's hideous! it can't be! it is! historic! then Ben took the other masks out of the bag one each catch he threw them their masks giggling and joking they tried them on just for a laugh with no serious intentions what did you waste your money on these for Marianne wanted to know so's we can rob banks Ben replied and they all laughed yes.

15   Sometimes in the Night

Mirando Mirando liked going up to the roof of Finn's. She liked the raw smell of unconditioned air, the splash of real raindrops.

No one ever saw her there. The others had no inkling. Not even Strobey. Poor Strobey. He hadn't a clue.

Sometimes in the night, when the traffic was stilled, she could hear a different pitch of noise, a remote low roaring. It was like there was some faint pre-rupture in the chronology membrane. It sounded like fire, and it *was* fire. It was the fire from every fire that had burned in the city to punish heresy. Hundreds of years ago. A low crisp crackling. And then she'd hear a sudden scream, followed by another. Then a deluge of screams, a huge wail of howling, of human agony, of human flesh melting like fat in a pan, popping and bubbling and squirting jets of fat, which ignited. It was like a physical presence, a surging tidal wave of human pain, all the pain in the history of this city, a boiling primitive atomic cloud of dark emotion, formed of all the warriors and the martyrs and the criminals, the ones who'd died in violence.

Hearing it, she was convinced of the rightness of what was about to be set in motion. And then the membrane would take her, too, the way it would take everyone. Into that sparkling mystery of mysteries. You always had to remember Norland's Final Thesis: *To see the future is not to see the future you will see.*

Suddenly, it was all over. The sun, still concealed by cloud, went down behind Highgate hill. It was as if a light had been switched off. Just like the Duplicate. When the silicon reading dropped to zero she appreciated the change. Edgar Allan Strobey was no longer Spectral. He'd become Real. Of course she knew that anyway. She had a direct link to the pair of Anarchs he'd wasted in the corridor. Spectrals, they were. No sweat. She had access to others.

Like his Duplicate, Strobey didn't know who she was. But she guessed he'd eventually locate her. That was what gave the game edge. The uncertainty. The never knowing if you'd win. No matter how good your experience. No matter how many runs you'd done before. You expected to win, of course. But you never knew until the end. And even then you couldn't always be sure. You saw your futures, but for all you knew they might be Astrar's. *Where did one world end and another begin?* Good Q. Lose and you'd find yourself in the Loop. Never knowing you'd lost.

The colours drained away from the clouds, the pale blue triangle vanished. The night came on. A police siren suddenly wailed nearby, down in the street. Mirando Mirando shivered. At moments like this she felt her own mortality. She knew she'd never see three-hundred again, but would she make it to her 350th?

She hoped so. For the sake of every Anarch.

16 Minimalist

Marianne lay low at Finn's, killing time. She'd become a movie buff. She spent her afternoons watching videos. A favourite was [deleted]. A weird, very frightening black and white movie about a girl who [deleted]. The car goes off a bridge and everyone else gets [deleted]. But as the film goes on you realise [deleted]. She's [deleted] she just doesn't [deleted]. And the dead are [deleted].

Marianne pushes mute. She's seen [deleted] times before. She prefers her own sound track. *Deserter's Songs*. The songs match the movie perfectly. Marianne sits inside the darkened cupola watching the picture slide by, while sad spooky songs fill the room, over and again.

She was trying to deaden all that dead time inside her. Sedate the rage. Be patient. Wait to get her perfect revenge. Everyone else at Finn's had their agenda (except maybe Strobey; she didn't understand him at all. Didn't trust him. Didn't like the way lately he always seemed to be watching them.) Marianne had hers. And not even Ben knew what it was.

What it was: *revenge.*

See? The others were given terms of between two and five years. All except Bob. The judge called them "An exceptionally dangerous and violent group of extremists determined to impose their twisted vision of the world on to society at large." *Violent?*, she thought. *I wasn't before. But I will be when I get out of here.*

It turned out Bob was really undercover officer D.C. Robert Buller. He got a special commendation. The Princess Royal handed it over. He had a photograph. Another one showed him exchanging friendly words with his Chief Constable. The words were affability, inclement, silence, royal, repletion, control and suppress. Buller's promotion came through six months later. Then more. One case buried another. Faces blurred. Years rolled. A dark angel rode on a whispering south wind.

Marianne faded in his mind.

Not him in hers. She never forgot. Her auburn hair turned the colour of dirty ash. It was the shock of prison. Of a keyless hole as big as Kant's eye. Of vagrants locked up for petty theft. Of drunks and foulmouthed whores. Somehow it had never occurred to her that they'd get caught. Or that certain actions might have unexpected consequences. Or what a British prison might be like.

There, she played it minimalist. She was cold, detached, polite. She did what the screws told her to do. Eyes turned down. Dumb. She wanted her remission. Quietly, calmly, she nursed her rage.

She came out of Holloway on a cold day in February. She walked down the Seven Sisters Road in a daze and a pair of too-tight shoes. The world had moved on without her. The cars looked different. She stared at her first Spacewagon. She was amazed by the number of off-roaders. They had big, ugly grilles at the front like for smashing something. She wondered what. There were red – not yellow - lines below the kerb. Everywhere people were holding mobile phones to their ears, and shouting. Her favourite broadsheet was three times the price it had been. She went into a coffee bar and asked for a coffee. They looked at her blankly. You didn't just ask for a coffee anymore. You identified type and size. Cappuccino. Gargantuan. It tasted better than the slop they used to serve. But she was shocked at the price.

She had a lot to get her head round. Deictic particles, the Spiral of Archimedes as the model for an auto-included regressive world, a sentence from *Jane Eyre* – "Profound silence fell when he had uttered that word, with deep but low intonation". She clicked her teeth in annoyance. It felt good. It was cold outside the paragraph. Last night's snow had thawed. She'd long since lost touch with the plot and with the other characters. She re-read her chapters and felt better. But now it was snowing again.

Miller she corresponded with for a while, then quit. She wanted to seem clean. She wanted the authorities to think she'd learned her lesson. That she'd given up on animal rights. She didn't want surveillance when she came out. She didn't want shitty undercover creeps making friends with her, pumping her, trying to find out if she was ripe for return. She wrote and told Miller she realized she'd been mistaken in ever getting involved with him (that part was true – he was the stupid fucker who'd introduced Bob to the cell, vouched for his enthusiasm and commitment). She told Miller she had discovered that the meaning of life lay in the Lord and realism. She begged Miller to avoid the heretical texts of B.S. Johnson and Ann Quin and ask for the Lord's forgiveness.

73

Miller wrote her an angry letter back, she didn't respond. She asked for a Bible and became pals with the chaplain. She prayed. She attended services. She read the novels of Julie Myerson. The authorities took note. They decided she was genuine. Special Branch marked her down as defunct. When she came out, there was no heat. Just snow, ice, scrappy flurries of thematic resonance.

She walked further down the Seven Sisters Road. She ignored the sign to Rio de Janeiro. It started to rain buckets and she dodged under a bus shelter. There she sheltered until the buckets stopped. Then there was a brief shower of buses. Then frogs. Then telephones. A chorus of faint, crackly voices shrieked at her from the mouthpieces. She remembered her medication and took it. The half-thawed phones sang an old number by Cornelius Cardew. The number was two-hundred and seventeen. She stepped out from the shelter, into a realm of whiteness and silence. The coast was clear. The ABC was showing *Magnolia*. She glanced back and saw it was *Memento*.

Marianne dipped into a newsagents and licked chocolate from her forefinger. She read the cards. She got a job in a realist back story, cleaning empty offices. She gave it up to become a keyboard operator. She earned enough prose to rent a room in a big, rotting Edwardian house in Leyton. The other rooms were full of Xs - ex-army, ex-married, ex-salesmen. Human driftwood. Their complexions yellow, their teeth brown, their shoes scuffed. Mottled skin, scurf, greasy pants, drowning in the years, going down, slowly. Herself, in truth, not in such good shape. A thick belt of flesh around her waist, years of sweet shitty fattening prison sludge. A house full of losers. Her room not much longer than a coffin. Her walls puffy with damp. What looked like soup stains on the ceiling. A threadbare carpet portraying a Chinese pavilion, in diluted mauve. Things were so bad her teeth chattered 'Mr Bleaney'. To humour the chaplain she went to church. Mainstream C of E. Niceness not nastiness. Sales of cherry cake to assist starving Africans. Equivocation on the vexed issue of bishopricks. She kneeled and muttered. She stood and sang. The congregation was old, with occasional whiffs of urine. The preech was young and smelled of pine and mint. Pink as a prawn, chubby and buoyant as a bloated smiley-smiley character on children's TV. He dribbled enthusiasm. He took you by the hand, laid his hand on your hand. He squeezed. He smirked his Christian certainties.

Once she was sure they were leaving her alone, she dumped on God. She would have liked to tell the preech to fuck off, what she really thought of him. But she didn't want to risk her cover. Instead she gravely informed him of a fictitious diseased relative in Birkenhead, who needed her twenty-four hour care. The preech nodded sombrely, a technique he had been practising ever since his ordination. He took her hand, laid his hand over hers. Of course, my dear. Our prayers will go with you. She went to pubs, drank Guinness. The colour started to return to her pale cheeks. She started to think about sex. Met Benjamin. Picked him up, really. Her first sex in over ten thousand words! She moved out of Larkin House into Finn's. A better class of decaying narrative structure. There she met the others, who recognised her from earlier in the text. There, very slowly, she shook off the shackles of verisimilitude and began to expel her voids and expand her mind, while Benjamin expounded strange notions, with potions and lotions and peculiar motions.

17 Finn's Again Warp

Ben was high.

Was on the roof, no one went there but him. Once, strangely, he'd found a wet footprint up there, decided it must have been his own, he liked the view, liked watching the overground trains, the line cut through the class structure like a knife, from Liverpool Street on the edge of the City and its wealth it descended into poverty almost at once, slipping through the sooty canyons of the original East End, for miles there was nothing but dark walls of stained concrete and blocks of flats which looked like the ones in old East Berlin, before the wall came down, ugly slabs of tarnished brickwork, bad parodies of play areas for kids, grey squares of sooty grass, poverty everywhere like bad weather, patches of tarmac hemmed in by high wire fences, grimy housing, streets choked with parked cars, a landscape of desolation, all that was left was to escape, into booze, drugs, blogging, movies, sonnets, travel, hit the road Jack, run, sink into the text of choice, words, sooty canyons was good for example, simple someone says in his head, one of the many whispering voices, his favourites the General, the Moor, Vladimir Ilych.

The line crawled through the dark, derelict, graffiti spattered stations of Hackney. At last it burst free of the suffocating tunnels and dark claustrophobic cuttings and all that seemed impoverished and stunted and curved across the mile-wide marshland of the Lea, heading for Walthamstow, postcoded E17 but not really East London at all, it had nothing in common with Whitechapel or Stepney or places like that, had started its urban existence as a suburb for upwardly mobile Edwardian clerks, after the Great War it became white working class, then, in the nineteen-sixties, because of the cheap housing, it became home to Asian immigrants, and now, in the twenty-first century, it was a honeycomb of diversity, the accents of Jamaica mingled with those of Sri Lanka, Albania and Afghanistan, but unlike most urban environments it had no ghettos, no divided territories of white and black and brown, or acute wealth and acute poverty, and the line flowed high over a network of terraced houses and crawled over the bridge above St James Street.

And minutes later the train glided in to Walthamstow Central, doors slammed, passengers got off, far fewer people boarded, the train lurched on its way.

Beyond Walthamstow Central was Wood Street, which was where Walthamstow in its north-eastern reaches started to become more affluent, this was where the houses had garages and drives, Upper Walthamstow merging into Highams Park, next stop the Tory heartlands, the Chingford line a dead-end track to a corroded Tory heartland, Ben had tried selling the paper there, hadn't sold a single fucking copy, made him remember the day after he'd seen *Notting Hill* on DVD and he went into Chingford Sainsbury's to get a bottle of rum and there was a woman in front of him, fur coat, high heeled shoes, a smell of perfume, she was buying *Horse and Hound*, Jesus

H Christopher, Ben hadn't even realised there *was* such a magazine, let alone that they sold it in Sainsbury's, of all fucking places, and in Chingford, where you never saw horses, where the only hounds were terriers on leads brought out by their smug *Daily Mail*-reading owners for the pre-breakfast shit, the mid-day shit, the last thing at night shit, left steaming on the pavement, though when you thought about it, it fitted, Chingford, home of Norman Tebbit and that bald guardsman creep who followed him, whose name had slipped Ben's mind, Chingford, its streets filled with 4-wheel drives and BMWs and smug bastards with safe jobs, he'd once come across a Mercedes sports with a sticker that read I AM NOT PARTICIPATING IN THE RECESSION, went back at night, it was still parked there, he sprayed FUCK YOU over the windows, over the bonnet, the lights, just about everything, he must have done thousands of pounds worth of damage, his modest contribution to the class war, the Moor would have been proud of him, who'd run down Tottenham Court Road smashing streetlamps, being chased by a thick plod, who of course hadn't caught up with the elusive superman of world revolution.

Arf!

On their way upstairs, Emma quickly told Edgar about what had been going on at the town hall, another made-for-TV Nazi drama-doc, movie people love Walthamstow town hall, the architecture is pure Nuremberg Rally, rectangular slabs and layers of concrete, brutalist 1930s classicism, *in the stripped-classical Swedish style popular in the inter-war years, particularly for grand civic buildings*, built between 1938 and 1941, all you have to do is run up a swastika and you're back there, and sure enough, that day a swastika is fluttering from the flagpole above the entrance.

The forecourt is laid out on formal lines with a central circular pool and fountain, the Assembly Hall flanking the forecourt to the East was completed to the original design of P.D. Hepworth in 1943, blah, blah, but not to the west, where instead there's the low, ugly, hostile fortress of the magistrates court, built to a sixties neo-paranoid design, Emma loitered by the big wrought iron gates, so did other passers-by, plus a crowd of students from the college next door, she gazed down the slope, the area in front of the town hall had been cordoned off, the film crew moved around with the self-importance of film crews, these people are SIMULATING REALITY, you can't get cooler, more important than that, Emma D-locked her bike to a railing, went to find out what they were filming.

An episode for a TV mini drama set in the second world war, this is where the heroine is taken to Gestapo headquarters for interrogation, Hitler's favourite design flutters in the breeze, on a balcony a guard in a grey uniform leans his rifle against the wall, lights up, slips on his Walkman and listens to the new Strokes album until they're ready for the next shot.

Emma splits, she's late, she pumps the pedals, weaves through the congestion, gets held up by the accident on Hoe Street. Back in May no one seemed to take Ben very seriously, even though he spent his days wandering around Walthamstow making notes, then Ben laid his list on them, the nearest bank was Barclays, on Hoe Street, just the other side of the railway line, they were nervous, incredulous, sarcastic, they laughed.

None of the others thought robbing a bank so close was a good idea, someone would be bound to see them running into the hotel, the same went for the Co-op Bank in the opposite direction, too close, also there had been two raids there in the past year, the bank had introduced double security doors and new colour CCTV.

They were never short of excuses, there were others, not too far away, but they also had heavy security, Ben wondered if they shouldn't try a building society instead, there were lots down the High Street, some (like the Nationwide) had the same double security doors as the banks, you had to press buttons to get in and out and the two doors never opened at the same time, try a robbery there and you risked getting locked in until the cops arrived, but they didn't all have that level of security, the Abbey National didn't seem to have anything apart from CCTV, and the Halifax seemed even more laid back about security, they didn't have CCTV, not unless it was concealed.

Ben was enthusiastic. Hold your horses said Emma, would that be the branch that's about fifty metres from the market police station? Ben grinned stupidly, he hadn't thought of that. Yeah, but we'd make our getaway in the opposite direction. Even though the High Street is always full of plods strolling up and down, said Emma, not to mention traffic wardens and security guys from the shopping complex, plus market traders, among whom there's bound to be one or two have-a-go heroes, not to mention the CCTV stalks.

Emma's right, said Strobey's Spectral Duplicate. Carrying out an armed robbery in Walthamstow High Street is too risky, people do it, I know, but they get caught.

Marianne enquired anxiously: this *is* all a joke, isn't it, question mark.

18   Darkness

"Get you a drink?" "Please." Daisy Spenser looked of the window. In the street below a man with a beard, his face contorted with rage, was shaking his fist at a traffic warden. "A lively place, the High Road," she smiled, as Scurr returned with a pair of gin and tonics.

"Yeah, I like a bit of urban realism. All night stores, the to and fro of motor vehicles, shit like that. Here y'are." He plonked the ice in her glass. "Two cubes okay?" "Two cubes is just fine," she replied, with a shocking ignorance of the rules of grammar. "Cheers, then." "Cheers, Andy." They drank their wine, unidentified, bound to be a crap one where Scurr is concerned. The drab dialogue creaked on.

"I been thinking about that Iris Scheist. I reckon we should get a search warrant. Check under the floorboards. I bet that's where Harold is. Probably wires to the hidden speakers, too." "But it's happened to other people. Only yesterday. There was a black guy. His wife vanished in the kitchen." "Fucking coons. Just confirms what I say. It's all a trick." "Andy! You know you're not supposed to talk like that." Scurr smirked. "It's what most decent people think," he said. "Especially in the force. You gotta remember that a cop shares the values of the lumpenproletariat. They're corrupt and conservative, so R we. Our primary function is to serve the ruling class and repress organised workers." "I don't think that's true for a moment. I think-" "Cut the political correctness crap, Daisy. Please.

Let's talk about you and me. You know I really like you, don't you? Like, *really* like you." "Andy, I barely know you." She stopped as he laughed. "What's funny?" "What you just said. 'Cos I'd like to *barely* know you, if you get my meaning." He sniggered. Daisy Spenser flushed. Their repertoire of expressions was simple but homely.

"I think I'd better be going," she said. "I want to be in a better chapter than this. I can't wait to get to an island off the Brittany coast and raise sheep."

"You alright? You look a bit off colour to me." "I'm quite all-" But her voice sounded thin and faraway. Maybe it had always been that way, she thought. Maybe I'll never be someone who speaks in a firm, decisive voice of the mendacious trajectories of hermetic realism.

She felt strangely weak. It might have been 3 a.m. on a warm electric night, a violet haze in the air and the smell of sewage and Coleman lanterns. Then the oldest spaceport on planet earth seemed to melt and she became aware of Scurr taking her by the hand, leading her towards his bedroom. "Nurr," she slurred. "Nurr. Plur. Ease." "Love you too baby," Scurr said. The expression on his face was ugly. A fusion of smirking and gloating. A true cop look. After that she was helpless as a doll in a neo-realist box.

Her arms lost all their strength and feeling. She flopped like rag. Her thought processes had shredded into rags and patches. Everything blurry and disconnected. Rohypnol, must be. The gin and tonic, she thought. It was in th-. His bedroom door opened on to a darkness, into which she plummeted.

She surfaced briefly into patches of light. Time bent and twisted, a mystery. She was aware she was naked. Scurr stood over her with a silver box. A tiny red light glowed like an ember. She fell back into blackness.

Later, another patch of light showed Scurr's hairy chest leaning over her. His face contorted. His lower teeth exposed, biting into his upper lip. She was aware of wetness and a burning somewhere in the lower half of her body. She was aware of Scurr, his torso shining with sweat. His cop face flushed and avid. His cop eyes bulging. Strange noises excreted from his cop lips, his wide cop mouth.

*

Cops aren't anywhere as smart or nice as TV dramas make them out to be, mostly they solve crime because someone grasses, Marianne learned a valuable lesson.

Do it alone, tell no one.

It was just a pity she didn't stick to that, that she trusted other people, that she ever allowed herself to get involved with the cell, that she deferred to a prick like Miller.

It was what happened with Miller turned her off truth and trust. She never told Ben about the security guard. She'd learned from bitter experience. She knew now not to trust a soul, not even a lover, because a lover might one day not be, could become a hater, unlikely, in Ben's case, but you can never tell. People change, love can turn to acid, people grow old, their ideas change.

Right now Ben might think Lenin was the greatest person in the entire history of the universe, but when he was in his forties question mark. Ben was an idealist, fine, so was she, in a different way, though for the present she'd given up animals, apart from the rats, the others pretended not to mind too much. She kept them in cages in the hotel cellar.

At first it was one, then two, now she had a dozen, she could tell Emma wasn't keen. The feeling was mutual. When Emma came in the rats went wild. But Marianne she never let them out of the cellar, and besides, they weren't wild ones, they were her pets, her special friends.

*

What happened was this.

It was six months before the Hindhead bust. It made her sweat to think how close she'd come. Once she nearly told Miller. If she'd done that blabbermouth would've been sure to confide it to Bob, and then she'd still be in Holloway, with years to go.

81

Close, yes., fucking unbelievably close, it was that era when all the AAF group seemed to do was *talk*.

They talked about picketing butchers shops, they talked about picketing supermarkets, they discussed animal laboratories, they agonized about what to do, did you target the company directors, or the scientists, or the people who worked there, did you get up a petition, write a letter, make a phone call, go further, they'd have to have a meeting about that. A meeting which would decide on another meeting. She was so fucking tired of meetings, she wanted action, she wanted change, to feel the world was starting to turn her way.

So she rented a Ford Fiesta in London for a week, drove it down the A3, as far as Butser Hill. She came off there, detoured, came back to the London carriageway, it was night, gone eleven.

She drove two miles, parked in a lay-by, walked down a private road. All these torture chambers are located at the end of private roads. She came at last to the target, only a brisk four minute walk, the petrol she was carrying slopping gently in the big red container.

There was a metal gate, it was locked, she clambered over it. No one emerged to challenge her.

There were four long low wooden huts. And it was true, it did look like a miniature concentration camp. The wire fence, the lighting. But no guards, no watchtowers, no people. It was a fully automated facility, food slipping down chutes at timed intervals, the liquid shit sluiced away into tanks, she could hear the clucking, a continuous fuss.

Marianne didn't bother looking inside. She went to the furthest hut and worked her way back to the first one, splashing the petrol along the walls. The night air was pungent with its reek.

It smelled good, the perfume of destruction. She was doing the hens a favour. She was putting them out of their misery. She poured a last trail to the gate, went the far side and tossed the match.

It went out.

Her nerves were beginning to go. Someone started practising a drum solo in her head. She tried again, the match went out again. She heard a car.

It was coming down the road.

She ran and hid in the bushes.

A false alarm, no car came, it must have been on the main road, she went back to the gate, climbed over it, lit a match and dropped it, a line of fire rushed back to the huts, the huts went up simultaneously, everywhere turned to orange daylight, she went back over the gate, ran to her car, even there the tops of the trees seemed edged by amber, but no one on the A3 took any notice, the traffic flowed both ways, headlights whooshed by, she got in the Fiesta, went back to London, was twenty minutes up the road before a fire tender came towards her, blue lights rotating.

Next day she drove to Yorkshire. In a service station on the A1 she bought a paper and read about the fire. It got more prominence than she was expecting, because of the security guard.

She hadn't known there was one.

She'd killed him.

He was in one of the huts, he was asleep. That's what the paper said, it did not say he was drink-sodden, whisky-zonked, that only came out at the inquest. The guard died from smoke inhalation, he suffocated. He was a single man of forty, the police strongly suspected arson, a spokesman for the animal rights movement denied all responsibility.

Shit, shit, shit. She never have torched the hut if she'd known. But how was she to know? It wasn't her fault, it really wasn't. If you choose to work in a place like that you get what you deserve. It was like being a guard at Auschwitz. If an RAF pilot had dropped a bomb, that wouldn't have made him a murderer, would it? Of course not. It wasn't her fault.

She stayed with an aunt, who lived in a village on the North Yorkshire moors. Marianne walked the moors alone. She listened to her aunt wittering on about this and that, obscure remote relatives, the royal family. But not the reputation of a popular local writer for oddity, wit and insouciance between 1738 and 1759, Hertz's discovery of the emission of electrons by the absorption of light, the Blütenstraub Aphorism #66 of Novalis.

Apart from wittering her aunt knitted. She watched too much daytime TV, for the Howard Hawks films she explained. She frowned, Hilda did. Hilda told Marianne she hadn't realised she was a vegetarian, Marianne left a day earlier than planned, invented an excuse, anything to get away.

She returned to London.

She took the car back.

The conical-shaped hollow muscular organ enclosed in the cavity of her pericardium thumped wildly in that brightly lit Formica-panelled rental office where she waited for a firm dark-sleeved hand on her arm, a polite request to accompany two cold narrow-eyed officers to a police station. It didn't happen, nothing ever happened. Nothing.

Whatever forensics they had, they couldn't link it to her. The story lingered a day or two, then fizzled. Nothing. Nothing to show, nothing ever. An unsolved crime. The papers yellowing, the years heaping up, no developments, the investigation quietly shelved, all done with, dusty drawers and cabinets packed with figments, murmurings, little by little losing all lustre, dust to dust, flaking, a shrinking stop, a black dot, over, all done.

19 Back Story

May morphed to June. TV daze of news, snows, snoozes, quiz choices, couch voices, bloopers, the papers, wheat beer, red wine, celebrities, that hat, those shoes, shows. Noise from nowhere. QUAND LA GAUCHE AURA LE POUVOIR EST-CE QUE LA TELEVISION AURA TOUJOURS AUSSI PEU DE RAPPORT AVEC LES GENS?

Then, in the second paragraph of chapter 19, Ben announced he'd found just the right fictional location. A building society in Stamford Hill. One of the smaller ones. The Chichester & Arundel. In fact it was closing down. A fiction – it had never existed. It had been gobbled up by one of the bigger outfits. This branch was like something out of the Edwardian era, imagine. Like, they didn't even have an armoured glass security screen. Just a counter, with three women behind it. And piles of banknotes. *Like they wanted to give it away.*

The last serious objection to the robbery back story was the

Spectral Duplicate's. It was getting nervous – in so far as a transferred projection entity with a silicon sleeker envelope and Cooper ghost attachments *can* get nervous. "There's too much traffic," said Spectral Edgar. "It gets in the way. You just can't make a fast getaway these days. Remember what happened to those jokers last month."

The Spectral Duplicate took a keen interest in the press. It processed the data on a page of newsprint in less than a second. It scanned voraciously, hoping to absorb material on Mirando Mirando. It had absorbed none – but it had learned a wealth of information about the primitive culture it was operating in. Like smash and grab, for example.

The jokers had been a couple of men who'd done an S and G at the Glitz jewellery store in the High Street. Their car had made it to Hoe Street before getting stuck in a long tail-back caused by a broken water main at the Crooked Billet. They'd abandoned their car and hidden in a back garden, where they were caught ten minutes later. "Traffic in London now moves at an average speed of nine miles an hour. We'd never make it." The SD had learned that statistic the day before. It had almost melted its bion-clip in shock.

"Bicycles," said Emma. "That's the solution. That's what we'll use." So they did.

Riding a bicycle was no joke for the SD. It needed immense seriousness, intensive bio-mass substitution, *and* eloid propulsion. It was considerably more difficult than fooling Emma into thinking she was having sex with it. All *that* required was intense bursts of energy, false aromas, cerebral manipulation. A phantom dick pleasuring her mind. As the Lincoln Orbital poet Wilshack Spoor famously wrote, *a Spectral Duplicate's days duplicate life's difficulties doubly*.

There were times Spectral Edgar wanted to tell Emma to ditch her contraceptive pills. No danger of her getting pregnant from a ghost out of the future. Then he remembered. Even if he could explain it to her rationally she still might not believe. There was a local religion which believed just that. It featured a smooth-talking Mary, hustle about some guy with shining wings. A religion in an advanced state of decay, admittedly. Nor was Emma into that jive.

85

All the same… Edgar gave a spectral shrug. A superfluous gesture since no one was watching. But it gave him a pleasant tingle in his spectral cortex. Sometimes even SDs need to relax.

A compressed attachment in the SD complete download supplied Strobey with the movie of his first robbery. He opened the multi-nano data display. The SD had thoughtfully edited it down to a coherent realist narrative during its spare time. Strobey watched himself shouting, "Hands up! This is a robbery!" But the girl behind the counter didn't play the game. She did not put up her hands. She just gaped at him. Gaped as in *stare curiously*. Gaped as in *open mouth wide*. Gaped as in *stare*, *look in wonderment* and *open the mouth wide in an expression of expectancy*, the movie informed him. "Cut the subtitles," he said irritably, and the words vanished.

Spectral Strobey pushed the gun nearer the girl's head. "Fucking do it!" (His Duplicate's grasp of the culture's vernacular was outstanding, Edgar thought.)

But the girl just went on staring back at him. Her eyes were pools of fear. She was paralysed by the powerful style. Her mouth emitted little strangled yelps of terror. "Just put those banknotes into this bag, dear," said Marianne quietly, pointing. That did the trick. The girl responded to a calm, commanding female voice. Obediently she started putting the banknotes into Marianne's Tesco carrier bag.

"Now define local colour!" Marianne growled.

"It's the representation in fiction of the landscape, language and customs typical of a particular locality, sometimes relying on a comic evocation of the surface peculiarities of that locality!" the girl barked, wagging her tail bone.

"You fucking do it too!" screamed Spectral Edgar at the other two cowering clerks. "And keep your fucking hands on top of the counter. Don't fucking try to press any buttons or I'll blow your fucking heads off!"

"It's the representation in fick-"

"Not that! I meant the fucking banknotes! Put the fucking banknotes in the fucking bag!"

The Spectral Duplicate wondered if it was overdoing the *fuckings* but the L-C RC display indicated it was doing fine. The Duplicate was beginning to enjoy itself. It wasn't used to giving commands.

Nether Time was an interesting place, it felt. Even if it did require frequent recourse to the Late-Capitalist Reality Checker.

The two older women looked as petrified as the girl. They'd been torn from the text, timetravelled back to a time even more primitive and barbaric than that of the Blair government, suspended under dripping limestone for ten thousand years, then abruptly taken back to Stamford Hill in the early twenty-first century. Ben held open his carrier bag. The robbers began hurriedly dropping in packets of banknotes.

Emma remained outside. She was wearing a blonde wig and sunglasses. She was waiting to intercept anyone who tried to walk into the building society while the raid was taking place. She'd seen a lot of movies and knew exactly what to do. It went like a dream.

No it didn't. It went like a piece of tired realism.

Ben left first. He got on his bike and rode off. He would meet them on the far side of the bridge. Strobey stayed inside while Marianne helped Emma put the bags in the panniers. The two masks, dropped into another supermarket bag, went into the pannier on Marianne's bike. Now it was Emma's turn to ride off, leaving Marianne to guard the bikes. A minute longer, then Spectral Edgar left. He stood in the doorway, slipping off his mask. Marianne left his bike propped by the kerb and started pedalling away. After a minute she glanced back. Edgar was following her.

Everything was it should be, apart from the slow backward spin of the bike wheels. No commotion, no excitement. No howling police cars or people running. Just a few cyclists pedalling along a London street. They turned off down Spring Hill, towards the river.

Emma and Ben were waiting on the far side of the footbridge, under some trees, just beyond the narrow U-gate designed to keep out motorbikes. When they saw Marianne and Edgar they headed off down the pathway beside the marina, in the direction of the marshes. On their left was a reservoir, hidden behind bushes and a grass embankment. Further over, a metre beyond the Samtron monitor, was a double CD set, the last track on the second CD "I Want To Vanish", an unfinished novel containing the sentence *'When I'm with you, I don't breathe quite right,' she said*, a story climaxing with the words *End of story*, and an anthology of essays translated by Mirra Ginsburg containing a paragraph which ends:

Przybyszewski could not write without a bottle of cognac; Huysmans – and he was not alone in this – used morphine. Andreyev drank the strongest tea while at work. Remizov drinks coffee and smokes. I cannot write a single page without a cigarette.

Further left still was Lenin, and on their right was the great sweep of the marshes. Bull rushes edged the pathway. There was a railway line up ahead. The Gospel Oak - Barking line, which connected outdoor religious delusions to madness.

A low, narrow tunnel bored through the embankment. The tunnel was designed for cattle, not people. Back in the days when farmers grazed animals on the marshes. It was just wide enough and high enough to get a car through - but not a Range Rover or a Transit van. Even on a bike you had to crouch over the handlebars and watch out your spine didn't hit the low, black metal edge of the bridge. It was dark and cold under the railway line. Plus the tunnel was flooded. Not deep enough to bother you on a bike but you had to keep going. Or ruin your shoes. It was as they went through the tunnel they heard the first faraway siren.

The cops!

20   The Cops

Daisy Spenser woke at four, her head aching, her mind filled with shots of Scurr.

She had her clothes on, was flat out on Scurr's sofa. Scurr sitting in the chair opposite her, smoking. He said you should never have had that second G and T, I did warn you, he grinned, and the tears began bubbling down her face.

You drugged me, she whispered. She ran into the kitchen, her glass wasn't there, a ticking by the sink, she saw it was coming from the dishwasher, pulled open the door, two glasses, so hot they almost burned, shiny and smelling of lemon, the evidence rinsed away.

Scurr stood behind her in the doorway, you have wonderful skin, he said. Flawless, not a trace of a bruise. A pity, really, what police doctors like to see is bruising, and juries too, big colour pictures of bruises do wonders for a jury's opinions. But those cases where there's no bruising, just one person's word against another, stands to reason something like that isn't beyond reasonable doubt, he grinned. I did a course in forensic science, bloody useful some of the things you learn, you know, sort of practical knowledge.

I hate you she said.

Pity he replied, I rather fancy you.

You bastard. I'll get you for this.

You can try but it's your career will get wrecked not mine. Nobody likes a snitch know what I mean. But keep your trap shut and maybe I can do you some favours.

Piss off she said.

Scurr held open the door for her.

Think about it, he said. No hard feelings, eh, he shouted, adding Not now.

His harsh laughter following her down the cold dirty stairwell forever.

*

Staying one step ahead of the cops didn't just rely on the traditional limitations of law enforcement agencies. Spectral Edgar left a nano-camcorder in a speck of dust to get aftermath data from the robbery. It transmitted inconspicuously from the high corner that contained the spider's web it had flown and clamped itself to.

"They were wearing *grotesque masks*," the cashier told police. She had to speak louder than normal because the alarm bell was still ringing. The rotating lights on the three police cars lined up outside sent slashes of blue light dancing around the walls. The spider slumbered at the edge of its web, undisturbed by the commotion or the camcorder.

The manageress stood below. She was leaning against the green wall, trembling. Staring with a puzzled upset dazed scowl. The cop stopped writing in his notebook. "What do you mean, grotesque? Like a Halloween mask?"

"Sort of. Sort of like a witch. Big staring eyes. Really *evil-looking*. And they was all three of them wearing the same mask." The cashier began sobbing again. "It was horrible. Horrible.' The policeman leaned forwards and patted her on the shoulder. 'Don't worry, dear. We'll catch them." But the police hadn't. Not yet.

The cashier was vague on clothing and accents. It all happened so suddenly. All that shouting and swearing. Wearing those masks. Later, when the cashier identified the mask, Chief Superintendent Buller, felt very, very old. It was a fact that the cashier *didn't know who the mask was of.*

"Yeah, thassa one," the girl had said, when the flying squad officer interviewed her again the next day. (NCs were smart little bastards. Prior to final dissolution the nano-cam had replicated itself and flown to the girl's hair, in order to maintain information continuity. NCs were invented by a team from Omniscience Incorporated on Level 17.)

A smart constable of the sort found in popular crime fiction but not in the police had managed to borrow a dozen masks from a local toy shop. A D.C. and the witness went through them one by one. Not Frankenstein's monster with the bolt through its head. Not that twee, creepy, big-eared creature from *Star Wars*. Not Dracula, not the werewolf, not Cilla Black. Well, maybe Cilla Black. On second thoughts: no. Definitely NOT Cilla Black.

"Yes! *That one. Thassa one*." The girl shivered at the memory. The flying squad officer leaned forwards. "The one of Margaret Thatcher?"

The girl looked blank.

"Who?" she said.

*

It was like one of those election night counting-the-votes scenes on TV. The four of them sitting next to each other at the biggest table in the hotel's dusty empty dining room. Each thumbing through the little paper piles in front of them. Except these aren't ballot papers, these are *banknotes.*

Sometimes they had to stop and start again. They were all lightheaded from the champagne they'd been sluicing. Plus flushed with adrenalin, relief, excitement. They did it. *They fucking did it!* They'd made it back to Finn's without being caught by the cops, a name derived from the early eighteenth century slang "to cop" meaning "to catch", the term "cop bung!" ("the police are coming!") having fallen into disuse, along with "copper-slosher" ("one apt to physically attack the police with a complete indifference to split infinitives") and "copper-stick" ("erect penis resembling a truncheon").

The plastic masks lay on a chair, next to the Czech handgun Ben obtained from a friend of a friend of a friend. Via a flat in a tower block in Tottenham.

When they'd each added up their pile they wrote down the amount on a piece of paper. Emma came round and collected them. Then she totted up the total while they all watched. Could be worse," she said with ~~a smile~~ her mouth. "Five-thou two-hundred exactly. Thirteen-hundred smackers each. So smile, Ben. Stop looking so scared. We did it. By Jove we did it!" Then she followed his gaze, saw what it was gave his eyes that conventional bulge of disbelief and terror. Marianne and Strobey, too.

It was a young woman, at a table the far side of the room. She hadn't been there moments before. She was wearing an oddly old-fashioned cotton blouse and long dark skirt that extended to her ankles. Her dark hair was done up in a bun, giving her a quaintly Victorian appearance.

On the table was what might have been the innards of a machine that lacked its outer casing. It was about the size of a television. It consisted of a series of slender rings, strung round a vertical metallic spine. The rims of each ring were dotted with what looked like small brown beads.

The woman was running her fingers along the beads in a manner that made Emma think of a blind person reading Braille. As her fingers ran up and down the strange device Ben realised that the rings were beginning to spin. The woman seemed oblivious of them. Then, as they continued to stare at the unexpected intruder, the woman and her machine seemed suddenly to be drained of colour. It was like they'd turned grey.

Ben realised with a shock that he could see *through* the woman. The table beyond hers was visible through her upper body. She seemed to be made of cloudy specks. A moment later she'd dissolved, along with her device.

He said: "Did you see what I just saw? A fucking *ghost*. I never believed in any of that shit before. Jesus! This place is fucking *haunted*." He went over to the table where the woman had been sitting. The chairs and tabletop were thick with undisturbed dust. "Did you see? *Did you see?*"

Yeah. They had.

"I don't like it in here," said Emma.

"Let's take our share and go." She took Spectral Edgar's hand and they hurried out of the room. Her delicate little hand trembled in his bio-energy detector glove.

Upstairs he put on an Enya CD and held her tight, soothing her with whisper words. The SD was neutral on the ghost woman and her device. It had no data and no programmed emotional response. Ghosts did not exist. Although there was a file on primitive folklore belief it wasn't worth the extra memory loading it into a spectral on a traject to that culture at that time. It therefore merely committed the scene to its sensory data bank, where it was catalogued by date and time, not content.

21   Strange Forces

Aphrodite woke to the sound of her doorbell, it rang, it rang again, it rang again, she turned on the bedside lamp, she looked at her alarm clock, four-thirty in the morning, *ding-dong ding-dong*, she went and looked through the security hole, the fish-eye lens showed the curved, distorted figure of a woman, someone she recognised, Aphrodite drew back the bolt, unlocked the door, opened it, *I'm so sorry, I didn't know where else to go,* Daisy Spenser, her face streaked with tears, can I come in, please, of course, what's wrong, let me make you a cup of tea, she went in, she cried some more, then, in three shockingly explicit pages she told Aphrodite everything about

[three pages deleted].

*

Ben was the least concerned by the ghost.

Apart from being troubled by aches in his copper-stick (which required constant lubrication) he was always seeing *strange stuff*. He knew there had to be a rational explanation. Professor Engels taught the materiality of things. The Prof was a man to be admired. You didn't mess with a man who had a beard that size. He was a prophet, a sage. A radical magus. All the same, the laws of motion of capitalism sometimes appeared to be stirred by other forces. Or were a plurality of incommensurable worlds themselves expressive of the physics of late capitalism, a question on the tip of his mind, toppling into its tip, dumped, forgotten, a day later, near Blackhorse Road, the question mark dissolving as a glint of something silvery in the sky caught his eye.

He glanced up to see what it was. The object was shaped like an hourglass, a kind of silvery eight. Against a grey, featureless sky it was impossible to tell how large or how faraway the object was. He had the impression of something of great size, at a great height.

Ben stared at it, baffled. It hung there, motionless, in complete silence. If it was a UFO it did not fit his expectations of one. It wasn't saucer shaped. There were no portholes. Its fuselage – the object was clearly some kind of craft – was dun-coloured.

He watched it for ten minutes, then grew bored. He turned away, then looked back.

It was still there.

He went back to the hotel to tell the others. He kept looking back at it, and it was always there.

Back at Finn's no one else seemed to have seen it. There was nothing on the news. Benjamin decided it was probably some kind of weather balloon.

93

*

Marianne was as shaken as the others by the apparition. It was weird. She wished now she had a dog, but she didn't, she had rats.

She went down into the cellar and spent the rest of the evening with them, she was training them, they were her pets. People were afraid of rats, which was silly. They were beautiful, she let them run along her arm, over her head. She adored animals. She was more afraid of the ghost than of any creature, but she wasn't really afraid even of the ghost, it was just an image out of the past, some kind of kink in time, she didn't pretend to understand. She felt that the woman with the strange device intended her no harm, and what was not tangible couldn't hurt, whereas a rat's teeth could, under the bare bulb dangling from what had once been the cellar where the beer and wine were stored her grey face evinced a strange smile.

*

Gone midnight.

Paint it black.

Ben had gone out to celebrate, Marianne was happy to let him. She decided to stay in his room and try to evince another strange smile, it wasn't easy. She wasn't into excess alcohol or uppers. The bottle of Magritte was something else, but she fought back temptation and let it stay on the shelf, a melancholy expression on its drooping blue face. She was strong, her lover was weak, and his weaknesses were another reason for keeping quiet about that fire at the factory farm.

Sodium moonlight illumines the dead street. Beech trees cause quivering shadows on the steel skins of the parked cars.

A double row of cars, all in a coma, both sides of the empty street. Waiting for daylight; waiting to be fired into life again. To fart their fumes and drink their petrol and beneath the bonnet stretch their oily limbs.

Miaow, says a black cat Ben hopes is real, skittering past. Tangerine lamplight washes over Ben's face as he sways towards

94

Old Rogue Palmerston Road.

Ben's stoned again. Uppers, downers, sleepers.   Plus Jack Daniel's. It all adds up. A firestorm in his mind. Layers of scarlet clouds building a warning in the sky. His vision a thing of ripples. Luminous specks darting to and fro like charged ions. His body battered and pushed off course by invisible forces.

He whispers back at them: I am Benjamin Scaravelli! He reaches out for a traffic sign, rests, then soars away across space to the next port.

A bus stop, a shelter on the shore of the great, slow river. Deserted at bleak midnight. He staggers, flies onward. Makes it to the next tree's cool solid trunk.

Going along Gainsford Road now. It all adds up. Affects your vision, yes. That time he was in Sainsbury's. Just went in for crisps and beer. Halted, sweating and shivery, appalled by the aisle with hundreds of tins of meat and the big sign: RAT FOOD.

Not forgetting that centipede in the kitchen back at Finn's Hotel. Every time he goes into the kitchen he catches the centipede on the hop. It's surprised, frightened, in a panic. It rushes off across the wall, wriggling and jerking. Once or twice he's tried to swat it with a zene. Then it stops, gets into focus, goes back to being just a dirty mark on the wall.

A deviant gene ran through Ben's family, explained the corporation man from Omniscience. Every generation threw up an oddity. His uncle Jack o'Beans, for example. Jack had a fondness for directing traffic. It was triggered by failed traffic lights. Every so often the lights would fail somewhere, and if Jack o'Beans came across the scene out he'd wander. Slap bang into the middle of the road. And start directing the traffic. He even had an official-looking cap and a fluorescent yellow plastic waistcoat, which he used to carry round. The full moon sent him crazy.

Benjamin leans forward against the howling silent storm. He moves on up Gainsford Road, navigating an invisible turbulence between the beech trees.

He embraces each of the seven trees on the odd-number side in turn. A moist dust of powdery bark attaches itself to his white raincoat like a dark mould. If there were birds in those trees they'd chatter to him.

They do, sometimes. A stream of electronic gabble. Sometimes you can decode the words. TUESDAY, a blackbird said to him once. TUESDAY! TUESDAY! TUESDAY! He ignored it, of course.

But the following Tuesday he nearly died. He was walking along Hoe Street and was just about to cross the end of Byron Road when he saw the car. It was coming down the hill fast, so he waited.

It didn't look like the driver would stop for him. Then he saw the car didn't have a driver. An A-reg silver Toyota. It went straight across Hoe Street like a rocket. By a miracle no one was passing at the time. CRRAAAASH! The Toyota went straight through the plate glass window of an estate agents. And vanished from sight like the jagged glass was teeth in a giant mouth that ate cars.

Drivers jammed on their brakes, people came running from everywhere and went into the shattered building to find the dead and injured. Only there weren't any. The estate agents had closed down four months before. And the car was very definitely empty. The owner had parked on the hill and hadn't put the hand brake on hard enough.

It reminded him of that scene in *The Omen*, the one where an evil force lifts the hand brake and David Warner gets decapitated. Strange forces everywhere. But the pills kept them in check. The pills put him on the road to the truth. Now he knew that the strange forces were in league with the laws of motion of capitalism, the cold dark tunnel under the track brought it all cascading back (rhymes).

That time he went for a jog in one. A long dark tunnel that seemed to go on forever. Ben had once had mental health problems. That was how they described it. Nowadays he was a lot calmer, relatively. As sane as the night is long. All the medication. Pills licit and illicit. Plus calming booze. Some people still called him Benny Bizarre (but not his friends at Finn's Hotel. They weren't like that. That's why he liked them and trusted them). It was the deviant gene. Benjamin knew he was partly fucked-up. But he didn't mind. The long dark tunnel seems to go on forever, and then you come to a place of bright, shining light.

Two years ago it was. Ben was on the platform at Walthamstow

96

Central, having just missed a train. He was standing opposite a Wonderbra hoarding. Being eyed ecstatically by a woman with breasts five metres wide. Benjamin didn't even notice her. There he stood on the edge of his feather, expecting to fly.

He raised his arms, like wings. Propelled himself off the platform. A girl further along shrieked. Ben landed heavily in the dark greasy pit between the rails, staggered. He missed the live rail by a fraction, and scrambled to the side. And then he set off into the tunnel. A fast jog down the Victoria Line! Words booming down the tunnel after him. "Come back!" screamed a London Transport man in a yellow plastic waistcoat.

"Come back!" The words distorted, flowing round Benjamin. Ache! Ache! Ache! Strips of light set like glowing jewels in the dark curving sooty walls.

This really happened. They had to stop all northbound trains at Seven Sisters. They had to switch off the power. They closed Walthamstow Central and Blackhorse Lane stations. Police and paramedics everywhere. A team going in after him. Police, LT personnel, a doctor, a shrink, four nurses. Waving their flashlights.

Too late.

Benjamin jogged all the way to Blackhorse Lane station. He would have liked to have gone on to Tottenham Hale but at Blackhorse Road he was seized, taken prisoner. Sedated. Sectioned. Taken by ambulance to Claybury. The loony bin. Drugged. Locked-up. Kept there for a year. Then released. Cured, ostensibly. A bit odd (who isn't?) but cured, and fit once more to join the company of zombies again. He discovered Saint Trotsky and the other elders of the Church of World Revolution. He discovered comradeship. And the folly of the other sects. Liberation!

He emerges from the cool, dark tunnel. Daylight washes over him. He's a free agent! A reddish globe the size of a football hovers above the adjacent playing field, eyeing him. When he winks at it the globe vanishes. He's in tune with the wildness at the edge of things – but he's also a rock solid guy. Cycling up Coppermill Lane with his mates. A perfectly sane and reasonable armed robber. Woo hoo! He falls into bed beside Marianne. Her face looks so happy. He snuggles up to her warmth. And falls asleep at once.

22 Infinity Died

Entering the room with Emma, Strobey waved at the other two. He knew at once that this was just moments after the third paragraph on page 31.

Despite the memory download it was still a shock for Strobey to meet people for the first time who'd known him for months, particularly in a paragraph revised during the week that Kaybrera Infinity died. The death was less than ten miles away. All that week the forecast snow refused to fall, out of respect. It would have been too trite, too obviously a cheap allusion to Auden's poem on the death of Yeats.

Marianne was somehow chubbier than he was expecting. She wore her hair cropped short, in the style of Jean Seberg in *Breathless.* She had eyes of intense emerald and looked faintly sullen. Strobey processed his spectral memories of her. With her fondness for dressing in black and her slightly pointed ears there was a faint resemblance to Nosferatu - or Star Trek's Doctor Spock.

Marianne was a bit wrinkly around the eyes. laugh lines. Strange, because she never laughed. There was a hardness inside her. A mixture of stone and ice, with lumps of dead adjectives. Maybe she was Mirando Mirando. Or maybe Emma was. The Duplicate said not. But the Duplicate hadn't found her. The Duplicate said she could be anywhere in London. *Big help that, thanks.*

If Marianne was cold, Emma was warm. She was sweet. Middle-class to the bone. An English rose, with cheeks to match. Strobey processed a spectral memory. Emma walks in beauty like the night. Emma walks in front of him down a short corridor. The corridor is narrower now than it was before. Matter is thinning. The glaciers are starting to crack up. Emma opens the door to their room. Inside, it's like a rain forest. Hot, with greenery everywhere. Emma adores plants. They fill the room. There are several varieties of fan palm, with big waxy leaves. There's a dwarf palm. A date palm, grown from a stone. The yellow-green fire of a *trifasciata laurentii* erupts in stiff silence from the big glazed clay vase, frozen in amazement at a blatant plagiarism. A japonica, a pair of fatshedra, a splayed, wilting aspidistra. A cyclamen on a shelf, its pale papery blossoms held aloft by thin stalks. A Firebrand. A Song of India, its streaked leaves reminding Emma faintly of chocolate and peppermint.

Most of all there are spider plants. Mature spider plants in big pots by the windows where most of the plants are clustered. There are tiny spider plants in little plastic pots on the marble mantelpiece above the fireplace. And there are spider plants spraying out from carved gourds hung from ropes nailed high up on the wall. At night a slimline convector heater on a low setting generated warmth. That summer she turned it off. It was too hot. Hadn't rained for weeks. Global over heating kicking in, again.

The aspidistra needs help. It is being strangled by the thin, repellent moustache of an Orwellio. There's a slim grey plastic watering can next to the Song of India. A quarter full. Spectral Edgar sits on her bed. Emma puts on *The Celts*. Mood music. They embrace. The intrusion network informs Spectral Edgar his spectral hair is being brushed by the tip of a spider plant. For the sake of authenticity, he reaches up to brush it away. Then he makes synthetic love to Emma for the first time. Afterwards she releases a drowsy smile, says "You're beautiful."

The Spectral Duplicate generates a returning smile. It does think of itself as pretty cool, and a considerable advance on the earlier Synth 34Zb model. "You have to say something back," its Motherboard informs its processor. The SD duly creates the illusion of warm affection in Emma's mental receptors. "I love you," the Duplicate whispers, choosing the number one hit in both the Hollywood movie and English liberal novel Current Decade Dialogue Download charts.

*

The meeting had been called in order to focus the reader's attention on the back story. They'd agreed the heat was getting too intense. Back of that was *der globalen Klimakatastrophe*. They shut their minds to it, concentrated on a better plot than entropy.

Seven successful robberies inside a month. The Met was reeling. Scurr blamed the influx of gays, all that political correctness shit.

And now the cops had grown wise to the two-wheel ploy. Last time the Finnsters had almost been caught. They hadn't been expecting the helicopter or the motorbike pack. Emma fled, abandoned her bike two blocks from the robbery. D-locked it to a street sign. Marianne drove the van, picked her up in the next street. A smart move, getting a clapped-out white Transit. They were everywhere in East London. The street after that she took aboard Ben and his machine. That only left Strobey's Spectral Duplicate. By this time the chopper was three-hundred metres overhead, directing the pack. They trapped the SD in Livingstone Road E17. A pair of big heavy cops in leathers and shades sat astride their bulky machines at the Hoe Street end. The SD turned at the kink in the street and registered a mirror image at the other.

A terraced house had a side entrance, a wooden fence at the end topped with trellis. The Duplicate swerved down the cold shadowy path. Concentrating its mind, it gave the fence a mild burst of atom loosener. The SD passed through it into the grounds beyond. Here the Duplicate found itself in an identical garden the far side, plus another side entrance. It was still managing to steer the bicycle, though it felt it was more *101 Dalmatians* than *E.T.* It came bursting out into the next street. No good. The chopper was directing the action, the pack was there too.

If it hadn't been a Spectral, that would have been it. SD Strobey went back to the house and forced the front door. Went inside, propped the bike behind the sofa, and sat there. It didn't have to wait long before a beefy, perspiring motorbike cop stood in the doorway, glaring in his direction. The SD projected an image of an empty room into the cop's narrow, desolate mind. No bike, empty sofa, empty room. The pig grunted like a cop. His leather boots creaked as he moved off to check the rest of the house. Returned, shouted to someone, "Must have gone out the back. No one here." Police radios crackled and leaked tiny staccato voices. Someone standing nearby made repeated non-specific references to sexual intercourse.

SD Strobey waited two hours, then left the bike at the side of the house and strolled back to Finn's. His spectral face auto-remembered to look tired, his spectral skin to sweat. The SD didn't

know what chemicals they used but it seemed to turn primitive
bipeds on. Well, Emma, at any rate. After they'd counted the cash
she took his hand and led him upstairs. It was like riding a bicycle
all over again. The effort put into making her think she was really
having sex. It threatened to exhaust his rapidly depleting energy grid
quota. It was a huge relief when Real Strobey turned up in the night
over the Thames estuary and took over his exhausting role.

*

Building societies were played out, they all agreed on that. It was
Marianne suggested the Regal Shakespeare Players. They were
coming to Walthamstow for four nights to put on *A Midsummer
Night's Dream*. At the Greek amphitheatre behind the Girls School
on Church Hill. A first-come first-served basis. Lots of dosh being
handed over. A gift for the taking, right?

Emma wasn't convinced. The ethics didn't seem right, somehow.
It was one thing to steal from the capitalist system. But a theatrical
troupe... Ben cut in, said it was, after all, the *Regal* Shakespeare
Players. A name like that, they deserved shafting. Plus these weren't
two-bit amateurs. They were professionals, the cream. Big money.
Fuck them. Besides, the Government subsidised them heavily. It
was really only stealing from the state. Emma began to think Ben
had a point.

Strobey volunteered to reconnoitre the site.

It was agreed. Tomorrow. Their last job. Then they'd retire. That
was part of the secret of being a successful criminal: knowing when
to stop. It was also a popular story line in successful movies.
Problem was, Strobey didn't really understand why they'd ever
bothered to start. He was still pondering this when, in the first draft,
Emma's cellphone piped a Moby tune. This was subsequently
changed to Asian Dub Foundation. "For you," she said. "Yeah?"
"Down in the street. Take a look," a metallic voice commanded.
Still holding the phone Strobey went to the window and looked out.

The traffic crawled past. A turbid Lizard 5 nuzzled the exhaust
pipe of a Tortoise 106, which was behind a rusting Panda. People
came out of Walthamstow Central opposite. No one seemed to

notice the ruby-coloured globe which hovered above the pavement below. It was about the size of a football and looked like it was made of a substance like glass. It hovered just above the heads of the passers-by. As he looked down at it the device flashed, as if someone had flicked on a bulb inside.

A noise of frying quorn dripped and spitted feistily from the phone. Strobey put it to his ear and the cell phone crackled with laughter. The voice returned. "Go to the scarlet globe," it said.

Strobey wondered if he had back-up. But he'd never known the TPT to send reinforcements. It was too expensive. Besides, it would be a waste. If you were any good you did the job. You didn't need a partner any more than you needed a spouse.

"Who in hell are you?" He wondered if it was Mirando Mirando. Was it a trick? She'd be expecting someone. But she surely wouldn't know it was *him*.

He repeated the question, but the phone was dead. Then, as if acknowledging the week's important death, a new voice with a faint Cuban accent said, "Here's a map made a few days before the English attacked the capital of the island… a rather rough sketch, but it accomplishes its purpose. It indicates with precision the Morro fortress across the bay… You may observe how the map distorts the characteristics of the city itself and its environs. It is believed that the map was made by an English spy…"

"I have to go," Strobey told Emma. "Intertextuality calls."

She looked puzzled. Nothing in the fiction of Libby Purves had prepared her for this moment.

Strobey held the phone to her ear. "The first part is ruled by dreams" the voice continued. "Drafts of reality drift through the cracks. There are composites, superimpositions, disintegrations of the-" A horn blared in the street, obliterating several words with the brisk efficiency of *highlight-delete*. "Madness is the love that lasts beyond death or necrophilia!"

Emma flinched and handed back the phone. No one had said anything like this in *A Free Woman*, praised by *Country Life* for its calm good sense, plain writing and warmth.

"What is it?"

"I'm not sure. A Spanish accent, I think. But I'm not certain. I think it might be an old friend of mine. A practical joker. Wants me to meet him outside."

"Don't go."

"I think I'd better."

He went out by what counted as the front door, in reality a service door fifteen metres to the side of the old disused entrance. The glass globe was waiting for him. It hung just a unit above the passing pedestrians. It must have been sending out a neural block - it was clear no one else could see it. Emma hadn't seen it when she followed him to the window.

As he walked towards it a pair of lips formed in the spherical material. "Just follow me, Strobey", the globe said. The lips smiled in a friendly way, then melted back into the hard ruby-coloured substance. The globe bobbed away towards the traffic lights on the corner with Hoe Street. Strobey hurried after it.

23 Collider

The hot week continued.

Buller loosened his tie, undid the second button on his shirt. He gave up altogether on his jacket but his armpits still leaked.

He was sleeping badly. Bad dreams, a rodent's tail slapping against his thigh, intermittent toothache. He still hadn't made an appointment to see Mrs Novoselic at the dentistry. He felt his control on things beginning to slip. His staff seemed strangely out of sorts. That new policewoman looked like she'd been crying. Aphrodite Cutter appeared distracted, distorted, disturbed. One morning she came in looking exactly like Picasso's 'Bust of a Woman' (1931). He did not like to see one of his officers with a nose which bore a strong resemblance to his own thick yet detumescent penis. It reminded him of its unemployment. Only DC Andy Scurr seemed his usually chirpy self. "Summer is icumen in," he quipped one morn, "Llude sing cuccu spryngeth sed and bloweth mede and groweth the wude nu."

The others were like Buller. They needed sleep, good sex, a break from whatever anxieties were troubling them. He wasn't exactly short of them himself. The robberies, the disappearances, the Collider opening... His head ached with information for the reader. The robbers on bicycles still hadn't been caught. The national press had picked up on the story. There had been sarcastic editorials about how these days the police couldn't even catch someone on a push bike. The Commissioner was breathing down his neck. It was a warm, oddly exciting sensation and for a moment he wondered if he was bisexual. Flushing, he hid the moment in the closet.

The Commissioner wanted them caught – and soon. And as a commanding officer with a fondness for hyphens and tabloid prose he was not to be trifled with. To top that, the disappearances were continuing. Every day there were two or three calls. He felt like he was in a science fiction movie (which, if this novel is ever filmed, he will be). Like, say, *Invasion of the Bombast Snatchers*. One of those ones where small weird things start to happen and nobody takes too much notice. One day the city is functioning in its normal way with a slightly verbose and inflated diction that is disproportionate to the matter it expresses, the next everything seems replicated with a ridiculous disparity between style and its subject matter. Though come to think of it, the local chief of police usually turned out to have been transformed into an alien himself.

Buller smiled sardonically, a side effect of opening that tin of sardons for breakfast. He was pretty sure he wasn't an alien *yet*. Despite all the stress he was under. He'd communicated the facts about the disappearances to the Commissioner. The response had been sceptical and unsympathetic. He could tell the top brass thought he was cracking up, while the cutlery and the copper warming pan muttered that they really couldn't say.

Grudgingly, the Ministry of Defence had been informed. Having decoded the grudge an official was coming down next week. Buller knew they didn't really believe him. Meanwhile his officers had to write reports and go through the motions of investigating the inexplicable. Fortunately even the local paper thought the episodes were too way-out to give them serious coverage. It cautiously downplayed them as conventional missing persons stories.

And now he had to give a press conference. The Collider was being officially opened in twenty four hours time. The sewer press scented the sweet perfume of trouble. ANARCHIST THUGS PLOT COLLIDER BLOODBATH the *Daily Vile* alleged. When he asked for their evidence the reporter faxed back a page from an Italian website. In semi-literate English it urged readers to "get up to Great Briton (sic) and smash the Coolider (sic) with internation (sic) solidarity and the iron fist of a workers everywhere (sic)." This ringing declaration, unlike his still throbbing tooth, did not keep him awake at night.

These days everything was spin. It made Buller dizzy and nauseous, like that giant teacup he had once been persuaded to sit inside and be swirled around in at a funfair in Poole. He had to give a press conference and assure the assembled sharks that there would be no blood on the day. The sharks hoped there would be, of course. And he intended to see that there wasn't. He didn't really think there would be, either. The Greens were a pretty harmless bunch, into organic root vegetables and non-violence. Their grasp of the realities of the capitalist state was as woolly as their hats.

He'd instruct his men not to use copper-sticks, unless in self-defence. No mass arrests. Keep it good humoured. What was the word? *Fluffy.* He winced. It was a word he detested almost as much as feuilletonistic.

*

Because of the demonstrations in the text and the demonstrations Ellis Sharp had gone on against the impending war on Iraq, against the outbreak of war, and against the subsequent military occupation, it had taken two years longer than planned to get the Zeilinger Collider ~~built~~ written.

The fictitious protest against the fictitious project had begun in a small way. Fewer than twenty miscellaneous Greens chained themselves to the old footbridge and the sign that read FERN ISLAND. They'd quickly been dealt with. But the arrests gave the protest publicity and soon others arrived to voice their opposition.

TV news showed the new protests. Young women lay down in the paths of bulldozers. Rebecca Lush got arrested again. Dozens more scaled the security fencing. Soon the police were there on a daily basis. But though the protests and Ellis Sharp's daily involvement in non-writing matters slowed the pace of the development, they did not stop it.

The footbridge was demolished and replaced by a four-lane concrete bridge lit by massive lighting columns that played beams of silver light across the sluggish brown river and the gashes in the earth. The old wooden sign was torn down and replaced by a vast illuminated metal hoarding that read ENTERPRISE AND DEVELOPMENT ZONE. A hundred metres beyond it a new road led up to a sign of similar size and design: the Zeilinger Corporation Welcomed You. A welcome muted by the rolls of barbed wire, the high fences and hundreds of security men in yellow jackets.

Day after day the protesters swarmed over the fences and ran towards the bulldozers; day after day they were dragged down by security men, or taken away in police vans. And gradually the Accelerator took form, based on Sharp's research into the largest particle collider in the world. He learned that bunches of particles focused down to the thickness of a hair were made to collide, with on average only one in about 40,000 collisions between the bunches producing a head-on electron-positron collision. He decided to cut all this technical stuff from the final draft and supply the reader with surfaces, not facts. And so it came to pass that the Collider resembled a series of joined together aircraft fuselages. Its tube-shaped foundations ran the entire length of the island and across the marshland to the north, on massive concrete supports. Above them grew the featureless grey shell of the building.

24 Eloid Propulsion

The device led Strobey left, out of Selborne Road. He passed Burger Bliss and the doorway beyond which he'd wasted the Anarchs with the erasure dust. That was only thirty minutes ago but already he had a heavy sense of the months and pages weighing down on him from his former spectral existence. He wondered if any research had been done into constructor fatigue induced by SD downloads.

He also wondered where in hell the globe was leading him – a subtly understated symbolic touch, he felt. It was like it had read his mind. The lips re-appeared. "Precisely so," it cried, confirming the leitmotif. "Important meeting!" the mouth continued. To Strobey's consternation the globe then jerked up to rooftop level. There it paused a moment, then accelerated away towards the clouds. A sleek white Ford Casserole drew up alongside him. There was an identification code painted on the roof, a rack of blue lighting along the front. Two men in dark uniforms inside. Cops.

A man climbed out of the back, held the door open. "Detective Constable Wilkey of Walthamstow C.I.D. I'd be grateful if you'd come with us, Mr Strobey. We have some questions we'd like to ask you in connection with a series of armed robberies."

Strobey, jolted by surprise, said "Sure." He got inside. He sat down. Wilkey got in. They moved off. It was funny. Three word sentences. Crude and simple. His headache worsened. Such poor prose. He needed air. Something richer, deeper. A complex oxygen. Felt himself choking. Please release me. Set me free.

The car passed a set of lights at emerald and entered a new paragraph. Strobey's headache was deleted. His breathing became more regular. He smiled at the thought of the police wanting to question him about crimes committed in a world where he'd only just arrived. They didn't know he *was* the police. Just far more highly evolved.

The Casserole edged its way along Hoe Street. The traffic was slow in both directions. Strobey wondered why the globe had facilitated the encounter. If it was a surveillance drone working for the TPT it would have been nice to have been told. "So what's all this about, then?" Strobey asked, trying out one of the TV drama dialogue downloads. But the cops had watched the same shows. "Later. Not now."

They went past the old, boarded-up cinema. Turned left on to Hatherley Road, down Elmsdale. The SD download shrilled something was wrong. The route they were on made no sense. "Walthamstow police station's that way. This is a postmodern journey, not a realist one."

"Hey,man. Where are you taking me?" Strobey cried, glancing

107

round for the author of his misfortunes.

"We want to show you something first," said Wilkey, who wasn't the person Strobey was looking for. Wilkey was a big fleshy man with a mole on his right cheek. His knuckles were densely coated in black hair. He exuded belligerence and a simian watchfulness. He seemed repetitious; he was perhaps copied from somewhere and not at all original.

They turned off Blackhorse Road, headed down Coppermill. The lines of terraced housing ended. They were entering the Lea Valley. Railings on either side marked the perimeters of a reservoir and a treatment plant. Grey anonymous buildings hedged by pipes and gravel trenches. A rotating arm watered a circle of sand. On the other side could be glimpsed an island of emaciated trees. Big black birds were clustered menacingly on the bare gnarled branches like an illustration from a fairy story. The style made him suddenly suspicious.

"Let me see your I.D."

Wilkey sighed. "Hoots, mon," he said.

"What did you want to show me? I demand to know!"

"Okay, okay," Wilkey sighed. "Show him, poor Jack." The driver brought the car to a halt and reached into the glove compartment. He pulled out a pair of brown suede gloves. "Verisimilitude," he whispered.

Poor Jack slipped them on and used them to display a crumpled Tesco bag. He let it hang over the seat, upside down. A few brittle flakes fluttered out.

Strobey knew what they were. He'd been pretty sure for the past 64 words. The ruby globe was all part of it. First a pair of black ones, now a pair of white ones. They weren't TPT. They weren't even cops. They were Anarchs.

A dozen violins screeched on the soundtrack as his thumb pressed down on the flute in his pocket. The beam cut through the back of the seat, through the driver's lungs and died at the ten metre cut-off point. The driver gasped and threw open his arms like he was about to hug someone. Then his head snapped back.

Poor Jack! With a low hissing sound like air escaping from a balloon he slumped forwards.

108

Strobey flicked the flute round and pointed it at the Anarch which had masqueraded as Detective Constable Wilkey. The Anarch seemed strangely unconcerned by the shooting of his colleague.

"That's not your real name, is it? And you aren't a cop. You're a pair of fucking Anarchs"

"Such perspicacity! And such a nice weapon. That's a slimline model 57 flute, if I'm not mistaken."

"Model 59, actually, buster. Modified. Triple the burn of a 57. With nano-chemical capability."

"Too bad mine's a thunder 60."

Almost the moment Strobey fired he realised he'd been fooled. As the beam cut through the Anarch the man winked and gave a smiley-face grin. A moment later he was gone.

Duplicates. He'd been fooled by Spectral Duplicates. The italicised recognition throbbed painfully inside him. While he throbbed the cushioned seat vanished beneath him and the car ebbed away into the random energy waste field.

Strobey fell a half metre to the ground and landed on his back. A jarring pain ran along his spine, reached the end, and sprinted back again, not breaking any records or bones. *Even the fucking car was spectral.* It was an unpleasant shock to learn Mirando Mirando had energy grids like that at her command. Plus a neural drone.

The sudden collapse of his certainties brought back vague memories of his research into the *nouvelle vague*. A shot man stumbled and staggered down a narrow, empty, sunlit street. A handcuffed man was tortured in a bathroom. A woman wearing nothing but a pair of high heeled shoes and some white tight-fitting pants crossed a room. There was a lurid red wall in the background. Four or five units of the crack between her plump buttocks were exposed.

Strobey felt a strange kinship with those figures from a precarious world conscious of its own artifice. The hard certainties of the conventional Hollywood movie were forever beyond their reach. Was Mirando Mirando the director of a movie in which he was the star? The ponderous diction made him start. He stopped. He considered moving to a walled city built of red adobe but knew it would never happen. Outside the old walls the spectral car honked

109

on the edge of his troubled mind.

The substitution and eloid propulsion involved in the preceding paragraphs didn't bear thinking about, so he didn't. They made him sweat, though. A modest but pungent trickle, with a tang of the receded tide east of the Ile de Gavrinis.

The worst thing was that Mirando Mirando now knew what weapon he was using. That's what the whole set-up had been about. A cheap trick from a thriller narrative designed to elicit information and emit the cheap perfume of suspense.

Merde!

Strobey headed back, back, back. To Finn's, to Finn's, to Finn's.

25   A Little Chapter of Big Yawns

Daisy Spenser yawned like a rhinoceros. She stood in the centre of the forest clearing. Sawdust lay all around her like soft, unnaturally yellow sand. She'd stripped down to her bra and panties as she sawed in the warm sunlight.

Her right elbow moved like a piston as she dragged the handsaw to and fro across the cut in the log. In her mind was the moment Aphrodite said, "I'm so, so sorry." Aphrodite yawned bigly, then hugged Daisy tightly. "You poor thing." Daisy looked at her with a tear stained face. It reflected images in reverse. She put the novelty hand mirror down. "You're so nice," she whispered.

Daisy had never had much luck with people. Her father was a drunk, her brother a coke head, her sister a pepsi liver, her mother dead of a severe third draft chill. Her first boyfriend broke her nose. She should have had him arrested but she was in love. She yawned like a cute sleepy donkey and looked at Aphrodite and smiled. It was difficult to know who liked *Mulholland Drive* the most, who kissed who first. Their lips found their way to each other across the centimetres of text. For a long, long time they simply looked at each other, marvelling at each other's adjectives. Slowly, tenderly, they stroked each other's nouns. Then, as if fulfilling some long suppressed commercial instinct, they both began to undress.

110

Sawdust lay all around Daisy like soft, unnaturally yellow sand. She'd stripped down to her bra and panties as she sawed in the warm sunlight. Her right elbow moved like a piston as she dragged the handsaw to and fro across the cut in the log. Muscles in her thighs tightened and relaxed as she maintained the rhythm of her work.

With a big yawn, Scurr watched from behind a tree. He licked his lips at the sight of her taut, beautiful body. Then he frowned, tasting blood. Stunned, he extracted the fleck of meteorite and realised his tongue had fallen from his mouth. It lay at his feet on the grass, wriggling like a small bloody fish. All that remained was a stump and a mouthful of hot salty blood. Scurr reached down to grab it and stuff it back into his mouth. But when his hand was about to close around it the tongue jumped away. He kneeled to trap it beneath both palms but again it skipped away. He emerged into the clearing, still pursuing his tongue. Daisy Spenser seemed oblivious and just went on sawing.

To Scurr's horror the prose continued. His tongue jumped on to the log she was sawing. Closer and closer it wriggled to the silver teeth of her saw. Scurr tried to scream but nothing came from his mouth but a gurgling sound. He threw himself forward to seize the tongue, and tripped. He heard his jeans tear and drop away. He landed on the log with a thump, straddling it like a horse. Somehow his underpants had gone, too. His penis flopped forward. Scurr gazed in fascination as the saw sliced into it. Daisy Spenser said nothing. Staring steadfastly ahead of her she kept on sawing, oblivious of the blood spurting from the stump between Scurr's legs. The sawdust turned into a liquid purple mess in which something was moving. It was Scurr's tongue. It swam towards him, slithered up his leg and hopped back into his mouth. He screamed and woke up as the press conference was ending. "So you have no real leads as to who is committing these robberies, Superintendent?" said the acned young man from the *Leytonstone Advertiser*, terminating his question with a slender yawn.

Buller yawned like the Golden Gate bridge and produced an insincere smile. "On the contrary. We are currently pursuing many different lines of enquiry. The public have been most helpful. The back story has, we hope, caught their attention." "But no imminent arrests?" "I'm afraid I really couldn't comment on that. Peripety and anagnorisis are outside my area of responsibility. Now if there are no more questions…" Buller mopped his brow, then reached for the bottle of mineral water on the stand. What he really wanted was a good stiff whisky. But that would have to wait.

The reporters shuffled out with their briefing packs. The six of diamonds was the last to leave. "That went reasonably well, sir," Aphrodite Cutter said, with a big yawn, after she'd seen the six and the three of clubs to the front entrance. "Yes, I think so." Apart from the difficult reporter from Leytonstone, the press conference had gone smoothly. Routine stuff, the usual guff about respecting the democratic right to protest but not tolerating any violent behaviour. A few statistics about police numbers and the cost of the operation. Only that one reporter had raised the unsolved bank robberies, and he'd brushed him aside. He could be hoovered up later with phone taps, blackmail and bribery.

No one had even mentioned the missing persons. Buller could go home now, get a good night's sleep. He yawned again, a real whopper. He had to be up early tomorrow. There was a 5 a.m. briefing at a local Territorial Army base for all officers involved, after which they'd set off for the Collider site in a convoy of coaches and Transits. It promised to be a long day of tired, second-rate writing.

26 The Amphitheatre

Strobey climbed over a low brick wall into the grounds of the actually existing secondary school on Church Hill, E17. He moved quietly under the big dark elms and round the back of a new classroom block. There was a full moon and the grounds were full of silvery light and a patchwork of shadows and atmospheric adjectives.

He emerged into a narrow, deserted car park between the block and the old main building. From there he walked round the side of a line of portakabins and emerged into an extensive garden at the back. He padded softly along a walkway framed by wooden archways and trellis covered in plausible climbing roses and ivy.

The amphitheatre was directly ahead when he came out of the leafy tunnel. It took several tries to get the spelling right. Surrounded by bushes and trees the amphitheatre was oddly out of keeping with the urban setting. Built on the whim of a local eccentric some seven or eight decades earlier in Nether Time, it looked like something from a dream or a surrealist painting. Circular stone ledges sloped down to the stage in the centre. It was a structure you might have expected to encounter on some sun-baked Greek hillside but not in grey East London.

The moonlight seemed only to magnify the amphitheatre's strangely unreal quality. Romantic associations caused a faint creaking in the background. Strobey moved round the perimeter and went into the pathways among the bushes. This was where the actors made their entrances and exits. Concealed from the view of the audience the pathways led between the stage area and an adjacent field. It looked a good enough scenario. Lots of places to hide. It ought to be easy enough to snatch the cash and make a quick getaway. Strobey went back to the amphitheatre.

He stopped, held back by the merest speck of punctuation.

Someone was standing directly opposite him, in the next line, on the far side of the bowl-shaped structure. A figure – a woman - wearing what looked like a tracksuit. A mask obscured her face. It was one of those theatrical masks with a fixed merry laugh for a mouth and eyes the shape of orange segments. The sort of thing you saw more often in illustrations than on any stage.

"Ill met by moonlight," the woman called out across the space between them.

Strobey recognized the blurred, chopped-up voice at once. He'd heard it often enough before. The difference was the mask. On the screens of Menzara she always preferred to use a feature distorter.

Strobey reached automatically for his flute but at once a tingling spread through his wrist. His fingers felt suddenly flaccid and helpless as Buller's penis.

113

"You would have been wise to stay on Menzara," Mirando Mirando said, in that familiar strange fragmented metallic voice. "There is no real future for you here."

"You invited me, remember? How did the message go? *Finn's. For All time.*"

"*Some invitations are best refused.* Lorenzo, The Book of Life, Chapter 9, line 14."

"Yeah, well I never was much into philosophy. History was my bag." Strobey wondered what she was using against him. He continued to claw desperately for the grip on his flute. His fingers had all the strength of wet paper tissue.

"Why Finn's Hotel?"

The leader of the Anarchs pointed silently to the rigid smile on her mask. "All in good time. Not long now."

"How long?"

"Soon. Very soon. Two hundred pages of single-spaced text at the most. When printed, possibly a little less. These matters are not always easy to judge. If the electricity cuts out, unsaved text might be lost, never to be retrieved. These are dangerous times for fiction." She began to step backwards, towards the bushes. At the mouth of a gap between two billowing clumps of erratic discourse she paused. "In two days," she said. "Novel time."

"Oh and something else." She looked right at him. "Before I left Menzara I met an old friend of yours. Januschka Orlando Two."

Strobey gasped like he'd been hit in the chest with a stun pellet.

"She told me lots about you. Lots."

The pellets rained upon him. He winced. *It was not possible* (but he knew at the same time that it was - and that it would require a substantial flashback).

Mirando Mirando emitted a tinkle of metallic laughter, stepped backwards into darkness. Was gone.

He quelled the boiling emotions inside him and went after her. His fingers thribbered and gliggered. They felt like they'd been burned. Mirando Mirando's disappearance had released him from whatever force was impacting on his arm and hand.

Strobey pulled out the flute and aimed it at the patch of darkness she'd vanished into. The slender pale blue beam penetrated it and went wriggling away in pursuit. There was a brief flash in the distance and a solitary, audible *pop!*

But Mirando Mirando must have been using a beam absorber, because when he caught up with the hit signaller all he found was a scorch mark on the side of a tree. He stood numbly under a dripping chilli tree and a hot chill spread through him. It was hearing Januschka's name again. Worse, hearing it on the lips of his adversary. He felt a cold blazing rouge infect his cheeks as he contemplated the whole incomplete TPT set up. Why did they send out agents on their own? He needed back-up. The odds weren't good. Cutbacks and economy measures never worked in the long run. For an enemy like her he deserved support in his short walks. Apart from her armoury, Mirando Mirando had spectrals out there. He knew he was good but was that good enough? He wouldn't find out until the end, and even then he might not know. Someone else was always pulling the strings. It wasn't like a first person narrative where the only two people to be fooled were yourself and the reader.

He remembered – or seemed to remember – or seemed to remember to seem to remember memories which might well have been synthetic – that long future afternoon in which he will go to see *Blade Runner* with a half-awoken Living Doll at a cinema running a Nether Time vid prog in the pleasure zone on level 1403 – and the major argument against giving him TPT back-up, namely that no one else but Strobey knew the first damn thing about Nether Time in Walthamstow. Someone else would just give themselves away in the first half hour. They didn't know the language, the culture, the history. Say the wrong thing and you'd end up getting sectioned, or deported, or made to deliver pizza leaflets down Milton Road.

Two days, she'd said. Two days time could only refer to the opening of the Collider. That was the back story which would become the front story, he felt certain. A reversal of the heist yarn, which was where the narrative began, centuries ago.

If you dipped your hand in, you could feel the outlines of old, abandoned writing. Stiffs lay motionless in banal prose, submerged in stagnant ditches. A green notebook held a motionless woman, tangled in inky growths. Odd jotted words and scraps lay all around. *I ain't done nothing wrong*, a man called out, but they took him away anyway. The neighbours told reporters the man hadn't been taking his medication. It took a van load of cops, a doctor, two psychiatric nurses and a social worker to remove him from the narrative. The man said his name was Strobey, but everyone knew him as Douglas Moog. In the chaos of his flat they found a blue file. In it were long descriptions of rooms without furniture. Rejection letters from agents and publishers fell across brief golden bolts of summer like flurries of winter snow. Ghost armies blundered on through walls and bolted doors, wondering if they would ever emerge into the warmth. The first psychiatric nurse and the social worker held Strobey as the second psychiatric nurse gave him his injection. The syringe was a flute. The nurse wore a mask and Strobey knew she was really Mirando Mirando, from the orbital Menzara.

Best not to think of such things. If the electricity failed he might lose part of his mind. Best to take your medication and hurry on, so he took out the blister pack, swallowed two of the pills, and hurried on.

On, deeper into the text, through shadows and blazing moonlight, his flute always at the ready.

*

Mirando Mirando must have scattered some scratch foolers around. He heard branches snap nearby and odd movements in the bushes. He distinctly heard her whisper his name from just behind him. He spent half an hour, flute in hand, searching for her.

Worst of all was hearing Januschka's voice. Januschka whispered that she loved him. The voice came from behind a clump of thistles alongside the boiler room. He searched there, knowing it was a trick. He knew Januschka wasn't there. She was thousands of years away from even being born. And he had lost her forever. Mirando Mirando was long gone, too. Staying in that place was a complete waste of prose. He climbed back over the brick wall and returned to

116

Finn's, where Emma, who was asleep, was about to fly through time and depart.

*

On the first night of the performance Emma went to buy a ticket. Somehow they'd pictured the Shakespeare Players selling them from behind a table in the car park, like for all the other kinds of entertainment put on at the amphitheatre. It was an unwelcome surprise to find you had to purchase them from a caravan. A big, corrugated silver American trailer-park type caravan. With a sales hatch set in the side.

Emma loitered, looking intermittently at her watch. Like she was waiting for her boyfriend, who was late, or something. The theatregoers had long since gone off to the show, which had started twenty minutes ago. She could hear the actors' voices in the distance, the occasional ripple of laughter.

A truck came in through the school gates and drove up alongside the caravan. Optimum Security it said on the van. Out of it stepped two stocky figures wearing security helmets. *Shit. This was heavy.*

Emma reported back. She didn't see how they really do it, not without violence. Which none of them wanted, right? Ben said they should meet up again in twenty-four hours time. By then there might be a new plot development.

27   Data Holdings

Januschka Orlando Two, exclamation mark.

It made Strobey sick to think that Mirando Mirando knew about her. Worse, had met her, talked to her. Had talked to her about *him*. He vomited. Mostly it was a sequence of dry, throat-scalding retches, with a gruel of marmalade, sweetcorn and some strands of lettuce.

Strobey didn't know anybody knew about him and Januschka – apart from Strumbert and his gang. It was hard to believe she'd really talked to Mirando Mirando about him.

He was having trouble concentrating on what Ben was saying.

"The development is this," said Ben. "I'll go up to the two security guards and squirt paint over their visors, blinding them. When they remove their helmets I'll zap them with this". He showed them a CS gas spray ("and no, you don't need to know where I got it from"). With the guards put of action they'd smash the caravan windows, get inside and grab the money. Three of them would do this – himself, Strobey and Marianne. They'd run through the school grounds to the low wall at the far side. They'd pass the money over to Emma, who'd be waiting there with the bikes. They'd pedal off down Woodbury Road, along Folkestone Road, then right, down St Mary Road. In the unlikely eventuality they were followed they'd easily throw off pursuit by going through the cycle gap in the cul de sac at the end. The only thing they'd have to watch out for was the CCTV stalk. Hopefully it would be pointing in any direction but directly down. If no one pursued them he suggested Emma get off at the junction with Forth Road and simply walk across the bridge to Finn's with the loot. The rest of them could dump her bike, then head off and dump theirs too. They wouldn't be needing them again, after all. If they just left them at the roadside kids would be bound to nick them in no time.

They talked. In the end, they agreed. Emma wasn't keen. She had a bad feeling about all this. There was no bridge near Forth Road. But she was out-voted. And as Edgar said, it really would be their last job. There was no way he was going to do any more. Get out while you're ahead. Strobey nodded in agreement. He hadn't heard a word.

*

Menzara data holdings are impressive but limited. The Library of All does not live up to its title. That title was dreamed by a jerk in the Lenitive Verbalisations subsection of the Department of Invention which dealt with Orbital Nomenclature.

The jerk's name was Michelangelo Einstein Quaron Junior. He had a wife named Douglas and a boy named Sue. He wore plaid trousers and affected a monocle. He talked in a loud voice. He had a high regard for his own importance and sense of style. He was a creep.

Q Junior was fond of blabbing about family values. Plus family tradition. The Quarons had once been big on the planet Humm. Then came that terrible day when, on a nostalgic return visit to Humm, Michelangelo went to see the wild fangfish in Lake Klimpt, slipped on a discarded slop-fruit skin and careered into the polyfiberG railings. That section of railings came away like they were nothing stronger than bamboo. Michelangelo fell into the lake below.

Splash!

Some blame must be attached to the unknown tourist who lazily dropped the slop-fruit skin, but the accident was largely the fault of a scandalous failure properly to renew the polyfiberG coating at the required moonly intervals.

It wasn't the fangfish which killed Michelangelo – they merely munched on his skeleton – it was Lake Klimpt. The waters of Klimpt are 73% dilu-acid. Michelangelo had time to scream, "Hell!" before his flesh dissolved. The private inquiry later decided that though the possibility of a mild expletive could not be ruled out, the probability was that he was attempting to shout "Help!"

Witnesses said he didn't even leave a stain. There was just a brief flurry of armoured fang-fish, as they crunched their way through their unexpected afternoon snack. Then the Lake returned to its pensive tranquillity. That tranquillity made famous in the poem by Chan-Jin Dallas III.

By the quiet waters of Klimpt
I sat up and laughed.
This is the joy of enduring
The ripples of a great loss.

The accident was widely reported on Humm. Two zylos later, on faraway Menzara, it made a short, sombre paragraph in the Library of All staff newsletter. It was also repeated in the Library Users Bulletin, where it was pleasurably received by one or two readers who were maddened by the Library's deficient holdings and who

119

felt its real name should have been The Library Which Has Everything Except What You're Bloody Looking For.

Strobey knew nothing of what had happened at Lake Klimpt – still less that only days after Quaron Junior's death his widow Douglas began an affair with his second cousin 57-Strobey-M3733. But he did know that the Library of All lacked some of the data he needed.

The Library depended for its knowledge on what was taken during past retrievals. Planetary emigrants took their back-up data with them when they left and lit out for a better life in a superior system. But it was all a question of storage capacity.

Interplanetary travel had never worked out the way the Nether Time dreamers had imagined. Those vast twenty-kilometre-long craft cruising the voids with a crew of eight didn't materialize. Long distance Projo propulsion required mimimalism. The space pencils held no more than four people, in a voluntary coma.

The pencils carried data coins and compressed holo buttons. What they could not take was material objects of any size or in any quantity. That in itself wasn't a problem. A holo button could reproduce the three dimensional appearance of every object in a museum. You could study surfaces (if not texture, density or weight). The real problem was that in any emigration – even in the mass migrations of two xenia ago - there was data not taken. On any planet – even on ones in an advanced state of technological development - there was always so much OMANC left behind.

OMANC was that vast variety of artefacts and documents which had never been backed-up, not even in a risibly primitive medium like a photocopy or a microfilm. The knowledge of all that OMANC in the voids - Original Material And No Copy – made every archivist depressed. It haunted them with a sense of absence – of data out of their reach. It niggled them with a sense of incompletion. Amid their data wealth, they were poor.

In Nether Time, at the last count, there were 19,342,782 unsolved crimes, lost literary masterpieces, stolen paintings, biographical enigmas relating to status six individuals, missing recordings, grey area assassinations, untraced manuscripts, un-holoed Etruscan vases

120

and miscellaneous conundrums of status twelve and above significance. (Oh, and 2,137 CUF - Curious Unclassified Fish.)

The data that might resolve some of these enigmas and losses was out of reach. Knowing this drove some archivists to suffer from Data Loss Syndrome. They locked themselves in their archives and refused to let anyone in. This invariably required the intervention of social services, a police tranquillizer team and years of help from specialist data therapists.

Others turned to drink, drugs, sex or – worst of all - politics. Archivist politicos were the worst. They might seem warm and smiley, they might hire SpinDoks who'd project them as best-buddy-folk, but what they dreamed of was Total Control. Every one of them was an incipient dictator. Their lust was for billions of files. Of total population knowledge. Fortunately none of them ever got elected to anything more substantial than the hydrocarbon sanitation committee.

A few archivists went AWOL. They found their salvation outside Menzara. They stole pods and went directly to the Nether Time slot of their particular expertise, desperately hoping to solve a mystery that obsessed them.

At first the TPT turned a blind eye. But the problem started to get so bad that action was needed. A dozen archivists were pursued to Nether Time locations. Eleven were terminated in libraries. The twelfth was decapitated inside a silo. On Menzara all archivists were banned from any Level that contained pods, technicians, time penetration software or any associated materials or personnel. The difficulty was quashed.

Januschka Orlando Two was an archivist. But she had no hankerings. Her interest in Nether Time was strictly academic.

28   Solidity Retrieval

Strobey first met Januschka Orlando Two in the staff coffee room at the Library of All. He was on the wrong floor. Staff was top, Users were below. He misread the arrows which gave directions. The arrows were the work of someone stupid in Design. The arrows were fancy, twirly, easily mis-read.

She was alone at a table by the arboretum window. He barely noticed her. He walked across to the hatch, slid his User card into the slit, spoke his order. An Earl Grey, large. A ciabatta roll filled with smoked salmon and cream cheese.

What he said impinged her consciousness. She was reading a book but his words cut through the prose, the track of her concentration. She frowned, said, "You don't work here."

Strobey turned, agreed he didn't. "I'm a User. Working on-"

"This is Staff Only," she interrupted.

She was wearing gold contacts, which gave her face a blank look. Her hair style was helmet, plain black. No stripes, no animate glitter. He wondered if she was a Loron. Lorons eschewed ornament. They believed in the one true meteorite. It was a huge chunk of rock on a loose orbit in the Kulik Tract. The rock was impenetrable *glaciara-irona*. It exuded from its interior a force that still hadn't been identified. Some sort of ultra-quionic radiation. Lorons believed that the rock was an entity. They thought the radiation effect was the entity *thinking*. They reckoned the Loron had dreamed the cosmos, which had taken material form. Lorons were completely nuts. They were usually people of little education who had suffered an early bereavement. They were tolerated under the Go Easy And Maybe One Day They'll Grow Out Of It legislation.

She was young, pale skin, looked severe. Disapproving. She didn't like him, he could tell. She didn't like rules being violated.

"I'm sorry. I thought this was the Users' room."

"Floor below. Follow the arrows."

The hatch pinged as crisply as a chapter of omniscient prose. His nutritious meal of anachronistic nouns was ready. He said, "I'm sorry. I'll grab my lunch and go."

She said: "That's a Nether meal. You doing a reality thesis?"

Strobey shook his head. "Nope. Strictly research purposes. I'm in the TPT."

"What's your number?"

"Eh?"

"Your user number. Here at the library."

"876135STR."

She grinned. "I thought so. I'm your deliverer. You've been driving me crazy for weeks. All those abstruse requests."

"Sorry. I have to go after a dissident. I don't have a lot of time left. Hence the data request overload."

Januschka's frown reappeared. "We're not supposed to meet. Librarians aren't supposed to fraternize with users. Especially not TPT personnel."

"You're right. I'll go."

But then she did a strange thing. This severe looking young woman put her hand lightly out and laid it on his arm. "Stay. It's not like this place is exactly crowded. Most people don't come in until after the mid-moon pulse."

Strobey looked at the mask of her face, wondering if that was a smile trembling at the limits of her mouth. Something weird was going on with the style.

"I promise not to ask you anything about your mission – or about that author who said of his characters *I may try to re-educate them*," she added – and then subtracted everything after the hyphen.

"Okay. Sure." He sat down. He sipped his tea. He swallowed his nouns. They talked.

*

She was a class five archivist librarian, specialising in solidity retrieval. Januschka Orlando Two was 27. She had Ph.Ds in chemistry, librarianship, Nether socio-history, plus simulation technique. Her expertise lay in transferring copy to its original format. She could transform data into sheets of paper which had all the appearance of documents thousands of years old. She knew a lot about texture, size and defunct inks. She reproduced books so authentic their pages released archao-dust when you opened them, making you sneeze.

Strobey had been pumping the Library of All for material on Walthamstow, for material on Finn's Hotel. For duplicates of the time's culture. He needed copies of the local newspapers. He wanted street data across the period of a century. He required maps, books, archival documents. Plus extras. A postage stamp, what it looked like. A bus pass. Weird outré stuff like that. Januschka had the job of supplying him. It was Januschka who created the materials which were delivered to the receipt orb at the back of his desk in his library cubicle.

Regular users were permitted to customize their cubicles. Strobey never bothered. He had no family pics to pin. No cosy souvenirs. He left it bare, saving Sharp the effort of a descriptive paragraph. Like his creator, he worked alone, oblivious of the hour. The Library, like the narrative, never closed. Strobey placed his data requests and waited. He remembered to take his medication. He came and went as he pleased. He lived off black coffee and amphetamines. He fingered the documents. He read through crackly old newspapers. He looked at grey photographs of street scenes thousands of years old. A crashed car. A demonstration. A schoolgirl accepting a certificate.

He read old history books. He checked out Finn's. He found an engraving of how it looked two years after it had opened. Smart. Successful. A four-horse carriage stood outside. Gentlemen wore boiler pipe hats. Ladies dresses exploded at the waist and trailed in the dirt. An advertisement recommended liver tablets.

Strobey's facial expression had a greedy edge. He was hardwired to get deep knowledge. His eyes shone with the glamour of a polished style. He was on a fiery plunge through history. He was feeling his way back to what it must have been like living as someone in a realist narrative in a primitive computer age society, back in the First Era of the Barbarians. He had to learn to try to think the way a primitive would have thought. How to live amid astonishing and irrational contradictions. How to accept the state of things. How not to howl in disbelief at the stuff on offer in the fiction section of bookshops. How to pretend to accept *the way things were*.

He had to imagine himself walking down a street, stepping to avoid animal excrement, while tense angry men in crude one-ton metal machines careered past at lethal speeds, trailing toxic fumes. Discarded food packaging lay on the ground, the pavement (as it was called) was cracked and uneven. Overhead a contraption of extraordinary crudity – it was called a jumbo jet – scarred the sky with a grey trail of poisons. And everywhere there was an anarchic swirl of noise and movement/the sense of a totally chaotic society beginning to run out of control. He felt his heart under pressure. Nervous anticipation. He could almost smell the past.

He learned how to regulate his breathing. His heart calmed. He ordered a book published in 1991. Then he went to the coffin elevator to get some lunch. That was how he met Januschka. He was tired. The arrows were too smart for their own good. He needed more amphetamines.

Januschka said she couldn't begin to imagine what it must have been like to live in a society like that. She screwed up her face in disgust. Its politics! Its criminal injustice system! Its television! Its liberal humanist fiction! All so *crude*. So *irrational*. So inhumane and coarse.

Januschka said she knew she'd never go down with archivist syndrome. She explained to Strobey she was happy where she was. She didn't think she could handle a real climate. Or a primitive society. Or novels praised for their remarkable, brilliant and meticulous storytelling, sound common sense and utterly convincing period re-creation, each nuance of behaviour brilliantly observed, with the breadth of a family saga and shafts of wintry humour, yet as light as Norfolk's summer skies. Or the abbreviated life span that was the inevitable consequence of a traject to the past.

Januschka was drinking blue juice. Her fingers were long and slender. Strobey wondered if she played an instrument. She should have done. Januschka finished her fried batterwings, went across and obtained a mug of fire froth. She came back to the table. She was wearing a black pin-striped suit that accentuated her slender torso. Looking like that, he was sure she was a Loron. But he said nothing.

She did not ask Strobey when he was making the transference. She didn't ask who the dissident was. She wouldn't have known it was Mirando Mirando. MM was old news. The flits had said she'd gone to Void Ten, a slot eight hundred xorks ago. The flits said the TPT had already sent four agents in pursuit. The flits told the pop the news they wanted to hear. Mirando Mirando was yesterday's woman. She was in the dead zone. She was gone. By now she was a

125

line of data on an ancient mortuary inventory. It was lies. But it soothed the pop. No journo questioned it. No journo wanted to fuck with their career prospects. They were the guardians of power – and they knew it. It was the reason for their goody bags.

"So why specialise in that era?" Strobey asked, puzzled. If she couldn't stand the thought of living back there, why care. Why the expertise. Why all those years of study, research, data retrieval?

Januschka explained. Januschka told him about the composer. Her name was Taha – Gabriella Cohen Muniandy Taha. She was born in 2048 and died in a scoot crash in 2091. She started out with three others in a group called Gasper, then went solo. Taha wrote and recorded over three hundred songs for the glister harp. Plus three symphonies (the Symphony of Upheavals, the Symphony for Six of the Defeated, and the Great Symphony of Saying No). Plus the soundtracks to *Imaginary Aliens*, *The Wrong End of Time* and *Brunner's Aye*.

Januschka adored Taha's music. It combined the hot, repetitive, insurrectionary urgencies and speed of desert music with the melancholy and contemplative qualities of certain decadent and decaying capitalist states of that era.

Even on her own planet Taha had not been that well known – at the time of her death she'd sold less than two million albums – but Januschka thought she was one of the greatest and most inspired musicians ever to live in that culture. Januschka had come across her work by accident. She'd heard a track playing years ago on a satellite show when she was on holiday in Bizarro. The song was called "Museum at the End of Love". At the time she thought it was the most stunning song she'd ever heard – melancholy and full of yearning but carried by a throbbing, unforgettable melody and the stiff, stabbing sounds of a glister harp. But when she'd gone in search of more of Taha's music she found it was virtually unobtainable. Or, rather, only obtainable after years of searching in unopened archives. By now Januschka had reconstituted over 70% of Taha's work. In fact she was thinking of producing a documentary about her. If he liked she could give him a Taha sampler.

Strobey said yes please.

126

29   Blown Away

The love that was written between Strobey and Januschka thrived on denial. At their fifth meeting in Staff Only he told her frankly he desired sex with her. But he made it plain it would be sex with a man who would be gone forever from her life in just a short time. It would be like beginning a relationship with a man suffering a terminal illness. He was headed for Nether Time very soon. No one returned from the past.

Plus there was his solemn obligation to the TPT. It was, after all, the first of the eleven pledges. *I, as a member of the TPT, do solemnly swear never to love any man or woman of any orbital, planet, moon, craft or other place, and hereby promise never to desire human company, or yearn, lust or suffer pangs for any sentient biped in any meaningful degree that might detract from the fulfilment of my mission, so help me Democratically Elected Commissar.*

The TPT frowned on sex with humans but tolerated it. But what was totally unacceptable was a relationship which endured for a period longer than two nights. So they'd have to transgress – but not in a big way.

Januschka said she could handle that. She quoted Spoor back at him. *What is brief can be more intense and sweeter than what is protracted.* When the time came for the rupture, she promised not to cry.

It was probably true she could handle the situation the best. Strobey had never been in love before. He didn't even know what it was. All he knew was sex. Like everyone in the TPT, he'd been visiting the Living Dolls for years. They weren't human but for their functions they were good as. You didn't go to them for conversation or company. You went for the contours of their synthetic flesh. For their smiling compliance with every human desire. When Strobey went to one he usually requested mute. He could do without the did-you-see-the-plazball-match-against-Mardlunk-United-yesterday dialogue. (He hated plazball.) He could even do without The Illusion of Simultaneous Orgasm Accompanied by Cries of Extreme Pleasure. He preferred to meet his body's needs in silence. He didn't

127

need the pretence that the Doll was anything other than a creature of synthflesh, wire and programming. In that, he was a perfect TPT player.

Strobey had had a couple of brief relationships with Menzara women. One had lasted almost nineteen hours. They had not been satisfactory, either sexually or otherwise. Strobey found it difficult to care about what his lovers chattered about. He cared little for fashion or celebrities or the goings-on in Menzara. Why should he be interested in a world it was his destiny to leave forever?

The women told him he was introverted, incommunicative, uncaring. They wept. They beat their fists against his taut chest. He fended them off with a languid raising of his arm. Their verbal and physical violence didn't touch him at all. Harsh brisk expletives and an arrow shower of exclamation marks fell harmlessly away into the gutter margins. His whole body was sheathed in arto-muscle, grown over the past decade. His heart was nothing more than a pump encased in a flex shield. Their weeping was nothing more than a behavioural phenomenon.

Strobey, you are so unfeeling!

He was, absolutely. Desensitisation was of the essence. In the TPT empathy was frowned on. The values that counted were cold, hard ones. In the TPT you were human - but you aspired to the perfection and genuine impersonality of a machine.

*

Strobey liked the Taha sampler. That combo of speed thud and sob-wailer was curiously effective. A glister-harp made a weird, compelling sound. Taha melodies started to play in his mind when he should have been concentrating on his Walthamstow research. The music intertwined with images of Januschka. He began to wonder what she was doing at that moment. He remembered the soft grip of her hand in his hand. His mind began to wander away from the book in front of him. His eyes scanned the text but he didn't absorb a word. His mind bulged with pictures of Januschka smiling, Januschka sipping blue juice, Januschka walking away from him, the taut dextro-leather trousers moulding themselves to her enticing contours.

A terrible thing had happened to the narrative and its style. Strobey had fallen in love. Luckily, he didn't know it. The penalty for emotional attachment was immediate expulsion from the TPT. But the rules designated states of feeling Strobey was incapable of recognising. For the time being he was safe. He was free to stare at the open book before him, and doodle strange drawings on his pad.

*

"I'm just going out to the shops. Won't be long." Emma had her coat on. Plus her new leather boots and the indigo beret which she liked to think made her look French and *chic*.

"Yeah, sure. See you later," Strobey said. He was reading the local paper. Some Couperin was playing, on a low volume. He'd found the CD in Emma's collection. She never listened to it. He tried it and liked it. Couperin's harpsichord stuff reminded him a bit of Geronimo Siffaoui's Mathematical Variations for Langotte, which he used to listen to repeatedly when he first joined the TPT. It was music that was cool and structured. There was no mush, no sludge. It cut like a knife.

Strobey turned the volume down even more so that the harsh distinct keys of the harpsichord merged with the clicking of Emma's high, steel-tipped heels. Strobey heard her footsteps recede down the rotting lino in the corridor. He opened the window, looked out.

She emerged from the door directly below and turned left.

He watched as she came to the traffic lights, waited for the change. But instead of turning off along Hoe Street, she crossed it and headed up St Mary Road.

He frowned, then quickly erased the cheap lazy gesture. Maybe she was going to the shops on Orford Road, but he couldn't think why. He went downstairs and out into the street. By the time he was across the five lanes at the junction Emma was approaching the corner with West Avenue. She went on, past the next turning, past the mosque.

He followed sixty metres behind. She never looked back. She went straight ahead, into the narrow alleyway that led past the Museum garden. He slowed his pace, waiting to see if she turned right, into the Vestry House.

No. Left. Through St Mary's churchyard.

Just before the churchyard there was the entrance to a car park. A couple of Transits were parked alongside the churchyard perimeter. Strobey stood by the gap between them and watched as Emma opened a gate into the churchyard.

She walked decisively, as if she knew exactly where she was going. As if, in fact, she'd walked here before. It was almost as if she knew about the earlier drafts.

This section of the churchyard was no longer used for burials. It was cluttered with big, ostentatious Victorian graves and unchecked vegetation. Stone crosses and big winged angels leaned at odd angles. Ivy smothered every grave. A lot of the stonework had cracked under the embrace of big hairy tentacles and repeated revisions. Rain and time had worn away the wording, rewriting had changed it. The graveyard was constantly expanding, a jungle of green, dark fertile life bursting between memorials of the forgotten dead. A slow, rising tide of grasses lapped the pedestals of the blank-eyed representatives of a petrified religion. In the background was a thesaurus, a cat and the old church. The church door was locked and protected by an outer door of thick iron bars.

Emma took no notice of any of this. She made her way along a narrow gravel pathway and halted before an enormous chest tomb. Then she did something extraordinary. She kneeled on the damp grass and put her hands together as if in prayer. And she began to weep.

Strobey scowled, perplexed by her mysterious actions and the language used to describe them.

*

A short sharp distance away in the Town Square something was going on outside the Centre for Lifelong Learning. A red fire engine was parked there. A crowd had gathered. Marianne went over to check it out. She was still at the back of the crowd when there was a *whoosh* and a pillar of acrid black smoke slid up, high over everyone's heads. A knot in her stomach tightened and she felt a little sick. Fire, and the use of the word "acrid", did that to her.

Flakes of burnt paper danced above the crowd. Black scraps zig-zagged downward, scampered across the square. The remnant of an incinerated page dropped at her feet. She picked it up. *O how shall summer's honey breath hold out / Against the wreckful siege of batt'ring days...* She let it flutter off.

Marianne pushed through the crowd and saw that the arsonists were librarians. They'd set fire to a large heap of books. But the incineration was legit. Nearby a temporary podium had been set up. The Mayor stood there. She was a sleek young woman in a fawn trouser suit. She began to address the assembled shoppers. Her lipstick was Vampire Red. She held the microphone with professional familiarity. Her speech was quadraphonic. The words boomed and crackled from speakers at each corner of the square.

"Here today to celebrate..." she was saying. "An end to an outmoded format... The Centre is now completely digital... More attractive to customers... Urge you all to come in and use the machines... Everything from established DVD classics like *Fahrenheit 451* to today's latest hits... including *Slashermaniac Three.*"

The speech ended. An elderly man shook his fist. He was shouting something abusive. Quickly a pair of policemen arrested him under the Terrorism Act and dragged him away. Marianne watched as they threw him into the back of a police van.

Back at the burning, the librarians plus a group of officials in suits broke into vigorous synthetic applause. The crowd stared, grew bored, drifted away.

The Mayor, the librarians and the suits went into the Centre.

Behind them the smouldering mound of books resembled a big red heart on a butcher's slab. It was veined with lines of fire. Smoke drifted across the square. Scraps of half-burned pages continued to rise into the air. Then the firecrew turned a hose on the smoking pile. It hissed once, angrily, and died. A cleaning crew came forwards and started clearing away the sodden, black mess. Soon there was nothing there but a big dark stain on the paving.

Then it started to rain.

*

Scurr said: "Gotta admit I never thought I'd ever get you to drop round and see little old me. Thought you didn't like me."

Aphrodite opened her eyes wide, then put the eye-widener down. "I can't imagine what gave you that idea, Andy." She held out her wine glass. "Got any ice? I know you shouldn't. But I love wine with ice. Especially on a hot day."

"Smashing idea. Back in a jiffy." He put his glass down and went into the kitchen.

When he returned she was staring down out of the window. The traffic was at a standstill. Somewhere a horn blew a continuous, angry protest.

"Great place, Leyton. I like a bit of life. All night stores, shit like that. Here y'are." He plonked the ice in her glass. "Two cubes okay?"

"Two cubes are just fine. The dialogue's great, too. It blows me away."

"Cheers, then."

"Cheers, Andy."

"I've been thinking about that cow Iris Scheist. It's time we mentioned her before the reader completely forgets about the disappearing people theme. I reckon we should get a search warrant. Check under the floorboards. I bet that's where Harold is. Probably wires to the hidden speakers, too."

"I very much doubt it. I agree with you that Iris Scheist may be responsible for her husband's disappearance. But I don't think it was intentional."

Scurr stared blankly. "I don't get you." (He didn't. He never would.)

"I think she *imagined* Harold out of existence."

"I don't understand."

"I'm not sure I do, either. But I think that's what happened."

"Fuck the Scheists. Less go to bed." Scurr crashed down on to the sofa next to her. His hand clumsily pawed her knee.

Aphrodite smiled. "Are you sure you're in any shape to have sex?"

"Warrerrurrr mean?" Scurr said, his voice skidding on the ice. Then the room darkened and he understood.

His eyes were slits of fury. "You swished thur drinks!"

"That's right."

The door bell rang. "That'll be the man from Curious Lacunae, come to take away *slits of fury*. Oh no it's not. It's Daisy! It's revenge time, Andy." She opened her handbag and produced a pair of orange-handled sewing scissors. She gave him a wink. The wink prodded him with its antennae. "Snip, snip!" she said. "Snip, snip!"

With a groan Scurr toppled forwards into the dark well that had formed in the carpet below him. The groan was no help at all. It popped like a balloon and he tumbled on, down into darkness.

30 Morphed

Emma remained by the tomb for twelve minutes. During this time a handful of people came through the churchyard – a cyclist wearing a stylish streamlined scarlet helmet, a woman pushing a buggy, a couple of middle-aged Indian men talking loudly in Punjabi. None of them seemed to notice Emma, who was as motionless as the tomb she knelt before. Then abruptly she stood up and walked away. Her sudden movement took Strobey by surprise. He had to dodge back out of sight behind the Transits.

She walked past the car park entrance and back down the alley to St Mary Road. She was obviously going back to Finn's. He waited a minute longer, then entered the churchyard.

The grass still bore the impression of where Emma had knelt. Strobey preferred to squat. He read that the massive tomb had been raised to the eternal memory of Mary Alice Meyrick (1813-1869). The name and dates were picked out in lead; they hadn't faded the way the inscriptions carved into stone had done.

Whoever Mary Alice Meyrick was, she'd been loaded. The memorial must have cost a packet. In the class structure of the

133

graveyard it came out near the top. Apart from its size, the tomb was decorated with stone wreathes and trumpet-blowing, scantily clad cherubs. The four corners had each once borne ornamental stone urns, but now one had vanished. The others were cracked and half-coated in lichen.

Strobey stood again, wondering Why? Why did Emma come here? And why did she weep for a woman who'd died well over a century ago? He walked slowly back to the hotel, wondering how he could ask without letting on he'd been spying on her.

*

The final robbery went like a midsummer night's D. The silver trailer was deserted, apart from the two women inside. They were sorting foolscap envelopes that bulged. Beyond, out of sight, the play unrolled. A male voice made a speech, there was a spatter of applause. The security truck came in through the school gates and drew up alongside the caravan. Out of it stepped two stocky figures wearing helmets. The caravan door opened. The smile on the clerk's face turned to puzzlement as she saw Ben.

His trainers made no sound as he ran up behind the two guards. The aerosol in his left hand jetted their visors with a yellow mist. They began to yank off the helmets. The aerosol in his right hand caught them full in the face with CS gas. The men opened their mouths to shout. Ben sprayed them again. They staggered back, hands over their eyes, gasping.

The women in the caravan stared silently

"Give me the money," Marianne said. She snatched the envelopes. She tore one open to check, saw the blue-greens, browns, purple. A solitary red fifty. She filled the carrier bag. She passed it to Strobey. They filled a second bag. That was it. They didn't bother with the coins or the complications of a long sentence structure. They ran. They darted between the school buildings, out of the paragraph.

Emma was waiting the other side of the wall. THE WALL MUST FALL said a sticker on a nearby lighting column. It quoted some statistics and then grew old and wrinkled and fell silent. Where that subject was concerned the writing was on the wall, Emma thought. She started – and reached out for a new beginning.

Strobey and Marianne passed her the two bags. Emma put them in the panniers and rode off. The others followed. On Forth Road, they transferred the two bags to Emma's rucksack. She walked a few metres back to St Mary Road and headed back to Finn's. The others cycled off to dump the bikes where they could be sure they'd be stolen. Emma left hers on Forth Road.

Charlie Jones, aged 12, watched from his house. Charlie was a smart kid. He might not have known about Borges's interest in plot as a teleological key to the world but he could do Aztec level 3 on the old N64 *Goldeneye*.

Charlie watched a lot of TV. He'd seen about the bike robbers on the London news. Charlie, his brain addled by police dramas which configured the representatives of capitalist repression as clever, wise-cracking admirable people, wanted to be a cop when he was older. Charlie watched the three cyclists. He watched the exchange of bags. Charlie left his house. He followed Emma round the corner. Watch out Emma! Be careful!

*

Emma was a little dazed by what she saw. Outside Walthamstow Central were twelve wild palms. They towered above the station booking office. The wind rustled their leaves. They looked purple under the lamplight. Their silhouettes against the sky were like frozen explosions. Explosions on sticks. It wasn't the time to check them out. It was probably just some marketing stunt. She went inside the hotel and waited for the others.

Charlie saw the palms. He thought they were cool.

He watched Emma. Emma went into Finn's. Charlie went back home. Charlie told his father. Charlie said what he'd seen. His father called the police. The woman who answered sounded bored. She sounded hostile. She sounded indifferent. She tersely thanked him for the information. She cut the connection. But somebody realised. Somebody was on the ball. Somebody acted. Somebody had been reading *The Cold Six Thousand*.

135

The phone rang. Charlie's father answered it. Soon a police car arrived outside. A pair of cops came into the house. The one who did all the talking was nice. Charlie liked her. She said her name was DC Cutter but he could call her Aphrodite. Charlie thought that was a cool name.

Charlie took her outside and pointed to Emma's bike, leaning against a garden wall where it had been abandoned. Aphrodite got the other cop to wait by it. The sentences grew longer. Aphrodite asked the child to show her where the lady on the bike had gone. Charlie led her round the corner as far as Hoe Street and pointed at Finn's Hotel.

"She went in there," he said. "There were also some palm trees there before. But now they've gone." Aphrodite asked him about the palms. Charlie described them in detail.

The kid was a fantasist. She'd wasted her time. Aphrodite walked Charlie home. She thanked him. Her manner was more distant now, though she maintained the charm. She got the other cop to put the bike in the back of the patrol car. He said, "Got them, have we? The robbers?"

Aphrodite Cutter shook her head. "I don't think so," she said.

"So what was all this about, then?"

Aphrodite smiled thinly and said thickly, "It looks to me like a case of lost property."

The other cop though it looked like a bicycle but said nothing.

*

"Nothing."

*

Scurr woke into darkness. Remembered. He was naked. In bed, in his flat. He remembered Aphrodite and the scissors. In a hot panic his hands went blindly to his crotch. *His johnson was still there.* He'd really believed the bitch was going to cut it off. It was a bluff. He relaxed. He grinned. All the loose ends were being tidied up. Then he felt the burning sensation on his buttocks. He stood up, went to the wall mirror. Turned and saw. Letters. Cut across both cheeks. In raw red block capitals. RAP on the left one. Scarred Scurr scowled. He hated that sort of crap music. You couldn't even call it music. It was verbal diarrhoea. On the right: IST. It was something to do with the commie left, he was certain. *International Socialist something.* Torture? Trajectory? Transfixion? Transfiguration? Trauma? Treatment? Trench? Triumph? Typography? Temulence? Theurgy? Transumption?

Blood continued to drip from the clumsy incisions.

*

On the M11 the traffic out of London was dense and slow-moving, like Buller's brain. He put on his CD of Mozart's Greatest Hits. Mozart usually calmed him down, but not today. The congestion began to add twenty minutes to his journey. His aching tooth began to throb again. Its deep bass pulses overrode the Mozart. Buller needed a drink, a couple of paracetemol. His knuckles whitened. His grip on the wheel was greased by sweat. When he at last drove into Churchill Drive the sun was a swollen misshapen disc embedded in a smoky haze over Chardwell Wood. He braked and waited until the lurid style had faded in the dusk of the coming postmodern night.

As the garage door opened Buller was furious to see that Thomas had left his bike leaning against the wall again.

He needed to cool down before he went in. He went out into the garden. He sat down on a newly imagined bench and stared at his carp. He prayed that Electrograd would not muddle the order of the middle pair of letters. The carp resembled a fleet of pale submarines quietly waiting in the sun-dappled depths. The sunlight contradicted the dusk but there was nothing he could do about it. The forecast had said something about a storm coming.

Occasionally one of his fish flicked a fin to maintain position. Buller stared at the grass. A small green beetle was making its way between the stalks, frantic. It was running from something but he couldn't see what. It was obviously symbolic.

He hurried indoors.

Inside, the TV was doing its usual perky idiot's monologue. His wife didn't turn her head. She was watching a home decoration programme. Builder Dick was making an economy coffee table out of what looked like egg boxes and an old tray.

"Have a good day?"

"Not especially. I'm hot, sweaty and tired. The unsolved armed robberies remain in that condition. I also have seven or eight unexplained disappearances. The traffic was terrible. I have the Commissioner breathing down my neck and it's strangely arousing. There's going to be a big protest against the Zeilinger Collider tomorrow. And my wife's a lush. In the circumstances, should I have had a good day?"

As he left the room he heard her glass break against the parquet floor. Buller didn't turn back. She could go get another bloody glass herself. Angrily, he stomped away upstairs and took a shower.

When he returned in the next sentence his wife had abandoned the sofa. Getting herself more booze, he guessed. But the big kitchen at the back was empty. Gone to her room, presumably. She was always taking naps before getting up for more shots of poison. On the table lay a note. GONE OUT, BACK LATE. TOM

What was "late" supposed to mean? He'd spoken to the boy before about being back by midnight. Tom had retorted that as he seemed to be the least important character in the entire narrative he didn't see why he shouldn't stay out for as long as he wanted. For all eternity, if necessary.

Buller opened the fridge and took out a can of lager. He tugged at the ring-pull, raised the can to his lips. Used it to wash down the paracetemol. Later he'd have a malt whisky. Just enough to get him off to sleep, fast. He went back to the lounge, where the TV was still babbling. *Why does everyone on TV have such white flawless teeth?* he wondered irritably. Why do they all look so fucking *happy?*

His slippers crunched on something. He realised Angie hadn't cleared up her broken glass. But then it was silly of him to think that she would. The slivers and shards were scattered along the floor by the sofa. He sat down at the other end. He'd clear up later. He could handle frags, glassy or opaque.

138

He flicked the mute button on the remote and switched to Teletext. He wanted to read what they were putting out on the news about tomorrow's demo. Buller tugged at the ring-pull and gulped down the cold delicious liquid. The warm glow of déjà vu spread through him. The text page numbers flickered past in the corner of the screen. And Angie called his name.

"Yeah?"

"Where are you?"

"In here. Watching TV."

"Where are you?"

Exasperated, Buller turned his head. Frowning, he said, "Are you in the kitchen? I'm in here, frowning, having turned my head in exasperation. It hurts, so hurry up with your reply."

"Fog," she said.

At first he thought she was cursing in a slurred voice. Only problem was, she was in the room with him.

He felt the hairs on the back of his neck, unlike the wrinkled unused length of tube between his legs, spring erect.

"Fog. Everywhere fog. Lost."

Angie's voice was only inches away.

He shifted the sofa, prodded the armchairs. Checked behind the curtains. Opened cupboard doors.

He went through all the motions of searching the room. But in his heart he knew there wasn't really any doubt about what had happened. The ventricles were no longer responding to each contraction of the auricles. The valve guarding the opening of the ventricle into the aorta was failing to close properly at each thump. And Angie had *morphed into a disembodied entity.*

31 Protest

For just a moment it was Saturday, 11.45 a.m. Then the moment was gone.

It was Saturday, 11.45 and one second a.m.

The Lea Valley stretched out below them, a curving band of green hemmed in by two slabs of dark urban sprawl. The green went on into a far horizon of cool adjectives. It died there, in a petro-chemical haze.

The Right Honourable Andrew Poffley M.P., Energy Minister, looked apprehensive as the chopper lurched, then dropped down towards a pear-shaped expanse of black water. If the machete hit him he was done for. He blinked the illusion away, and once again he was an important person being transported in a helicopter which ran as smoothly as a bourgeois realist novel. The machine's racing shadow resembled a wildly spinning distorted windmill as it skimmed across the reservoir surface. "Nearly there, Mr Quixote," said the R.A.F. liaison officer as the Sikorski S-76 tilted to the left and began its final descent to the Collider. No, he can't have done. *Minister* was surely the word, the word, the word.

To Poffley it looked like they were going to hit the water any second. A dull hot panic flared briefly in his chest from an earlier draft of his career. He wondered about the obituaries the papers would run. He knew he'd come across as a good party man. In other words a dullard. He'd long since shelved what little youthful idealism and principle he'd ever once possessed. His betrayals were etched in the wrinkles on his face. He didn't really stand for anything any more. Only the oily party line, no matter how irrational, reactionary or self-serving. Ah, how Sharp hated members of parliament – especially the sleek rabid sharks of New Labour and the shifty spivs of the Conservative benches. Not forgetting those 17 Lib Dems who didn't bother to turn up to vote against Blair's fantastically authoritarian house arrest bill, which, had they bothered, would have been defeated. You can always rely on the fucking Lib Dems to let you down. (Hot thoughts on a cold, cold morning, Thursday 3 March 2005 – the admirably well-read reader sturdily echoing young Jane Eyre: "his gripe was painful, and my over-tasked strength almost exhausted.")

Abruptly the reservoir vanished and they cruised over a road and a patch of marshland. Beyond the marsh was an expanse of grassy scrubland. It was crowded with extras in a medieval battlefield scene before the filming of the battle. On one side was a vast, ever-shifting crowd of people. There looked to be thousands and thousands down there. Facing them was a long line of police assembled behind temporary metal barriers. Behind the police line rows of white police Transits had been lined up to make a secondary barrier. Beyond them were the reinforcements – clusters of nouns, twenty strong. The roar of the helicopter blotted out any sounds from below.

"Quite a crowd," Poffley called out to his aide. He had to raise his voice to be heard above the roar of the omniscience. He grinned nervously. It looked like an alarmingly large number of people had gathered to protest against the opening of the Collider.

"Quite a lot of police, too, Minister."

They passed over a bridge and the glinting sliver of water that the bridge pinned to the planet's surface. A long tube-shaped grey structure appeared beneath them. The Sikorski seemed to lurch to a halt. It hung in the air, swaying gently. Then it sank through the crisp clear prose to an empty car park below.

*

In the command vehicle at the far end of the car park Buller yawned bigly as he watched the chopper descend. He'd had another bad night, sleep-wise. Two nights in bed alone. He wasn't used to it. Anxiety clawed him in the dark. He punched it in the genitals and the cat jumped out of bed with a satisfying screech of agony. How Sharp loathed hairy quadrupeds!

Buller didn't know what to do about Angie's disappearance. It was, to name check one of his least favourite author's favourite movies, bad timing. What with everything he had on his plate – a toasted mcguffin sugared with disappearances, bank robberies and the Collider opening. Plus it was so absurd. That it should happen to him, of all characters. He'd have to report it, of course. But not yet. Luckily Tom hardly seemed to come home at all these days. If he was aware of his mother's absence he didn't show it. But then, can an absence be aware of a parallel absence? he wondered. He felt as helpless and perturbed as Iris Scheist or the ageing Nietzsche.

He needed to get the demonstration over with first. He couldn't have not turned up for this – not if he wanted to keep his job or his reasonably prominent position in the narrative. There was also a

lead about the latest robbery. A kid in the previous chapter had
claimed to have seen some suspects. But the kid had seen other
weird stuff that didn't make any sense. Cutter thought the child was
a fantasist. Well, maybe. But the child insisted he'd seen a suspect
go into the derelict hotel across the road from the tube station. He
could also do Aztec Level Three. Best not to write the brat off just
yet.

Buller instructed Cutter and Scurr to organise some surveillance
of the derelict hotel. He'd paired them deliberately. These days
they crackled with antagonism towards each other. He wanted them
to pack it in. Buller deplored contrariety, countercurrents,
contradiction and negation. He didn't want stuff like that on his
team.

A nearby estate agents had co-operated. From a dusty unused
office on the agency's top floor Finn's Hotel was now under 24-
hour observation. So far the only thing the observers had reported
was a woman who stood on the roof, watching. The surveillance
team reported she did it regularly.

They said it was like she was waiting for something to happen.

*

The Minister stepped from the helicopter and shook hands with the
project's director and a group of officials. Above their heads a red
balloon from the demonstration drifted past and out of sight.

Even in the empty car park, well behind the lines, the chanting
seemed very loud. "Co-lie-durr-no! no! no!" the crowd howled. The
mantra was repeated three times, then melted into ragged applause,
cheering and the squealing of whistles. Then it started all over
again.

Some of the protesters had drums. The steady beat sounded like
the thumping of gigantic hearts and an overheated narrative rhythm.
They gave a menacing edge to the day, Buller felt. His own pulse
seemed to quicken to match the rhythm. He glanced back at the
screens which transmitted images from the mobile surveillance
units.

142

"No trouble yet, sir," Aphrodite said. She sat between two other women officers at a desk which faced a wall of screens and switches. Messages crackled to and fro on the police radios. Behind them two more officers sat a similar desk which faced the opposite side. Here a much bigger screen displayed a plan of the site and the disposition of the opposing forces.

The command vehicle was the size of a small removals van. A door opened to the cabin at the front where the driver and an armed back-up were drinking tea and reading the *Sun*. Daylight poured into the interior from the armoured bubble dome in the roof. The dome provided a safe viewpoint in a riot. Buller sat in a swivel leather chair close to the brushed steel steps that led up to the dome. Sitting there he sometimes felt like a submarine commander. In the leather chair he was in total control.

"I think something's happening near the bridge." Aphrodite leaned forwards to switch one of the cameras to zoom. "Some kind of skirmish." She shivered and popped a pill. "Looks like we might soon have the narrative excitement of EXTREME VIOLENCE."

32   Control Room

The Director, Colin Nixon, was an eager young man in a suit and tie. He'd been headhunted from Banal Realism. He shook the Minister's hand and stood for a moment or so, respectfully listening to the faint clink of broken principles.

Nixon led the Minister through the lobby into a cool, plausible air-conditioned reception room, where a model of the Collider was laid out on a table. The Director began earnestly pointing at aspects of the model while babbling statistics and explanations. Detectors, he said, were used to look at the tracks made by the new particles produced by the collision of accelerated particles. Tracking detectors captured the trajectories of individual particles. Calorimeters measured energies.

Poffley attempted to look engaged by this portentous information, but his mind was elsewhere. The morning before Poffley had kissed his wife goodbye at their large detached home on the shore of a Cumbrian lake. In the afternoon he had put in an appearance at the

House and dealt with constituency business. After dining with colleagues he'd gone to his Westminster flat where from 10 p.m. he'd spent a memorable two hours in bed with his blonde German research assistant, Ingrid. Ingrid was 27 and an exceptionally enthusiastic and innovative lover. It was difficult to think about quantum physics when the image of Elise's deliciously naked body kept returning to his mind. But at last the Director's sleek, monotonous monologue came to an end and the Minister was escorted through to the Collider control room.

*

Colin Nixon decided this would be the best time to explain. When it was just himself and the Minister, with everyone else trooping after them, unable to hear what he was saying.

He got it over with quickly.

"You will see a book. One member of our team believes that when you turn on the Collider this book will be teleported in time," the Director smiled. "Pardon this harmless indulgence. I know you are not here to see conjuring tricks. It probably won't work. But if it does it would be… of enormous significance."

The Minister nodded gravely, with that slow, desolating windswept expression that graves have when they incline towards you. He didn't have a clue what the fellow was talking about.

As they approached the control room, a pair of automatic glass doors slid back. Inside, half a dozen scientists in white coats stiffened to attention amid a blur of fingers on the keyboard. "Before too many decades have passed this method of fixing prose on a screen will seem weirdly archaic and writers will talk to their machines," said no one. No one added, "The room, like the computer screen before the impact of the first letter, was a clinical white."

The control panel bore a resemblance to the one in the Sikorski, the MP thought. Lines of switches and lights that resembled coloured beads. A solitary red button on a kind of raised pad. Above all this infobluff a large plasma-glass window opened onto a section of the Collider's enormous tubular structure. Resting on the base of the tube beyond the plasma-glass was the book the Director had mentioned. It had a gilt spine which glittered under the bright fluorescent lighting.

*

The Minister began with an old joke. He always began with this joke. It relaxed people. It made them like him. "It is believed that the universe began some 15 billion years ago – a time which pre-dates even the successes of the present Government." There was a moment's pause, then a polite ripple of laughter crossed the void, initiated by his private secretary.

There were about forty people present – the Collider's top brass (bronzed and beautifully polished), three from the base, Poffley's own team, and about a dozen journalists and photographers. Poffley recognised the science correspondent of the *Times* – that was good – and the photographer from the *Guardian* – that was bad. The photographer fellow was a pest. He always tried for an unflattering shot which used either a peculiar camera angle and grotesquely exaggerated the subject's nose or chin or went for something comically inappropriate in the background which made the subject look absurd. Poffley glanced quickly behind him to make sure there were no slogans which might be amputated to make him look foolish. He hadn't forgotten the time he'd fronted the 'Made in England' campaign, which, hedged by colourful union jacks, patriotically urged the housewife to buy local diseased meat and pesticide-impregnated fruit and veg, rather than foreign varieties. The *Guardian* snapper managed to get a shot which showed him with his mouth gaping vacantly in close-up, alongside only the first three giant black letters of 'MADE'.

The speech, on with the speech. The scriptwriter, a successful television comic, had included a joke about the Big Bang, but aides had deleted it on the grounds of being too risqué. The memory of the suppressed joke brought a fleeting image of Ingrid to the M.P.'s mind. He quickly moved on.

"With the valuable assistance of a blue-ribbon panel... the scientific and technological challenges of the future... combination of public and private finance... the science that underpins a modern

145

society and drives our economy... particle physics crucial in understanding the laws that control the make-up of matter... delighted to be here today to open the Zeilinger Collider... the biggest linear accelerator in the world... cutting edge exploration of anti-matter... neutrinos... black holes... wormholes... on behalf of the Prime Minister and the government...would like to congratulate everyone involved in this magnificent new project."

When the applause for this rubbish had died down the Minister stepped forward to press the button that turned the Collider on. Once again he glanced quickly behind him but it was just the same as before - a bare, white wall. He moved over to the panel and let his thumb rest lightly on the small red button to give the photographers time to take their photographs. He groaned inwardly, seeing the *Guardian* man sink to the floor and point his camera up at a forty-five degree angle. The bastard was zooming in on his chin. He would look dreadful in the picture, he just knew it. But he maintained his rigid professional smile despite the pain of the groan's bristles as it ran amok in his small intestine.

Poffley prayed that there would be no trouble from the protesters. If there was, he knew the papers wouldn't be interested in running a picture of him standing by a control panel. Instead they'd go for something sexy, like fighting, damage or a blood-spattered face. But he supposed that that would mean the *Guardian* man's picture would be junked. He thought: every cloud has a silver lining. Then he wondered what had happened to him. It was bad enough speaking them; now he was even *thinking* in clichés. The Lord whispered in his ear, "I'll see what I can do, mate."

As he maintained his stiff, frozen smile and his banal realist posture Poffley grew apprehensive. He was suddenly aware of the chants of the protesters outside. "No! No! No!" they were screaming. "Co! Lie! Durr! No-no-no!"

But the disruption, when it occurred, didn't come from the protesters beyond the police lines. It came from inside the room – and then from tangled time, tantalising transferences, tempting tintinnabulation, tawdry tangrams, tangential tableaux, talkee-talkee, and other textual teases.

146

33 Frenzied

"Don't!" yelled a voice from the back of the officials and technocrats gathered in the control room. Faces turned in surprise, muscular movement forming the integument of the various foreheads into attractively patterned transverse wrinkles. The eyes of the reporters lit up - deep blue for the *Telegraph*, a watery yellow for the *Guardian*, a deranged purple for the *Mail*. They scented a story different to the one they were there for.

"Don't press that button, Minister!"

The demand came from a small, elderly-looking man in a crumpled black suit. The knot of his tie had slipped down across his chest. He seemed faintly dishevelled and desperate. His eyes bulged urgently from a wrinkled, tired-looking paragraph.

"Don't do it!"

The Director scowled. Displaying a shocking ignorance of modern copyright law, he recognised the voice as belonging to Dr Lund. Lund was one of the project's associate directors. He had been coming to the Director regularly in a number of flashback scenes which will shortly occur. In recent days he'd been urging Nixon to consider the American maniac he'd been named after and to delay the opening of the Collider. Lund claimed it might be dangerous, with irrevocable consequences for matter. His argument was simple, grandiose - and preposterous.

He'd given the Director a theoretical paper illustrating his point. The Director had irritably glanced at it but no more than that. It was speculative bunkum. It was hocus-pocus. Gobbledygook. Mumbo jumbo. Fiddle-faddle. Frenzied nonsense about splitting infinitives and fracturing time. Colin Nixon could not pretend to understand all of it – his own scientific qualifications as project director were distinctly lacklustre. He had been appointed to his position because of his administrative skills and his willingness to downsize where necessary. He was a man of his time and his time was now. He was respected where it mattered: by those in power and authority. Whereas poor Lund…

Lund's theoretical work had been brilliant in its time. But now he was a man in his late fifties. He was past it. He'd once had original ideas and a quick, sparky intellect. Now all he had was bees in his bonnet and abnormal amphigoric tendencies. Nixon had done his best to fob the fellow off with perfidy and tergiversation. But Lund had not been satisfied with that. Now he'd decided that the experiment should not go ahead at all. He claimed – put simply - that it would disrupt time. A preposterous idea, barely worthy of a teenager whose mind was addled with science fiction.

"Dr Lund, *please*," he hissed. He would never forget that terrifying display of snakes on the quayside at Paimpol. "Now is not the time."

A pair of black security guards had stirred from the margins of the narrative. They knew they would never have families or names. Even if they were gifted with the rudiments of a face it would at best be a blank ebony oval containing nothing more sophisticated than a dry smile, a look of grim determination or an angry snarl. They moved either side of Lund, the worst paid characters in the entire narrative, on less than six euros an hour. They were waiting. They looked to the Director for orders.

Lund responded with a loud yelp. It turned into raucous laughter. It was an old party trick he used to entertain drunken visitors. Now it was suddenly enormously useful. "Time is what you will break, my friends! Shatter the membrane and we are lost! History is at an end!"

The journalists were beginning to grin with pleasure. A loon! A crazy scientist! A real live nutter! A boring photo call was now suddenly turning into something potentially much more interesting and newsworthy. The photographers raised their cameras. They didn't shoot, not yet. They were hopeful of something spectacular. Perhaps the mad boffin was going to launch himself at the Minister. Hit him, maybe.

Lund's face was not beetroot red with passion, as originally written. Not even an alcoholic East Anglian turnip farmer (of which there are many) could have had cheeks quite that colour. But it was lurid and empurpled – more like beetroot juice in a kitchen sink, diluted by tap water, draining away from a split vacuum pack.

Lund's eyes bulged. He looked like an angry frog (supposedly). He had so much to tell these idiots and so little time to say it! He could feel the rage gurgling in his throat. Such style! It was like standing knee deep in a roomful of petrol trying to tell a child with a box of matches not to light it.

Lund raised his arms and pushed away the security guards, whose beefy shoulders were now nudging him with a strength and power fed by hundreds of burgers.

The Director strode across to him. "Stop it, Lund! Now!" the Director furiously whispered, like a publisher whose most commercially viable novelist has just delivered the first 1,000 page instalment of his next book, which has turned out to be a near future comic jape of stupefying intertextual dimensions, which the publisher anxiously anticipates will be coolly received by reviewers as alternately tedious and effulgent.

"Otherwise I am dismissing you here and now for gross misconduct! For Nietzsche's sake, man! The press are here. The Minister is here. Don't be insolent! Don't make a fool of yourself! Stop this now, I beg you."

"THE BUTTON MUST NOT BE PRESSED!" Lund shrieked. In his youth he had lived among a school of peacocks, which regarded him as one of their brightest pupils.

The security guards were big tall muscular stereotypes, in uniforms which aped those of the Metropolitan Police. The guards looked expectantly at the Director, who reluctantly nodded. "Permission to start moving your limbs granted. Remove him, please," he said crisply, clenching his fist around an empty packet of Prawn Cocktail which had mysteriously found its way into his pocket. He felt certain it had been dropped by one of the marchers on 15 February 2003.

Everyone - apart from the journalists - stared, appalled. The Minister stayed where he was, his posture frozen. The air conditioning was unbelievably cold. Not believing how far it was below zero, he said nothing. He hardly noticed his immobility or his silence, since this was the condition of most literary characters most of the time. He was pleased to find that some use had been found for his facial muscles, which composed a perplexed expression. He was trying hard not to frown. Frowns are the diarrhoea of narrative self-indulgence and lazy excess, he felt. It was fatal to let your

149

professional expression slip or open up when press photographers were at hand. They were just waiting to catch you out yawning or picking your nose. If you weren't careful you could easily find yourself on the cover of *Private Eye* with a curving-bladed balloon embedded in your head.

"Nothing."

His hand was beginning to ache as it hovered in the air above the button. He tried not to look angry for fear of that frog simile. But if his photo opportunity was wrecked by a red-faced man in a dishevelled suit he would NOT be a happy man.

It wasn't, he was. Lund was dragged from the room, still shouting. The photographers' cameras whirred as they simultaneously shot the moment. But they guessed their pictures would not be used. It had ended in anti-climax: the man hadn't attacked the Minister. It was a let down.

"One of our colleagues, I'm afraid, Minister," the Director said. "My sincere apologies. Lund is due for early retirement later in the narrative. He has a severe personality disorder, exacerbated by personal tragedy and work stress, I'm afraid. His lunches are liquid and he rarely returns from The Newton's Wake until late in the afternoon. His wife died not long ago, leaving him all alone in Hangover Square with nothing for company but a copy of *Onder de vulkaan.*" He concluded, as if this finally clarified matters: "She was from Amsterdam."

The Minister adopted a grave expression – fixed, metallic, orphaned, enduring, with the incinerator hidden from view. Politics had taught him many valuable lessons in survival. One of which was that in times of crisis *keep quiet.* Express yourself only in the blandest and most rubbery of terms.

"You will destroy *everything!*" Lund shrieked, re-appearing in the doorway. Then he grunted with pain, almost as if someone had punched him in the kidneys. Perhaps someone had. The physicist went limp and was half-carried, half-dragged away.

The Director coughed loudly. "My apologies for that most unfortunate interruption," he said, addressing the room at large. The postcode was E17 4UU. He had quickly regained his composure. "I regret that even among a distinguished scientific community such as ours there are those who cannot resist a whisky decanter in the morning."

There was an outbreak of good-natured laughter. The reporters grinned. A piss-head, eh? Ah, well. Not surprising, really. Appearing in a narrative like this. No bloody windows or daylight. No unproblematic mimesis. It would drive anyone to drink.

"I am afraid Dr Lund recently suffered a very sad bereavement, which appears to have unhinged him more than anyone could have guessed. We shall see to it that he gets the very best medical care. Now, shall we proceed, Minister?" He beamed at the politician, using the orthodox sequence of flashes to be seen every night in Southwold. Poffley strapped a professional smile over the metal plate and lowered his forefinger to the shiny red button.

34   Opera Faustiana

Some five months earlier, written only yesterday, Lund had given a talk on the ghost radiation aspect of quantum theory to the Burgess Institute in Kensington. Ghost radiation was the jargon for negative energy. It was something that could be read about in the science pages, then used to show that Lund knew his stuff when he spoke about it in the context of the positive energy of matter in transit. You could prop up a wormhole with it, hypothetically. Make time travel possible. Dazzle the reader with theory.

The woman was in the third row of the audience in the steeply banked auditorium. In her late twenties, probably. She was at eye level with him and vaguely disconcerting. With her shock of red hair, her scarlet lips and her smart pin-striped suit. So different to all those balding, portly scientists in brown cardigans. He felt her eyes boring into him as he spoke of single electron detectors and split existences.

Afterwards, along with five or six others, she stepped down to the stage and spoke to him. She apologised sweetly for the perforations her eyes had caused. The others were merely freshly minted old associates, there to exchange pleasantries (peasants, pheasants, connections with crescents). But Red Hair had something weighty to communicate. When the others had finished and stepped aside she

151

smiled and silently handed him a slip of paper. Sketched on it was an astonishingly heavy diagram, with some scribbled equations.

He saw at once it showed a silicon beam and a Cooper pair box joined to an aluminium loop. Her mathematics made him take a sharp intake of breath - his eight-hundred and fiftieth so far. He glanced back at her with profound respect, and more than a little puzzlement at the prose. She seemed so young, so fresh. Knowledge like that was usually the preserve of older people. When he complimented her, she smiled wryly and said, "I'm older than I look." Then, having got his attention, she passed him another slip of paper.

This one made him start as if he'd been touched by live electricity. His mind left Liverpool Street on the Central Line and accelerated towards Hamilton Drive. Her theorem proposed a quantum superimposition of massive particles enabling spatial transference via the absolute duplication of every atom and electron. It came accompanied by calculations, sketches, new equations, paratext, marginalia and a splash of Rosemount Shiraz Cabernet 2003 in the shape of the island of Bearnaraigh. Lund felt his old heart beginning to thud, so he transferred to a new one. In the background his friends waved their farewells. He heard one of them say, "Lucky devil," and laugh.

The woman – she told him her name was Dr Myra Nandow – invited him to accompany her to a nearby coffee shop. They strolled down the wide, quiet tree-lined street and turned into a side street near the Cromwell Road. She led him into The Coliseum, all silver tables and chairs and hexagonal mirrors plating the walls. To his surprise the staff really was Italian. "Da questa 'opera faustiana' è tratto il film diretto da John Huston e interpretato da Albert Finney e Jacqueline Bisset", the proprietor remarked. "Quarto rampollo di una ricca e morigerata famiglia di commercianti metodisti, Malcolm Lowry nacque nel 1909 a Merseyside, in Inghilterra," his brother-in-law replied.

Lun and Nandow drank cappuccinos. They talked.

She wasn't English, he could tell. She spoke it perfectly but her accent gave her away. It had a slight East European edge. She explained she was from the Cobain Laboratories, in Lithium. Their

152

equipment and funding was mediocre, all the effort went into theoretical physics. She thought she'd recently made a breakthrough but her boss had dismissed them as wild fantasies. In Lithium, if you are a woman... She shrugged, Lithiumanian style, with a thirty degree sideways lurch.

That was why she had come to Lund's talk, she explained. He was the only person she had ever heard of who might understand. She had read his *Towards a New Theory of Quantum Superimposition* and thought it was a marvellous book (she pronounced it "marff-luss"). Lund flushed with pleasure, then returned to their table. His book had so far sold 37 copies and only the previous week he'd received a letter from his publishers brusquely informing him the book was to be remaindered.

Dr Nandow said she herself had attempted to set down her ideas... Would he mind reading her manuscript? she wondered. He would be able to spot any flaws. Perhaps it might be published?

Lund explained that the market for serious, technical books on quantum physics was very, very small. He couldn't really hold out any hopes in that direction. Had she considered writing a collection of satirical short stories in which the President of the United States masturbated over Inverness? Something along those lines was bound to be immensely popular in Nebraska. But he said he would be very happy to read it. Very happy indeed.

She explained that she was returning to Lithium the next day. Dr Nandow handed him a large jiffy-bag, wrote down her address, and shook his hand in a solemn, formal manner. He watched her walk away down the street, out of the chapter.

35 The Book

Nystagmus? No. Lund niddle-noddled, numbed by Myra Nandow's manuscript. It was fantastically advanced. It was like *The State and Revolution* meets *Naked Lunch* and *Infinite Jest* via *Plus Oh!* He read it through in a single session, fuelled by black coffee and a large tumbler of Glenmorangie.

Plus oh! he thought. This woman is brilliant. She is luminous, florid, intelligent, perfect, noteworthy, a gem. She should be working with us, on the Collider project. In fact, it's as if she had been working with us. She knows exactly what we're aiming for. Better than that, she *understands*.

Lund knew he had to see Nixon, get her on the team. The Director would like her (Lund frowned: someone like Nixon would be *certain* to like a woman as young, attractive and nicely turned out as Dr Nandow). Myra Nandow was wasted in Lithium.

He was excited, too, by her suggested object for teleportation. *A book.* That would be perfect. It would be fine and dandy. It would be excellent, beautiful, shapely. By comparison with anything experimental done so far it was a phenomenally large object. It would be the theoretical equivalent of displacing the Empire State Building. He calculated that the displacement would only take minutes, but all the same. If they set it up for the Minister, when he officially opened the place... Holy smoke! It would create a sensation! To see something *disappear into time* and then rematerialize minutes later!

It would be a moment every bit as historic as the invention of the wheel, or splitting the atom, or the discovery of the double helix, or the first time the Michelin man stepped on to the moon, or the wedding of H.R.H. Prince Charles to Lady Diana Spencer, July 29 1981.

*

"I haff an idea," Lund said. Sometimes when he spoke like that you remembered he wasn't English. What a hoot! It wouldn't have been so bad if he was American, but *Dutch*. The Director had once had a very bad experience in Amsterdam. There was a police officer shouting at him, it was raining, his trousers were twisted round his socks. He held the entire Dutch population responsible for his humiliation. Even now the memory of it made him flush with embarrassment, which was probably why his constipations were sometimes as lengthy as a year. But he would never talk about what happened in Amsterdam to anyone. He didn't want to remember it. He stamped on the memory, moved quickly on.

"This book. I sink I can make it *move*."

154

"Move?"

"In time. Make it *phut!* Vanish! Just like that."

Lund's mouth cracked open with excitement. With distaste the director observed the staleness of the accent and Lund's old, yellowed teeth. There were gaps. The director grimaced. It was the constipation again – and the lacunae. Some people didn't seem to understand that times had changed. Image and presentation was everything these days. Bowel movements in fiction were now not only not necessary but even frowned on. It wasn't enough to be smart with your prose and characterisation. You had to get out there and sell yourself in the market place. You had to get funding, grants, prizes. You had to persuade industrialists and research committees and government ministers. The old days of just asking nicely were gone. Those kinds of committees had gone. You no longer had to justify yourself to a bunch of dishevelled scientists who were long overdue for a haircut, had egg stains on their ties and smelled vaguely of lab chemicals. People like Lund, in fact. Couldn't the fellow afford a dental plan? The Director wondered irritably. He might at least buy himself a tube of tooth-whitener and a subscription to *Time*.

Lund continued to grin. He'd been frozen in the posture since 2002 and now it was March 2005 and the world had changed. He was thrilled to be back, and showed it. He stretched out his arms and did a little dance. Lund reminded the Director of a floppy, crazy rabbit in a cartoon. "Yes, sir, I sink we can make this book disappear!" Lund said (he was beginning to sound like a cartoon character, too).

"I see," said the Director, nervously.

"According to the eighteenth theorem of Ludwig Spenser, time is relative to the velocity of the particle in collision with decelerated matter!"

"Spenser?" said the Director. "Eighteenth theorem?" He looked puzzled. He *was* puzzled.

"Don't you worry. Is a jock. I just make it up! Words is nothing! It is too *long* to explain. This is what counts." He reached into his briefcase and pulled out a volume praised by the *Daily Telegraph* as an entertaining and dazzlingly innovative work, a dizzying gallop across the wild frontier of contemporary fiction. He put it back and withdrew an A4 pad. The Director noted the words DISCOUNT BARGAIN PRICE and THREE FOR THE PRICE OF TWO blazoned on the scarlet cover. Inwardly he sighed, the sigh taking the form of a very large, curling wave.

Lund fanned open the pad. Every page was covered in mathematical calculations and formulae, done in Lund's erratic hand. There were inked-in arrows, doodles, ban-the-bomb logos, and, once, a smiley have-a-nice-day face. Bearnaraigh nuzzled Eigg, both islands empurpled by the setting sun.

"I say we put this book in the display zone for our distinguished visitor, mister government minister. He switch on the accelerator and *phut!* This book is moved in time. Approximately three minutes to future! The minister wait three minutes and *phut!* He catch up with the book! The book return to our own time. Of this I am certain."

The Director was aghast at Lund's Dutch English. As for time travel! The man was mad. Not just mad but unbalanced, deficient, aberrant. Yet Lund seemed serious. Nixon was not, at first, persuaded. He never read science fiction, let alone metafiction. He believed in truth, stability, realism and parliamentary democracy. But Lund's bubbly enthusiasm eventually wore down his hesitation. It might be less than £3 a shot but Asda's Cava wasn't bad at all. Interesting new islands formed on the calculations, which it would be necessary for him to locate in his atlas. Lund was, after all, no Tom o' Bedlam. The Director had to concede that Lund, though lacking in many social skills (combing one's hair, dressing smartly) had a first-rate mind. Lund had depths and qualities he did not pretend to understand (Lund's attraction for that fabulously beautiful and smart woman who had married him, for a start).

"If I may suggest a book, Herr Director..."

"I've told you before, don't call me that. You make me sound like a bloody Nazi. What book?"

"I am sorry, Herr – I mean, uh, Director. May I suggest something by the greatest Englishman of all time."

The Director wondered who. Winston Churchill? Henry VIII? David Beckham?

"I refer to Chick Spur."

The Director was still baffled.

"To his sonnets."

It suddenly clicked who Chick Spur was.

"Let me think about it." He closed his eyes.

In 1817 an interview with a Tewkesbury chair-maker who was a direct descendant of Shakespeare's sister was published in *Monthly Magazine*. "The name had proved of no use to him than as furnishing jokes among his companions, by whom he was often annoyed on this account. On the writer presenting him with a guinea he declared it was the first benefit which had arisen from his being a Shakespeare."

Lund put the pad back in his briefcase and took something else out. He said [quietly/loudly], "I haff a copy here." He laid the book on the desk.

The director picked it up and opened it. A cloud of dust erupted from its innards. Digital enhancement produced a face that winked. The dust fell gently across his suit like snow. It settled on his lapels. It drifted across his mouth. He swallowed it, inhaled it, began to splutter and gasp. Tears wobbled in his eyes. He turned to the title page. *Shakespeare's Sonnets*. Underneath someone had written in an elegant hand, "To my darling Henrik. With you to the end. From Kirsten."

There were kisses.

So that's what Lund's first name is! He flipped the book open, then shut it. He shut it crossly, which was a mistake, as it forced out a fresh wave of dust. The dust settled across his dark suit like dandruff. When he tried to brush it off it turned to powder and left a smear on the fabric and on his fingertips.

"It will work. Believe me, it will work."

The Director steepled his fingers, thinking fast. Churches! Fire! Nazis! George W. Bush!

Lund was an infuriating scruff but there was no real question he was the brightest man on the project. His permanent glow was a tribute to all those years spent in the presence of radioactive materials. No wonder he adored *Silkwood* and Homer Simpson. If

157

Lund said he could make the book move through time, he was probably right.

It was sensational. And what a gimmick! Nixon decided he'd say nothing to anyone in advance. It would just be between Lund and him. Afterwards, he'd take all the credit. Lund was easy enough to manipulate. He was just a character in a narrative that Nixon was writing in his mind. The man didn't care about promotion or money. He could be deleted at any time. Or, like Mr Rochester, he could be mutilated and blinded as a consequence of the actions of a filthy, deranged woman! Nixon liked that idea. It would be a doddle. Of course, Lund would have to share the Nobel Prize with him, but that was no problem. Lund would be a whimpering wreck in a wheelchair, with Ray Charles glasses. He, Nixon, would do all the talking. He'd be the person that people would remember. It would be like Crick and Watson all over again and that bloody woman whose name he couldn't remember.

Which was precisely the point.

The Director beamed affably. He leaned forwards confidentially. His sentences unfolded clumsily. "This is really most exciting, Lund. Your idea is excellent. For the moment I think we must keep this between just the two of us. But I'm sure the minister will be most impressed. As will everyone. Splendid work, Lund. Splendid work!"

Lund squirmed with pleasure and grinned. Then he removed his hand and wiped it on a grey hanky studded with flecks of emerald. Lund buttoned up his trousers. "And these book is okay?"

"Absolutely. Shakespeare. What could be more appropriate? The unity of literature and science, funded by industry. The essence of a forward-looking culture!" He added, "But we will say nothing in advance. Just in case it doesn't work. Don't want to make fools of ourselves, eh?"

"It will work. I haff proved this. But there is further work to be done. I haff not yet explored the consequences of such a displacement. Or the reader's reaction to all the comic stereotyping. Holland is an important market."

"Consequences?"

"For decelerated matter subject to displacement. What it does to the chronology of the membrane of the enclosing matter."

"Ah, yes. Fascinating stuff. Well you carry on with your work, Lund. And well done!"

"Please. My book."

"Ah, yes. Of course." The Director handed the sonnets back.

Lund's eyes shone. Perhaps the dust was getting in his eyes too. Or maybe it was just the contamination. "It was a gift from my wife."

The Director remembered. The poor woman had drowned. On holiday, swimming. Taken by a powerful current of authorial indifference. No sooner born than deleted.

"Yes, yes. We are all very sorry for what happened, Lund. You know you can have a sabbatical any time you want to. Three months abroad, travel, we'll be only too happy to fund it. We might even be able to transfer you to a more mainstream work of fiction. A thriller, perhaps."

"Yes, I know. Everyone has been most kind. But my work is my vacation."

"Very well, very well. We'll put the book in the Collider. But we won't mention anything about time displacement, eh? Then if nothing happens we won't look like bloody fools. Got that, Lund?"

Lund departed, leaving the Director dabbing at his jacket. He'd have to get the bloody thing dry-cleaned now. But what the hell. If Lund was right this was going to be a very big story. He could see the headlines. *Top scientists crack time puzzle.* The red tops would be even better. *Boffins in time travel sensation.* He smiled with complacent satisfaction. It was going to be so big it wouldn't be long before he'd be on the TV news. He rather liked the thought of getting close to Natasha Kaplinsky.

She provoked in him a swooning admiration.

He began adjusting his tie in subconscious expectation.

He wondered if she'd ever met someone with a keen interest in auto-erotic semi-asphyxiation.

159

36   Stop Dice

The interview with Dr Nandow was what first triggered Lund's doubts.

The problem was, she couldn't be interviewed. She was untraceable. The laboratory she'd named did not exist. As for Lithium! Had he misheard her? Written something down wrongly?

It was like that second sentence in the second chapter of the Quartet edition of *Berg*: "I an albatross, never to fly in a direction taken a million times before." It read oddly. You wanted to go back 13 unlucky years in time and check the Calder edition. But even first editions didn't always help. "More sharpe to me then fpurring to his fide, For that fame grone doth put this in my mind, My greefe lies onward and my ioy behind" was the text of the 1609 Quarto, which had clearly been put unclearly together by a drunken compositor with six missing teeth. In later years turnstile hyphens, wrought-iron semi-colons and genial easygoing modernizations had infested the text.

Dr Myra Nandow did not seem to exist. She was not employed by any scientific establishment in the world. Next Lund tried universities, polytechnics, colleges. Even schools. Zilch. No search engine could locate the name.

He had been tricked in some way. But why? The book experiment was harmless enough. The transference would be severely restricted in both time and space. What could be the problem with that?

Consequences. Would there be consequences – side effects or slide effects - outside the experiment? He had complacently assumed there would be none. Perhaps he was wrong.

An image suddenly flicked in his mind. He was in his local park, standing at the lakeside, idly watching a child throwing a lump of wood into the murky water. With a great splash, the wood sank out of sight. A moment later it bobbed up again. And that was his book experiment, wasn't? Making something disappear and then re-appear in the same spot.

But what he hadn't considered were side-effects. The consideration produced a strangely soporific feeling. He felt unexpectedly feverish and began to lose consciousness. Time passed, and then he came back to where he was, feeling nauseous. He held a blister pack in his hand. His head throbbed. The circular wave that spread out around the wood moved slowly across the stagnant surface. A plausible duckling bobbed up and down as the wave passed below it. A water lily's leaves swelled and fell. Then a tiny surge rushed across the strip of mud at the lake's edge and lapped around his shoes. A sudden cold sensation in his left foot made him back away and examine his sock. That was when he discovered that the sole of his shoe had split from side to side. And he'd only had the wretched shoes a month! He squelched his way angrily home.

Consequences. Unforeseen, unconsidered effects.

A cold panic began to grow inside Lund. He watered it with a gallon of anxiety. He grabbed his A4 folder and frantically began jotting down facts and figures. He felt the pressure of plot and action tightening around his windpipe, like the fat, greasy fingers of a publisher's accountant.

*

In those last twenty four hours before the Minister's visit, Lund worked at his calculations like a man demented – or a dreaming Scotsman off Manhattan, lying in his bunk under the influence of heroin.

He looked terrible. His cheeks were hollow. Inside them lay gigantic unfinished manuscripts. *I often wondered how far out a man could go without being obliterated...* There weren't just bags under his eyes but suitcases, whole shelves of them.

Weeks of sleeplessness and anxiety could be measured in his gaunt, drawn face. Chalk was just one of the substances being used and abused. Lund had become nervy and bad-tempered. He exploded with anger when little things impeded the smooth flow of his day. The bad writing had to be gathered up and patched together again.

He shouted at the girl in the office when she put sugar in his tea by mistake. She burst into tears and ran from the room, a thousand salty tadpoles howling for the restoration of naturalism. It was granted. Back in his office Lund had to make a brusque, bad-tempered apology, full of banal adjectives.

An awful vista had opened up in his mind. It resembled a suburb of Manchester. He blanked it out with a surge of smoke from an exploding research facility. *What would happen if the Collider didn't transfer a solid object in time in one direction?*

They'd been sleepwalking on the project. He saw that, now. Since reading the scene with Angel in *Tess of the D'Urbervilles* his whole outlook on life had changed. It was like planning a big explosion and thinking everything would be thrown in a single, narrow direction. But what if it wasn't like that at all? What if time split in different directions, at different speeds? What if the effect was localized? What if, like Hardy's version of his novel, the text was tampered with from edition to edition? Or was subjected to as yet unknown and uncomprehended variables?

He saw now that he needed to switch off the question marks - and that switching on the Collider might have an effect every bit as devastating as the triggering of a massive thermo-nuclear device. But *might* wasn't good enough. Nor was the language. He had to prove it. Worse, he had to unleash yet more dogged narrative in order to prove what those consequences might be. He could barely understand them himself.

He caught theoretical glimpses, no more than that. All he had was an image of time twisted, compressed – and then abruptly released. Time out of control. Time running in different directions. A wall of clocks, all running at different speeds.

He was sure he'd seen something like it in an old movie. Clock hands whizzing forwards, others spinning backwards. Some gulping the hours in seconds, others crawling with the slow, malevolent movement of a viper getting closer to its prey. People worried about global warming but what about the menace of overheated prose? - or the stark memory of that frightening snake exhibition at Paimpol, obliging him to flee hand in hand with Mme. Pointu along Rue Salvadore Allende.

He felt himself going slightly mad. Freddie Mercury howled in his mind. An unseen hand turned a master valve. In the darkness of the living room the phone began to ring. "The days are over! I leave

162

after breakfast with fifteen hundred things to do at home!" an American called out, further along the ward.

Lund sensed he was surrounded by fools. No one would understand the science – or the glistening coils of allusion. But it must be done, it would be done. He'd prove it. He'd appeal to the Director to halt the official opening until more research had been done. Lund grimaced, merry as a grig. It was all that bloody woman's fault. The one in red. She was the one who was responsible. She'd set the ball rolling. She'd grimed him with her stop dice. She'd started something big. She'd set him a trap and he'd plunged innocently, eagerly, stupidly into it.

For the thousandth time he wondered who she was.

He knew it was only a question of turning the pages to find out.

37 Belgians

Over by the bridge a section of the crowd had broken down the security fencing and was trying to push its way through the line of police.

Ben Scaravelli led the charge, and others followed. But not the women. Marianne hung back. She didn't want to get arrested by a paragraph of vicious realism. Her cover as a born-again plausible character would be well and truly blown. They'd put Special Branch on to her again and she didn't think she could handle fending off Triffids. Surveillance would fuck everything up. That would spoil the plan.

Emma stayed with her. She didn't believe in violence. Also, she felt sick. She was pregnant with narrative possibility. She wanted to lie down on the grass, rest a while.

She decided to go to the back of the crowd and rest her head on her marijuana pillow. By this time Marianne was nowhere to be seen. She'd dipped out of sight, only to resurface in the next chapter. The protesters were a sea of faces in a lake of bland description. Everyone seemed to be moving in different directions. She'd even lost sight of Edgar.

Strobey followed Ben. He knew this was his last chance. It was obvious why Mirando Mirando had come to Walthamstow. It was nothing to do with Finn's Hotel. That had been a complete red herring. Enough of that! He would cook the herring by the light of the moon, long and slow in an oven dish full of spiced vinegar. He would cook it at gas mark eight, until the bones melted away and love itself had rest.

She was here because of the Collider, exclamation mark. She was obviously going to get it to do something radically different to what had been planned, exclamation mark. The bitch had postmodern tendencies, exclamation mark. Was she going to blow up London? Only half inflate it? Strobey had no idea what Madame was intending. But somehow he had to get inside that building and rewrite her plot.

Ben ducked between two cops, quacking. He was through the first line. Ahead of him was a scattered line of white Transits of Venus. He saw coppers spilling out of them, glistening with prejudice. How they loathed poofs, pakis, asylum seekers, social security scroungers, women and lefties! The cops were holding small round shields and truncheons. Behind him he saw Strobey. *Good ol' Edgar!* The line had completely broken now. A hundred or more protesters (more – 127) were sprinting across the grass to the main Collider building.

Ben reached the Transit cops. They stared at him. They glared at him. Hatred flared at him through their visors. Ben aimed for the gap between the nearest two clusters. He dodged past the first group. He was gonna make it!

The movements of the boiler-suited men were stiff and clumsy. It reminded him of the moon landing the Americans had faked. A truncheon swished through the air, missing him by several miles. A strange pressure seemed to be building up inside the story. Strobey grinned. He surfed the good vibrations. He followed.

The cops had formed up into a line of stationary words. Strobey could see Ben beyond it, being chased by half a dozen angry officers. He did what he'd done to get through the earlier line. He ducked down, put his arms over his head, and hurled himself between the nearest two cops. *Quark! Quark!*

A truncheon slammed into three of his lumbar vertebrae, making him livid, then black and blue. But he was through! Then a boot

164

came out in front of him and he tripped. It was like *psychedelic*, man. Saturn hula-hooping like crazy, man.

Strobey landed face first on the rough ground. It felt like a giant step for mankind, but was just grass. The drugs do work! he thunk, grinning. His breath sounded like the tide dragging down a shingle beach. The beach resisted fiercely. In the end the tide withdrew.

"You're under arrest!" a voice shouted in his ear.

Then another voice said, "Fucking forget it. He ain't worth the fucking paperwork or the fucking descriptive effort involved in fucking processing him at the fucking nick."

A rain of truncheons and boot kicks began.

Strobey so wished it had instead been a harmless torrent of gently descending bowler hatted bourgeois Belgian males with briefcases.

38   An Incandescence

The tip of the Minister's beautifully manicured forefinger touched the button. His finger smelled good. Soap and a scented wet-wipe had long since erased the sardine odour which lingered when its frolics ceased in Elise's gash – not to mention all those imperial gallons of Iraqi blood. The dainty finger slowly increased the pressure on the button and the Minister continued to smile the smile of a man who knows how to give a parliamentary researcher a really good time in bed.

Flashes bathed him in splashes of silvery light. A further flurry of flashes flickeringly followed the first fast flurry of flashes. An incandescence flooded the room. The Minister felt for a moment like God, spuddling the whole earth. It was a good feeling. How he would have liked a legion of tall, winged creatures who would fly off and zap his enemies, who were many!

And yet.

Was it his imagination, or did the voices seem very much closer than before?

Voices?

The photographers had finished. The Minister increased the pressure of his thumb and felt the button sink on its spring. It gave

165

an almost inaudible click and a scarlet light came on at the centre of the panel.

The bombardment of electrons and positrons began.

*

The Director flinched furiously at the flaming flashes. Angry was he. Very, very angry. He'd humoured that cund Lunt by letting him pot that ficking buick in the conducktor. And the bastard had almost ruined everything. The ingratitude made him want to choke. He just hoped that bloody book was teleported. If it wasn't he'd impersonally strangle Lund himself.

He wished now he'd insisted on a decent science book – a classic. A book everyone admired - something like *The Double Helix*, say. Or the one about time by that freak with the squeaky machine voice. *Shakespeare's Sonnets* was no doubt an admirable book (Nixon had not himself ever read it; Tudor verse wasn't his bag). But it wasn't exactly relevant to quantum physics, although Shakespeare was, of course, important for tourism and trade.

He was fortunate Lund hadn't been picky about which edition. The Director had managed to get hold of a very nice copy with an expensive leather jacket and gold lettering on the spine. It had class. It looked good. That was what counted in a book.

Lund's theory had been that the book would disappear. It would be displaced in time (he'd finally calculated) by three minutes and thirteen seconds. Into the future. He'd produced a bundle of calculations to prove it.

The Director opened his eyes. He felt a hot flush of anger spread across his face.

Shakespeare's Sonnets was still there.

*

Januschka lived in a strategic flashback in a high-density urban complex on Level 63. It was where people on middle-to-low incomes were located. The housing consisted of racks of three room apartments accessed by speed tubes. Each apartment had subsidised dream screens, to make up for the lack of a view.

On his first visit there, Strobey saw that Januschka had chosen stars in space. Her apartment was configured like a space ship. Not a real one, of course. There was nothing romantic about a space needle. This was a dreamship design, with articulated brushed steel tubes looped above the all-white furniture.

Her Loron idol rested on a glitter plinth. A holo of a planet with six rings drifted to and fro below the curved ceiling. Her bed was circular and made of stretched ruberium.

A stalk robot brought him a drink of Enhancer # 5. Five minutes later they were naked together on the ruberium. They held off for as long as possible, enjoying the touch of skin on skin, of the tip of a tongue, teasing, touching, tweaking. Soft, low spontaneo-astral music played, adjusting its tempo to the rhythms of their lovemaking. It was all so different to the rough, quick sessions with a mute Living Doll.

Januschka's eyes were great pools of desirio-plash. Her laughter was as delicate as those flicker fish he had once seen in a tank on the Moon of Drifting. Her pleasure, when it began, was a sudden intense shuddering suction that made her face twizzle and cantart. A cheap, sickly perfume filled the chamber, which he recognised as Essence of Biological Hyperspace. He knew, then, that he wanted to quit the TPT and stay with her. He held her in his strong, muscled arms and told her everything. How he'd long overdosed on steroids and used substitute piss to fool the drug wardens. How his mission seemed suddenly barren of purpose and interest. How he wanted to stay on Menzara, with her and spend many repetitive sentence structures in her company.

She told him not to be hasty. She told him to be careful. She told him he was commissioned and if he gave up now he'd be punished. She warned him repetition can only go so far. He risked being sent for twenty years to a patrol ship on the perimeter of Void Eleven. They'd be nothing for him there but Imago Sessions with the rest of the crew. She urged him not to make any impulsive decisions. They should enjoy each other while they had the time. He didn't have to decide just yet. His mission was still some units away.

167

Strobey knew she was talking sense. He respected that. Acumen, perspicacity, discernment. He loved the way she unbuttoned his defences, cocked her head, pursed her plump lips, opened her voluptuous mouth, and gave him level-headedness.

He blew her a kiss from the hatch of the speed tube and said he'd see her at the same time the next time.

The hatch closed and he was hurled off to Terminus 101.

*

The Minister opened his eyes.

He hated this.

He was used to being photographed but these *paparazzi* seemed insatiable. Wave after wave of exploding flashlights washed across his frozen features. Drained of colour, his complexion was that of pale stone. They were vampires feasting on his pinioned anguish.

The incandescence was painful. The dazzling reiterated whiteness seemed as if made of arctic fire or the monstrous last four blank pages of his copy of *Counter-Clock World*. The flashes bored into the retina of each eye, gouging them with an acid flame. Pure whiteness seemed to pour into the two agonized slits in his face, filling his vision, his mind.

He screwed up his eyes to shut out the fire. He raised his forearm against the trajectory of the rhetoric. Camera motors whirred like demented wasps. Shutters clicked and snapped like a frenzy of feeding piranhas. Bars of red light tracked down across his closed lids. Bulbs of shimmering scarlet danced in the vein-meshed dark. An overheated style filled the paragraph like a cloud of furious wasps.

Then it was over. Dazed, thankful, trembling a little, the Minister opened his eyes.

He wondered if that drunken scientist had been right, that pressing the button had triggered some kind of catastrophe.

He was relieved to see everything was normal. The press photographers were putting their realistic-looking cameras away. Reporters who for a moment had all seemed to be staring at him quizzically now turned from his cool gaze and began chatting

168

among themselves. Unheard but plausible-looking background conversation began, just like in a bar scene in a TV soap.

He'd pressed the button. The facility was now officially open. The journalists had their story. It was all over now, baby blue.

"Minister? Are you alright?" The Director was at his elbow, looking anxious. The elbow seemed loose. There was a twist of black hair there which might have been escaped wiring.

"No, I'm half left!" That was the joke in his school playground 37 years earlier. But now he was a man, with a public air, pubic hair, a piddling heir.

"Yes, thank you. I was dazzled for a moment by those wretched cameras. But I'm fine now, thank you." He was back in smooth professional mode, now. He was in total control. He could manufacture authoritative dialogue for any occasion. You could ask him any question you wanted, he'd give you a slick answer. If he didn't know the answer, no problem. He would say That is a very important issue which I'm glad you've raised. Rest assured we are looking into as a matter of urgency. When this matter has been fully investigated the Government will act appropriately. On that I can give you my word.

His word being: ambition. Or dream. The dream of every cabinet minister that one day it would be them at Number Ten. And not the present holder, who was clearly no longer up to the job. And getting there required diplomacy and flexibility. That was the core of his philosophy. Treat everyone as if they were your friend. Charm them. Make them feel you are really interested in them and their pathetic molecule-sized problems. Make them feel you are going to do something about it. Seduce them. Emotionally screw them. Get their votes. Only then can you open the aerostat's gated panel and piss down on them.

He beamed at the Director, as if this moment was the greatest one of his life and not just another tedious PR job. But Nixon looked distracted.

"Oh excrement!" Colin Nixon's gaze had wandered back to the conductor. What he saw made him feel sick. He could not believe it. *The book was gone.*

169

The Minister looked at him. He said nothing but a flicker of amusement seemed to dance briefly in his blue eyes. It was doing the twist, and the music was by Chubby Checker. He had the feeling Nixon's day was going wrong every which way. Which didn't perturb him at all, just as long as it didn't fuck up *his* day. In fact he was rather enjoying the Director's discomfiture. *Schadenfreude* is a seriously under-valued emotion. Everyone at Westminster knew that.

39 Many Rivers to Cross

The interior of the police command vehicle was full of realism. Messages crackled from police radios. The camera operators zoomed in on the crowd. Close ups of faces mouthing unheard words filled the screens, then vanished as the camera panned. Aphrodite was sipping at a lukewarm cup of tea when it happened.

A strange shimmering seemed to occur inside the vehicle. It was as if a big, invisible wave was briefly churning its way through, disturbing nothing but the vision of anyone watching. Aphrodite felt nothing as it rushed past her. A micro-second later it was as if nothing had happened.

"Did you feel that nothing?" Buller said. "It was as if nothing happened."

Aphrodite nodded. The camera operators turned and said, yes, they'd felt nothing too. A couple of them looked scared. They knew that Dr Johnson had authoritatively defined the novel as "a small tale, generally of love" but they had heard a rumour about a novelist who Sôseki Natsumè introduced to Japan in 1897, comparing his masterpiece to a holothurian. This is a bizarre sea animal: "one cannot tell where its head or tail is." Natsumè showed a clear liking for the famous episode in that novel involving Phutatorius and a roasted chestnut.

"I don't know what it was. I'll go and find out."

He returned after a minute or so, saying that no one else had noticed anything unusual. But he looked faintly anxious. He did not tell them that the ripple effect had obviously coincided with the Minister switching on the Collider. Was it some sort of radioactivity? Or something harmless? He wasn't a scientist, he didn't know. He'd never heard of anomalous narrative transgression, let alone cyberpunk. It bothered him that no one else had seen what he and the others in the command vehicle had seen.

He hoped they weren't all going to get cancer in twenty years time. Like people did who'd watched atom bomb tests.

Uneasily, they all went back to their three dimensional activities.

*

The guards manhandled Lund to the rear of the facility. Here there was more realism, situated around a loading bay where deliveries were made. Hard dirty grey surfaces dappled with old oil stains. Everything was concrete, was basic. No frills. No outlandish vocabulary.

Beyond it, a small car park and a gate with two guards inside an adjacent hut. The guards worked the automatic gate. Beyond the hut a small service road extended to the front. A solitary police van was stationed here, just in case. Eight bored cops smoking and reading newspapers that reinforced their prejudices against asylum seekers and gypsies. But all the protesters were on the far side, by the front gates. There was no action here. Not until the guards and Lund appeared. One of the cops put down his paper and idly watched.

The gates swung open. One of the guards pointed at the service road.

"Mr Nixon says you have to go home, sir. And you must not return until he says so."

That was fine by Lund.

He ignored the service road and took the dusty brown pathway across the common. Heading for the marshland and the landscape beyond.

The cop went back to reading about what the 22-year-old soap actress had got down to in the hotel room with a famous Hollywood movie star three times her age.

*

Strobey stepped from the hatch of the speed tube into another flashback from the future set in Januschka's apartment. And found himself face to face with Void Archangel Strumbert.

"You, Strobey, are a bloody fool!" the Archangel screamed. He looked furious. His throat scar had turned ultramarine in colour. Behind him stood four sullen guards holding para-blasters. "Do you know what you've fucking done? All that fucking training and you fucking well get into *this*!" Strumbert gestured at the white bed. Above it, on the sex screen, surveillance footage played retro shots of Strobey and his naked lover.

"I'm disappointed in you, Strobey. I've a good mind to send you down for forty years for this. How do you fancy living out all that time on a Labeorite? Hand-cutting blitter stone, living in a cold dormitory on a fucking great rock, shit food, a zap-collar round your neck, and nothing for entertainment but jigsaw puzzles. And you can't even play with yourself because on Labeorite colonies they numb the prisoners' dicks for the full length of their sentence."

"I wouldn't like that at all, sir." Indeed not, forsooth!

"You don't like my narrative; you look almost sick" (what Mr Rochester says to Jane Eyre).

"Then get back to your training programme" (what Void Archangel Strumbert says to Strobey). "From now on you will be restricted to the TPT zone and will be obliged to wear a surveillance brooch at all times. And that includes trips to the little room and the Dolls, understand?"

"I understand, sir." Strobey saluted. "Sir…"

"She got away. We'll find her. Her transgression is much more serious than yours. Seducing a TPT member is a very serious offence. She'll get fifteen for that. Now forget her."

"I wouldn't exactly say I was seduced, sir."

The Void Archangel's face darkened. It was that cool new try-a-different-ethnicity lotion he was using. "Strobey, I do not want to hear your *fucking opinions*. These gentlemen will see you safely back to where you belong. Now *fuck off*!"

"Thank you, sir. Fucking off at once, sir."

He fucked off back to the TPT zone, where he went back to fucking Living Dolls until the day of his sexless traject.

He never saw Januschka again. And they never told him what they'd done to her. And he knew better than to ask. Asking meant *residual feelings*. He knew he mustn't permit himself anything as destructive as that.

*

The reservoir looked Mediterranean blue in the sunshine, reflecting an omniscience which Sharp brought back from Sardinia on the day of Paul Foot's funeral.

On an island in the middle big black birds sat on the branches of a tree stripped of vegetation. They looked like they were waiting for something. They reminded Lund of vultures in a cowboy film. Something was about to happen, but they wouldn't understand. Only Lund understood.

Only Lund knew the consequences of that bland, foolish politician pressing the red button. Probably by now he'd already pressed it. The membrane would have been ruptured, the continuum cracked. Time itself would have been damaged. Time itself would from that moment be warped like a car squeezed between a careering juggernaut and an out-of-control tanker full of hyper-realism.

He'd gone without sleep to understand it. He'd sat up until dawn scribbling wild theorems, anarchic speculations. Shimmering towers of figures danced before him. Calculations giving birth to a swarm of buzzing, sting-bearing possibilities. Lund was unshaven, wild-eyed, a little deranged. *They* thought *he* was mad; *he* knew *they* were deluded.

The fools had shattered time! He'd worked out the mathematics of it. Before, time had been like a slow, ancient river, following a predictable course along a predictable channel. Now all that was gone. The river was in flood and had broken its banks. Time had flooded space. Time was rivers, and waterfalls, and lakes, and seething gutters. But now it would flow backwards as well as forwards. You might grow old inside an hour. You might find yourself shrinking back into your childhood. You might blunder into the shining streets of a city not yet built.

173

He'd done his best to make them see. But it was too late now. He was past all that. He really didn't care anymore about the bourgeois novel and the collapse of its polystyrene worlds.

*

Lund came to the abandoned industrial estate. Economics had killed it a decade earlier. Politicians had mouthed promises of syrup and hope, and then the syrup dissolved into a toxic acid and the promises burned like paper. A long forgotten minister had done a photo shoot here once, years back. The Westminster member was long gone, accompanied by his testicles, his stomach, his little whining cloud of journalists and photographers and shiny, scuttling dung beetles.

Nothing ever really changes, Lund thought. Then he grinned to himself, thinking: leastways, not until *now*.

Downsizing, asset-stripping, cheaper labour in the Third World. All that was left were the ghosts of heavy industry and a nineteenth century realism. Warehouses with roofs open to the sky. Big grey buildings with ducts. Stagnant narratives encrusted with dialogue of the dead. A paralysed crane, its neck broken, feathered with rust. Chimneys which would never leak smoke again. Thistles growing where crowds once hurried. The car park surfaces cracked. Even the weeds seemed grey. A powder of soot clung to the walls of the dead warehouses.

He walked through the ruined site, absorbing its melancholy. Desolation lay everywhere, like a grey, blotched moss of the soul. There was bad karma here; purposelessness streaked with giant tear tracks. All employment gone, lives crushed, labour twisted into dust. The ghosts of middle-aged men wandered here, a layer of fat around their stomachs, a cancerous ache in their intestines.

It was as if thinking of these vanished figures had conjured one of them into existence. Someone came slowly out of a dark doorway in the derelict factory ahead of him. But it wasn't a man, it was a woman. She walked towards him, smiling warmly.

"Dr Lund," she said. "I felt I had to see you again. To thank you for your work."

174

For a moment he was puzzled. Then he realised it was Dr Nandow. She looked completely different, now. Her shock of red hair was gone. Her scandal of breasts was smaller. She was no longer dressed in a smart trouser suit but a dozy, floppy skirt.

He said, "You used me, didn't you? You made me create something that now those fools have gone and started."

"I didn't *make* you. I just helped along your ideas. You were half way there already. You just needed a push. You would have got there in the end, but I couldn't wait any longer, I'm afraid." She smiled. The rhythm demanded one. "I just didn't have the time."

"Who are you? Where are you from?"

"Does it really matter? I had to change your world to change mine. It doesn't mean things will automatically be worse. It just means things will be different." She gestured at the ruined industrial site all around them. "I mean, this is hardly success, is it? And as for the naturalistic fiction of late capitalism!"

Lund searched for a suitable gesture but there was nothing there, just a decayed shrug and a broken headshake. Anyway he didn't want to talk to her. He was through with dialogue. What would be would be, as Doris Day had understood. The thing was done and that was it. The matter was closed. In the end he shook her hand. Then, removing his hand from the end (which was circular) he said, "Goodbye, Dr Landow. Or whoever you are. I must leave now. I have an appointment to keep."

She watched him walk slowly away between the broken buildings until he disappeared from sight. Then she headed off briskly, back in the direction of the Collider. A helicopter rose up from the distant horizon like a tiny black dragonfly and went skimming away towards the city, following a delicate track of similes.

Bill Gates didn't like that last word. Bill Gates scribbled a wavy scarlet line beneath it. "That word's not spelt right!" Bill advised, in his warm, friendly billionaire's voice.

Ellis Sharp smiled. Heck, Bill was darn right! He'd typed 'smilies'. Shucks! With a chuckle, Ell corrected the error. Ell was tired as a two-day turd. He went off, made himself a mug of coffee. As he drank it he read an interview with French rapper MC Solaar. "Who is the world's greatest lyricist?" the interviewer asked. MC

175

Solaar replied: "Leonard Cohen, for his metre – his flow – and the way he tells stories. I also like Jimmy Cliff, especially his song 'Many Rivers to Cross.' "

40 Dark Steps

Beyond all those ruins lay the river.

Lund came to it. He had crossed many rivers in his life. Here there was a concrete embankment. The water was a dull brown. It moved sluggishly. And Kirsten was waiting.

Far behind him the membrane was broken. Behind him time was careening. Young men would find themselves growing old and grey. Others would be slimmed and smoothed to mewling infants. He didn't care. He was locked into an unending present. He had no place forwards to go to. He mustn't keep Kirsten waiting.

There were some dark steps that led down into the river. The cold didn't bother him at all. The water greeted him without pretence. It was there to do what he wanted it to do. Lund didn't hesitate.

He kept walking long after his head had gone under. He walked along the cloudy, powdery bed of the river. Jeff Buckley sang 'Hallelujah', on a loop. Weeds shimmered gently in the slow current of prose. Dark umbrellas of curving leaf cut the blue shimmer leaking down from that layer of oxygen and delusion called the real world.

Thin grasses swayed like slow, drugged dancers. Big knots of entangled weed hung above him like green chandeliers. JB cut out mid-song. Fragments of Malcolm Lowry sentences floated slowly past. Somewhere nearby the musicians from the *Titanic* began playing a muffled, melancholy tune.

The fine strands of weed reminded him of Kirsten's hair. He walked on, raising small dark clouds with every step. The cold pressed against his cheeks like winter. And then he saw her. She came towards him, smiling. Slowly she opened her pale arms and they embraced.

They lay down together on a dark bed with a cold, lumpy mattress. A surge of silt washed over them, covering them like a sheet. Their time in this fictional world was over. Lund lay beside her, happy at last. He closed his eyes and shut the chapter down.

41 Tasty

"We'll be at Chelsea in ten minutes, sir."

The helicopter's whale-shaped shadow swooped across the greenery below, then broke up into triangles and squares and danced across the rooftops of Stoke Newington like an animated cubist canvas. The Thames glittered distantly.

They were there in next to no time.

The Minister ducked and waddled across the pad, the turbulence from the spinning rotor blades running wild fingers through his hair.

The sleek sexy style made him think of Ingrid.

*

At the heli-pad it wasn't his usual chauffeur, Brian. The driver explained Brian hadn't turned up for work. He was off sick. The alternative chauffeur's name was Fred. He was fat and bald and spoke with an accent fermented over five decades in Tower Hamlets. Fred explained he usually drove for Environment. He didn't normally do Energy. "Where to, sir?"

The Minister named the street next to the one where Ingrid lived.

Fred fingered his shiny cranium, as if checking it was still there. A wise move in a postmodern narrative. Then he put on his Chairman Mao cap and they headed off towards Battersea and the end of capitalism.

"You can drop me off at the corner. I have some shopping to do. Updick & McEwans herringmongers has some superb descriptions of bream and lobster."

"Very good, sir."

The chauffeur was looking at him rather oddly, the Minister felt. But he said nothing. They arrived at the corner he had suggested. When he got out of the limousine he tripped on something and almost fell over. He grabbed hold of the door frame just in time.

"You alright, sir?" The driver was still scrutinising him as if there was something strange about his appearance.

"Fine, thank you. It was nothing. Goodbye." The Minister looked at the limousine and frowned. Earlier it had seemed like a standard car from the ministerial fleet but now he realized it was much bigger. Surely Environment didn't get larger, better cars than Energy? He prickled at the thought of it.

The car moved away through the late afternoon traffic. The Minister glanced down, annoyed to see that he was standing on cloth from his trousers. Had he torn them? Now he realised *both* trouser legs hung slack. Perhaps his belt had broken. Perhaps that was why the fellow had given him such an odd look.

In fact it *was* the belt. He felt a bagginess around his waist.

Poffley's eyes narrowed. Strange forces were at work. The belt hadn't come undone. It was as if he'd grown thinner. His legs, too. His trousers were baggy clown's trousers, several sizes too big for him.

His shoes, too.

In fact all his clothes were too big for him. His hands had disappeared into his jacket. The sleeves hung loose like his hands had been amputated at the wrist.

Attempting to move, he almost tripped again. *What the fuck was going on?* Nothing like this had happened to any of the characters in those magnificent novels by Dan Brown. Whatever it was he had to get to Ingrid's. And fast. He could tell that people were beginning to look at him, like he was a street weirdo. He tightened his belt five notches. How slim his waist was!

As for his trousers: all he could do was roll them up to what would once have been his knees but now was no higher than his ankles.

His shoes seemed enormous, many sizes too big. He had a flash of childhood memory: plodding heavily about the house in his father's big shiny office shoes, as anchored by gravity as any deep-sea diver.

He was shrinking.

But the idea was absurd. It was impossible.

He had another memory from long ago. Watching *The Incredible Shrinking Man* on someone's portable TV. His student days, a naked girl, the letters of Engels, a trickle of incense.

Holding the girl close beside a monochrome flicker. The perfume of her meat rendering luminous the story unfolding itself across the room. A man alone in a strange, gigantic world. The black and white saga of an American husband reduced to battling spiders.

Wasn't it some kind of proto-feminist fable? He could barely remember. Anyway, what in hell did it matter? It was not relevant to his plight. The American, he remembered, had been doused in radiation. Poffley had left the girl in the morning. She'd wept. He'd abandoned her just as he'd abandoned his foolish dreams of revolution. He'd become sensible and moderate and sensibly flexible and moderately pragmatic. He'd forged links with business. Bondage. But he'd never been near a nuclear facility in his life. They'd all been privatized. They were nothing to do with Energy anymore.

The memory jolted him to an awareness of where he'd just come from. That fucking Collider. What if that red-faced piss-head scientist had been right all along?

No. Impossible. Believe that and you might as well believe in Lenin. As he had done, once, stupidly, when he was 16 and knew no better. Luckily a red-cheeked elderly Stalinist with a fondness for opportunism and apologetics had set him on the right road, to reformism, reaction and a rewarding career in the PLP.

He had to get to Ingrid's.

He set off on his epic journey to the next street, swathed in a giant's cast-offs. It was more like wading than walking. People were openly laughing at him. They were only lightly sketched generalisations but they seemed dreadfully real. Some were pointing.

His legs seemed to have grown shorter still. He tripped on his trousers and this time he fell.

"Penny for the guy!" a youth jeered.

Shit, shit, shit!

He felt a quick cold surge fill his Calvin Klein underpants with the contents of a dredger.

179

*

"Yes?"

Ingrid loomed above him in the doorway, her heavy German accent as adorable as ever. Or was she Swedish? It was so long ago he could barely remember.

"Yes?" the sexy young continental woman repeated. She scowled down at him. "What do you want?"

"Ingrid, it's me!"

She glared down at him and looked puzzled. She was struggling to remember her name. Was it really Ingrid? Or was that from an earlier draft?

The Minister realized how small he'd grown. She looked twice the size. His eyes were level with her waist. What fantastic breasts! They loomed above him as might a pair of perfect shining planets to an astronaut on a fabulous voyage of discovery.

"It's me! Andrew!" he squeaked.

He was shocked at the change in his voice. His heart began pounding, then became dolorous. He realized what it was. He wasn't growing smaller – well, not exactly. He was growing younger. He'd turned into a boy. A mere child. A nipper. A young tyke. His body was accelerating backwards in time, at speed. He clapped a hand to his brow: the wrinkles were gone. He fingered his scalp. The twin bays where his hair was beginning to recede had vanished. Momentarily forgetting Ingrid's presence, he unzipped his trousers and pulled aside the big, slack underpants. His pubic hair had vanished! His penis was pathetic! No bigger than his little finger…

Above him, Ingrid stared incredulously. "You dirty little boy! You are pervert. Go away ziss instant or I shall call ze pliss!"

"But Ingrid! Please! Listen to me! Let me explain!" he squeaked.

"I am calling ze pliss!"

She slammed the door.

It was like a wire had been pulled. A siren wailed instantly in the distance. He must have been reported by a postmodernist.

Shit!

180

The dredger emptied another load from the stinking depths off Canvey Island.

The Minister retreated to the gate. He staggered clownishly along the street. He had to hold the waist of his trousers almost up to his eyes in order to move. Shit oozed into his shoes. His shoes squelched. The smell made him want to puke.

He dragged himself to a plausible structure with steps out the front that led down to a basement flat. It looked closed-up and empty.

He fumbled and slithered his way to the bottom. He scraped off as much of the faeces as possible. Next he removed his heart from his sleeve and wiped his filthy palm there. Next he went down the steps. Next he curled up in the dark porch formed by the steps to the flat above. Next he had the sensation that a needle had got stuck in the groove of an outmoded narrative format.

His jacket was now big as a blanket. He pulled it up to his neck. The night came on. He felt small and lonely and miserable and lost. It was like the first time he'd stood for the council and lost by just 17 poxy votes.

He began to cry.

*

The Minister realized he must have dozed off. When he woke it was night. High above him ragged white scraps of cloud raced across a clear sky filled with stars and monosyllabic nouns.

Imprisoned by language he found it difficult to move. While he was asleep he'd grown even younger. His arms were chubby and tiny. So, too, his legs. He realized he'd pissed himself.

He wailed. He wanted comfort and kindness. He wanted help.

He wanted his mummy.

Language was lost to him. He could no longer articulate words. All he emitted was whimpers and glubber-globbers.

That was when he saw movement at the top of the steps.

An animal.

At first he thought it was a dog. The animal came slowly, cautiously down the steps, its nose alert for danger. Its tail was bigger than a dog's. In the streetlight it looked grey and lean and mean.

It looked like a wolf but it was no wolf. This was London, after all.

It was a fox.

The creature padded over to the Minister and glared down at him with hungry eyes. It pawed his jacket. The Minister glubberglobbered softly and felt the warmth of fresh piss across his chubby thighs.

The fox licked the Minister's face. It liked what it tasted. It raised one of its paws and slashed an opening in the Minister's plump pink cheek.

In the street above the traffic was as loud as always.

No one heard anything.

No one saw a dark shape at work.

The creature's back arched and its sharp, avid face bored into its prey. The rib and jaw muscles tightened as it splashed and feasted in the unlit porch.

If the thought fox could have chuckled, it would have chuckled. This was good. Very, very good. A bit greasy but it didn't really mind.

The Minister tasted even better than Kentucky fried rat.

42 Day's End

After the Minister's departure, the Director looked again at *Shakespeare's Sonnets*. They rested there with a reassuring solidity. He was convinced now that they had been there all the time. Their apparent disappearance was obviously some kind of optical distortion. Light shining on the observation screen combined with his own sense of stress, probably.

Then his face whitened as the book disappeared again. The blood of his bloodless existence was drained from him, yet he survived. And the book was gone. Just like that. There one moment, the next: gone. Vanished. Into undernourished air. The Director felt tired. The baseless fabric made his head ache. He needed an aspirin.

He went to his office, moving very slowly in the heat. The heat, yes. He hadn't been much aware of it before. Sure, the West Antarctic ice sheet was cracking up but that wasn't his fault, was it? He couldn't help emitting carbon dioxide, could he? He wasn't the only person who ate a tin of baked beans for breakfast, was he? The Gulf Stream didn't run through his fucking garden, did it? Heck, he needed his Lexus Model RX300 with 4-level air suspension, leather upholstery, air conditioning, 9 airbags, electronic traffic avoidance and 3 litre V6 engine just as much as the other families on the gated estate where he lived.

But Jeez, it was hot. The heat had the density of fabric. He tried to remember where he'd come across that word before. Only recently, was it? His memory seemed to be going, just as the heat was building up. Now hot air seemed to fill the corridors. Someone was broadcasting a speech on the environment by the Prime Minister. In an earlier draft he wondered where all the reporters had gone. Now he knew. To Whitehall, for the speech.

So hot. Stifling. Maybe the air-conditioning had broken down.

Nixon moved groggily towards his office chair. He needed a rest before moving off again. He sighed. What a bloody day! He'd cut himself while shaving, his wife's period had stained the bed sheet, someone had been beheaded in Iraq, and the abattoir had run out of water. But at least the Minister had opened the damned facility and departed without any major incident.

The Lund affair was as good as forgotten. The fellow would never be allowed on to the premises again. The board would surely back him on this. Gross misconduct, beyond any question. Shouting at the Minister like that. The man was a disgrace.

Strange how tired the prose felt. Watered-down interior monologue. It sapped the will to go on. He felt like an old man. It would be nice to hire one and humiliate him. Preferably a physicist. Nixon just about managed to get out of the chair. He went into his private bathroom to get some water to swallow the tablet with. Tablet?

Its mirrored interior gave him a terrible shock. He was hallucinating, surely. The bathroom was no better. In fact it was sick as crazy. The wiring was loose again. Plus there was a ghost in there. The ghost of an old man. Staring at him out of every mirror.

"Who the hell are you?" he demanded, watching the old man's lips move in synchronicity with his own words.

The Director raised his arm. Secretly he had always liked *Triumph of the Will*. "Now look here…" he began. But his words sounded weak and slow. The ghost mimicked his every gesture. He moved closer, just as the old man did. He stared hard at the brutally mottled face. Liver spots everywhere. That faintly repellent dappling of the elderly. The skin hanging in flaps. Drooping. A face cracked and fissured. A caricature of maturity. Ears stuffed full of disgusting grey hair. An eroded, incompetently shaved cliff face.

Except for those eyes. Eyes never aged. Despite the frame of sagging flesh, he knew those eyes. He knew it was *himself.*

The recognition, obvious to the reader, came to the character as a great shock. The voltage was strong and harsh as the prose and went straight to the heart. His reflection revolted him as much as if maggots had suddenly tumbled from his raw flaky nostrils. He pawed at the ghost, fumbling to hit it. He attempted to erase it.

He turned, disgusted. He heard himself fart. A screeching trumpet blast that seemed to mock his decrepitude and lack of control. His body had gone slack and helpless. He was a bag of wind. That orifice foully filled that office.

He felt revolted with himself, with everything. Time, like the working class, had finally risen up against the Tsar. His power was gone. Suddenly he was old and weak. His skin felt like paper. His whole identity felt fragile as a necklace of consonants and vowels. When he scratched his scalp experimentally with his fingernail a tiny shower of commas fell to the floor.

"Must, get, Lund," he grunted. His pig mimicry – oink! oink! - was superb. "Must, talk, to, him."

Everything was wrong.

He was dying on his feet. He looked and felt eighty years old. Not possible. But Lund was right. The accelerator had damaged time. Time was screwed. Time was accelerating. Time was running crazy. He needed Lund to sort it out. Only Lund understood.

The Director remembered the Sonnets, flickering in and out of existence. He set out on a slow, painful trudge back to his desk. He was worried he'd fall. If he fell he knew his bones would snap like polystyrene.

He made it.

But now his desk was different. It had rained a yellow dust. The powder was everywhere. It was like a sandstorm had hit the room. He could just make out the shape of the phone. It was a pale bulge in the sand.

He strained to pick up the phone. It had the weight of a brick. He could barely hold it with both hands. He called his secretary. "Get, me, Lund," he whispered. "At once. Bring him. Here." Exhausted, he let the phone drop.

A young woman bustled into the office. She must be one of the new secretaries, he thought. He didn't recognise her. She had a strange haircut with something colourful embroidered around the crown of her head. She was wearing a futuristic white shimmery outfit which emphasized her petite breasts.

When the young woman saw him she began to scream.

*

Lund could not be found.

Lund was gone.

"Lund's not here, sir," the paramedic told the Director. "Maybe he'll come visit you soon."

He was humouring the old man. The old man claimed his name was Nixon but it was not unknown for elderly Conservatives to reinvent themselves as dead American war criminals. Only the other day Ronald Reagan had walked in, looking very confused. Nobody knew who Lund was either. Nor was it clear where in the hell the old man had come from – possibly the upper circle.

The secretary said when she first saw him she thought he was a ghost. It was like he was made of glass. He was so pale, so thin. He kept saying he was the Director. Director of what? they wondered. He was obviously confused. The likeliest possibility was that he'd somehow managed to find his way out of an old folk's home. The poor old sod. He looked buggered.

As the paramedic kneeled over the Director he saw that the old man was dying. Even as he started to unbutton the man's shirt he saw the man's puzzled, anxious eyes bulge. The old, wrinkled body shook in a last spasm. It was like it was freeing itself from a narrative it could no longer control.

The paramedic laid the suddenly slack lifeless body back on the floor and spoke into his brooch.

*

The day was over.

The Minister's helicopter had long since passed overhead and vanished from sight. Crisp packets blew about across a vast area of crushed, flattened grass and mud. Pages from abandoned newspapers fluttered here and there like injured birds attempting smileys. An abandoned bottle glinted in the late afternoon sun. But though it kept signalling to the sky, no rescuers came. A little tear dribbled from the bottle's eye.

The last of the demonstrators had gone and the contractors had arrived to dismantle the lines of security fencing. A final convoy of police vans drove away up the narrow road out of the valley. The Collider staff had all returned home. The car park was empty. All the gates were locked. There was no one left but six security guards drinking coffee in a control room filled with CCTV screens.

The blood-red sun, swollen by heat haze, was beginning to settle over a darker haze that marked where the first draft represented the distant skyline of Tottenham. The only sound was the clatter and crash of security fencing being stacked up and the faint roar of Bach's St Matthew Passion from a blue Hitachi ghettoblaster.

A man driving a forklift truck shouted something to a pair of workmen who were lifting the panels one by one, freeing them from the connecting steel pins. It was a tranquil scene, pretty as a picture.

A thudding sound made one of the workmen carrying a fence panel turn and look. And a pair of hands fluttering and swooping across a keyboard made the words that evoked the thudding sound

186

and the fence-carrying workman turning to look. And a cerebellum conceived the QWERTY keyboard design and others conceived the technology that made possible the shining screen where the words were put. And the cerebellum that controlled the pair of hands was produced by sexual intercourse between a woman who'd worked in a toffee factory and a man who'd jumped out of the toilet window of a train on the outskirts of München, who'd met at a swimming pool. And they were evolved from marine amphibians. And the thudding resembled a drum – one of those African ones that some of the demonstrators had been beating on earlier in the day.

It was not a drum. It was an animal. An animal of a type none of those who turned to stare had ever seen before. At first glance it looked like a very large pig – a big, solid animal on small, muscular legs which the workers had seen in *Week-end*, edited by Agnès Guillemot and Odile Fayot. But it was more streamlined than that fat pale pig. And it was moving much faster than a pig can move. And unlike a pig it had a tusk protruding from its brow.

"Merde!" The workman realised that the beast was running towards him. Was charging him, in fact. Like it was a fucking rhinoceros, or something.

He'd once met a Zimbabwean who'd been charged by a rhino. The Zimbabwean said the thing was to stand still, not flinch and stare the rhino right in the eyes. The rhino couldn't handle people who did that. The rhino would put on its brakes, halt in a cloud of dust, then turn and amble away with an *only-kidding* expression on its armoured face.

Sod that. He ran.

He had no spare energy to scream or shout to anyone. He just ran to his van. Twenty metres, fifteen, ten.

He could hear the thunderous thudding, sensed its terrifying proximity. It was a sound he had heard on many soundtracks.

He tore open the door to his van, breaking some perforations in the paper. He jumped inside. He'd be safe there, inside language, in a paragraph of his own.

He realised what it was. A boar.

He'd seen a picture of one on TV only a few days earlier. On a quiz show for morons. But boars were extinct, weren't they?

187

Frantically he reached for the ignition key in his pocket; frantically he attempted to insert it. But his hand shook so much with fear he couldn't do it. Another spasm of déjà vu – the shaking hands with the car keys had been done so often in movies.

Boars are extinct. This is fucking unbelievable. If ever there was a moment for italicisation combined with an expletive this was surely it.

There was a shuddering crash which reminded him of a collision he'd once been involved in on the M25 – a stab of memory so aural, so shiveringly tactile, it brought to mind that sequence of books he'd once ploughed through when he'd worked on a farm outside - was it Oinville? Dedicated to Gaston Calmette, and conforming to the text of an edition revu et établi sur les manuscrits autographes par Pierre Clarac et André Ferré, if he remembered rightly.

The van's suspension lurched and the entire chassis shook, rattled and rolled. The boar's tusk punctured the door panel. In the first draft the tusk burst through "like it was passing through a sheet of paper". Over time the panel had thinned to what it really was. The tusk pierced the workman's right thigh and moved on to impale his left thigh as well. Every bone the tusk came into contact with splintered, broke or was dislocated. It tore through muscle tissue and sliced veins and arteries. Then the boar retracted its now bright scarlet and slippery tusk. As he died, Jason (for that seemed to be a suitable name for a mythic proletarian with an interest in blondes) could not help but think of the skinned rabbit in the murdering-of-the-mother scene in *Week-end*.

The boar snorted, beat its forelegs against the ground, then turned and scampered away up the valley, back in the postmodern direction it had come from. The workman's mates, who'd been staring in disbelief at the script, ran towards the van. Jason hadn't said anything, so hopefully he was okay, they thought, clinging obstinately to their realism.

As they approached the van they saw the windscreen. It was as if someone was playing a hosepipe against it from inside the van – a hosepipe that squirted blood and melodies from *The Wild Bunch.*

The first one to open the van door turned back and fell to his knees. He muttered a short prayer, crying out for help and

188

consolation from a humourless, white, elderly, bearded all-controlling entity presumed to hang out in some other dimension of the cosmos.

He was rewarded for his sycophancy by being struck on the head by a particularly painful hailstone. Next he was convulsed by vomiting.

A shower of wet, glittering sprats spurted from his gob. And then the thunderstorm began.

*

Sheltering from the torrential rain, the third worker dialled 999 on his mobile and called for an ambulance.

They did what they could for Jack (which was no help to Jason, who felt very neglected by the retention of elements of the original draft). One of the workmen reckoned you shouldn't move badly injured people, so they left Jack slumped in the driving seat. They put their coats over him and waited for the ambulance. It seemed to be taking forever to arrive.

Meanwhile the blood just seemed to come welling up out of Jack's legs. His face was chalk white, his whole body cold as ice. Things didn't look good. The style was EE (everyday/easy). But matters were much better for Jason, who was dead. "At least now I won't have to put up with the heat o' the global warming or the furious winter's rages!" he'd chirpily reflected while his vision dimmed and the ferryman kindly helped him aboard the gondola for a trip to locations used in *Don't Look Now*, followed by a sojourn on that distant isle.

The rain stopped, the thunder ceased, the sun came out. The workers linked hands and sang "I Can See Clearly Now". Then they brought the other two vans over, together with the fork lift truck. They re-assembled the security fencing, constructing a double circle of defences in case the loathly beast returned.

"Where the fuck's that ambulance?" somebody said.

That's what they all fucking wanted to fucking know. They were fucking shaken, fucking scared, fucking nervous. They might never have erections again (they didn't). That bloody animal must have escaped from someone's private zoo. That illegitimate personage deserved to be sued down to his last cent. Jack's life was screwed, that was obvious. He'd probably be fixed to a wheelchair for the rest of his days. Then, in the distance, they saw help arrive.

And stared in disbelief. From the disbelief direction, coming across the marshes, was a horse and cart. In the cart, which had a red cross painted on the side, was a nurse and an old man, the driver.

The nurse was a middle aged woman, wearing a nurse's costume that went down below her knees. She stepped down from the cart, scowling at them.

But before she could say a word, one of the workmen shouted, "Who the fuck are you? What the fuck's this? Is this some fucking joke?"

The nurse strode briskly towards him and slapped him hard across the face. "Wash your filthy mouth out, young man! And may the Lord God forgive you!"

She gave them a withering look from her extensive collection. "And what, pray, is the meaning of this?"

The workmen gawped. The old man in the cart stared back at them, goggle-eyed. Sharp went off to google. Next day he was back. One of the workmen was set in motion and mutely led the nurse to the van. He threw the paper door away.

To his amazement the driver's seat was empty. No Jack, no blood, no hole in the door. Nothing. Not even Jason.

A clatter made him turn. The letters on the keyboard were starting to fade from the daily battering Sharp gave them.

Jack was stacking fence panels about a hundred metres away. He smiled and gave a cheery wave. He was as unpierced as saviour who pops back a few days after his crucifixion to reveal, with a juicy grin, that he's actually a vampire, and it needs a stake in the chest to do the business, not nails in his bloody wrists or ankles.

The nurse said grimly, "I am in no mood at all for folly of this kind. I would have you know that I am Sister Sadie. I am a woman of substance in these parts. Let me say this to you. Extra-diegetic narratees are bad enough but to combine this device with blasphemy is intolerable! It is grossly irresponsible of you to waste the

190

responsible reader's time in this way! I shall see that Sir Hartley Harris is informed. I happen to know him well. He is a Justice of the Peace. Perhaps you did not know that. He is a great believer in whipping."

And then her eyes widened.

A dull, slow thumping noise came from the west, and they all turned and stared. "What a chapter of turning and staring this is turning out to be!" chirruped a bird [insert bird of your choice]. They turned again and stared at the bird. The bird sat on a nearby wire, gabbling in a language which could only be deciphered by persons of acute sensitivity. Then they turned and stared in the original direction.

From behind some trees which had not been there a minute earlier, a woolly mammoth emerged into view. It was gigantic, bigger than an elephant. As digital imagery went it was a lot more solid and plausible than the animals in *Jumanji*.

"Oh defecated human waste!"

The workmen turned and ran towards the Collider. But the Collider building had vanished. In its place was forest. And all around them, suddenly, were ferns. And the ground underfoot was squelchy and wet. Their feet sank into soft mud.

The nurse climbed back into the cart. It promptly tipped over, sending her and the old man flying into the ferns. She emerged, her white uniform copiously splashed with mud. "Sir Hartley will make you pay for this!" she shouted, shaking her first, her face red with make-up. And then she heard something move in the ferns beside her, and glanced down.

An enormous snake lay there, curled up, staring at her. It had two slits of darkness for eyes and a body about as thick as her own.

It began to move, like a drowsy penis suddenly alerted to the presence of a warm, nude female form. It hissed. A tongue like a slender glistening catapult of dark elastic shot out, then retracted.

Shaken shocked spattered Sister Sadie shrieked.

191

43 Rats

Buller drove home. He felt coldly satisfied with the way the day had gone. The demonstrators had failed to break through the police cordon. The trouble that there was had been contained. No one on either side had been killed or seriously injured. There had been fewer than thirty arrests, for public order offences. The Commissioner would be more than happy with the last four sentences.

But Buller was not a happy man. How could he be? His wife had melted away, like the others. It was beyond him – and so was she. He was used to a conventional crime narrative. His days were spent in the company of centripetal selves, not centrifugal elves. And worst of all, if he couldn't somehow find her – if she hadn't in some mysterious way returned – he would have to do something deeply humiliating for a man in his position.

He would have to call the police.

*

Buller left the garage door up. He decided not to go indoors straight away. He stepped back outside into the garden. There was acid in his guts he needed to quell. He wanted the sense of peace and tranquillity his garden and pond gave him. His carp reminded him of the existence of other, calmer worlds.

The blood red daylight had seeped away now. Venus burned brightly, low on the horizon. The goddess always grew depressed at dusk.

The evening had a soft, warm, velvety quality. Like a good malt, it was something to consume in slow, gentle shots. Buller breathed in the sweet fictitious landscape, which smelled of pines and freshly cut grass. He walked over to his pond.

The surface looked different, dappled with grey shadows that were not usually there. At first he thought someone had thrown rubbish into the pond. Then he saw that the motionless floating objects were all the same size, all shaped into the same stiff curl.

192

His heart churned so badly at first he thought it might have turned into an archaic container for milk on a nineteenth century Dorset dairy farm. Or perhaps he was experiencing the first thrilling electrical stabs of a full-blown cardiac arrest. But no cream was produced and there was no stoppage of his policeman's dull, conservative pulse. The words flowed on, and he knelt, shaking with shock and anger. He lifted one of the carp from the water. Guderian's glassy eyes gazed blankly back at him.

Dead, all dead. All nineteen fish.

There were streaks and patches of something on the pond surface; a faint aroma of something that smelled like methylated spirits.

His fish had been poisoned.

Someone had poured a toxic chemical into the pond.

Buller felt his bowels begin to burn and loosen. He hurried indoors, to the toilet off the utility room at the side of the garage. He tore down his trousers and pants, sat down on the bowl – and screamed in pain and surprise.

He was aware only of something vicious and small and frantic, something with razor sharp teeth that had its grip on his flesh. On his delicate familiar necessary balls! Something that had been crouched inside the bowl, a creature with malicious beady constable's eyes and whiskers, a fucking rat! Boring into his soft flesh, taking mouthfuls of testicle, he was being fucking crucified, he was in fucking AGONY.

Through a mist of pain and shock and monosyllables, Buller started to beat down on the rat with his fists, trying to smash it off him. In a moment of swelling horror he heard its long tail slapping and thrashing against the curving porcelain sides.

A solitary spray of blood shot sideways and splattered a small Cezanne reproduction that hung on the wall, framed by seashells. But punching didn't work, he had to reach down and grab the rat with his hands, feeling its hot squirming sleek body.

The rat snapped at him with bloodied teeth and mouth, ripping a patch of flesh from Buller's right wrist. Grunting and sobbing, Buller finally detached the rat from his bloodied, burning scrotum.

He hurled it against the wall. The rat slid to the floor, leaving a slug trail of glistening purple. It crouched there, evidently unhurt, eyeing him. Its tail slapped and flickered as if it was wondering what to do next. Buller clamped both hands across his crotch, protectively. Blood oozed between his fingers. He seemed to be on a high strange plateau of pain. He was in agony yet he was also detached and calm. The style was superbly realist. Then Buller heard the door open and turned to see if it was Angie.

But Angie was long gone. She was in a different dimension, now. Instead it was a woman he didn't recognise, yet felt somehow he knew.

She, evidently, knew who he was. Her hair was spectacular in its quantity, length and lurid scarlet colour. She looked a bit like a witch, he felt. "Buller," she said. "I've waited a very long, long time for this moment. I used to dream about it every day I was in prison."

Buller frowned. A gigantic force manipulated him. He was trying to remember, he couldn't. He was in such pain, such confusion. Such fear. Then the woman put a hand to her head and wrenched the wig off. Underneath it she had short, cropped greying hair. She looked much older, now. Old and worn. And then he remembered. Animal rights. She was that bloody animal rights woman he'd put away ages ago.

Marianne smiled. "I see you do remember, after all. Anagnorisis is essential to all conventional crime narrative, n'est ce pas? Though the genre is quintessentially reactionary. As Ernest Mandel remarked, Disorder being brought into order, rationality restored after irrational upheavals: that is what the ideology of the crime novel is all about."

"You killed my carp. You bitch! You killed my fucking fish!"

Marianne said nothing. It was as if she was enjoying the music of the residual alliteration.

"And I thought you were supposed to care about animals. Fish killer! Pervert!"

"To kill the thing a person loves best," she said at last. "I think that's the best revenge there is. And next to your fish I guess that like any man you love your Philip K. And your balls. Goodbye, Buller."

194

He was aware of her pulling something from her pocket. Fluff. A bus ticket for Bury St Edmunds. A gun.

At first he thought she was going to shoot him, but then he saw it wasn't a type of gun he recognised. It was bulkier than any gun he knew. Also there was a needle protruding from the barrel. A needle gun? He frowned. He was starting to overdo the frowns, he thought, but the director told him to shut it and just do as he was told.

"They use these in safari parks To sedate the animals, when necessary. Surgery, dental work. So it should work on a pig, I'm thinking."

She pulled the trigger and he felt the dart puncture his left arm.

"I've another little surprise for you." She stepped back out of the room and came back a moment later wearing a cowboy hat. Two melons were stuffed into her blouse. "Didja know Dolly Parton's most embarrassing moment was when she entered a Dolly Parton lookalike competition – and didn't win!"

Buller gawped like a gulpin.

Marianne went out again and returned carrying a large blue plastic crate. It was the kind of storage box they sell in home and garden centres, for storage. There were holes in the side, like she'd been practising on it with the tranquiliser pistol. From the crate came a squeaking, as if it contained working machinery that needed oiling.

Whatever was in the dart was working fast, Buller realized. The pain was gone from between his thighs. But his body felt stiff and sluggish and very heavy. He tried to stand up but couldn't. His limbs had been going to SWP meetings and had now gone on strike. His body was refusing to obey orders, which was out of character.

"I shall call the police," he said thickly. Or was it, in a thin, reedy, quavering voice: "I will call the thick police"?

Confusion, confusing.

Marianne laughed lewdly. "No, I think someone else will do that. To report finding a body. Or should I say *human remains*. For you, buddy, the jokes are over."

She opened the lid of the crate, tipped it, then stepped quickly back out of the room. Buller heard the key turn in the lock.

Out of the crate scampered a dozen more rats.

They paused for a moment, sniffing, looking around. They stared at Buller with interest.The bravest rat sprang on to his lap and looked up at him to see what would happen. Buller tried to shout but his lips felt paralysed, without feeling.

The rat moved forwards and took a quick, exploratory bite. Buller managed to make a muted, gargling noise, nothing more. His gullet glittered in the sunlight. The rat took another bite. The others, seeing this, could hold back no longer.

A moment later Buller was smothered in the creatures.

44   Driftings

Emma felt unwell. Not her usual self. More fictitious than expected, with a touch of fever. Her mind seemed cloudy.

She remembered losing the others in the crowd. Far, far more people had turned up for the demonstration than she'd been expecting. She wondered what had happened to Edgar. She caught a bus to Tottenham, took the tube back to Walthamstow Central. *THIS IS WALTHAMSTOW CENTRAL. THIS TRAIN TERMINATES HERE. ALL CHANGE.*

It was all she could do get across the road and into the hotel. She felt her way very slowly upstairs like a mountaineer low on oxygen. Opened with immense effort the door to her room. Crossed with immense effort to the bed. Collapsed on to it. Fell asleep at once, utterly exhausted.

A single bar of white space contains who knows how much lost time? Emma woke, still drowsy, to a room filled with raspberry sunlight. The atmosphere in the room felt thick as syrup. It was an effort to move. She was reminded of the big clumsy motions of an astronaut on the moon. Her movements were slow. Someone had drugged her in some strange way she didn't understand. Sweet flavours jostled on her tongue. She rested on her bed. She listened to music. She felt plubicious, and wondered what that coinage meant. It didn't appear to be counterfeit. Someone intervened with all nine Beethoven symphonies. She liked the Pastoral Symphony the best. It matched her mood. It washed over here, languid and dreamy. The slow movement.

Someone put a pillow behind her back and gave her books. She read all those big old Victorian novels she'd never had time for before. She lost herself in *David Copperfield*. She wandered through *War and Peace*. She completed *Vanity Fair*. She ate almost nothing. But sometimes when she woke there'd be a cup of hot sweet tea at her bedside. Sometimes a plate of bacon sandwiches.

She never saw who did this or cleaned the grill or put out the garbage sack in the wheelie bin. Like a prince of the House of Windsor, she never thought about it. Like a member of the proletariat who votes Conservative, whole sections of her thinking seemed to have been shut down. She found it difficult to make connections. One moment there were gigantic food mountains being set ablaze to keep prices high, the next famine in the third world. One moment there was global overheating and melting glaciers, the next a full page advert for a truly fabulous 4 X 4. One moment there was dampness on the ceiling and a huge rise in her rent, the next she was warned that asylum seekers had been stealing from her purse and gypsies camping in her garden. But she didn't have a purse! She didn't have a garden!

Her mind was emptied of Edgar Strobey. She had no past. She lacked curiosity about the state of things. It was like regressing to childhood. Someone benign was looking after her, attending to her needs.

She never went out. She was aware that something strange had occurred outside. There was no traffic, no people. She never heard sirens, now. Nor any trains. The trains had stopped running.

One morning she found herself at the window, not knowing how she'd got there. She felt lighter than air. It was as if she was a creature of consonants and vowels, arranged on a white rectangle. Portrait, not landscape.

She looked out at the derelict station. Ivy had started to grow up the walls. Tufts of adjectives sprouted in the tarmac of Selborne Road. As the weeks passed the colour green took hold and began to spread. Emma noticed ivy slowly climbing the walls. She told ivy to stop but ivy took no notice. Ivy was a good climber. Soon, leaves were framing her window. The window screamed it was innocent but it was put away. Soon it was like staring out from a tree house.

Though there were no people in Walthamstow there was plenty of wildlife. Birds sang. Poo-tee-weet! Poo-tee-weet! Poo-tee-weet! Once a tiger walked slowly past. And then the driftings began.

Emma knew she'd always been aware of the driftings. You saw them sometimes on sunny days. Out of the corner of your eye. A quick, yellow movement, like a flash of sunlight reflected from an opening window. A translucent swirl. A greyish blur where someone has just dropped out of sight behind a picket fence. Like a ghost passing by just outside your vision, slipping inside a wall when you turned to look.

A wall covered in cracks and centipedes. The centipedes scuttled out of sight, the cracks healed. Nothing was ever there in full focus. But the driftings grew stronger. They were scraps of text from earlier versions of reality. They were jottings from old notebooks. They were sudden impassioned scrawls on the backs of A4 size planning papers. On the other side of this world lay bureaucracies searching for order in a changing world.

"The opening hours are a time when a majority of people are at work or are not expecting the ambient noise levels to be low," a spokesman for the committee explained to her. "The use of matching roofing materials will help the roof extension to blend in with the character of the original narrative. The extent of impact on the surrounding area is considered to be negligible. All corridors give access to a remodelled real world. The site is within an Uncontrolled Postmodernism Zone and is therefore is unlikely to disturb the amenity of readers of Hornby model lifestyles, chicklit, bourgeois liberal realism and other commercial structures in this ancient heritage neighbourhood."

The committee ebbed.

New driftings invaded the old hotel. Emma began to see strange things. A creature from woodland myth, half naked, half swathed in moss, with antlers sprouting from its wild hairy scalp. It crouched on the table in her room, as if about to spring. It stared. It became wintry and bleak. Then it slowly dissolved, with six paracetemol.

Later that day she saw her own mother, who was dead. But it was her young mother. She was laughing and holding a bucket and spade. Emma moved towards her warmly. How happy her mother was! She was laughing proudly. She was with a child. The child seemed familiar. She realised it was herself. Mother and child walked through the wall as if it was no more than a projected image.

Emma followed them into the next room. They disappeared. In their place was a man in some kind of space suit.

He sat in a streamlined pod about the size of a car. It was made from a silver-grey substance, which pulsed and rippled like skin on something alive. Emma went towards the pod and touched it with her forefinger. To her shock her fingertip stung with heat. The man turned and said something sharply to her in a strange language. He shook his head. It was a gesture that had lived on for another ten thousand years of narrative.

A vanilla-coloured unicorn entered the room. It cropped the grass. Its horn was golden. The carpet was grass. A delicious-looking green. Tasty enough for a salad.

Emma yawned and went back to sleep.

Once, she woke up and saw herself. Emma stood at the bedside, smiling down at Emma. "You are just a simulacrum," Emma said. "The narrative needed you. Don't worry, in time you'll find out what it's all about." Emma smiled and left the room, and Emma went back to sleep.

She sensed that something had happened to set things free. Months had passed since the previous paragraph. The sun shone. Selborne Road had long since turned to a green waste of ferns and exotic palms. It rained a hot rain that made the jungle outside steam. Monkeys began breeding there. They chattered and screeched as they mounted one another, or hung from a single straggly hairy arm, staring at the orgy. There was only one season now: summer.

She was happy. She had all the books and music she needed. She didn't miss the others. She frowned. What others?

She tried to remember them. She had a dim sense of ghosts, scraps of threadbare voices. The ghosts had no names. They dissolved into mist.

One day she dreamed there was a machine which was a cross between a television and a typewriter. She typed a message on to the screen and the message was transmitted to a similar machine stationed in Scotland. But the television told her that the message she had sent could not be delivered. *This is a permanent error*, it advised her. It ticked her off for her folly, gibbering at her in machine language: XhwgtZWN0IGhpb SBjbcmlv ZC4gIEphbllbCB zIGhhbmR3cml0aW5nLiAgVkGhpcyBFnZSBzb2llIHByaWWlA it sputtered, in a metallic voice full of spikes and static.

Some days she saw flying saucers. High in the sky.

They spilled from the ribs of craft the shape of gigantic cigars. They cruised silently overhead. They knew she was there but they didn't bother her. She saw that there was nothing to fear.

One day she woke to hear the wail of a train. She looked out the window, saw a black steam locomotive huffing and puffing its way up the overgrown line. It was towing four brown carriages.

It drew into Walthamstow Central and stopped. Doors slammed and people got out. She looked down at the passengers. They were dressed in the fashion of a hundred years earlier. The women wore long skirts that trailed against the ground. The men wore waistcoats and stovepipe hats.

She knew she was seeing ghosts. The passengers poured out of a brick wall and moved through the waist-high grass. Then a man in a uniform appeared at the end of the platform. He blew a piercing note on his silver whistle and raised a green flag.

The great pistons of the locomotive began to turn.   Puffs of smoke boiled up from the train as it gathered speed. It formed a swirling spectral ribbon of smoke that curled and coiled, then ebbed into nothing at all.

One day she looked down into the street and saw someone she'd once known. She couldn't remember his name. Was he an old lover?

There was so much she couldn't recall. He didn't have a description. He was just an outline, cutting his way through the tall grass with a machete.

He looked up at her. He called out: "We must patch the membrane! Stop the flow!" He moved on and out of sight.

The next day she saw that the ivy was dying. The grass outside turned yellow. Patches of tarmac began to reappear. The sentences grew shorter.

One night she woke. It was three in the morning. She felt nauseous and ill. She knew something had changed, something was wrong.

She shivered. She felt sweaty. She lay there trembling, alert.

She could hear odd noises. Whisperings. Odd scuffling noises. Muffled thuds. Something was being organised in the darkness.

She felt afraid. Something was wrong. The room was grey and colourless. She pulled back the curtain and looked out on to a grey, dirty street.

Everything had returned. The tarmac, the litter. It was five in the morning. The street outside was empty. She opened the window and looked out. Further down the road a line of white Transits were blocking the road.

She looked the other way and saw that the intersection was empty. Along St Mary Road she saw more vans in the street.

Dark figures wearing baseball hats and carrying weapons clustered in groups. Men wearing boiler suits and helmets were gathering with their shields.

Emma yawned. She went back to bed.

Almost at once there was a new chapter, which started with the sound of a door being smashed down.

45   Parade of Ghosts

Crash!

They came in through the side entrance where Strobey had wasted the two Anarchs.

They battered down the front door and poured across the derelict reception area.

Scurr led his troops up the stairwell.

They rushed the empty bedrooms.

Aphrodite commanded the search of the ground floor.

As more and more of Finn's Hotel was searched, the adrenalin of the officers began to ebb. Everywhere was dense with dust and neglect and desolation and depressing adjectives. It was a place of emptiness. No one had lived there for years, that was obvious.

Scurr kicked a bedroom door open, his anger rising. A fucking waste of time, this was. And then he saw Emma. She was sitting up in bed. She looked frightened.

Scurr said: "Don't move. Armed police. You are under arrest."

Emma opened her mouth. She said something Scurr didn't hear. Her lips continued to move.

Scurr scowled. He moved towards her and seized her wrist. His fist closed on air. She faded in front of him.

He took out his truncheon. He battered the bed with it. Dust jerked upward, cloudily. He tipped the bed over, broke one of its ribs. He trashed the room. He ripped down the curtains. He was sick of tricks.

She was nowhere yet he had seen her. She was fooling him. He refused to be fooled. He trashed everything. He recirculated the dust. He whacked the walls. He walloped the wampum.

Aphrodite found him there. Scurr was flushed and furious. He was sat amid wreckage, on the brink of tears. He'd seen Emma with his own eyes, he knew she was there somewhere. Hiding. But he couldn't get to her.

She wasn't with the others.

*

They found the others on the fourth floor. The cops ran upstairs. They searched every room. Empty, empty, empty.

Then someone heard a sobbing sound. Faint cries, as if for help. The cops pounded upstairs.

At the top of the last flight was a wooden door painted bright. The lead cops had a battering ram. It was a sawn off telegraph pole, customized with a pointed steel tip. The brushed steel tip was scratchy and gouged with the memory of many broken doors. Six cops held the pole and charged the door. The bright panels collapsed. The door was wrenched from its hinges.

They burst through into a room of shining light.

A faint mist seemed to hang in the air beneath the banks of fluorescent lighting.

From out of the mist stepped the disappeared – an old, bewildered man, a black woman who was wearing an apron, a nude, shivering young woman whose skin glistened with water droplets. A tired-looking, faded blonde. Other spectral figures who stepped forwards from the mist and whose shadows took on human contours and colouring.

Somebody whispered, "Isn't that Buller's wife?" Someone else said, "Yeah, looks like her."

The disappeared approached the cops stiffly, suspicious, perplexed. Daisy Spenser put her jacket around the naked girl. "There, there," she said. "You're safe now. You're back inside a naturalistic story."

"Who kept you here?" they were asked, but each bit-part actor and actress was mute. Too overwhelmed to talk. Too deprived of dialogue to say a word. They were led away downstairs, to be asked questions that none of them would be able to answer, and to be reunited with their loved ones in an imaginary, unwritten subsection of the story.

Emma, who was standing at the foot of the stairs, frowned at this parade of ghosts. There is no fourth floor, she thought. "Who are those people? And why is the hotel full of police who are transparent?"

One of the transparent police was staring at Emma. It was Aphrodite, frowning across the dark landing at the faint outline of a woman. But the outline faded and she decided it was just her imagination. She followed the others downstairs, while behind her the stairs thinned and vanished, along with the fourth floor and the room of mist and shining light.

Emma watched the transparent policewoman fade into nothingness. She realised now she was just the same. She wasn't anybody, really. She was just a ghost, a fiction, a thing of scraps and patches. Someone had made her and used her in some way. Now she'd been cast aside as being of no further use.

Perhaps I never really existed, she thought. She looked down at her arms and realised she could see straight through them. Her entire body was transparent, in fact. She was just a pair of eyes, staring at an insubstantial world.

Her mind began to fold itself up, getting smaller and smaller. Her vision turned to a grey mist. She realised she was coming to an end. Her after-life was over. She was used up, over, finished with.

She shrank to a black dot. The dot turned white. She was nothing, now. A ghost gone into an Arctic white, in a world where the ice and snow was exactly 90gsm deep, and the texture of offset cartridge paper.

*

The door wasn't locked.

Aphrodite entered the room and glanced quickly round. A poster of Karl Marx on the wall, shelf after shelf of books. Political stuff, mostly. Placards with sticks on were heaped upside down in one corner. WORLD'S NUMBER ONE TERRORIST. BLIAR.

A floorboard squeaked as she went to check the filing cabinet in the corner. Aphrodite reached down and moved the scrap of threadbare carpet by the bed. She looked round for a tool, saw a wooden ruler. Slid it in the gap between the floorboards and levered the loose one up.

She saw the banknotes at once. There were hundreds of them, stuffed into the gap between the joists. She glanced back at the open door. Shouts and crashes came from all over the hotel.

Quickly she let the floorboard drop back into place. She replaced the carpet. She snapped the ruler in two and dropped the pieces behind the filing cabinet. What am I doing? she thought. Her pulse was going mad. Whish! Far calls! Coming, far! it burbled. She thought of Daisy, of Scurr. She knew exactly what she was doing.

Another officer appeared in the doorway. "Nothing here," she said. "Just a lot of books."

They went on to the next room.

*

The search was over. Everyone had left five minutes ago.

Almost everyone. On the second floor a muffled thumping and grunting came from the open doorway of one of the bedrooms. Aphrodite went in and found Scurr.

She looked at him, perched on a mound of bedclothes and smashed furniture. "Time to go," she said.

He looked at her with hatred in his eyes.

"No," he said. "Time to stay."

And from his back pocket he took out a knife. Scurr giggled. "It's a Sharp one. One poke with this and you're deleted!"

46   The Moor's House

Ben Scaravelli arrived at the junction of his desire. He was feeling good. He was in the mood for a swelling anthem. Mike Scott singing 'Love Anyway'. The Internationale. Yah-wooooooh!

Ben had been arrested, charged with assaulting a police officer and released on bail. His comrades would be impressed. He had form, now. He was just like Lenin and Trotsky.

He glanced for the twentieth time at the old photographs, wondering if he'd recognise the General. Ben knew he'd be visiting some time that afternoon, but he didn't know precisely when.

He set off along the street of terraced houses and banged the heavy iron knocker on the door of number 41. A pale-faced woman with a shock of dark hair opened it. Her eyes looked tired and strained.

"Please give this to your father. He's in terrible danger. Only these can save him." Benjamin held out the six pills in the palm of his hand.

"What are they? And who are you?"

"A sincere admirer. A friend. It would take a lifetime to explain. These are antibiotics. Only they can save him. If he doesn't take them he will die this afternoon. Of that I am certain."

"Are you a doctor?"

"Yes, a doctor! The General sent me. The matter is most urgent, believe me."

She nodded stiffly, like a nineteenth century woman. "Very well. I shall do as you say. If you are certain the General ordered it."

"It is what he wants, beyond question."

Afterwards Ben went back to the junction and waited. A little after three was followed by a quarter past, then half past, then several paragraphs of uncharacteristic realism, which began with a carriage.

It drew up outside number 41 and a tall, distinguished-looking gentleman stepped down. Ben hurried down Maitland Park Road after him.

The General had been worried for some time about his old friend's health. In the past two years Karell had suffered from an inflammation of the covering membrane of the lung. In search of fine weather and a cure for his pleurisy his friend had travelled to Algiers and Monte Carlo, to Enghien, Geneva and Ventnor. But by March his condition had worsened, and he was suffering from an abscess on the lung.

The same woman who'd spoken to Scaravelli earlier let the General in. She told him that the doctor had already delivered the medicine and told him that her father was in his usual place. Perplexed by her story, Engels hurried upstairs to the study. His old friend was slumped in an easy chair at his desk. Evidently he'd fallen asleep. Engels gave him a friendly prod in the shoulder blades. Marx started and sat up, giving a little grunt. "Eh? What's that?"

"It's me, Moor! Wake up!"

"Uh? Must have nodded off. What time is it?"

"Ten past three on 14 March 1883. You know you really should lay off the opium. It's all Trocchi's fault. I knew once you'd read *Cain's Book* you'd never bloody well get *Capital* wrapped up. If you OD and leave me to piece together your leftover manuscripts I shall be bloody pissed off. I can tell you. Opium's bad for you. It makes you look hideously old. Plus you're getting confused. Just say no."

"No. No can do. It's that blasted lung. Hurts like hell."

"Now what's this nonsense Tussy tells me about me sending a doctor with some special medicine? It's quite untrue. I hope it's not a plot. An associate of that damned Vogt trying to poison you."

206

"Perhaps I can explain," said Ben, stepping into the room. "Your friend, General, is in serious danger. If we do not act quickly he will die. I have read three biographies of Dr Marx and they are all in complete agreement about this fact. I have come from over a century in the future to tell you this."

"One of those damned time traveller chappies, eh?" Engels barked, grinning. He wagged his spinal extension and pumped Ben's hand. There was a rush of fine fresh enthusiasm. "Delighted to meet you, sir."

Engels's grip was firm and strong. Not a trace of Singapore or an old man's tremor. The slight shimmer must be the heat, Ben decided. "We really must get you away from here," Ben urged. "To a better part of London. Where the air pollution isn't so bad. As it happens I know the perfect place. In Essex. It's just outside London but it has two stations and you can catch a train into town any time. A pretty little place called Walthamstow. It's right on the edge of Epping Forest, and there's the Lea Valley. Clean air, and perfect for walks.'

*

And so it was that in May 1883 the members of the Marx household carried their belongings out into three wagons waiting in the street (one for the household goods, the other two for the Moor's books and papers). They trundled slowly off, to Tottenham, over the ferry bridge and on to Walthamstow.

They moved into a modest terraced house five minutes walk from St. James Street station. Here, in the invigorating atmosphere of Walthamstow, Marx's health made a rapid recovery. Engels came up on the train from Liverpool Street two or three times a week. It was almost like the old days.

Having been warned by Ben that he did not have much time, Marx got a grip on himself, enjoying surge after surge of serotonin. He chucked his Trocchis out. He gave up opium, and inside a year had worked furiously to complete volumes two, three, four and five of *Capital*, with a smaller 800-page appendix on the future of the novel under late capitalism.

Novels would, Marx predicted, grow more fragmentary, factual, allusive and reflective, expressing the alienation of the creative personality and the artist's engagement with the everyday capitalist realities of contradiction and the dialectic. Marx prophesized a great future for science fiction, which he described as the greatest of all the genres.

A few enigmatic late jottings appear to foresee a new kind of writing known as "past-modernism" (though the handwriting is admittedly very shaky and is open to various interpretations).

His life's work over, he instructed that the legend MARX HOUSE 1884 be inscribed upon the front of his house. "We shall compete with the lighthouse which I predict will be built just up the road in 1893. If those pestilential Pentecostal religious arseholes can have a false beacon for the proletariat, we shall give the workers a materialist alternative!"

Marx lived long enough to see the stonemason carry out his instruction. The very next day, on 22 December 1884, he died. He was buried in Queens Road cemetery, Walthamstow.

In order to confuse vandals and naive materialists who confuse biographical trivia with the essence of a writer's work, Marx instructed that, as a jest, after a suitable period of time had elapsed, a preposterous and grotesque statue ("I give special instructions that it should look nothing like me at all!") be erected in Highgate Cemetery.

MARX HOUSE can be seen even today. In 1925 Walthamstow District Council was very briefly replaced by a soviet of workers' deputies, who, at the suggestion of 'Red' Reg Huddle, changed the name of the street to "Marx House Road." This was subsequently amended during the Restoration by the Conservative administration of 1926, which altered it to "Markhouse Road", by which name it remains known to this day.

Ask at the local museum what MARX HOUSE means and they will tell you the house belonged to a Swiss watchmaker, a Mr Marx. He was so proud of his new house that he felt like putting his name on the front of it. 1884 being the date on which it was built. This is a fabrication put out by the Pentagon. After the revolution, when Ben Scaravelli is made Commissar of Culture, the red flag will fly over the museum, the truth will be told, and crocodiles of schoolchildren from across the land will troop to Walthamstow to learn and be inspired.

*

Ben laid the bunch of roses at the foot of the modest plinth in Queens Road cemetery, then mounted his bike and began to pedal away.

Coming round a half-moon curve his front wheel hit something and he found himself catapulted over the handlebars. He collided with a stone angel and a splash of orange light flashed across his vision.

The angel seemed to have been weeping and was tilted forwards as if weighed down by trouble. Ben stumbled back to see what it was that had brought him of his bike. It was a book, a big heavy hardback edition. *Alice's Adventures in Wonderland.* Inside, in faded copperplate handwriting, *To Ben from the General, with sincere best wishes for all you did for the Moor.*

Then a metal whirlwind roared overhead.

Ben looked up to see the white belly of a police helicopter. "Armed police! Throw down your weapon!"

The revolution had begun!

A throb of elation ran through him. More throbs followed as he swallowed another lyricism tab.

He picked up his Kalashnikov and began running through the forest of ancient gravestones. Grey puffs of dust peppered the graves as he ducked and weaved among the nouns and verbs. He was Ben Scaravelli, hero of the revolution!

He was invincible.

Forwards!

47   Hell hound on her trail

Forwards!

Aphrodite ran downstairs. The wooden steps seemed to have grown bigger since she'd walked up them. She had to take longer and longer strides. The text seemed to have enlarged itself since her first appearance. Or maybe it was the tropological qualities of the hotel.

The lobby was deserted. All the other police had gone. The dusty floor was patterned with a chaos of ribbed boot prints.

A dark skinned woman swigging from a bottle of rum sang

A Benky foot and a Benky leg
For Charlie over the water.
Charlie, Charlie.

But she was in another story. There is always another side, always. The woman wasn't there. The lobby was deserted. The dusty floor was patterned with a chaos of ribbed boot prints.

Scurr was just a few paces behind Aphrodite. She could hear his panting, almost feel his hot breath washing against the back of her neck. Hell hound on her trail, psycho slasher, fucked-up racist rapist copper. In terror, she ran from him. To terra, she ran.

The big door locked against her. A huge door. And herself strangely shrunken.

Scurr towered above her with his knife, his silver slicing angry blade. "Gonna. Cut. You." His words spat, his fury rampant. He had a granite hard-on. Was gonna cut her first, then give her one, give her two. Back and front. A total revenge, and some. For that shit she'd carved on him.

His breath spurting in quick short jets. A faint stale gush of ancient burger meat, dead minced cow smeared with a squirt of luminous mustard, a tidal drift of bad beer.

And Aphrodite aware of herself growing smaller, slimmer, younger. Like she'd been slipped acid. Like she was heading down to wonderland.

It wasn't possible.

She danced beneath the arc of his anger. She ran out of the room. She saw the smashed window, the stool. Shrinking, growing younger all the time, she climbed through. Ignoring the hot liquid fire when her calf dragged against the serrated glass. The blood pouring down to her tendon, into her shoe.

210

She hit the street running. She fled along Hoe Street. Her floppy clothes flapping. Her dark blue skirt close to her ankles.

Scurr smashed more of the glass. He clambered through after her. He tore his trousers. He muttered obscenities.

She heard his feet slapping the footway.

"Police!" he bellowed. "Stop!"

No one tried to help him.

Passers-by grinned. Or just stared from faces of stone.

Aphrodite zig-zagged through the shoppers. She was fourteen, going on twelve. She was young and fit. Scurr had the lungs of a heavy smoker, the sluggish limbs of a man who'd downed four pints at lunchtime. She was outpacing him.

Her breasts were not so much shrinking as *retracting*.

Weird.

*

Aphrodite was outpacing him.

She was a small, slippery shape flickering amid the passers-by like a slender fish amid slow swaying weed.

Scurr noted the lights at red, the stationary car, the solitary driver. A bald guy, podgy, sixtyish. Sitting in a blue Ford Fiesta at the lights on Hoe Street. "Out!" he said. He punched the man in the kidneys. The man gasped. His complexion turned to chalk. Scurr dragged him away from the wheel, dumped him on the road, scribbled some graffiti, climbed in.

The lights turned to green.

The car behind hooted at the man in the road to get out of the way.

Scurr pressed on the accelerator pedal.

I'll get you, bitch.

*

Aphrodite ran across the zebra. She skipped along the elephant's back. She ducked under a giraffe. Another zebra, flat out. She headed out over the huge piano keys. She'd go up Richards Place,

Browns Road, Milton Road, the alley at the end. Lose the psycho in the one-way system.

The Fiesta came at her with a low roar. She turned to glance at its dead eyes, its lunging bonnet. It locked on to her vulnerable skin and bone. Scurr's lips were drawn back, exposing his yellow teeth, his snarl. She could see his knuckles. They were white with the intensity of his grip on the clichés.

A micro-second later the fender smashed against her right shin. The bonnet slammed against her chest.

She was flipped upward, smacked against the windshield. The glass shattered. The glass subsided softly, then sprang back like rubber.

Aphrodite Cutter was catapulted over the car's roof.

A slow arc took her down to earth again. She hit the blacktop with a noise like breaking eggshells. She bounced and flopped, came to rest. One leg bent back against the knee. Her eyes shut.

Months later she opened them. A woman with ginger hair was leaning over her.

"Don't die," the woman said. "*Please. Please don't die.*"

She saw it was Daisy Spenser.

Behind her a girl in a yellow T-shirt was pushing her bike along the pavement. Aphrodite closed her eyes.

*

Scurr was on a roll.

He was hot as mustard.

He rocked.

He braked hard, hearing the long drawn out squeal as the blacktop grated the locked rubber. The windscreen was a frozen blizzard. He glanced back at the rag doll in the road. It looked like it was beginning to leak. He laughed.

He lit off up Richards Place while the zombies were beginning to assemble and gawp. No one followed. Fucking stupid zombies. Paralysed by their curiosity.

Turned right, then right again. Across Hoe Street to Hatherley, then through the back streets back to Finn's. It was derelict, after all.

He'd hang out there until the suspense plot had blown itself out.

48   A Woman Again

Scurr done a bad thing to Aphrodite. Aphrodite want revenge. Aphrodite know she have to kill Scurr. Where Scurr? Him in Walthamstow. Somewhere.

"Excuse me, little girl. Where do you think you're off to?"

The hospital orderly towered over her, smiling. He held up a hand like an old-fashioned traffic policemen directing cars.

"To get Scurr, of course."

The orderly frowned, and she realised he was a replicant. The machinery shallowly implanted beneath his face but deep in the fibres of his mental processing.

"I don't know who Scurr is," the replicant responded, in a hollow tone. "But you mustn't leave the ward. You really mustn't. You've had a very bad accident, you know. In fact you shouldn't be out of bed at all. I'll take you back and tuck you in, then go get you a nice sleeping pill."

Aphrodite was tired. She was in no mood to hold a debate with a replicant. "Listen, buster, I'm leaving. And I don't want no fucking sleeping pill. That asshole ran me down. It's payback time."

The man's face registered shock at her language and accent. The kid was only ten! It was disgusting, the way standards were falling. He blamed television. "Now listen, missy. You are going straight back to bed. And I'm going to give you a little injection to put you to sleep. You need rest. And I shall tell your mother about your rude word. Believe me, I will."

"Fuck you, fatso." Aphrodite darted between his legs, reached up and squeezed hard.

The man let out a screech of agony, doubled up and slid in two halves to the floor.

"You. Little. Bitch," he wheezed.

He had a malfunction of the valves and damaged wiring in his chest. Aphrodite followed through with a quick chop to the back of his neck. He fell silent, head lolling over his chest, dreaming of

213

pork, which was how security found him ten minutes later.

Aphrodite split. She was growing stronger all the time. Bigger, too. The splits joined together with automatic resealing fluid. She slipped out of the hospital grounds and began jogging through Banal Suburb.

*

Aphrodite knew she had to arrest Scurr. Attempted murder, that's what it was. She came over the ridge, fast. The sunlight hit her cheekbones. She flinched at the burn, eating into her skin. It felt toxic.

A shock. Ahead of her, everything was changed. Walthamstow was gone. All she could see was forest. It sloped down from the ridge towards the distant river. She tried to remember its name but there was a hole in her mind. The notes are not consecutive, they go on and on, like a tapeworm, a soft enchanting simple enticing devilish voice seemed to whisper.

Behind her were broken cities, smoke bubbling up from wreckage. A confusion of inexplicable images. Her ears still seemed to hold a memory of colliding metal and shrieks. But now the sky was clear and calm, the crunching machinery and human pain switched abruptly off. Now she could hear a blackbird, piping its song.

The bird came shooting out of a nearby tree, making her start. An old trick, that. She wasn't falling. She refused to go back to the beginning. She was sticking to 48.

Sceptically, she scrutinised the bird. Its trajectory was too kinked, its wing movements too stiff and slow to be plausible. The song sounded pre-recorded.

Aphrodite tried to remember if the nurse had told her about the blackbird but there was a hole there too. All she knew was that it was important to go on. Scurr was down there somewhere, going about his business. Unaware she was locked on to him. Unaware she was returning from the dead.

The forest below looked massive, emerald, unreal. Its mass was matched by that of the vast blue sky above. She tightened her eyes,

214

tried to focus on the faraway river. It slithered and shone. Its soft simple outline seemed to go fuzzy, then snap back into wiry focus, then blur again. Maybe it was her eyes, the sunlight, the burn, exhaustion. She hurt inside. The pain was there in her cheekbones, plus deep behind her eyes. Plus in her shoulder blades.

Her shoulder blades dripped pain. She could feel the individual drops as they trickled down her bone structure. Pain was yellow in colour. Her ribs were dripping. Drop after yellow drop. She could see this quite clearly. Plus the bigger drop that was snaking its way down her spine. It was pear-shaped and scabrous. It scraped each vertebra in turn with steel brushstrokes.

She clenched her right fist and switched it off. She was whole again. She didn't hurt now. A dove was distantly coo-cooing. Aphrodite felt at peace. Her familiar old self had returned. It had been on a long voyage but now it was home again. She'd fixed herself with a number 26 at 72 on 33rd but she'd taken the cure and had just gotten through. She was a woman again, no longer a little girl.

A woman in a strangely altered world. It held a slight shimmer, a faint vibration. Tiny currents pulsed through everything like specks rotating before her eyes. Abruptly the currents ceased. Solidity returned. Matter shrank to twists of black ink. Scenery collapsed into an alphabet and shaped itself in a new form. Black holes imploded into tiny black dots. They scuttled to the ends of sentences and crouched there, not moving.

The ridge she was standing on was some sort of tumulus. A structure from a lost age of iron. A giant grass-covered mound which rose out of the forest like a bare island surrounded by a sea of gently-rippling language. At first the immense forest seemed unbroken. Then she saw the finger of smoke, some distance away to the south. A tiny drift of blue smoke that soon lost its outline and colour and melted away. That had to be the hall. Aphrodite didn't waste any more time. She skipped down the steep grassy embankment and plunged into the forest.

*

215

Twenty units later she emerged from its ultramarine depths in a cloud of thought bubbles. She imagined a road and one appeared. It took another five units to reach the hall.

The road was narrow and uneven and deserted. It sloped downward between the trees, rutted with hoof marks and the imprint of cartwheels. Aphrodite jogged along the strip of dusty grass in its centre. It was cool in the shadows cast by the trees.

Ahead of her a yellow band of sunlight slashed the shadow. Another band, out of sight, played Weezer covers. The butchered shadow marked the junction with a side road. Aphrodite skipped through a blaze of light. She took the new road.

A sign flashed past. *To Skye*, it might have read. *To Skaz*?

It moved too fast. She wasn't sure.

Two hundred metres further on Aphrodite saw the hall. She tried to remember its name, why she was going there.

The hall was set just back from the road. It stood alone, hemmed in by forest.

There was space at the back; a lawn, a big ornamental garden with rose-smothered arches and diamond-shaped flowerbeds lurid with primary colours.

The hall was three storeys high, timbered, isolated in a handsome paragraph. She counted a dozen windows. It was a rich person's home. A horse was tethered to a post by the front door. A spectral drift seeped from one of the tall brick chimneys.

Aphrodite glided along beside the hedge that fronted the house. At its centre was a brick gatepost. She reached it and stopped. Her heart was grinding inside her like a piece of frenzied figurative language. She felt hot and giddy. She reached out to steady herself on the gatepost.

This place was Thorpe Hall. A poet's house. The one who'd written *A lovely nutbrown face is best of all.* A line she treasured.

A pair of huge plausible earthenware pots slumbered either side of the front door. Passing between them she could smell the pungent scent of opium. She was in the wrong place, but what was the right place? She couldn't remember.

The door was open, so she stepped inside. A big hairy dog loped across the dark interior towards her and sniffed her. It decided she

216

was worth a quick lick. Then it went back to the fireplace and settled itself by the fireside.

She rose in slow motion up a narrow flight of stairs and passed along a short corridor, not touching the timbered floor or the rushes strewn there. Through a doorway she saw a man bent over a desk.

She leaned over his shoulder to read what he was scratching on a sheet of paper. "Where I *was* tomorrow is where I *am* today, where I *would be* yesterday," was not what she read. The paper was brown and the sheet was much bigger in size than modern paper. *From my poor house at Walthamstow in the Forest the second of January 1575,* he'd written.

Then the author became aware of her presence and turned to face her. The poet looked tired. Hardly surprising, since he was 471 years old, though by gas dweller standards he was a mere infant. But though haggard and wary, it was a kindly face, she imagined she thought.

The man was wearing a preposterous white ruff which pressed up against his chin. He looked like a turkey. "Oh," he said. "It's you. I thought it was Ralegh. He said he'd be here by nightfall."

"Ralegh?" Aphrodite scowled. *Who the fuck was Ralegh?*

The poet scanned her mind and decided to shoot some fact. "Walter Ralegh. Sailor, explorer, historian. And poet. My stuff influenced him a lot, you know. He pilfered some of my best rhymes. Not to mention my mission statement. *Tam Marti Quam Mercurio* – 'both for Mars and Mercury'. Meaning: *I fight for the god of war but I can write like an angel.* I love his epitaph. He wrote it himself, you know. I know it off by heart. Hey, cool cat, let me recite it to you. Forget Keats and Lenin and Khan. Of all the material cited in this text I think this is the funkiest:

Even such is Time, which takes in trust
Our youth, our joys, and all we have,
And pays us but with age and dust,
Who in the dark and silent grave,
When we have wandered all our ways,
Shuts up the story of our days:

217

And from which earth, and grave, and dust,
The Lord shall raise me up I trust.

"It's too bad he's going to have his head cut off in 43 years time. By the way, what *is* the time?"

Aphrodite looked at her watch, then saw her wrist was bare. She remembered the nurse had removed it after the crash. She swayed, feeling giddy again. "It's Scurr I'm looking for. You haven't seen him, have you?"

The poet didn't answer. He wasn't there. His foolish dialogue had gone, along with the desk. The brickwork crackled like electricity. A white flash jolted her backwards, out of the vanished house.

She swayed on the tarmac pathway, beside a grass verge which held in its trembling clutch an empty bag of Golden Wonder. Instinctively she reached out for the railings beside her. Cops like bars.

Someone flicked a switch and the soundtrack changed. The silence of the forest was displaced by a three-second screech of Shostakovich, a few plangent chords of Damien Rice, and then the distant hum of traffic. A car came past.

The house, the forest, everything was vaporised. The road was wider, surfaced in asphalt. It was now lined not with trees but parked vehicles. Where there had been nothing but forest there was now a sprawl of allotments. Rows of terraced housing sloped away back up the hillside.

She realised she was standing on the pavement outside a red brick primary school. On the corner of a nearby side street an Asian shopkeeper was standing in the doorway of his shop, staring. Slightly suspicious of her.

Aphrodite wriggled her shoulder blades and clicked her body back into Ostensibly Real Time.

*

It seemed to be her day for meeting writers.

A carriage pulled by four horses stopped beside her on Forest

218

Road and a plump, jolly-looking man with a red face and a smart brown wig offered her a lift. His face seemed familiar. She wondered if they'd met at a crime conference.

She climbed aboard. "Thanks. Don't I know you from somewhere?" The coachman tapped his whip on the flanks of the front pair of horses and the carriage moved off. Aphrodite was surprised by its discomfort. It jolted and shook and reminded her of being inside a machine at a theme park. The structure creaked like a ship at sea.

The man introduced himself. "Sam Pepys, ma'am. Always happy to help a charming lady who requires assistance. Now my dear, I'm not going to beat about the bush. I'm sure you'd like to earn a shilling, wouldn't you?"

Without waiting for a reply he tugged at his fly. A small dun-coloured penis flopped out. (She'd seen bigger. Much bigger.) He beamed at her. "I want you to give me a little squeeze, my dear. Until I spend myself. That's an easy way to earn a shilling, isn't it?"

His breath smelled like old cheese. Pepys spat into his right palm and began to massage his lubricated member. Slowly it began to enlarge itself.

"Go fuck yourself, you dirty old pervert," Aphrodite retorted. She clenched her fist and brought it crashing down on to his crotch.

A greenish pallor flooded Pepys's cheeks. He bent in pain and began to retch. Aphrodite opened the door and jumped out. The coach must have been going at about ten miles an hour. She hit the footway, stumbled past a red pillar box, and managed to stop outside a shop selling second-hand filing cabinets. She watched as the coach clattered away in the fast lane, its great wooden wheels silently rotating backwards. Then it melted away and became a petrol tanker.

*

Further along there was a lay-by with a bus stop. She waited behind a longhaired young man for the next 123.

"Have you been waiting long?" she enquired of the other prospective passenger.

"For all eternity, ma'am. Despite her enticing name, Fanny would never let me have carnal knowledge of her. She broke my heart. I was reduced to whores, ma'am. And caught a dose, of course. Now I consume mercury for my sins."

"You poor fellow. What did you say your name was?"

"John Keats, ma'am. You know, *Season of mists and mellow fruitfulness* and all that jive. I come to Walthamstow often. My poor sister lodges here. I declare she is almost as wretched as my poor self. Tell me, frankly. What do you think of my work?"

"A cop's got no time for poetry, buster. Except in television drama."

Keats frowned. "Television? Pray, what is that?"

"A device for transmitting moving images. In its own way as synthetic as your bogus early nineteenth-century dialogue."

"Quite so, ma'am. Quite so. Now if you'll pardon me."

"Don't tell me. You're going to cough and splutter and spit up some blood."

"Quite so, ma'am."

But they were interrupted by the arrival of the 123. Aphrodite climbed aboard and pressed her Oyster card against the yellow blister. The gigantic machine began to move. Aphrodite sat down and strapped herself in for the centuries long voyage to Walthamstow Central. As the bus pulled away she realised that Keats was still standing at the bus stop. She gave him a wave and he grinned. Just three more and he'd have enough for an ocean!

No: delete, delete.

He held up a bloody handkerchief and feebly gestured back.

49   Muscle Action

Scurr dozed for a while on the sofa in his flat. He woke to an itch. An itchy ass. A torment of tiny flickering needlepoints. A ring of fire.

He unzipped, pulled down his pants. Felt between his legs for that little dark wrinkled button-mouth.

Scurr fingered its grease, its warmth. He raised the fingertip to his left nostril, sniffed his own intoxicating odour of faecal decay. Went back once more and scratched again. Sniffed again. It was better than drinking in glue. He'd done that as a teenager. Glue was metallic and muzzy and left him feeling sick. This was different. This was a perfume of the earth, of darkness, of dung and perversity. He could sense sorcery, a devil crowding the fetid gloom, urging him on. Promising graveyard delights, unimaginable foulness.

He felt his innards shift, felt and heard a quick sharp trumpet spurt of gas from his anus. The tumbling of half-digested food in the soft, misshapen vat of acid that was his stomach. He could picture the gases bubbling, the blocks of disintegrating food bleeding a froth of air.

The itch wouldn't go away. The prose style was driving him insane. He shivered, wanted to howl. It was all too distracting. Normally realism gave him easy, lazy dreaming. Big soft women told him he was sensitive and clever and a fabulous lay. The sex was delicately narrated, yet graphic. His nudity excited him, made him hard. Not now. An itch like this he couldn't contemplate jerking off. No solace there, his dick was pitiful and wrinkled.

He scratched and scratched the place until his forefinger was tipped with bright wet scarlet. This was madness, torture.

The tumble of broken-down food in his guts was getting worse. He could picture it, a sludge of onion, carrot turned to a soft orange mould. Biscuit pieces with the texture of sodden tissue.

He had his pants off, he was lying there on the sofa, three perfect spots of blood dappling the pale surface. The gut-twist sharpened, it happened, he felt the thrust, saw it happen. A sudden stabbing pulse of sensation in his ass, then the snake's head shot out.

It came out straight and hard as a stick. A slime-shiny tough muscular brute, a bright red he thought might be his blood but wasn't. Its scaly body segmented with delicate black lines. With a convulsive flick of its tail it was born, his baby. At once it changed. Its slender straight body shivered into curves. It raised its head between his legs like the parody of an erection. Two slit eyes regarded him blankly. The snake gave a slight hiss. Its tongue flickered out, sampling the fetid air. Then it slithered off the sofa on to the carpet. It made for the TV. A slime trail smeared the screen as it flicked across it and jumped to the shelves above.

Scurr saw the blood dripping there. It was oozing out of the row of cheap paperbacks on the bottom shelf. The snake dipped its slender head into the mess and drank greedily.

Afterwards it turned and gave Scurr another of those cold, hard stares. Then it flicked itself off the shelf, shot across the floor, and vanished under the door.

*

Scurr remembered the letters carved on his buttocks. He reached for the scabs and scraped a few more flakes off. He felt a wetness as the wound re-opened. Fresh blood was on his fingertips. He'd dealt with Aphrodite Fucking Cutter. Now all he had to do was find that bitch Daisy. When he did he was going to punish her. Punish her, day after day after day. Punish her with his fist, with his knife, with his johnson. Especially with his johnson. The very thought of it made him harden. Drool trickled from one corner of his mouth; he sucked it back.

Scurr put his clothes back on. He felt cold and sweaty. The clichés had given him a hangover. Hair o' the dog, eh? He went into the kitchen and found a can of beer. He tugged the ring-pull, slurped it down. It tasted warm and stale. What maddened him was the way things had changed. He didn't really understand how or why. He just knew they had. There were blanks and confusions in his mind that had never been there before. They were barriers to finding Daisy. He had no idea where she was. It was all he could do to remember her face.

He went down the stairwell and out into the street. He almost slipped on a dead baby. *Another fucking dead baby*, Scurr thought irritably, kicking the flabby object aside. There was another one at the kerb. A dog was tugging on an intestine. Its head was tipped to one side as it gripped the grey ribbon of tubing. The ribbon

222

stretched like rubber. A revolting stench of old meat and shit and rottenness poured into Scurr's nostrils like a fluid. He could feel the stink spreading inside his head. He shook it, to clear the mist.

Scurr walked past the dog. He walked on through dirty, empty streets. He felt dizzy and ill-at-ease. From behind the wooden sheets of the boarded-up Burger Bliss he could hear the screaming of a woman being tortured by the Government Anti-Dissident Squad. Scurr wondered why anyone would want to oppose the Government. Didn't they know how dangerous that was?

Further on, by the new post office, the bodies of many dead Arab children floated by. They were about two metres above pavement level. Once Scurr would have wondered what kept those stiffs afloat but now he was past all that. He just wanted to get to the Paradise Disco, fuck a blonde in a cubicle, have a shot of hip-hop-happy-hooby-hoo-ha, and go back to his apartment, get more sleep. *Dead bodies*, he thought. *They're everywhere these days.* He remembered a time when there didn't seem to be any.

At the very end of the street a man with a bright red face was on his knees, staring at a thistle. He was obviously drunk. "Dee-ye-ken-Jimmie?" he shouted, incomprehensibly, to no one in particular. In fact he seemed to be addressing the thistle. Scurr wondered maybe the guy thought he was speaking into a microphone.

"Mack!" the man added. Then he sagged forwards, crushing the weed. He lay motionless.

Scurr went across to the fallen figure. He rolled him over on to his back. The man was a number nine. He stared up at the sky. He didn't seem to see Scurr. His face wore a look of extreme happiness. Scurr took the man's wallet, then kicked him in the head until the cunt's eyes were wide shut.

Scurr walked on. He took a piss against the window of a dress shop. He heard the sound of a bass beat. He reached his curtained destination. He danced a while, found a lean blonde, had her the way he liked, had his shot. Went home.

Slept.

Next morning out there by the kerb: a few grey bones, like bits of a discarded chicken.

*

Scurr was once again on a roll. He was clean and pure as butter. What a day! He was feeling good. He was king o' the world. He was cruisin' for a bruisin'. He hummed the latest number one:

I can see
That you an' me
Is gonna be
In eck-stah-seeeeeee...

He walked the streets. He was looking for trouble. He was pleased when he found it.

"Stop right there, sunshine!"

Scurr stood in front of Strobey, making him stop. His eyes burned. "Open the bag."

"Why?"

"Because I fucking say so."

Strobey groaned. His legs and back were purple with bruises from the beating he'd received at the Collider demo. He'd managed to get back to the hotel, only to find it empty. Strobey knew he had to get back to the Collider and destroy it. He had his flute tucked into a sock and was carrying a blue sports bag. It contained his remaining supplies of vanassium. He held it open.

Scurr rummaged in the bag and picked out one of the packets.

"Oy, oy!" he honked. "What's this, then?"

"I wouldn't touch that if I were you."

Scurr sarcastically echoed him.

"I really wouldn't. It will hurt you. It burns. It's vanassium. On a ten second setting. It's lethal."

"That's a new one on me." Scurr smirked maliciously. "I've never heard of van-whatsit. Good is it?" He raised the packet to his face. Before Strobey realised what he was about to do he'd put his tongue out. The soft pink wet tip touched the erasure dust.

Scurr didn't have time to scream. The dust ate away his tongue and began to bore its way down through his throat. The Detective

Constable's only reaction to what was happening to his body was written on his face. His eyes flashed puzzlement at the violence of the realism, then shone with fear, then swelled with agony. They bulged out like marbles, red veins stretched against the whites. The dust formed a tiny toxic inferno, a plummeting needle. It cored out his torso in three seconds. Blood rushed into the gap, came out of the burning hole between his legs.

It had all happened so fast Scurr was still standing. Adjectives and similes spurted in every direction. It was hideous – but also (to all who hate cops) hilarious. Scurr looked like he was a woman, pissing a jet of scarlet fluid. Muscular spasms contorted his ash-grey face, stretching the skin tight, dragging his mouth open. The gums of his teeth were bloodless and taut. He looked like a skull. Muscular spasms raised his arms.

Then he fell.

He was clinically dead. It was the harsh muscle action induced by verbs which kept him jerking and shuddering. Then holes began to appear across his uniform and his chest and stomach collapsed. By the time the cut-out kicked in, the pool of meat sludge that had formerly been DC Scurr was unrecognisable as something which had once been inhuman.

Strobey thought: *Well, I did warn him.*

50   Soft Layers

Marianne looked out of the window. At first she thought Selborne Road was flooded. At third she realised it was now a river.

Finn's Hotel stood alone in a lush meadow. There were no other buildings, just fields and hedgerows, and, far to the west, the bare, sloping hills of Stoke Newington. Cattle grazed in the fields. It was a bucolic, unreal scene, like something from before the Great War.

A boat came into view in the distance. Marianne could shortly hear singing. "So Long, Marianne", was it? It was a rowing boat, containing four people. They were talking, laughing, occasionally breaking into song. She smiled as she realised that her smile was at the start of the sentence and that in the boat Emma was at the front. Her nipples were hard as tiny pebbles. She waved gaily at Emma's

225

svelte form. Edgar was behind her, rowing. Ben was sitting on the seat at the rear. He held up a wine bottle in one hand and waved at her with the other. She felt a pang of jealousy, and wondered why she'd not been invited to accompany them. The pang pricked her again and she swatted it with a copy of *Time Out*. She wondered who the woman with long blonde hair was, sitting opposite Ben. Only her back was visible.

There was a new burst of laughter, as if someone had exploded a balloon joke. Marianne felt a flush of anger. The plumbing of her jealousy was bust and she was emotionally drenched. She had a paranoid suspicion that the joke was about her, that everyone was looking at her, that someone was planning forcibly to expel her from the warm, gently humming world of a sunlit screen into a harsh foreign land of paper and poor sales, where she'd wind up on a shelf, her spine touched by no lover, her jacket never opened, neglected and lonesome and growing yellow and dusty with age.

Benjamin looked very drunk. He stood up and began bellowing. His bull impersonation was superb. So was his cock. And so was his Albert Finney act. "My name is Blackstone," he slurred. "William Blackstone. Frontiersman." He winked: "A bit of a big fish in these tranquil waters, eh?" He began to sing

Row, row, row the scow
Gently down the stream!

But there was nothing gentle about his demeanour. He swayed, as if about to fall in, but regained his balance.

He threw the empty bottle at a duck. She hated him for that. Then he pulled down his zip and urinated into the river. Marianne flushed with rage at the thought of him with his scow tied up in the canal at Flushing, without her. The casual way he was exposing himself to the blonde woman was repellent. The blonde herself seemed quite unperturbed by it. Her plump shoulders shook with laughter. Everyone in the boat seemed to think that Ben pissing was quite the wittiest thing imaginable. Then he sat down, his limp member lolling out of his open fly.

226

The rowing boat was now level with the hotel but showed no signs of pulling in to the small wooden landing stage below. Instead Edgar rowed on by, in the direction of St Mary's. Afterwards – coming, ready or not! - he thought he'd head to Shooter's Hill and the sign to Ypres, then on to St. Anton and San Anton'. After that, go back to Pittsburgh and count up to thirty.

The blonde woman looked up at Marianne and stared right at her. With a stab of perceptual knifework – horror - amazement - Marianne saw – realised - recognised - that the woman was *herself*. Her duplicate in the boat looked up at her, and tore off her blonde wig. She raised her arm and pointed up at the hotel window.

"Murderess!" she screamed. "You killed that security guard! He had a child, who was taken into care! His mother died of cancer! You will pay for your crime! Watch out for the tumbler!"

And then her face developed a network of fissures, her complexion went from a dull yellow to an dirty white. Her short cropped hair turned to silver bristles, then dropped away. Marianne of the boat was now a bald, wrinkled, drooping old crone, with twinkling malicious eyes, every inch a picture book wicked witch. Ben had fallen asleep. Strobey rowed east as if nothing untoward was happening.

And Emma had vanished completely.

*

Marianne woke at dawn. Something was making a tiny tapping noise in the room. In the grey light she saw that there was an upturned glass on her bedside table. She knew it hadn't been there when she'd turned the light off five hours ago.

She stared in horror at what was inside the up-ended tumbler. Who had captured this monstrous thing, far worse than any poisonous spider?

The cancer scuttled around inside its glassy cell, looking for a way out. It was a pale reddish phenomenon, faintly slug-like. But unlike a slug it had scores of tiny legs. They whirred in agitation, running in a narrow circle. The body looked like the dark slimy inside of a throat. It was exploring where to go next. She felt

227

frighteningly vulnerable. She sensed it eyeing her through the glass.

When it arched its back against the walls of its tiny prison it left a smear, like a bloodied finger. It wanted its freedom. It wanted out, in order to be in. It wanted release from that hard, transparent prison. Freedom to crawl up her leg, or along her arm. It would settle on her skin, then submerge. It would sink between her veins and arteries and nest in the soft warmth of a muscle. Then it would begin its business. Empurpled, with piles, it would eat her up, feasting on her until she died.

Marianne shuddered and ran from the room. An earthquake tried to trip her as it played the bare floorboards like piano keys. Even before the door had closed she heard behind her the terrifying sound of glass shattering.

She ran.

*

Ben did not return until next morning. Marianne woke as he opened the door. She remembered a frightening dream. Something about a trapped insect.

Ben came in noisily, as if he was still intoxicated.

"Enjoy the river trip, did you?" she said, aggressively.

He looked at her blankly. "What?" he said.

"In the boat. With the others. On the bloody river."

His eyes widened, forced open by the enormous pressure of an old narrative convention.

"What boat? What river?"

She dragged back the curtains, and winced at the bright light. She pointed. "That fucking river."

He looked out, shrugged. "I don't get you," he said. "There's no river. And besides I've been with Marx and Engels. I am guilty of nothing except a banal shrug."

She looked beyond him. Traffic was moving up and down Selborne Road. A surge of people came out of the Walthamstow Central exit, as if a tube train had just arrived.

"Hey, look!" Ben said. "There's Edgar. I wonder where he's been." He frowned. The pressure was still high. "That's funny."

228

"What is?"

"Two black men. They look like heavies. They seem to be chasing him."

*

Benjamin said he was going to go back to the Collider to try and find out what in hell was going on. Marianne said she'd go too.

A pair of sharp shining machetes appeared beside their walking boots. They cut their way through lush, billowing adjectives to the end of Selborne Road. Some weed-draped ruins by what might once have been the junction with Palmerston Road were probably the old multi-storey car park, Ben reckoned.

They chopped their way round the back of it and came to a narrow path through the jungle that seemed to mark the route of the old High Street. They followed it between dense, lush overhanging trees until they came to the marshes. Ahead of them, a thistle-bordered path threaded its way among the reeds.

They came at last to the River Lea, much wider than when they'd last seen it. Someone had constructed a crude, narrow paragraph containing a wooden bridge on stilts. When Marianne stepped on to it the entire structure creaked with implausibility. "I'll go first," she said. He protested, but she insisted. He did that, but she did this. He underlined the words *at the portal*, *congeries of facts* and *beyond words and in a mystical way*, but Marianne erased them with a rubber and laughingly blew the gritty remains away.

She made her way cautiously across the next paragraph, gripping the thin noun slung between trees either side of the river. She had almost reached the far side when she heard shouts and cries behind her. Looking back she saw what looked like tribesmen dressed in dirty furs. They were chasing Ben along the embankment. His foremost pursuer had a bow and arrow. The tribesman halted and took aim. Marianne screamed. It seemed impossible the man could miss. Ben turned, saw, and without hesitating, dived into the river.

Its muddy brown surface barely rippled as he plunged into its depths. The seconds passed. He did not reappear. She wondered if he was hiding under the bridge, as people being chased often are in

229

adventure stories. She wondered if the primitive tribes of the Hackney marshes ever read the bestsellers on sale in W.H. Smiths.

The tribesman with the bow had turned it in her direction. Once again, he began to take aim. She sprinted off the last two metres of bridge and hurled herself into the dense jungle. Bushes with waxy green leaves bigger than rhubarb plants slapped her face. She ran on, making lewd suggestions, hearing yelps and shouts in the distance. She kept going, crashing onwards through tall grasses and tunnels of overgrown vegetation, until she was exhausted by the over ripe style. She crawled into the black heart of a vast flowering bush bigger than the biggest rhododendron. Inside, beneath the outer layer of green leaves and purple and white flowers, it was dark and wiry, and the ground was carpeted with a soft layer of dead, dark vegetation and sickly sweet-smelling clichés. She lay down and curled up and waited. She wondered if Ben would ever emerge from the previous paragraph.

Once she heard a faraway shout, then nothing. Only later did she become alert to the sounds of the jungle. Birds released long, liquid, repetitive calls that were answered by distant warbling. Once, something scampered through the branches overhead. Something else – a lizard, perhaps – scuttled past in the dark shadows, slapping a small brown tail.

The next day Marianne found her way back to the river, led there by a strange force. The tribesmen were gone and there was no trace of Ben. She followed the riverbank, heading inland. For days she met no one. There were apples and bananas on the plum trees. Deer came and looked at her. Coconuts thudded to the ground. The sun shone. Music from classic Walt Disney cartoons played from amplifiers in the trees. She kept on, heading worstward ho, into the postmodern interior. She was smiling like a newsreader. She felt happy at all the narrative attention she was getting. She felt a slow phosphorescence in the fabric of her reality.

That was the last time Marianne ever saw Benjamin Scaravelli. Still wearing a dreamy smile on her face she was abruptly ejected from the text.

*

230

Aphrodite took one last look at the lambs. They tottered on spindly black legs, clustering around their mother. She smiled and gently shut the wooden door to the shed.

On the far side of the meadow a light had gone on in the kitchen of the small stone farmhouse. She could see Daisy moving around in there. Beyond the farmhouse lay the thin strip of water that separated the little island from the mainland. It was a rich, royal blue in the last light of day. The setting sun had turned the dark granite cliffs a warm bronze colour. A few waves slapped gently on the rocks by the shore.

Neither of them had ever regretted what they'd done. They quit the Met and discovered their talent for raising animals, growing courgettes and melons and making gruyére in a cheesy modern woman's romance. On this island off the coast of Finisterre they were self-sufficient. There were ample stocks of cliché to see them through the harsh winter that lay ahead. Tomorrow Aphrodite would take the dinghy across the strait to the little pier and the lock-up where they kept the 2CV. She'd drive to the market in the quaint little town of Piat d'Or, where they sold their produce. They made enough euros to keep going. Plus there was the money from the hotel. It seemed like an eternity ago. She'd gone back with Daisy and they'd taken the lot. It had made them feel excited, dangerous. Sexy. The deserted hotel was a turn on. They stripped off, made love on the bare carpet, banknotes fluttering all around them.

Smiling at the memory, Aphrodite breathed the fresh, clean air and set off across the meadow to the farmhouse.

*

Benjamin woke with a headache. The headache looked a little shamefaced as she pulled her clothes back on. She leaned over the bed and kissed him lightly on the temple. "Stay cool," she grinned, as she skipped away, out of his room, out of his life.

His throat felt like it was full of specks of river mud. He tried to cough it away but it stayed. He sipped some water from the glass at his bedside, but it made no difference. In the end he used the

231

vacuum cleaner attachment. *Slurrrrupppp!* – and the dust was gone.

Benjamin remembered fragments of a strange dream. He'd gone to see Karl Marx, and then he was in a cemetery with an automatic rifle, and then he was on a river. There was an embankment and a London Underground sign. On a plastic chair a mad-looking woman with a pen wrote *Double up now double up. Look sharp.* But already the details were going, cut to pieces by the sunlight pouring in the room and by his waking into full consciousness and by the delete button.

He looked out the window. Selborne Road was empty. Weeds sprouted around the derelict station. Letters were missing. **WALT C AL**, the sign read. He glanced back at the empty bed. He wondered what had happened to Marianne.

Tumbleweed blew by. There was sand in the air. It formed on the window ledge. It was yellow and pure. He remembered a bay in Dorset. His long ago childhood. A helter-skelter. Swings. Another life.

A man swaggered into view below. It seemed like he'd just stepped out of Finn's. Below, Benjamin could hear the sound of a honky tonk piano, the sound of a crowded, noisy bar.

The man wore leggings. A cowboy hat. The leggings flapped. He had a belt slung around his waist, holsters. Another cowboy appeared. They squared up to each other, forty metres apart. They drew. The noise of the shots reverberated. It sounded like frying popcorn. The first cowboy went down into the dirt. A dark stain spread across his back.

The victor strode away. Selborne Road was deserted. The corpse slowly began to dissolve. Soon it was completely gone. A jaunty unseen orchestra began playing the theme from *The Magnificent Seven.* Ben's pulse quickened. He felt brave. He wanted to go out and save the population of an exploited third world village from the predatory gunmen of capitalism. He dreamed of a final stand. He wanted to take a score of fascists down with him, like the man at the end of *For Whom the Bell Tolls.* He wanted to do a whole lot better than Ché, whose politics were lamentable. Fuck Ché. Ché was an empty pin-up. Serious revolutionaries had Lenin on the wall, not a Latin American playboy.

232

More tumbleweed blew by. It reminded Ben of breakfast cereal. Gigantic balls of shredded wheat. Faraway over Tottenham he could see a twister. It swayed its way through an estate. Tall buildings began to disintegrate. Rectangles of panelling winged across the streets, then fell to earth amid a flurry of minor debris. The sky beyond was the colour of a livid bruise. Mauve cumulus leaked egg yolk. Style shone everywhere, like a coating of syrup.

Ben leaned further out the window. He could see a pile of bodies in the bus station. A hand protruded stiffly in a Hitler salute. There must have been thirty or forty corpses. Birds wheeled above, on tiny bicycles. Occasionally they darted down to take a quick, nervy peck at the dark flesh. The bodies were those of Indians. They all had red bandannas around their foreheads. The stench of putrefaction from split entrails drifted his way. The newspapers were full of stories about a cannibal who'd eaten the brains of one of his victims. *The streets and the grey buildings around Victoria depressed me*, he read. Benjamin flinched, dipped back into the bedroom. He'd read somewhere that flinching was something to do with Norwegians at Whitby. Whereas dipping involved gravity, slumping, reaching the depths.

He dragged down the old heavy sash window against the earlier drafts. One of the greasy ropes snapped. The window fell like a guillotine. It slammed shut with a heart-rending crash. The air seemed cold and congested. A song played. A woman with a sore throat invited listeners to take another little piece of her. Mud, shock gel, breathing difficulties. Fragments of ancient valentines.

Benjamin turned. He was used to being spun round and made giddy by dope. He was suddenly aware there was a man standing there in his room. Plump, elderly, looking a bit like a Victorian bank manager. But on his waistcoat he wore a large yellow smiley-face button. It read: HENRY JAMES, and underneath, in smaller letters, FAMOUS NOVELIST. Ben said aggressively, "You never mentioned the genocide. All those dead Indians. Why not?"

The novelist had his thumbs dug into the pockets of his grey striped waistcoat. Henry James shrugged. "It didn't seem important. It wasn't what interested me."

"You're so fucking complacent. If you don't mind me saying so."

233

Henry James nodded gravely. He seemed unperturbed by Ben's abuse. "You may say so. You may say anything you like."

Henry James had grey skin, grey eyes. He began to dissolve. He became a portly outline. The outline turned to little more than a line of dots. The dots began to change position. They re-shaped themselves. Ben realised they were time particles. He'd studied the science at school. He tried to remember the formula but all he could see was his old quantum physics teacher, Rosamund Einstein. She was a tall dried-up spinster. Once she'd been beautiful but now she was craggy and lined like she was made of limestone. Her face had the faintest dusting of blonde hair that you only noticed when she fell under the scrutiny of bright sunlight. She pointed at the blackboard with a cane. Numbers were scrawled there.

"And that is all you need to remember in order to pass your examination," she said. Then she burst into a star shaped silver incandescence, like a firework. Benjamin's eyes swam with a vision of sparks. The water was cold as the Atlantic. The sparks turned black and became time particles. They re-formed, making a much taller man than the novelist. The dots joined up. They became the firm outline of a tall, bearded man. The man took Ben's hand. He squeezed it. His hands were hairy and mottled. "Tell him to go on!" he cried. "He translates by phenomena, which is nonsense! Point out that the dotted lines are to be kept in the text!"

An ambulance wailed past below. A wash of blue rushed across the room, erasing the bearded man. Ben brushed the back of his hand, getting rid of the pressure of the bearded man's firm grip. He tried to drag the window up but it wouldn't budge.

Ben went to the next bedroom and opened the window there instead. Dust showered him like soot. Cold air rushed in, smacking his skin. He leaned out and looked down the street. The ambulance had halted by the bus station. A yellow digger was loading dead Indians into the back of the ambulance. Paramedics in green struggled to close the doors on the corpses. The legs were giving them trouble. The bodies were rigid as iron bars. In the end they managed it. The ambulance did a U-turn and came back past Finn's. It turned the corner on to Hoe Street. It went out of sight.

Ben guessed it was heading out to the Lollard pits in the barren lands at the edge of Leyton. That was where they usually dumped the disappeared. He sat down. He poured himself a glass of Glenfiddich. He turned on the TV. Shining happy people shone happily. They shared their excitement and amused pleasure. Things were fantastic! Fabulous! Great! Truly terrific! They laughed. They chattered. Trailers were trailed. Commercials popped his brain.

Benjamin zombie-watched. He put the world out of mind. A shining happy weather girl appeared. She told him there was a deep depression heading his way. This revelation was sponsored by the Washington Energy Corporation. A row of merry cartoon cats sang a jingle. *It's so eee-zee with WEC, eee-zee, ee-zee with WEC!* They were displaced by a sombre middle-aged white man in a suit. He exuded gravitas. He spoke like he was making a major government announcement. *WEC*, he said. *Bringing power and light just when you need it most.*

It was at that precise moment that the grid failed, plunging Walthamstow into total darkness.

51 Power Gone

Strobey sat alone in the empty train. Luckily it was at a station when the power went. He wished he'd noticed which one. Leicester Square? Charing Cross? What line was he on? He'd been too deep in his book to notice. *For a long time I have felt that writing which is not ostensibly self-conscious is in a vital way inauthentic for our time* he read, as the brakes were applied and the train emitted its conventional rumbles of indigestion with added hissings.

The doors opened, no one got on. The doors closed. And all the lights went out. The train's throbbing engine cut out. Blackness everywhere. And silence.

The driver must have abandoned the train and fled, like God when he saw Nietzsche coming. Strobey knew there was no point in waiting for help to come. There was no point in praying, either. You were only praying to yourself. Religion was just jerking off your mind. It might make you feel good but there was no one else involved. When your ship started to sink it was better to know that the lighthouse was an automatic one, there was no one there watching through binoculars, organising a rescue, running down to the boat shed. No help would ever come. Just a lonely crowd of beaming metaphors and similes.

The doors were shut. He tried but he couldn't force them apart. If he'd been able to wedge something into the join it might have been possible. But he had nothing. The only way out was through a window or a wormhole.

He removed a shoe and used it as a weapon. He smashed the heel against the glass. Nothing happened. He had to batter the pane repeatedly before he heard a cracking noise. He ran his palm over the surface of the window, feeling for the crack. He found it and aimed his shoe there. He began to beat against the panel with increasing fury.

A fragment fell away with a tinkle. Soon he had made a bigger hole. But beyond the first panel lay a second sheet.

It took him over an hour to batter a hole big enough to allow him to squeeze through. He went through feet first, praying this wasn't one of those curving stations like Waterloo on the southbound Bakerloo line, where there was a perilous gap between the platform and the train.

He landed clumsily and tripped on something bulky. A body of bad writing. He managed not to fall. The floor was sticky with blood or spilled juice. Whatever it was he moved hurriedly away from it. He held out his arms like a gassed tommy in the Great War. His fingertips touched the back of the platform. He felt his way along the tiles, hoping it wasn't a urinal. He came to the entrance to a cave. His footsteps echoed in the emptiness. Steps led upward. He followed them.

Someone screamed faraway and the echo of it whispered its way down the stilled escalators and the windless tunnels where no trains came.

*

236

Strobey walked across the enormous mosaic surface. The abstract patterns of square and triangular tiles were broken up by miscellaneous images. There was a red London bus, the face of Winston Churchill, some clouds. The clouds shimmered slightly as he looked at them, as if on the surface of a vast jelly. But the ground beneath his feet was solid as stone, his footsteps crashing out loud and clear. He found himself stepping over the image of a serpent. He smiled, realising it was a representation of the Loch Ness monster. Then the mosaic ended and he walked up some steps into a vast, deserted gallery of paintings.

They were renaissance masterpieces and they bored him. Chubby naked cherubs with wings fluttered around the shoulders of muscular bearded men in cloaks. Chariots, trees, spiky mountains against blue skies, reminding him of the cover of a Jackson Browne album. A pink, plump woman with an enormous torso was exposing her left shoulder to a leering satyr with hairy buttocks. Various bland Madonnas clutched various small, banal Jesuses. He remembered how as a child he had been shown a similar picture and had asked why Jesus had a dirty omelette floating just above his head. How everyone had laughed! Everyone except himself. Then he remembered it was one of the false memories that Januschka had generated for him. He remembered he was not a native of this planet or this time. But his memory of this awareness was fading, he sensed it. It showed he was coming to the end of his time.

If he did not find Mirando Mirando soon he would lapse into an earthly coma. He would continue with his identity as Edgar Strobey, never knowing he had ever been anything else. He was aware of these confusions massing like clouds above this great gallery, while inside he hurried on through a dreamy labyrinth of paintings.

A door opened into a wrecked office. The nameplate read INFORMATION SERVICES. A filing cabinet lay on its stomach. Its mouth had vomited a swirl of A4 sheets.

A woman with dark trim hair lay on her back in the wreckage, naked from the waist down. Her bruised legs were spread wide, like scissors. She didn't move. Her pale stone face was puffy and blue. Black blood was congealed across her chin. A pair of flies waded in

237

it, quenching their thirst. She had to be dead. The language had no mercy.

"Fuck YOU!" a voice bellowed behind him. He turned. It was a man, a dishevelled drunk. His shirt flapped down over his baggy trousers.

Something else: the man had a hand gun.

The drunk raised it, grinned stupidly.

Fired.

A strip of lighting overhead shattered and went out. Shards of fine thin cream-coloured glass fell like snow. Went tinkling across the polished gallery floor.

Strobey ran.

In the Titian room someone had the biggest painting down. A group of youths stood around the great canvas like it was a urinal. Pissing on to it. Watching them, Strobey felt a slight ache in his bladder. Later. He retreated from the gallery and went on.

At last he came to the painting he was looking for. "The Hay Wain" by John Constable, R.A. He read the words on the plaque, which contributed nothing to his understanding of the canvas. It was much bigger than expected. And the painting more ragged and impressionistic. What in reproductions seemed precise and compact now seemed smeared and rippling with movement.

Perhaps it literally *was* moving. It seemed to ripple, like a curtain blown by a sudden draught. But it was just the time membrane, passing through the fabric. Strobey, looking abstracted, looked again. His eyes retracted from their long stalks and focused on the figures in the painting.

He remembered a Nether Time movie he'd once seen on the vidscreen in his cubicle at the Library of All. A girl was abducted and locked inside a painting. She remained there, looking mournfully out, growing older, until one day she turned grey and vanished. He shivered. Voices could be heard faraway. A fragment of a speech by Margaret Thatcher briefly played, then cut off in mid sentence. What a foul, vile old witch she'd been. Her honeyed tongue stuck deep up the threadworm-writhing anus of the Chilean torturer. And now there was a new soundtrack, like that of a football

238

crowd, released from the stadium after their team has lost six nil. The voices sounded angry and vaguely malevolent.

Strobey walked over to the corner to get away from the stench that seemed to rise up from those words "Margaret Thatcher". He sat down on the chair for the attendant, who was lying on the floor in a puddle of beetroot juice.

Now the voices were growing louder and nearer.

Moments later he heard the sound of running footsteps and moments after that a mob burst into the gallery. It was made up of young bearded men; red-faced, perhaps drunk, wearing loose baggy clothing like caliphs in some Arabian nights' fantasy. They went straight to the Constable and began manhandling it from the wall. Somewhere far away an alarm began to shrill. The great golden frame fell to the ground with a crash. One of the men tumbled to the floor, howling in discomfort and clutching his knee. The mob began stamping and kicking the canvas. With a cry of joy someone managed to break through the canvas. "Joy!"

Putting someone's toe in the gash, someone helped someone to enlarge it. Others joined in, shredding it with their hands or knives. By now other paintings were being torn down and trashed. Then the crumpled, jagged canvases were snatched up and taken away. The mob ignored Strobey completely and ran off, leaving him in a room of empty and broken picture frames. A few shreds of painted canvas lay on the immaculate floor. He made out the wheel of the hay wain and slipped in into his pocket as a souvenir. Then he left the building.

Returning across the mosaic floor he went out into the open air and realised where he was. In front of him was Trafalgar Square. The day, once bright, was now heavily overcast. A raw, acrid smell stung his nostrils. He realised it was smoke. Smoke everywhere. Smoke boiling up from the square below, where half a dozen bonfires burned. The nearest two seemed to consist of paintings and gilt picture frames.

On the far side of the square lay a pair of ninety degree angles and beyond them a road filled with overturned vehicles belching fire and thick black oily smoke. Strobey realised the buildings surrounding the square were also on fire. *This was even better than the great poll*

239

tax riot which brought down Thatcher! someone had typed in italics on a scrap of paper which drifted slowly past at eye level.

Strobey descended the stone steps. Half way down he passed a man squatting, with a dreamy expression on his face. The man was naked from the waist down. His legs were covered in thick black hair. The man was defecating on the step.

Nearby, a couple were having sex on the pavement.

Strobey walked past them and down into the square. Many of the revellers seemed to be drunk, were waving bottles or swigging from them.

"What giant propensities she had!" one of them leered, quoting Charlotte Brontë.

Strobey went on into Whitehall. Opposite the banqueting hall lay the bodies of two guardsmen. Their faces were smashed up and blackened and one of them had lost both eyes. A big dark pool of blood spread around them across the paragraph.

The gates at the entrance to Downing Street were lying buckled.

The Prime Minister's residence was a crumbling inferno. Big hot pieces of burning debris came floating down through the air, crackling. The cenotaph had been sprayed with words for sexual intercourse, excrement and a puckered orifice.

As Strobey was approaching Parliament Square there was an explosion and he saw the statue of Winston Churchill disintegrate before his eyes, and vanish into smoke. A great whoop came from a vast crowd on the grass.

Parliament, too, was burning. Strobey suddenly grinned. There was his housemate Benjamin Scaravelli! Ben was below his bigger namesake. He was standing on a makeshift wooden platform, addressing a substantial crowd. A sound system boomed out vast, distorted words. *Lution!* he heard. *Ling class!* "Hey, Ben!" he screamed, waving an arm. "It's me, Edgar!"

The sound system died. Scaravelli stopped in mid sentence. He glared across the silent crowd to where Strobey stood. Strobey felt a sudden sense of foreboding. This was reinforced by the music on the soundtrack – quick sharp inbreaths of violin.

Everyone had turned to stare. Strobey became aware of his *difference*. He was wearing jeans and a T-shirt but everyone else

240

was in a strange baggy Arabian nights' costume. Ben brought the microphone close to his lips again. "Over there, comrades! A class traitor!"

A dozen turbaned youths approached Strobey. One was waving a broken bottle. Why had Ben said such a terrible thing about him, he wondered? It was unreal. A scene from a nightmare. *Any moment now I shall wake up and this genre writing will stop. Any moment now I will look back and see that it is not Ben at all, it was never Ben. I am dreaming all this.* His guts burned with clichés and very short sentences.

Strobey fled past Portcullis House and on towards Westminster Bridge. Shouts behind him alerted people ahead of him. Strobey saw a line of baggy-panted men form a line across the bridge. He was trapped.

The men ahead of him looked implacable, their arms folded, waiting for him.

Behind him the mob drew closer.

He had no choice. Either be beaten to death by a crazed mob or jump.

The river below seemed a sickening distance away. At least three vomits. It was like jumping from a plane. He wondered how high you had to be before impact with water made it like hitting concrete.

"You is gonna DIE!" shrieked the nearest youth, his eyes avid with murder, an extraordinarily large dagger in his hand.

Strobey jumped.

52   Slipstream

The dark surface of the water rushed at him like a wall. The waves were lashed by a strong wind blowing in from the west. Strobey felt his skin cracking. The skeletons of thesauriosaurs formed a pattern across his closed lids. A harsh, papery whiteness filled his brain. The thesauriosaur bones collided and splintered into C8IAAAwc CAAAV QgAA DgLAAB MCw AATQs !!!!!!!!!!!AA M8LAQAA ByaWF0Z SBiZ Whhdm lvdXI gYm90aCB3a XRoaW4gdGh! Banks of lights flashed, alarm bells went off, went silent, darkness, just the whistle of the wind. This is what it must be like to be in a car crashing head-on at a hundred miles an hour, he thought. Nausea piped through his tubes, a greenish burning swelling soup.

He hit the river.

The water wrenched at his clothes as he plunged down, down, down. His trainers flicked away like scraps of paper. His T-shirt was dragged off by a maniac. Fingers of cold stone tore at his jeans, the whores of death, trying to snatch them away. His face felt as if it was being pummelled and punched by a score of enraged assailants. Down, down, down he went, into the darkness and the cold and the mud.

He rested. He dozed.

Though his eyes were open he could see nothing.

It was dead of night. A cold liquid fog obscured everything. His lungs felt squelchy and old. The shock gel had an odour that reminded him of hair lotion mixed with disinfectant.

His body had been slotted into a vice, which was being turned, squeezing out every drop of warm blood.

And then gravity was altered and he was aware of himself rising up through the murk, like a soul towards paradise.

*

Swans everywhere. Then arms, reaching out for him, hauling him aboard.

His rescuers took him to the south shore and dumped him there. They were men in drab brown jerkins with lined, red faces. They spoke to him in an accent he couldn't understand. When he tried to talk to them they whispered among themselves.

"Well, it was hard, but what can a body do? I'm like to look sharpish," he explained. More whispering, fingers tapped on skulls, and then they walked off, leaving him standing on the wooden quayside. He gazed round at a different, older, greener London. Smoke rose into the sky from a thousand chimneys. Everything seemed the colour of mud.

Strobey walked past a structure which faintly resembled the Globe theatre. It was a lot dirtier-looking than in the downloads. The theatre was the colour of dirt, apart from scraps of blue and gold on

242

the limp flag hanging from the pole which rose out of the roof. A man was urinating against one of the walls.

Strobey felt a little drunk, despite having touched no alcohol. He guessed it was something to do with the time membrane. He wandered on. He wondered if Mirando Mirando had won. He wound his watch, or tried to. He didn't know why he'd made that ghost motion. His watch was gone, ripped off by the river. Its batteries were drowned and silted. He was out of the river but still inside it. The flow took him on through these streets of mud. It was like Mirando Mirando had ruptured a dam that controlled the passage of time. He tried to remember how she'd done this, but someone had punched holes in his brain. His memory of things was patchy. He realised his old identity was ebbing fast. He knew somewhere he'd been the fifty-third son of someone. On a spaceship, was it?

The membrane broke. Something jolted him there. He slipstreamed into his old shack in the TPT zone. He was back with the Archangel. He'd just been given some important information. He said, "I'll check out the history. Offhand, I can't say it means anything to me. What were the precise co-ordinates, sir?"

"A station. Walthamstow Central. In some city called London."

Strobey frowned. "I think I've come across London. In my reading. It's all a bit vague. I need to check."

"Get started my boy. Soon you won't have any time for reading." As he said this, Void Archangel Strumbert frowned. Through the glass he could see his bodyguards retreating into their pods. They moved backwards, with strange, jerky, motions. At the same instant all the objects in his field of vision seemed to ripple, as if a massive but invisible wave was passing through everything. The pods and the Turtle shimmered, the giant pines lost their stiffness. A passing blue eagle suddenly rose and fell like something bobbing on the surface of a choppy sea. Strobey stared down at his body. Even his arms and hands seemed distorted and slightly unreal. His hands became webbed, then the paddles melted away and his fingers came back.

"Wah," the Void Archangel began. "Whirr, arr. War. Aw." Strumbert's speech was slurred and meaningless, like he was blind

243

drunk. The Archangel wondered for a moment if Strobey had drugged him. Or worse, poisoned him. Then remembered he'd had nothing to eat or drink. What's more, the young recruit looked as perplexed and aghast as his commanding officer. He, too, was trying to articulate something.

"Wash. Ip. Thar," he began to remark, but the effort was too much. Something seemed to be twisting his throat and tongue. He had a sudden desire to lie down on the floor.

From the corner of his eye Strumbert saw movement, colour. There, on the screen beside him, was a woman's face. She was singing a low, melancholy song of return.

I am coming home,
Home to sweet Menzara.

Her unaccompanied voice was strangely haunting. Then an instrument began to play in the background. A sadden-mewler, by the sound of it. Long, reverberating chords shimmered and spread, like the aural equivalent of those invisible spreading waves.

Menzara is free of time.
Menzara's chains are gone.
Dance with the passing of the five moons,
Dance to the dying sun.

And singing this chorus, the woman began to dance. Behind her, the Bohren Shield glimmered like a dull emerald curtain. She moved to and fro against it like a swimmer. She dived into its marbled depths and vanished, then re-appeared, bathed in a silvery light.

She said she was Mirando Mirando, but Strobey knew she wasn't. He recognised her face. She was someone he knew. He tried to remember who but couldn't. There was no precision to his thoughts. His mind was like soup. He saw that Void Archangel Strumbert had fallen asleep and was snoring. Outside, the bodyguards also lay asleep. Strobey yawned. He felt strangely relaxed. Mirando Mirando was coming home. Menzara would soon be free.

As he nodded off he remembered the name, and smiled. Everything was going to be fine now. Everything was on the level.

While he slept, the strange rippling carried on through every level of Menzara, on through space, heading for Evanescence and Lincoln and all the other orbitals.

*

He was jolted back. He slipstreamed down a dark, sparkling torrent. He glimpsed the jagged spines of mountains, the abstract splashy swirl of a galaxy. Now time was pouring every which way, in swirls and eddies, surging on one way, curling back another. Black holes sucked on planets, swallowing them like tablets. He felt himself tumbling through the cold air, down towards a dark estuary. He knew exactly who he was. He was Edgar Strobey, now. He was a prisoner of Nether Time. His Menzara core was set to dissolve.

Now he was in a strange, distorted city of narrow alleyways and over-arching wooden houses. The structures were dark and old. His tongue tasted of soil. The scene before him was bending as if every facet was made of rubber. The trunk of a street tree split open and turned into a mouth, like something in a fairy story. Everything had a cartoon existence, its physical properties turned to infinite flexibility. Something seemed to swirl him forward like a feather.

The scene sharpened its focus. Ahead was a miry carriageway which ran between drab timbered buildings. At the flick of a switch the street was filled with people and noise. Children were shrieking and jeering. An extraordinary sight, a man on horseback but facing back towards the tail, led by a grim-faced, slatternly-looking woman. FOR HORDOM said a paper tied to the woman's head. HE DYD HOR HYS WYFFE explained a sign on the man's head. A couple of grinning urchins pelted the man with mud. The woman swore at them and they ran off. Her accent was Cornish; thick and guttural.

Trumpets sounded from a barge on the river. It cruised slowly past, propelled by lines of rowers in a sumptuous green livery. A couple dressed in gold and scarlet sat on elaborately carved chairs in a cabin at the rear. They stared straight ahead. Strobey thought the

245

man looked a little like himself. The woman's face was very familiar too but he couldn't put a name to her.

The river was full of snow white swans. There were hundreds of them. Strobey had never seen creatures like that before. On the orbital the only birds were multi-coloured holograms, written to a phoenix template.

Choking black smoke came rushing down the street. Strobey gagged at the dense, overpowering banality of it. When it had rushed past he entered the hole in the air. He saw someone had lit a bonfire in a square at the far end of the studio. A crowd of extras cheered. As Strobey drew close he saw there was something black tied to a post at its centre. A sequence of close ups showed that it was a disfigured human being. The clothes were burned away, the body was a mass of scorched, blackened, popping flesh, that spat fat and fire, pissing fire…

He retched as the smoke swirled around him, smelling of burnt meat.

"A Pentagon spokesman denied the victims were civilians and said it had no knowledge of any involvement by U.S. troops," a soft, friendly woman's voice was saying. "And now other news. There were smiles all round today as villagers in the little Scottish seaside resort of Penge helped coastguards finally free Wanky the whale. Wanky, who became trapped on the beach last Friday - "

53   Floodwater

He lay on the carpeted floor of a small mirrored cubicle. The nausea had returned. He wanted to vomit but all he managed was a few, dry, retching coughs. His throat burned with pain.

After a few minutes Strobey forced himself to his feet. The willpower involved was enormous. For a few giddy seconds he trans-shaped himself into olive, pomegranate and mulberry, then his head cleared of mythology. The image of a wild, unshaven, flushed figure glared back at him in the harsh fluorescent lighting. He drew back the tiny bolt and opened the door. Ahead of him was a faintly surreal sight: a rack of women's underwear. On the wall was a reproduction of 'Oww, God, Mom, the Dog He Bited Me'. The door closed silently behind him. He realized he was in a department store. In women's clothing, in fact. He'd been in the changing room. A woman assistant frowned at him, then lifted a telephone and began talking into it.

Shoppers moved to and fro among the aisles. Women dawdled by the racks, not talking of Michelangelo; fingered items; took clothes from the hangers and rested them against their bodies, examining the effect in mirrors. A bored child squealed its impatience to be gone. Strobey walked past the knickers and stockings and a tub of giant teddy bears, heading for the exit. He was almost at the exit when he heard shouting.

At first he thought they were on to him. He looked back. But the teddy bears were still paralysed by the drugs that made them smile. The shouting was coming from outside, not from the store.

Outside was a blue sky, sunshine. But the air was cold, like winter.

The first thing he saw was Death.

Death was about four metres high. Its yellow skull and blank eyes emerged from a long dark robe. The apparition had stick arms and bony fingers. The arms were being manipulated by a pair of arms which came from the creature's ribs. He looked lower and saw that Death was wearing a pair of dirty trainers.

It was some kind of demonstration. People were banging on drums, blowing whistles.

Some held placards. NO WAR, the placards read.

He wondered what war this was, what year this was. With time warps and U.S. imperialism you could never be sure. Heck, it sure wasn't an old war, you could tell by the clothes people wore. They looked modern. A bald, red-faced man in his fifties began thumping a scarlet cake tin with a wooden spoon. Strobey winced at the din. He moved away.

The man had produced a harmonica. The tune he was murdering sounded like "Yellow Submarine". Or maybe it was "The British Grenadier".

Strobey wanted to be away from this place and these people. The faint sound of the harmonica pursued him. By now the tune the man was torturing sounded like "Auld Lang Syne".

To one side of the square there was a grassy knoll. Strobey headed across the square and on to the grass.

At the far side was a car park, a picket fence. By the fence were two men, looking across at something the other side. From that direction he could hear the roar of a crowd, then the crack-crack-crack of a faraway firework. But one of the men by the fence was aiming a rifle and Strobey knew exactly when and where he was. He didn't want to be there either. He ducked down by the nearest car and hurried in the direction of the train line.

He climbed over a wire fence and ran up an embankment. Gravel crunched under his feet. Everything seemed plausible and solid. The style was sturdy and visual. There were a dozen parallel railway lines in the paragraph, each one with a long line of stationary wagons. Strobey clambered up on the nearest wagon and found that it was empty. He slid down inside. His shoes made a clanging, reverberating noise. Overhead the sky was still blue. An airliner moved in slow silence dead above. He took off his jacket and made a pillow. He lay down and rested his head.

He slept.

*

When he woke the square was empty and the sun had removed all the triangles and gone. He realised now where he was. The wagon had been erased and he'd been gently relocated to the grass. The grassy knoll next to Walthamstow bus station. Just beyond that was the old hotel.

He didn't have far to go, now. Thirty pages maybe.

Scaffolding covered the station. A gigantic snowflake had been erected above it. A workwoman was attaching loops of wiring to its complex lattice-work patterning. From the wires hung clusters of coloured bulbs. Strobey half-wondered what the snowflake was promoting, but he was too tired to really care. He entered Finn's through the shattered front door. The hotel had been trashed.

248

Everything was broken. There were scorch marks where people had lit fires. He walked upstairs, stepping carefully around broken glass and fragments of broken furniture.

Emma's bedroom had been ransacked. Her CDs were gone, her books lay scattered across the floor. Pages had been torn out. The bedding was missing but the mattress remained, and the bed was still intact despite being broken into pieces by Scurr. Strobey lay down on it in the final draft and was once again soon asleep.

*

When he woke the sun had gone down for the second time that day and the room was in shadow. He realised Emma was sitting in the armchair, staring at him. She smiled. "It's good to see you, Edgar. It's time we talked."

There was a great sadness in her face, Strobey thought. He said, "It's like years have passed. But we only left this place this morning. I think someone's fucked with time. What I mean is I *know* someone's fucked with time. I was sent here to stop her. And I've failed. But soon it won't matter any more. Soon I'm going to forget all that. In fact I *am* forgetting it. It's leaving me, I can feel it. Soon I'm going to be nothing more than your boyfriend."

Emma stared at him. "Are you high on something, my love?" She frowned. She knew that Sharp was everywhere but she felt His presence most when His prose was intrusive, unstable, decreational, asphyxiating the banal gabble of realism – as currently it was not. "You're not making any sense."

He disdained her ontological sagacity and ignored her question. "And where the hell did you get to, anyway?" he said. "Disappearing like that. I was worried."

"I went off to talk to an old acquaintance of mine."

He glared at her, jealous. "Who?"

"His name's Lund. You've never met him."

"An old lover?"

She giggled. "Hardly that. He's – well, not my type."

"So who, then?"

249

"He's a scientist. He was working on the Collider. A brilliant guy. Without him, none of this would have been possible."

Edgar scowled. "None of *what*?"

"This." She nodded at the broken window. The broken window winked back. Through its frame could be seen the floodwater down below. Walthamstow Central was an island in a brown lake. It protruded above the surface like a fat, squat oil rig. The track was twenty feet below water. "The membrane has been breached. The currents are flowing freely. Nothing can stop it, now. The future is gone and the past will change forever."

"What the hell are you talking about?" He stared out at the flood. "What the fuck is going on? If this is the drugs talking, baby, then gimme, gimme, gimme!"

"Close your eyes."

"What?"

"Close your eyes. I want to show you something."

He sighed heavily; humoured her weightily; let the clichés flutter lightly.

"Now open them."

He stared in disbelief.

What an amazing twist!

*

When he woke the sun had gone down and the room was in shadow. He realised Emma was sitting in the armchair, staring at him. She smiled. "It's good to see you, Edgar. It's time we talked."

There was a great sadness in her face, Strobey thought. He said, "It's like years have passed. But we only left this place this morning. I think someone's fucked with time. What I mean is I *know* someone's fucked with time. I was sent here to stop her. And I've failed. But soon it won't matter any more."

Emma said: "I don't quite know how to say this, Ed. I decided in the end the language of a TV drama would be best. The thing is I can't take any more! You're not the person I fell in love with. You've gone all weird on me. Your drug taking's got completely out of hand. You promised you'd stop. You lied to me! You've just gone on, mixing uppers with downers, drinking to excess, smoking dope. And worse. You've started hallucinating, did you know that? Either that or you're a paranoid schizophrenic. All those voices in the next room. They aren't in the next fucking room – they're in your head! And these stories of yours. About coming from an orbital in outer space, when all the time you really come from Brighton! And all that far future shit. Your mission to save the world. A mixture of James Bond and Arnold Schwarzenegger. And this stuff you've been writing. You say you're writing a novel. Well listen Jimmy, the world is full of sad fucks who say they're writers. I've looked at your drafts and buster none of it makes any sense! You should pull your selves together and take a look at what sells. Who reads Alexander Trocchi these days? Get real, Mr Eddie. Stop filling your head with all that science fiction trash for twelve year olds. Dan Brown is the man. He touches the soul of the common woman. And what are you? A traveller from an advanced culture? Somehow I don't think so."

"I can't believe you just said all that," Strobey said. "The style was dreadful. Quite out of character. I'm deleting it RIGHT NOW."

He lurched forwards, but Emma was gone.

Only her ghostly outline remained. Her tangible personality had left the room in a blaze of realism. Was that her next door with Charlie Meadows, jiving to G. Love's amazing album *The Hustle* (Universal Records, 2004)?

Strobey picked up a materialized axe and with a chuckle began to chase after her through the enormous empty hotel. The chuckle ran alongside, its tongue lolling, wagging its little tail. Strobey produced a huge, warm, freshly minted demented grin. How he had always idolised Jack Nicholson in *The Shining!*

54   Just Words

When he woke the sun had gone down and the room was in shadow. He realised Emma was sitting in the armchair, staring at him. She smiled. "It's good to see you, Edgar. It's time we talked."

There was a great sadness in her face, Strobey thought. He said, "It's like years have passed. But we only left this place this morning. I think someone's fucked with time."

"They have. Take a look." She pointed out of the window. Through its cracked pane could be seen the floodwater. Walthamstow Central was an island in a brown lake. It protruded above the surface like a fat, squat oil rig. The track was twenty feet below water. "The membrane has been breached. The currents are flowing freely. Nothing can stop it, now. The future is gone and the past will change forever. Close your eyes."

"What?"

"Close your eyes. I want to show you something."

"Okay." He closed 'em.

"Now open 'em."

He stared in disbelief.

"*Januschka*. What in hell are you doing here? And where did you get that amazing twist from? It really suits you, you know."

Then it hit him, what she'd done. She'd performed an act of dissidence! She'd grabbed a pod from somewhere and done a traject. He was appalled. She was nothing more than a criminal!

Januschka bowed her head. "I came here. For you. Because I love you. I couldn't bear it after you'd gone. I had to see you again. I want to live the rest of my life with you. I want to grow old with you. I know this place isn't what we're used to, you and I. But now it's the only place we have." She held out her arms, palms upward, pleading with him not to delete her dialogue.

"No! You're crazy! This dialogue is criminal. Do you know what you've done? This is terrible." It was no time for sentiment. A lifetime's training taught him what to do. He reached for his flute. He felt completely calm. He said coldly, "Januschka Two, it is my duty under Section 27 of the Menzara Orbital Penal Code to liquidate you for Time Dissidence."

Januschka sighed. "Have it your own way, buddy," she said, in a voice that wasn't hers. The contours of her face seemed to blur, and reconfigured into that of an old woman. Her hair was grey and sparse. A spray of lines ran out from around her eyes. The skin on her neck was loose and cracked as a reptile's. She looked about three-hundred years old.

Strobey relaxed his hold on the flute. "You're not Januschka," he said. He sounded weary but relieved.

"I am, and am not. I was and was not. I was your lover. But I was always someone else."

"Yeah, I can see. You're a fucking *witch*.'

The old woman smiled. "Yes, I think you could say that. Only no broomstick or cat. Personally I have no great enthusiasm for hairy quadrupeds with claws. Though I gather they're incredibly popular in this lamentably primitive culture."

"You're not Emma, you're not Januschka," he repeated dully. And then it hit him, who she was. His fingers flexed round the flute, but it had gone. He glanced down, looking for it. Something bobbed just outside the broken window, distracting him. A small red balloon. Another anomalous phenomenon. Outside, it had grown dark. As he watched, the bulbs on the giant snowflake flickered into life. He saw now that some of the bulbs had been arranged to form a name. It was picked out with blazing scarlet bulbs. MIRANDO MIRANDO, they read, and underneath, in green, IS HERE!

"I see you've worked it out, smart guy. I'm afraid it's true. I'm Mirando Mirando. But I was – am - Emma. And I was – am - Januschka." She laughed. "Let's just say I get around."

"That's not possible. Januschka and Emma were both *young*." He looked at her in disgust.

She smiled. "Aw, come on, lover. Don't be like that. I was wearing vlopes. The principle is just the same as cosmetic surgery, lipstick, false teeth, a padded bra or a wig. A vlope can make anyone beautiful. Besides, we had good times together. No regrets, eh? Let's face it, you were never in love. Neither was I. It was just sex, after all. A good experience. But it didn't mean we wanted to do other stuff together, did it? I mean to be honest I always found your conversation a little *limited*."

Strobey felt sick. He'd heard the rumours about bio-envelopes, had never really believed them. He said, "I think it's revolting. I'm *young*. You're *old*."

253

"Hey, easy soldier. I thought TPT members weren't supposed to have feelings. Besides, our age gap is only 272 years. Admit it, at the time you didn't notice a thing. You were horny as hell. Me too. No regrets, eh? From now on, let's be *friends*."

Strobey had heard enough. He saw the flute lying on the floor. It was resting on a torn strand of pillow case. He had no recollection of dropping it, but he must have done. There were grey spaces in his mind, he knew it was to do with ebbing of his Menzara identity. The very core of his being was thawing. Soon he would be just another dumb biped lost in Nether Time. But he wanted to finish his mission before that happened. Take the bitch out for all time.

Besides, it was personal. He said accusingly, "It was Anarchs killed my parents. Your people. You're all just a bunch of killers."

Mirando Mirando looked tired too. And sounded it. She said in a sad, weary voice, "The truth is, Strobey, late capitalist narrative convention requires an amazing turnaround in the plot towards the end. This is yours. Think of it as a birthday present. Happy birthday!"

Eagerly Strobey unwrapped the paragraph. "Both your parents were Anarchs," Mirando Mirando continued. "They were leaders of our movement. That's why the Menzara Council had them vaporised. It wasn't an accident, it wasn't mindless sabotage. It was a targeted assassination. The Council does it all the time. It saves the effort of a trial. Juries don't always play ball in trials. Your parents were planning to split. They had their traject all worked out. They were going to take you with them. But Strumbert got to them first."

"Strumbert?" Strobey said thickly. "You're lying. It's so thin it's transparent!"

"I'm not, but I can understand why you don't believe me. He's always been in charge of assassinations. It was a pretty neat policy, really. The Council arranged to kill the top Anarchs, then blamed the deaths on Anarch terror. Plus they got the kids. What happened to you happens all the time. Quite a few TPT people have Anarch parents. Of course, they never find out. And even if the information is given to them, they naturally reject it. Their minds have been fucked with ever since they were children. All that realist narrative

254

purporting to tell the truth." She smiled. "Just like everyone else's. Remember the nitrus bomb that went off on the Island of Longing? That was Strumbert. He was even prepared to kill 25,000 holidaymakers if it helped to smear our movement and boost his budget. Strumbert also organised the Construct super-cruiser collision. And all those stupid DESTROY EVERYTHING NOW Anarch messages – they were bogus, a fraud. We never did infantile stuff like that. But it worked. Military force never defeated us but ideology was starting to. That's why I had to split. Get back here and rewrite the future to stop the crap flow. Of course, I know you'll never believe all this. But I still had to tell you. And it's because people like you are really one of us that the movement has decided to treat you kindly."

"Kindly?" Strobey said sarcastically. "You land me in this postmodernist shit hole with my Menzara core about to go, and this is *kindness*?"

"Astrar's Delusion is always better than permanent extinction. Repetition is better than termination. To be sealed in a loop is better than to be sealed in a tomb. That's what it says in the secret text messages of Razana Anansi Anarch. Makes pretty good sense to me."

"This is all bullshit. This is just *words*." She was tricking him in some way, he knew it. She was killing time. Well, she wasn't going to fuck with *him*. He lunged at the floor, his fingers reaching for the flute.

Incredibly, it jerked away. Its slender perforated piping began to shimmer. It transformed before his eyes into a pale blue snake. The snake crossed the room in a few flicks of its body. It curled up at Mirando Mirando's feet, like an obedient dog.

Then through the broken window a red balloon drifted into the room.

It burst, releasing a cloud of tiny scarlet particles which swarmed towards him, coating his face, his eyes. He felt scores of tiny needles puncturing his skin, a numbness spreading across his face. He tried to claw them off, but there were more on his hands, stabbing into his fingers, making them go floppy. A prickling surge of pleasure poured through him and he lost consciousness.

255

55 Imago-Goggles Off

A faint ache still layered the inside of his temple as Strobey took off his imago-goggles. He blinked, adjusting to the old reality once more. He was the first one to come out of the simulation.

He looked round at the others in the dimly lit circular room. Their fingers were beginning to tap out simple tunes on invisible pianos. Their bodies moved slightly in the plectron chairs. They were slowly returning to consciousness. He went over to the hatch and asked for a cappuccino. "At once, Mr Strobey" the hatch replied. "Your usual bone china mug with the William Morris design?"

"Please."

He took the coffee over to the nearest porthole and looked out. As always he saw the lacy swirl of curling incandescence that was the Glorian Nebula. As always he was reminded of the pattern in a slab of marble. As always he remembered the Nebula was the remains of a supernova explosion from the second cosmic war against the Edgers. (4 Steppen 02 – 19 Steppen 127). It was where it had been after the last imago game, and where it would be after the next, and the next, until help at last came. Strobey looked at his watch. Only another five hundred years before the rescue ship *One Day More* arrived. Continuing to stare, he sipped his coffee and waited for the others.

Aphrodite was the next one to return. She yawned as she took her goggles off. Looked across at Strobey and said, "How long was it that time?" It was the first thing everyone wanted to know when they came out.

"Seven weeks," he said

Aphrodite smiled sleepily. "Our best yet."

"Yeah, pretty good. I wasn't sure about the ending. A bit confusing, I thought. But overall I preferred it to the previous game. That hardboiled private dick working for multi-millionaire crooked businessman scenario, complete with sexy, double-crossing wife, all set in the late Barbarian era. It was so fucking *clichéd*."

"Buller loved it. So did Benjamin."

"Yeah, well, Buller would. And Benjamin takes too many DreaMURs."

"Someone talking about me?" Buller grinned. "And since I couldn't help overhearing, yes I damn well did prefer the previous game. This one stank. From a strictly personal point of view. I mean to say, getting eaten alive by rats. Whose fucking idea was that? Come on, own up. Who pre-programmed *that?*"

Aphrodite said, "I did, of course. You were my boss. Therefore I had to get rid of you. How else is a lady to get promotion?"

"Not a very nice way, if I may say so. In fact, I still feel distinctly *ragged*. I need a bloody scotch." He went over to the hatch. "Havana Reserve. And fake it better than last time. The last lot was muck."

"Your adverse comment has been acknowledged," the hatch said, in a stilted mechanical voice. "Under the Satisfied Company Personnel Policy you will receive a written reply to your complaint within ten working space days. If you are dissatisfied with the reply you receive you may indicate the reasons on the consumer response form, which will be transmitted to the chief executive, who will reply to you within one space month."

"Not when we're five hundred fucking light years from home he won't," Buller growled.

"Your remark is not within the parameters of my understanding," the hatch said in a mechanical voice.

"Forget it."

"Under company recording policy made available to you in the contract you signed please recall that I am obliged to remember everything. Please do not be alarmed. You are reminded that all personnel conversation in public areas of the ship, bio-status information and miscellaneous data unrelated to the primary transaction materials will be deleted one hundred years after the voyage is ended, as required under the Federation data protection act of 8 Steppen 3023."

Scurr came through next. He groaned and clapped a hand to his temple. "What a complete bastard I was. I hate myself. I need a drink."

"I've ordered something which in theory ought to be very tasty indeed. But don't hold out your hopes. There are some things even

257

an advanced liquid simulator can't manage, and a good stiff drink is one of them."

"Its gin and tonics taste perfectly okay to me," said Aphrodite. "But right now I need a nice cup of tea." She went over to the hatch and requested an infusion of Echinacea and raspberry. No sugar, no milk.

More and more crew members began to wake and climb out of their plectron chairs. There was the usual joshing as a queue formed for the nutro hatch. Daisy Spenser was chatting to Scaravelli. She was no longer young and freckled but now her real self, a dark, tall, elderly woman with grey cropped hair.

"I absolutely refuse to be the bad guy next time round," Scurr said. "For the next two games I want to be the hero. Everyone agree?"

"Hold on to your quadro-speeders. We're not all returned yet." Aphrodite nodded at Mirando Mirando, who remained comatose in her chair, the imago-goggles still enclosing the top half of her head. With the goggles on, her head resembled that of a Voratian wasp. Aphrodite went over and touched her gently on the shoulder. "Wake up, Mirando. Time to come home. Everybody's waiting." And then she said, "Oh, shit."

The others turned, sensing the fear in her voice.

"I think-" She made a strangled noise. Was having probs with speech.

It came out in a rush.

"I think she's dead. She's cold as ice. Get over here quick, Buller. You're the doctor."

Grim-faced, Buller did as she'd asked. He felt Mirando Mirando's pulse. He took a frond-pin from his jacket pocket and stuck it into her upper right arm. He looked at the reading and frowned.

"She is," he said.

He added, in a puzzled voice: "And I don't understand why."

56   A Downward Plunge

A faint ache still layered the inside of his temple as Strobey took off his imago-goggles. He blinked, adjusting to the old reality once more. He was the first one to come out of the simulation. He looked round at the others in the dimly lit circular room. Their fingers were beginning to tap out simple tunes on invisible pianos. Their bodies moved slightly in the plectron chairs. They were slowly returning to consciousness. He went over to the hatch and asked for a cappuccino. "At once, Mr Strobey" the hatch replied. "Your usual bone china mug with the William Morris design?"

"Please."

He took the coffee over to the nearest porthole and looked out. As always he saw the lacy swirl of curling incandescence that was the Glorian Nebula.

"It gets boring after eighty years, doesn't it?"

Strobey turned and saw it was his wife. "Yeah. A bit like marriage."

"Aw, come on!" said Mirando Mirando. "No need to be tetchy. Just because I won the game. And you lost."

"That's bullshit. Didn't you understand? *I* won. Not you. You were eliminated. You ask the others when they wake up. I zapped you good and proper."

"I'm afraid that's a delusion. Just like our marriage. Just like this place, in fact. And all your memories. There is no Glorian Nebula. That's just a rather crude variable holo. I simulated it in less than five minutes. Ditto the ship. You are not on the starship *Amy Foster*. You are not stranded in space awaiting a rescue ship that won't arrive for another 500 years. You are not passing the time playing imago games with other crew members. They exist – but not here." She gestured at the other figures, sitting peacefully in their plectron chairs. "These characters are entirely spectral. Look."

She winked at Strobey and the other crew members began to dissolve, along with their imago-goggles. When they'd gone their chairs dissolved too. Strobey suddenly found himself standing on a small flat silver disc, surrounded by the vast dark sparkling wastes of space. He realised it must be a simulacrum because though he wasn't wearing a spacesuit he didn't die. He could hear the amplified thudding of his heart. His breathing sounded like the gravelly suction of rapidly retreating waves on a rough shore.

Mirando Mirando vanished, along with the rest of the room.

He stared at the remote, vast Glorian Nebula. It looked real enough to him.

Then the outline of a silver tree trunk began to form in space about twenty metres away. Its roots protruded down into nothingness like shining hairs. The trunk sprouted branches, the branches spread an emerald embroidery against a sheen of sparkling emptiness.

A golden cat materialized on the lowest branch. A sheriff's star was clipped to its right ear. The star swelled and expanded as if it was a balloon being inflated. The cat disappeared behind it. The balloon was white. As it grew bigger, so did the name printed across it in tiny black letters. The letters were in capitals. The name became legible. The balloon exploded. A crimson incandescence. The name "SCHRODINGER" throbbed in red bars in the mist below Strobey's closed eyelids.

He opened his eyes. The name was still there, but the letters were melting. Seconds later only the "O" and "N" were left. The letters skipped position. NO, they read. Then the "O" began to swell, obliterating the "N". It expanded towards him, a rubbery black globe. It shone with a strange glossy brilliance.

Strobey flinched from the impending impact. The globe exploded, making an odd slurping noise. The noise morphed into laughter, an entire chorus of it, echoing. It was as if thousands of mouths were roaring with irrepressible merriment.

Someone switched the raucous laughter off. There was an abrupt silence, a sudden icy gust. It was getting cold. Out there, beyond the stars, a storm of unimaginable magnitude was getting up. It would radiate outward for a billion years. He felt this knowledge in his bones. Strange messages jostled in his mind, transmitted from somewhere deep inside him. Strobey wondered if someone had once implanted a neural expansion device inside him without him knowing.

His eyes adjusted themselves to the returned darkness. The tree was still there, the cat was still there. The cat's face was unmistakably Mirando Mirando's. She looked at him and gave him a slow wink. Then the tree faded, the cat began to melt away. A

260

moment later there was nothing but the winking eye. A second later, nothing.

He was alone in the universe, standing on a disc not much wider than his cubicle at the Library of All.

He looked down and to his horror saw the perimeter of the disc ripple. The rippling morphed into a jerking movement, as if an invisible force was pulling at it. Morphed into a contraction of matter, the material supporting him. The disc began slowly to shrink towards its centre.

He stared down at his feet, like a man on a sandbank far from shore with a cold black tide rushing in around him.

The last scrap of disc disappeared from beneath him. *This is only a simulation*, he told himself. Then he felt an icy gust against his flesh as his body plunged downwards, towards the Thames estuary.

57 Varieties

In the darkness the bulbs on the giant snowflake flickered on and off.

Emma said: "What you don't realise is that Finn's Hotel is built over a resonance fault. Remember that elementary chrononaut physics you did in your first year at TPT College? Marina Schmidt IV theorized that every Red Triangle system contained two resonance faults. Cracks in the membrane that permit entry. And re-entry. Think of them as security card slits. They have no tangible physical existence. They aren't like fault-lines in the earth's crust, though there are rough similarities in their effects. They exist as concentrated space-time matter. Circular plates approximately two units in diameter. In themselves they are nothing. But if you can activate them... That was Schmidt's theory. But of course no one's ever found a resonance fault. Leastways, not officially. But a remote explorer team once located one using a meeron detector. It was an accident. They were looking for ziridium liquid and instead got a signal of a kind which even the ship's Mother couldn't identify."

"Don't tell me. Coming from Finn's Hotel."

"Finn's Hotel didn't exist back then. The area was just forest. The nearest bipeds were primitives living in a hut two surface micro-units away. But the information was brought back to Menzara. Marina Schmidt knew what it meant. And her best friend was my grandmother. Who, shall we say, recognised its potential. By the time my mother got here the planet had moved on a few thousand years."

"Your mother was a dissident?"

"Yeah. She's buried in the churchyard of St Mary's. She did well for herself. The tomb is really big. She married a city merchant. But of course I'm going to re-write all that. I know she won't be happy staying dead. She knew I'd get here eventually and rewrite her. She once managed tried to rig up something to send a message to me, but she didn't have the materials. It just bounced back to Finn's. Your SD should have told you my mother was involved when he saw her, but of course a non-physical entity is nothing special to a spectral duplicate. It's there in your download, but it's not highlighted. That's why you missed it. Hell, nobody can be expected to relive all that time in its totality. All you can do is speed-process, right? Hope that the search engine gives you what you need. Problem is, not everything is coded that way. Anyway, I got mom's message in the end. And now I'm going to rewrite her century and get her out of it, back to Menzara. Along with the rest of our family. It's only right that a daughter should give her dead mother a better future."

This junk was enough to make Stroubey laugh, but he didn't. He said, "Even assuming I believe all this theoretical shit, how do you activate the so-called resonance fault?"

"Simple. You create a quantum ripple." Her eyes twinkled. It was just reflections from the giant snowflake. "It needs to be reasonably close to the fault."

"The Collider?"

"Yeah. The Collider. The moment it was turned on it created the ripple. Which activated the fault. Which moved. Creating slippage. Think of it as a time earthquake. The shocks go out in every direction. For anyone in the vicinity it's chaos. Time goes backwards, forwards, whatever. Stuff from the deep past returns.

Matter from the future passes by. And anyone who appreciates what's going on can head off back through the Bohren Shield to Menzara. In time to take advantage of what's about to happen there. Of course, what nobody knows is how long the effects last. And not even Schmidt calculated one strange side-effect I've discovered. Namely, that when you change time you can also change space through desire. When you re-write someone's world you also give them the freedom to re-write and delete. It turns people into creators. They want someone out of their lives, whoosh! – they're gone. Like a novelist deleting a character. Scary, huh? And I guess it lasts as long as the time change. Schmidt calculated about the equivalent of a year, but she's the only one who ever thought about it. Long enough, at any rate, to re-write a lot of past and future history. And of course something like this has never happened before. Space exploration was always thought of as sending ships out across the cosmos. Such a masculine concept, if I may say so. Re-writing the original creation seems more preferable."

She gave a dry smile, then snatched it back and swapped it for a sexy, lubricated one.

"Men just want to penetrate. But women prefer a different kind of friction."

*

Strobey felt exhausted. "If I could go out of life now, without too sharp a pang, it would be well for me," he thought, just like Jane Eyre.

He entered Finn's through the shattered front door. The hotel had been trashed. Everything was broken. He suspected a pang was in the vicinity. The worst sort - sharp. He walked upstairs, stepping carefully around broken glass and fragments of text and broken furniture.

Emma's bedroom had been ransacked. Her CDs had gone, her books lay scattered across the floor. Pages had been cut out and sliced like a postmodernist with a fondness for collage had passed thru. As in the aftermath of a great love affair, the stained bedding was gone but the mattress remained. The broken bed was still intact.

263

Strobey lay down and was quickly anaesthetized by a leaking hookah. A hooker caught him in a dream of green sheets, where her stubby fingers found novel uses for a rubber band. When he woke the sun had gone down, the share price of British Gash was up, the moon had moved sideways, Venus was in the ascendant, the room was in shadow, and apparent typos were in reality not. Emma sat in the armchair, staring. She smiled. "It's good to see you, Strobey. It's time we talked."

"About all this? About what's happened to us?"

She nodded. "I take it you've never heard of Astrar's Delusion?"

Strobey hadn't – any more than he'd heard of Gangemi, Genette, Gombrowicz, Gytisolo, Grass, Gass or Gray.

"It was Astrar who set up the TPT, back in 2397. They don't talk about him any more, of course. An embarrassment. All that time you spent in the Unending Forest learning about this shitty little planet and you never knew your own Orbital history! That's typical, if I may say so."

It was a trick of some sort. He didn't believe a word she said, apart from the ones in the Oxford English Dictionary. "The TPT was established in 2444. By Menzara's son. That's what I was taught. That's what I believe."

Mirando Mirando stifled a yawn. She tossed it aside. She wasn't a sentimentalist where small furry narrative vermin were concerned. Plus she was tired, in no mood to argue. "For a while everything was fine. TPT personnel went off after Dissidents, never came back. But then in 2402 along came a target TD Astrar couldn't quite resist going after himself." She smiled. "My daughter."

Strobey frowned. "That's not possible. The Bohren Shield doesn't permit you to have a daughter in the twenty-fifth century."

"I guess another thing they never taught you was Norland's seventh thesis. If the Bohren Shield can be penetrated twice at the same location then chronology reversal becomes possible." Mirando Mirando raised her hand, anticipating his objection. "I know, I know, according to your physics this is impossible. Just as our presence here to these people is, in their terms, impossible. But imagine for a moment that what I say is true and that my family can do such a thing."

264

Family? What the fuck did she mean, family? He said: "There is no seventh thesis. Every schoolchild knows that."

"Humour me. Listen to my tale. Astrar came after my daughter. The Princess of the Anarchs! Quite a target. In fact he followed her here, to Walthamstow. Not, of course, the Walthamstow that we are in now. An older, earlier Walthamstow. Late nineteenth century. Finn's Hotel had just been built. Everything was brand new. The mirrors and windows sparkled. Maids in crisp white bonnets waited on the guests. My daughter waited there for Astrar. She knew he'd come. And I'm afraid he was no match for her. She disposed of him the way we always dispose of TPT agents. Humanely. Not using your methods – violence, weaponry, erasure dust. She sealed him in his own Loop. She transferred him to Repetition. You know what the Loop is, don't you, Strobey? It's a vacuum. It's that zone where time repeats itself unendingly. In the morning Astrar arrived to liquidate my daughter. He had many exciting adventures. He believed he encountered and eliminated her. But it was all spectral. We Anarchs call it 'Astrar's Delusion'."

Her voice hardened. "It is the fate which awaits every member of the Time Penetration Team. Including you, my friend."

Strobey reached for the flute in his pocket. His hand no sooner touched it than the whole of his right arm tingled and froze. A localized paralysis. He looked up and saw Mirando Mirando. She had a wand. She was pointing it at his arm.

"Is that a flute in your pocket? Or are you just pleased to get close to me?" she didn't say. What she said was: "When I shut the door you'll be in the Loop. Forever. So say bye-bye to Menzara. And enjoy your Delusion!"

She cackled like a Walt Disney witch and headed out of the room.

He had to stop her.

Remembering the Lenin epigraph Strobey tried to run, but it was like his feet were glued to the floor. Strobey thought: It's my mind. She's in my mind. I need a shield. He remembered the Anarchs who'd waited for him at Walthamstow Central. He remembered their shooters. He thought: Mirando Mirando is full of shit. The Anarchs use weapons! All that stuff about humane disposal is garbage!

The feeling came back to his arm. It surprised him so much his hand relaxed. The flute slipped out of his grasp and clattered on the floor. He knew he had to get to her before she left the room so he left it there. Treacle sucked at his shoes. He tore them free and ran across the room.

She was just closing the door as he grabbed the knob and wrenched it back.

Mirando Mirando looked suddenly scared. She tried to drag the door shut but he was too strong for her. Instead she let go. He wasn't expecting that and fell back against the wall, still holding on to the door.

By the time he got back to the doorway she was near the end of the corridor.

He projected his mind, caught her in its net.

Her costume seemed to melt away. Suddenly she was nude, still running from him, her buttocks rising and falling as she ran.

He span her round, and she smiled.

She was superb. Golden flawless skin, full gorgeous breasts, a perfect triangle of pale hair over the dark slash between her legs. A faint reek of sexual juices came to his nostrils. He felt the beginnings of an erection.

"We could have such a good time together," she smiled. "We could rule this planet. We could make it a world even better than Menzara." She cupped her breasts, parted her legs a little. A fabulous invitation.

She shouldn't have mentioned Menzara. It reminded him of his parents, of who he was. In some far chamber of his mind he saw their shuttle collapse in fire and plummet into the Lake of Ice.

She tried to thwart the memory, offered herself to him, hot and panting and greedy. Images of their coupling fluttered through his mind. He saw it from every angle – behind, above, sideways. His penis was massive, big as a stallion's. He watched as he pierced her, massively, and she howled and shivered with pleasure.

He shut it all out and screamed, "You are Mirando Mirando, Anarch, and it is my duty under Section 27 of the Menzara Orbital Penal Code to liquidate you for Time Dissidence!"

He hadn't reached the end of the sentence before she changed. The goddess impaled so fantastically on his quivering giant prick moved backwards with a slurping, sucking noise. The golden skin darkened and became blotchy. Cracks and wrinkles spread across her surfaces like a shattering windshield. Her pubic hair shrivelled and dropped off, revealing raw, diseased flesh coated in scabs and dripping sores. Her howl of sexual ecstasy turned into a snarl of agonized rage.

Lines from a song by Edwina Josh-Wah pierced his mind:

Orbital woman with a manufactured past
Guess I'm seeing the real you at last.

Clusters of glistening sticky worms dropped from Mirando Mirando's black, encrusted armpits. They slithered towards his shoes, crawled over them. White creeping things swarmed across her bald head. She jerked backwards, hissing, her eyes slits of sly, emerald cunning. "Qu'est-ce que c'est déguelasse?" she whispered, and he felt a strange quick slippery language enfolding him like a net, worms probing his flesh, crawling higher.

Strobey raised his flute and fired.

He went on firing until the last of the twenty needles had gone.

Mirando Mirando shrank and thinned into a dark, whirling pillar. As each fresh needle transfixed her writhing core she shrieked in pain and fury.

Finally she exploded.

A foul stench filled the corridor. The walls looked like they'd been splashed with a greyish soup. The soup sank hissing to the floor in slow, wrinkled waves. A brownish, unpleasant dust hung in the air. Now there was a scorched, metallic smell.

Strobey ran past it, through it, outside.

It was a glorious summer's day. The sky was blue, the sun was shining. A blackbird was singing on a high branch.

Strobey felt good. He realised what all this meant.

He'd broken the Loop.

He could go home! Back to Menzara.

Whoo-hoo!

267

It was a strange thought. He felt a little dizzy, a little intoxicated. She'd been fucking with his mind, but that was all over now.

Sweet things unfolded inside him. He could taste the change in his personality. He was beginning to feel a rush of new emotions. He was weirdly elated. Wild thoughts stampeded down shining grids.

Maybe he'd get married. Have kids. Leave the TPT and start over. Become a deep space explorer, or a Titan player, or a poet. Something crazy.

No hurry. He'd have plenty of time to think about stuff like that on the traject back.

But first he had a little private business to attend to.

58 The Museum

It was a Sunday morning, the edge of dawn. Everything was grey. Strobey drove through the deserted streets of the city to The Museum. It started to rain, he switched on the wipers. A faint headache, otherwise he felt fine.

Everyone else was staying indoors that cold, hostile morning. Strobey couldn't exactly blame them. He would have preferred to stay in bed with Emma, her soft warm nude body against him. Would have preferred to stir her gently into wakefulness, touching her gently, nuzzling her breasts. Arousing a wetness between her legs, scenting the beginning fire of her lust. Rocking together, fucking hard until slimed with perspiration and the oozings of love. Then coffee, breakfast, the Sunday papers in bed. Then more fucking.

Not that Sunday. He kissed her lightly on the cheek. She muttered something about romantic clichés, then went back to sleep. He dressed quickly and left. He had business to do. He wanted The Museum to himself – or as quiet as it would ever get. The Museum was the only one in the city that was permanently open. *Time Out* said Sunday just after dawn was the best time to go if you wanted to avoid the crowds.

He drove along the one-way system through Bank Quarter and on across the Victoria Viaduct. The lights stayed green all the way to the Embankment.

Out on the river a solitary black barge was moving slowly downriver, toward Hinge Bridge. It looked like the coffin of a giant, floating aimlessly away on the tide.

Strobey drove on. He went past Charred Cross Station, round the great black marble Plinth of Longing. On top he glimpsed the heroic figure of the Imperial Onanist, Admirable Lewd Neilson. Neilson's black scarf was tied across his eyes and his right fist squeezed a marble cock two metres in length. A jet of water curved in the air, then fell like a fine mist to the square below. In summer young women stripped naked and cavorted there, believing in the old legend that the mist brought fertility.

Then he was past and going down Mildew-Mawl. He turned right at the Buckingham Sewage Plant and went between the big open gates into Reverberation Park.

Some Los Angeles geese flew by, high in the sky, their great golden necks unmistakeable even on that gloomy morning. One of them screeched, and its screech duplicated itself among the vast bowl-shaped spadula trees at the centre of the park. The remote tinny screechings drained into a faint, fading metallic whispering.

On sunny summer days the park was full of sunbathers and lovers and children playing. Today it was deserted. Someone had turned off all the fountains. The skin of the whales and dolphins was streaked with rust and green stains. Rain danced in puddles on the gravel, made the motionless cars shine and glitter. The rain made the grass look greener and fresher than it really was.

Getting a parking space wasn't a problem that early. At this hour there were half a dozen vehicles, no more. Strobey pulled in close to the entrance and went up the vast flight of steps.

The Museum might almost have been designed for President Carlos Wand himself. It was a vast neo-classical monstrosity of the sort that pleased major league tyrants. Banal statuary of huge muscular naked gods and goddesses lined the exterior walkway beyond the tall stone columns. The marble giants had blank eyes and empty expressions and the rainstreaks made it look like they were lost in some equally immense melancholy.

The museum doors were open. He crossed the lobby. His footsteps crashed and reverberated like small explosions in that spacious stone emptiness. Strobey hurried across to the ticket clerk. She was a small, dark, severe-looking woman of about 40, with her hair done up in a bun. She was reading a book but put it down as he drew close.

"Yes?"

"One, please."

He gave her five euros and she passed him a plan of the Museum. The turnstile clicked and he pushed past it. He saw that the book the ticket clerk was reading was a novel, *Unbelievable Things*. Pulp trash, by the look of it, and an author he'd never heard of. The woman seemed vaguely familiar, like he'd met her once, many years ago. But he didn't say anything, it would have sounded too much like a crude chat-up line. He pushed through the turnstile.

Beyond it, forty metres away at the centre of a dome-shaped vestibule, stood Angelino DiNarco's legendary sculpture "The Woman Ascending Gives Birth to a Hundred Dreaming Unicorns".

Strobey stood before it and gazed reverently at its complex, enormous structure. The woman was naked, her huge buttocks resting on the ground, her thick thighs spread wide. Out of the crevasse between them surged a flow of unicorns, intertwined, rising like missiles into the sky.

The ones at the base of the sculpture had limbs the size of railway carriages. The very highest unicorn was three hundred metres in the air and just one centimetre in height. It was invisible to the naked eye. From the tip of each unicorn's horn sprouted scores of delicate wire shapes which expanded to form bizarre branches and extensions. Some were draped with papyrus, others dangled polystyrene pots. Some tinkled faintly like wind chimes, others twisted and glittered like mirrored mobiles.

It was said that the entire contents of human history could be found represented literally or symbolically somewhere in this sculpture. Strobey had no difficulty believing it. The woman's torso was covered in engraved patterns, barely decipherable words

270

in dozens of languages, tattoos which showed sailing ships, maps of tiny faraway countries, patterns of distant solar systems. DiNarco had begun work on this masterpiece at the age of four; she finished it on the very last day of her life, aged 103.

A brass plaque gave a potted history of DiNarco's career and explained the significance of the sculpture for the benefit of tourists from Bejing, Tokyo and Nova Zembla. Strobey glanced away. He'd read six books on the artist, he knew all that stuff. Beyond it was a large sign:

WELCOME TO THE MUSEUM OF LOST POSSIBILITIES.
PLEASE LEAVE UNATTENDED ITEMS IN THE GALLERIES

Ignoring it, Strobey went through Cute Gigantic Skeletons and Erotic Pottery into Imaginary Furry Animals, Football Fever and Television Waste. He hurried down the Corridor of Extinct Royalty and through the Gallery of Extraordinary Delusions. Beyond it, in 22nd Century European Painting, an attendant wearing a Magritte bowler hat was dozing by Broznan's "Turbulent Clown". In the background a song by Nina Simone was playing.

The painting was almost as famous as DiNarco's sculpture. It showed a clown with his hands tied behind his back kicking at the door of a prison cell. The clown's face wore a look of extraordinary ferocity and despair.

Strobey touched the man lightly on the shoulder and the attendant jerked awake.

"Manuscripts? Gallery 20. Go through there, sir, and it's the third gallery on the left." Strobey thanked him and went on.

The manuscripts section formed part of the Sheer Genius Gallery. One half was devoted to the classics, the other half to Unpublished Fiction, Unfinished Verse and A Hundreth Sundry Jottings.

Strobey frowned at the manuscript of *Love's Labours Found* and *Shakespeare's Diary*. The scratchy, slanted Tudor handwriting was mostly unreadable. Keats's "Ode to the Dead of Peterloo" was easier on the eye. Not that he was really interested in either writer. It was Khan's stuff he wanted to see – or rather one item in particular.

He hurried past the manuscript of Emily Brontë's second book *Raw Meat* and Charles Dickens's pornographic novella *Naughty Nelly's Naked Nights*. Finally, by the far wall, he found the glass cabinet devoted to Khan. His eyes scanned across her six volumes of poetry and seven books of postmodernist fiction. And there, at last, it was. Her diary, open at the page he wanted to see. He bowed over the temperature-controlled armoured plexiglass cabinet to absorb the full impact of her faded ballpoint:

Walthamstow Central? Wasn't that where Strobey took off to in Nether Time and broke the Loop? Seems a long time ago, now.
Lisa Kamanzi Khan, 57 Steppen 3063

His own pale face stared back at him from the glassy surface.

A tiny shiver appeared in his right cheek and ran down his chin. The cabinet exploded, showering him in a wave of hot wet fragments. His head broke into sheets of pain. Fire lapped Khan's diary. It crumbled before his eyes. The flames lit a fire down a crack in his mind. At that moment he remembered who the ticket seller was. He turned and, yes. It was her, standing at the gallery entrance. She was holding a semi-automatic flame pellet dispenser.

Mirando Mirando fired again and scores of small black discs showered around him. They exploded on impact. Cabinet after cabinet burst with a shattering effect. Pillars of fire rose up from the exhibits. Shakespeare's faded brown signature darkened into blackness and vaporised.

Strobey ran.

59   Thank the Archangel

Through gallery after gallery he sprinted, heading for the roof.

The sound of explosions and breaking glass followed after him like an incoming tide. Faraway he could hear sirens wailing and alarm bells going off.

Now great sheets of metal began to unfold from the walls and close protectively over the exhibits. Moments later the sprinklers started. Strobey ran on, half-slipping on the soaked floors.

He came at last to the top gallery. He burst out of the final Salvation Room and into a deserted coffee bar. At the far end, by the window, was a balcony with half a dozen circular tables and chairs. An ancient Catatonia track was playing.

The view over Londinium was amazing, but he had no time for that. He pushed a table against the wall at the far end of the balcony, put a chair on top and mounted the chair. It screeched under the weight of Strobey's need, his quick rough urgency.

Strobey's fingers stretched over the ledge at the top and felt something metallic, like piping. He had no real choice, now. He hauled himself up slowly until his feet left the flimsy plastic chair below. The brickwork ground against his chest. It was only a noun but it hurt. He dragged himself over the edge just as an explosion below him disintegrated the plastic furniture. Chairs and the twisted discs of burned tabletops went showering down into the park below. Strobey stood up, looked around.

The roof of The Museum was flat. Nearby there was a water tank, a pair of satellite discs, a structure with aerials attached. Beyond them was the glider.

Unbelievable! (But something stirred in his memory.) A nifty, gleaming, sleek, beautifully moulded mini-glider. He took hold of the handle and dragged it towards the far edge of the roof. He was amazed how short the sentences were at this height. He was knocked out by the repetition. He came back at once, amazed how light the craft felt. It was like it was made of paper. For a horrible moment he thought maybe it was. Was it just a fucking art exhibit, not a real aircraft at all?

No, it was real as real can be. Thank the Archangel!

He manoeuvred the words until the cone of the craft was pointing out over the edge. All he had to do now was get into the tiny cockpit, strap himself in, and use his hands to waggle it over the edge.

A fucking big "All".

But did he have a choice? He did not. A clicking came from the keyboard and explosions rocked the air. There was a disturbance, back there by the water tank. Shrapnel had sheared through a pipe. Water was jetting up convulsively from the rupture. Water was pissing from the sides of the holed tank. Water was beginning to spread across the roof towards him.

Then he saw her, still in her uniform.

How the fuck she'd got on the roof he had no idea. Not the same way he had (he remembered the showering furniture).

However, she was there. A cool, calm smile on her face. Like she knew something he didn't. Holding in her right hand the pellet gun. A big, round, clumsy device. It looked like inflated plastic, reminded Strobey of the water guns of his childhood. She was watching the water slide towards him, weighing up her options.

Strobey climbed into the seat, didn't have time to use the belt, began frantically to push the glider along. It didn't budge. Panic yammered in his chest, he started to rock the craft. Make it seesaw.

She decided to fire: fired.

A score of pellets shot from the big whore mouth of the muzzle, rose in a slight arc, then plopped to the ground. Looking so harmless. Bouncing merrily across the dark tarmac roofing, skipping and bobbing and hopping along like a kid's toy.

It was time to fly.

Strobey climbed out again, stood beside the fuselage and pushed. The glider tipped at a crazy angle and began to go. He fell forwards into it as it went, as the pellets went off. Close, one after another, a piercing explosive roar that breathed a hot fiery breath over him, that pushed an orange whiteness over the wing. He smelt the toxic wastes of burning plastic.

The fucking wing was on fire!

"The time for action is past!" she called out to him. "The time for reflection has come!"

Then she was gone, the roof was far behind, he was being spun round and round in a torture device that would go on forever.

Twisting and twisting until it smashed into the grass far below.

Crazy shapes whirled across his vision, a blurring that slowed. A dark twist of obscurity transformed itself into words, a sentence, a grove of spadula trees. He saw the circular lake at their centre, saw his own vast swollen face in the magnification of a shaving mirror, his jaw aching and puffy after the extractions, a dribble of blood running down the cold throbbing surface of his skin. His face vanished, displaced by specks which might have been the lake's ducks. The glider was heading straight for them.

Then something kicked him in the guts, he gasped, the control bolt prodding into his stomach, his face slammed forwards and smacked into the instrument panel. He pulled back, brushed a wetness from his eyes, was puzzled by a dozen pairs of eyes staring back at him, his own eyes, had they ever had a colour? he wondered, hard to tell, they were just there, a four letter word replicated in the twelve clock faces containing a circle of figures, where needles flickered and fell, and outside, through the cracks and gaps in the cockpit's hood, blue. Blue, everywhere.

He realised it was sky.

Morning had broken like the first morning, the glider had hit a thermal, was doing what a glider should do. Cruise gloriously level across the land below.

Top o' the world, ma!

A cold roaring accompanied these events, tore at his hair. He realised it was the hatch, not secured. Wrenched it down, flicked a handle.

A sudden silence enveloped him.

When he was certain he wasn't going to crash he dared to look back. The Museum's windows leaked fire and smoke. From the roof an enormous pillar of smoke was rising as he watched, growing in volume, adding boiling layer to each new boiling layer. And there on the roof a solitary figure, waving perhaps.

Entirely surrounded by a circle of fire.

Serve the bitch right.

Bye bye, baby!

Smoke swallowed her, and she was gone.

60   It Ends At The Shore

The glider cruised of its own volition towards the big river.

It drifted in silence. It crossed the sprawl. The city streets far below stood out with a clarity you only ever saw on maps. The human mess down there was gone. It was too puny to see. Strobey dry-swallowed. His body began to relax. The fear and the tension were ebbing fast. He felt safe. He would start a new life, now. Lost in a nether world, but free. Mission accomplished! And a whole new world to explore...

The thermals lifted the delicate craft and bore it on towards the sea. One day, he knew, he would go there. He had old friends out there. "Drop by any time," they'd said. They raised sheep on a farm in Finisterre. He'd promised to take Emma there, and he would. But not today.

The glider's right wing was blackened and shedding tiny fragments. The fire had blown out in the descent but you could see the damage. The titanium alloy of the skeletal structure beneath was exposed, along with shreds of poly-anthium fibre. But he wasn't afraid. He felt strangely confident of landing safely.

Now he could see Hinge Bridge far below, where he'd driven earlier that morning. The glider took him on, past Bister Fortress and the wharves, past the Isle of Dregs and its shining domes. Then fields, the great salt marshes of Virginia Plain. Galleons and battlecruisers far below him. And the great Flood Gate itself, its copper islands like a line of helmets sunk across the estuary.

He turned on the radio. Nina Simone was singing "Sinnerman" but the song cut out before the end. A pompous Second World War BBC Public Announcement Voice was saying, "And the river was once a mile wide at this point. In the year 894 the Vikings sailed their longships here, on their way to attack Hertford. Two centuries later the land began to be drained."

Strobey tried another station. On Walthamstow Baroque "Drain You" blared until annihilated by a sound like a shotgun. Next Mozart, sweet and boisterous. It was displaced by one of the songs from *OK Computer*, the one about cops. Then that too was terminated, replaced by Babyshambles. Then a Weezer song, his favourite, the one about a butterfly. Suppressed by Smug Voice, which returned with a solemn announcement: "The first-ever mention of Walthamstow is in the Domesday Book, 1086, where 'Wilcumestou' is recorded as having one-hundred acres of meadow. This is a landscape subject to change after change after change. And now, in the age of the internal combustion engine and a late capitalist economy, it makes a great escape route for robbers on

276

bicycles. These facts have been brought to you by Burger Bliss, home of the juiciest burger you ever did taste!"

Somehow the BBC voice had turned into that of a man from Texas. Strobey twiddled the dial again, caught a screech of Beethoven's Ninth. Then a woman with a heavy German accent broke in, shouting: "The accelerator will produce not only higher energy but also a higher luminosity! The probability of a collision between particles! Never been achieved before! Will reveal the behaviour of fundamentals! Matter which has never before been studied!"

It sounded edited, mutilated, wrong. He twiddled the dial one last time. All he got was a tortured electronic banshee wail. Strobey gave up on the radio. He reached under the seat and found what somehow he knew would be there.

Time seemed to have speeded up, or maybe he'd been in the museum much longer than he'd realised, for now it was almost dark. Way out ahead was the rim of the land, a ragged line of shingle beaches and grey dunes under ceaseless assault by the Sea of Nothingness beyond. Everything was dimming, going grey...

Strobey put the device on.

Not long now.

*

His skin crackled with a sharp effect as he came through. Consonants tingled inside his suit. The Thames estuary stretched out around him, the waves lashed by a strong wind blowing in from the east. In the distance the cranes of a freight terminal were lit up like X-rays of robo limbs. Beyond lay a harsh, papery whiteness.

The jet-chute pack came softly alive and lowered him through the darkness.

On the shore of a new beginning, Edgar Strobey stood waiting. Strobey slowly raised his arms and stepped towards his double. As they merged, the TPT agent felt the data rushing into his brain. He stood still, eyes closed, absorbing the download. Memories, experiences, detailed narratives. Last chapters, first chapters, seventh chapters. A sense of nausea and overload merged with a strange prickling sensation.

Afterwards there was nothing to do but discard his jet-chute in the water and set off for the nearby station. *There is no traject back,* he thought. It disturbed him for more than the obvious reason but he wasn't sure why. He listened to thirty minutes of birdsong until a train arrived and took him to Fenchurch Street. He walked along Seething Lane to catch the tube at Tower Hill. In less than an hour he was approaching the end of the Victoria Line. The blackness beyond the window ended in a rush of artificial light. The platform slid into view.

His name was Edgar. Edgar Strobey. A good name, he liked it. He felt strong and confident. His fingers lightly touched the pack of erasure dust in his pocket. Strobey smiled. Everything was going to be fine, he just knew it. He'd done the VR runs so many times he knew what to expect.

The silver train halted.

"You have now arrived at Walthamstow Central," a voice crackled from the PA system. "All change here. This is the end of the line. All change, please."

He felt jaunty as he joined the crowd pouring along the platform towards the exit. He started humming "Menzara Woman, Can This Really Be The End?" A fantastic song. It was number one on Level 17 for over a year. A timeless classic.

Out of the tunnel and into the concourse where the crowd segregated into three groups. The ones – four or five fit young men – who went bounding away up the two-hundred concrete steps. The minority who queued to walk briskly up the left-hand side of the escalator, hurrying home to their lovers or their cats. The majority who swirled around the base of the stairwell, jostling for a slow ride up on a slatted silver step. He joined the ones waiting for that ride.

After that there were only the ticket gates, then two short flights of stairs.

Processing the data download the only thing that really bothered him was how he'd managed to fire his flute when he'd never picked it up from the floor. A stray thought flicked the consideration aside. Where does one world end and another begin?

278

In time he'd work out the answer to that. Meanwhile he had work to do. Strobey moved in the direction of the daylight, where all the future behind him was waiting.

All change here.
This is the end of the line.
All change.